WATER
UNDER THE
BRIDGE

WATER UNDER THE BRIDGE

a novel

KELS & DENISE STONE

BETWEEN THE SHEETS
PUBLISHING

Published by Between the Sheets Publishing

kelsdenisestone.com

Copyright © 2024 Between the Sheets Publishing LLC

All rights reserved.

Paperback ISBN: 978-1-964675-00-8

ebook ISBN: 979-8-9864169-5-3

Water Under the Bridge

Editing & Proofreading:

Manu Shadow Velasco at Tessera Editorial

Caroline Acebo

Cover Design: Chloe Friedlein

To my burnout, you almost won, but not this round.

Chapter 1
Avery

SOMETIMES YOU HAVE TO GRAB LIFE BY THE NECK AND CHOKE IT real good. My dad used to say that often; he always cut straight to the point.

Except, right now, I'm the one being choked. And not in a good way.

Exactly thirty minutes ago, I was meant to be at a pivotal job interview for a position that could launch the career of my dreams. Instead, I'm speeding through New York City in my four-inch stilettos like a panicked ostrich fleeing from a predator.

I'm fucked. So magnificently, absolutely, heinously *fucked.*

The elements are against me.

The unseasonably scorching heat and thick humidity cause sweat to pool down my back. My bra is drenched and resembles the Pantanal wetland I visited in Brazil almost ten years ago.

Oh, the joys of being a woman. A *very* late woman.

Whatever bad luck woke up with me this morning and caused me to type in the wrong address into my GPS app, I want it to go away.

Can you hear me, world? No more!

I take a large step onto the road, and the crossing light immediately flips red. A few cars screech their horns at me, and I match their rage by releasing a few expletives into the air above East Fifty-Seventh Street.

This is New York City. A red light is a *suggestion*, not a rule!

Okay, it's most definitely a rule, and I need to avoid working myself up right now. The last thing I need is to battle an all-too-familiar wave of anger about my day.

I gulp down a deep breath of thick air and try not to gag on the aroma of garbage. It's a smell only the people who live here can tolerate. But I spent too many humid summers around New England cleaning up riverbeds to be afraid of a bit of trash.

Inhale. Exhale.

After what feels like an eternity, I finally see it: ***O**ceanic **R**esearch **O**rganization.* The cerulean signage is brightly displayed on the awning of the *Enviro* glass building, flanked by concrete skyscrapers, each big industry name that resides inside decorates the entrance. The forty-five-floor building is budding with green venture capitals, humanitarian organizations, nonprofits, and companies like ORO.

I brush my hands over my previously pin-straight hair and tuck my blouse back into my navy pants.

More sweat collects above my lip, and I dig into my tote, hoping to find something to wipe it away. I sift through a bottomless pit of lip balms, pens, and my interview notes.

I really should spend some time cleaning this thing.

My fingers brush against an old gum wrapper. I fish it out and use the minty film to wipe away the moisture above my mouth. An older woman watches with a hint of judgment. Frankly, we share the horror.

I try to stay positive; this disaster of a day could be much worse. I still have a few sips of my toffee iced latte, and my heels haven't melted into the steaming pavement.

I make my way inside the building. Enormous photography prints are on display around the lobby, showing a group of polar bears napping on a glacier and lions roaring atop a ledge.

I bet these were taken by renowned *Global Planet Magazine* photographers just like my dad. The thought immediately dampens my mood.

Ignore it. Eyes on the prize, Ave.

If only my teen self could see me now: covered in sweat, buzzing from caffeine, and minutes away from meeting the incredible Joanna Benbart.

The daughter of billionaire Charles Benbart and the sole heir to his massive fortune, Joanna had no interest in her father's private equity business. A true trailblazing activist, she left the comforts of her privileged life to start the Oceanic Research Organization. Her company fuses innovation and advocacy to solve the greatest challenges facing our oceans.

I hope I can accomplish even a fraction of what she has by the time I'm thirty. Only five more years to become the most extraordinary woman on the planet. No big deal.

Pulling my ID out of my wallet, I hurry to the front desk and catch a glimpse of the security guard's name tag.

"Hey there, Tim, I've got an eleven a.m. interview at ORO!"

Tim glances at the ID before typing something into the computer.

"I'm sorry, ma'am," he says. "We only have an Avery Sock listed here."

Of course.

I laugh a tad too loudly. "That's me! A common typo."

It's most definitely not a common typo.

Did I mistype my name on my resume?

Before I have the chance to review the folio, Tim picks up the phone. He mutters something to a high-pitched voice on the other end of the line, eyeing me suspiciously.

Do I look like a fraud?

After a few exchanges with the phone receiver, Tim gathers enough proof of my identity and business here. I try to avoid my watch, but I catch the numbers *11:42 a.m.*

Tim finally returns my ID and directs me toward an elevator bank. When I make my way past the turnstiles, I notice one of the cars has its doors open, and I sprint for it. The clacking of my heels echoes through the lobby, resembling the sound of spilled marbles.

"Please, hold the door!" I call out to the hint of a person I can see inside, but the gates begin to fuse together. "Please, please, please!"

Inside looms a towering, dark-haired figure repeatedly pressing a button.

A button I can only presume is meant to close elevator doors on women in distress.

It works.

I stop short of the entrance, inches separating me from the jerk dressed in a dark suit that looks unnecessarily expensive.

His piercing eyes meet mine in a superior glare that so easily screams "I'm the sole owner of this elevator, and I win." There's a hint of a smirk on his bowlike lips before he's hidden from view.

Ugh!

I shake my irritation away, jump toward the call button, and smash it incessantly. The other car takes forever to arrive. While I wait, I pull my folio out of my tote and glance at my resume. The carefully typed header reads *Avery Soko*. I knew there wasn't a typo!

I press the folio to my chest. Exhausted, I stare at my unkempt reflection in the metal doors. Despite my damp blouse and frazzled appearance, I still look some*what* professional.

Another car finally arrives. I step inside and find the twenty-third floor. The final drops of my latte swirl in the glass tumbler in my hand.

ORO Headquarters, here I come!

A leather briefcase shoots between the steel, forcing the cage to reopen.

No. No. No.

Three men rush into the elevator, barely acknowledging my presence. They appear to be in their mid-thirties. All of them are wearing jeans and look as disheveled as I feel.

"Sorry!" blurts the largest of the bunch in a thick Scottish accent. "We're running late!"

I want to shout that I was running late *first*. Instead, I keep my cool, suppressing a scoff.

The skinniest man presses the button to their destination, and the group continues their small talk until the largest one of the bunch informs them that their meeting is actually on the sixteenth floor. Not the fifteenth.

Before anyone can respond, the large man pushes past the others and presses the button for the sixteenth floor. His movement sends his thin companion stumbling backward into me, and the remainder of my latte spills all over my things.

Time stands still as my blouse changes from a pearly white to a deep brown before my eyes.

The urge to scream appears in my throat, but the only thing that comes out is an exasperated "Why?"

"Look at what you've done, Ollie!" scolds the only man in the group who hadn't spoken yet.

Ollie gives me a look filled with pity and chuckles. "Sorry, lass."

I glare at him, unable to comprehend how this mammoth man has the nerve to laugh at the unfortunate circumstance.

"This isn't funny."

The presumed leader of the group clears his throat, likely attempting to defuse the situation. "You've ruined her entire shirt."

"I can fix it, Mattie!" Ollie says. His large fingers quickly begin undoing the clasps of his dress shirt.

We all watch in terror.

When Ollie reaches the third button, Mattie slaps his hand away. "Seduction isn't getting you out of this mess."

I let out a reluctant chuckle, the knot in my chest loosening.

It's okay. It's just a little *stain. I'm just a* little *late.*

"We're so sorry," says Mattie. He gestures to the thin man, now awkwardly pressed against the opposite side of the elevator. "Robert, give her your sweater."

Robert opens his mouth to protest, but Mattie shoots him a very icy stare.

Begrudgingly, Robert pulls off his gray sweater and hands it to me. He extends his hands, offering to hold my folio, coffee mug, and tote while I wrestle with the saving grace of my new top. It smells like citrus detergent, and I shove the woven fabric over my head.

I take my things back from Robert and give him a warm smile.

"Thank you," I say to him.

Ollie shoots me an overly friendly wink and a thumbs-up as though this trade is a success.

The elevator jerks to a stop on the sixteenth floor, and the doors open to a reception area with signage for Lemon Venture Capital.

"This is us, guys," announces Mattie.

Ollie shoots me another apologetic glance and then the poster boys for disaster depart the elevator.

I shove my coffee-soaked folio back into my tote and tuck the gray sweater into my pants. I'm glad Robert has a similar frame to me because my new top only bunches around my wrists. It's definitely not the outfit I wanted to wear today, but it'll have to do.

I take a long, deep inhale, then exhale the irritation inside me. A spill isn't going to ruin my day.

I close my eyes in the silence before the doors open on floor twenty-three.

I got this!

Finally exiting the box from hell, I take in the ORO waiting room and its cerulean velour couches. Blue and green murals depicting wild ocean waves and colorful sea creatures adorn the walls. My gaze drops to the floor, and I make out the image of bone-white seashells decorating the tiles.

A receptionist sits at a large driftwood desk in the middle of the space. She notices me and waves me over.

After checking me in, she leads me down the ORO hallways, which are as magnificent as I'd always imagined. Everything and everyone is on display behind the glass walls that line each corridor. Employees sprawl in different seating areas, huddling over their laptops or speaking to their coworkers. A few people in jeans and company hoodies walk by, and I feel slightly overdressed. But first impressions are important.

We finally arrive in front of a large boardroom, where the receptionist swipes one of the many key cards she's holding and ushers me inside.

"Hang tight for a few," she says with a toothy smile. "I'll go get Joanna."

She closes the door behind her and leaves me alone.

The floor-to-ceiling windows reveal a stunning skyline of Midtown Manhattan. In my almost three years in New York, this might be the best view of the city I've ever seen. My lips curl upward. My luck is finally improving after this morning's circus.

A quick knock forces my attention to the door. Where I expect to find Joanna stands a petite woman. She steps into the room wearing a wireless headset and a yellow sundress that clashes with the solemn expression on her face. She seems to be about my age, although her copper curls and large eyes make her appear much younger.

"Ms. Soko?"

"Yes, hi." I walk over to her and extend my hand. "Please call me Avery."

"My name's Molly Greene, and I'm the lead Executive Assistant at ORO." She gives me a soft handshake. The kindness in her voice soothes my worries about running late. "We'll have to push the interview back by an hour. Feel free to make use of the office's amenities while you wait." Her eyes scan my wardrobe. "Are you cold?"

I know the best thing to do is pretend the oversized men's sweater I'm wearing isn't out of the ordinary, but the words spill out of my mouth before I can stop them. "There's a giant coffee stain underneath this thing."

Why did I say that?

Before I have a chance to take back my ridiculous overshare, Molly takes a step closer. "I'm not as tall as you"—she regards me—"but we're about the same size."

"Um, that can't be right." I don't try to hide my skepticism. She's a whole foot shorter than me.

"I may be small, but I have a long torso." She chuckles, eyeing me once more. "Let me grab one of my extra blouses for you to change into."

My heart warms with gratitude. "Are you sure?"

"Yes, don't worry about it." Molly gives me a polite smile and then walks toward the door.

"STOP TELLING me there's no paper in this tray!" I squawk as though the machine is arguing with me.

After I changed into the new top, which fits very snugly around my shoulders, I dried my laptop with my stained blouse, then pulled up my notes. I needed to reprint them. Finding the copy room housing the printer was easy, but getting the printer to work is an entirely different story.

I bend over, trying to click random buttons, but I'm met with a blaring error message. **No Paper.**

Over the noise, footsteps enter the copy room.

"Our printer doesn't have the means to defend itself against rambunctious women," a deep voice drawls behind me, sending an annoying shiver down my spine.

"Let me fix it." A masculine hand reaches over my shoulder.

"I got it." I swat the stranger's fingers away and turn around to confront the know-it-all behind me.

The jerk towers over me, his broad shoulders occupying most of the empty copy room. At five nine, I stand comparatively tall among most men, but he still manages to peer down at me even in my heels. I tilt my head back to get a good look at this guy.

My stomach somersaults.

Mere inches from me stands the man who closed the elevator doors in my face.

"*You!*" I gasp when I meet his brown eyes.

A pair of thick, dark eyebrows rise in amusement, and his lips curl into a subtle smirk. A sharp jaw complements his masculine features.

He's very, *very* manly.

Like, the kind of manly they'd cast to play a brooding villain in a film. Maybe that's what he's here to do: film a commercial for ORO where he's the bad guy, like one of those big oil lobbyists, and Joanna gets to take him down with one of her motivational speeches.

I'd love to see that.

My attention returns to how my borrowed blouse stretches across my chest. The fabric around the buttons is barely holding itself together. I start to feel particularly exposed.

We stare at each other for a minute too long, and then the printer whirs pulling my attention away from him.

Presentation notes. Joanna Benbart. Dream job.

"You're printing from the wrong tray." He reaches over me again, making no effort to acknowledge our previous run-in.

"It says to print from tray one." I face the machine, nudging him out of the way with my elbow. "Tray one has paper!"

He lets out a small chuckle, and for the first time, I notice a hint of warmth in his dark eyes that reminds me of the maple trees back home in Vermont.

If not for the blatant arrogance in his features, he would be somewhat attractive.

"I can help," he says. I catch another hint of his smile as he steps around me and presses a button on the printer. The machine suddenly whirs to life.

Okay, who am I kidding?

This man is handsome in a way that screams he never tries too hard before a woman falls for his mysterious, smug act.

"Thanks, but I can figure it out." I turn to face the ancient technological monstrosity before me. This thing is oddly out of place for an office that feels so modern.

"Then hurry up," he says in a manner too curt for my liking. "This is the only printer in the entire office, and you're holding up the queue."

"Just so you know, this is a terrible way to apologize to someone after you close the elevator doors on them."

"I don't know what you're talking about."

His refusal to acknowledge his part in my morning makes my jaw tense.

The man stands beside me as though he has nothing better to do with his day than watch paper come out of a printer. It seems he actually fixed this darn thing.

I take a deep breath to fill the quiet, and the faint hint of woodsy forest musk tickles my nose. It's beyond distracting.

I blow out a breath. "Can you just come back in a few?"

"No," he says. His pointed look sends irritation through me once more.

"Fine," I reply and flip my hair over my shoulder.

"I haven't seen you around the office. Are you new?" There's genuine curiosity in his deep voice.

"I have a meeting with Joanna Benbart today."

"Oh." His eyebrows furrow before he takes a short step away from me.

I'm not exactly sure what causes the sudden shift in his overbearing stance, but he doesn't leave the room. Instead, we stand in awkward silence while my notes finish spurting out of the printer.

What on earth could he possibly be doing in this office? Regardless, I should warn Joanna that some jerk is accosting people in the copy room.

I grab my papers and organize them into a neat stack.

Another brief laugh escapes him. "Not even a thank-you?"

Is he mocking me?

"Not for a heartless suit," I whisper, hoping my words are out of earshot.

"Can you repeat that?" his voice commands. "I think I missed it."

I whip my head toward him. "There's something jammed in my throat."

His eyes open wide, and his head tilts to one side.

Did that come off inappropriately?

I feign a cough to cement my point and tuck my papers under my arm. I sidestep him and start walking back to the location of my interview.

"Nice shirt," he sneers loudly after me.

I'M FUMING in the boardroom when Molly knocks at the door. I leap up, returning her smile.

Ms. Benbart follows her. My breath seizes in my lungs as the reality of the situation hits me.

This is it. This is *her*!

My head begins to spin. I'm going to pass out from excitement.

A job here is so coveted that the mere application took two weeks to complete and was followed by a month-long review process with the hiring manager, after which I finally earned the opportunity to present my pitch.

If only my dad could see me now. Our dreams are on their way to coming true!

"Hello, Ms. Benbart." I try to dull the elation in my voice. *It's a typical day, and everything is fine.* "I'm Avery Soko. It's *so* nice to meet you."

I pride myself on holding back the avalanche of praise and tidbits I've thought about Joanna for most of my life.

She reaches over and grasps my outstretched hand. The icy blue of her eyes starkly contrasts the long gray curls splayed across her shoulders. "Likewise."

"I just wanted to apologize for my scheduling mix-up."

She smiles dismissively and takes a seat at the head of the table. I recollect myself and stand next to the television, which displays my first slide.

I open my mouth to speak when someone knocks on the door.

"Great!" Joanna says in a somewhat patronizing tone. "ORO's new chief operating officer, Luca Navarro, will be joining us today. Hope you don't mind."

"Not at all," I assure her.

If karma exists, all the times I paid it forward weren't enough because *the* heartless suit walks across the room and sits next to Ms. Benbart.

He barely acknowledges my presence. He sets his eyes firmly on the television, clearly expecting me to proceed.

Molly taps her pen gently on the conference table, a somewhat unsubtle suggestion for me to begin and be quick about it.

Despite my shaking hands and burning cheeks, I pull in another deep breath and deliver what I hope is the best fundraising strategy pitch the world has ever seen.

Chapter 2
Avery

"So, how'd it go?" Lily yells into the phone. The sound of a university campus invades the line.

"Well, when I got off the train—" I begin before she promptly cuts me off.

"Ave, I want all the details, but I'm already four minutes late to my next lecture, so just the recap."

"Right." My best friend, who also happens to be my roommate, runs on a tight schedule between classes and bartending. "It was fine."

"Did you meet Joanna?"

"Yes, and the brand-new COO."

"*What?*"

"Ugh, I don't want to get into it. The guy was a massive jerk."

"Look, I just know you blew them away," Lily says.

"Thank you." I sigh.

"Go have a celebratory drink on me. I'll see you tonight." Lily ends the call.

A minute later, I get a notification for twenty dollars on my phone's payment app with a message: *love you, you're gonna save those turtles!*

I chuckle at the text and tuck my phone back into my tote. She's always supported me, even if she pokes fun sometimes.

I'm thankful Lily snuck under my defenses all those years ago. After one of my late-night study sessions at the beginning of my senior year, I strolled into the only bar open at 1:00 a.m. on a rainy Tuesday in Chapel Hill. Lily, who happened to be working the night shift, poured me a generous glass of wine and listened to me vent about my overbearing ecology professor. Then she told me about a guy she was seeing who brought her an annotated book every time they hooked up.

I try not to think about how long it's been since I even considered dating, let alone found someone who would put in that much effort. But why would I need a boyfriend when I have a best friend like Lily? We've chosen to be there for each other through the best and worst of our adult lives.

I'm running on fumes after my long interview and incredibly in need of a distraction.

There's the sting of a freshly formed blister on my right foot, Molly's small blouse is still suffocating me, and my sweat-drenched hair has been wrestled into a frizzy low bun.

I could go straight home to the Upper East Side, but I would rather sulk around a group of strangers than sit alone in my apartment.

I aimlessly stroll down Fifty-Sixth Street until I finally notice a seemingly cozy Irish Pub. Behind the tinted glass windows, stuffed leather chairs are scattered around the bar, and there are a few casual patrons hanging around. I make my way inside, sit at the corner of the somewhat sticky bar top, and read over the menu. It's 3:00 p.m., and I'm practically starving. I scan for something fried and crunchy, needing a hug from the inside.

"Hey!" a slightly familiar voice says behind me, but the weight of my day makes me ignore it.

"Hey, you're the woman from the elevator," the voice says again, and I turn around to see one of the men from earlier.

Ah, the ringleader of the group. What was his name? Matt? Mattie?

He starts making his way toward the empty seat next to me and slumps on the opposite bend of the bar, facing my right.

"What will it be?" the bartender asks, saving me from what could have been a very awkward interaction.

"A glass of Chardonnay and a large side of onion rings." I smile. "Thank you."

The bartender nods, taking away my menu.

"I'll have another whiskey sour, Maureen," says elevator guy. His messy, jet-black hair tips forward when he nods to the bartender. His lips purse together as if he's lost in thought.

He's probably here to reclaim Robert's sweater. "Right, I have something of yours."

I pull the gray sweater out of my tote, but Mattie taps his hand on the bar. "Please keep it." One side of his mouth curves up, and he tilts his head toward me. "We sorta owe you one for ruining your shirt."

I give him a polite smile, which I hope conveys a *please let me wallow in peace* expression, and take a sip of the wine Maureen sets before me. I pull out my phone and attempt to distract myself with some outstanding emails until my sizzling-hot onion rings arrive from the kitchen.

I take my first bite and still feel his focus on me.

"They're so great, right?" His words force my attention back to his side of the bar.

I nod and take stock of his features. Kindness emanates from his deep-blue eyes. A five o'clock shadow coats his jaw. I scan his wardrobe. Mattie sports a graphic T-shirt with the word *Plastech* printed on it in emerald green.

"My company," he says, pointing at the name. "Or who knows what it'll be after today's failure of a meeting."

I frown. "If it makes you feel better, I'm likely to remain unemployed after the day I've just had."

"I'm sorry if my team had anything to do with that."

His apology seems sincere. I turn to face him and smile. "Don't worry about it."

My forgiveness does little to ease the tension in his expression, but I honestly didn't blame him. My morning has been frantic since I left the apartment and had to run back upstairs because I forgot my coffee tumbler.

But the worst part of my day was how little of Joanna Benbart's attention I'd been able to capture with my pitch. Her partner chewed through everything in my presentation until it was bare bones, yet I'm confident I held my ground against him. It was like he had fun trying to get under my skin. Even if he was ruthless and made me want to pull my hair out, it was kind of thrilling to answer each question without pause.

The chaos of the day weighs on my mind. I should probably look over my budget when I get home, especially if I don't get to work at ORO after my catastrophic interview.

Last time I checked, I had about two months of living expenses saved up from my previous job. I worked as an assistant for a couple of career philanthropists, Foster and Deborah Adams, who were *very* generous. My salary helped cover my Columbia University graduate school tuition, rent, and a little extra.

Looking back now, I regret not taking the family up on their offer to remain employed after graduation. I should've thought my backup plan through, but ORO was always going to be the priority.

A deep sigh from the man beside me brings my attention back to the bar. The sad look on his face hasn't lifted. There's no reason we should both sit here, lost in our own fears. I'm better than that.

I push my plate of comfort food between us to share. "Let's start over, yeah?"

He looks as exhausted as I feel, but his eyes brighten. "I'm Matthew Hudson." He pops one of the onion rings into his mouth. "The big guy today is Ollie Anderson. My other colleague is Robert Stewart. Both are licking their wounds right now at our temporary offices."

"I'm Avery Soko."

"So, wanna talk about it? Or we can sulk in silence and eat our weight in fried food."

I spend the next hour explaining every detail of my day to Matthew. He does a great job listening and nodding at all the right places in my story, giving me another apology when I explain I have been wearing a different stranger's shirt since earlier this morning.

Then it's his turn to fill me in. "I'm the CEO of an environmental tech firm."

"Oh, what exactly do you guys do?"

"We've created a technology that uses proprietary AI to separate trash from fish in our oceans."

"That's really innovative!" I gasp.

I've been keeping an eye on some of the recent tech developments in the conservation space. It's precisely why I was so excited for my interview today. Each time I come across something revolutionary, I immediately want to be a part of it. If I worked on ORO's development team, I would help allocate funding to projects like Plastech's.

Well, that and, of course, I'd get to learn from Joanna.

"It is." Matthew sighs. "But if our pitch today is any indicator of our future, we may not last much longer."

"That bad?" I ask.

"We're in desperate need of funding for a new mission on Gaya Island in Malaysia," he explains. "Our biggest issue is scalability. Once we run out of cash to operate, we're done."

"Before I went into my master's program, I spent two years at a nonprofit that conducted a lot of research in that area." My cheeks lift.

"No way!"

"Yeah, I helped on the fundraising team. Tell me about Plastech's current strategy." I'm already reaching my limit for talking about work today, but my professional background forces my curiosity. "How long can you guys sustain yourselves?"

"Most of our start-up capital came from angel investors." He shrugs. "At this point, it'll be easier to shut everything down than exhaust the remainder of our funding."

Ah, the elusive angel investor. I nod knowingly.

They're frequently wealthy individuals who enjoy partaking in passion projects but refuse to stick around for the ongoing work.

"And you've maxed out your leads?"

Matthew doesn't answer. Instead, his head slumps solemnly while his lips form a tight line.

The urge to intrude on Matthew's predicament is overwhelming.

I don't know if it's the wine giving me a second wave or the sense that I've likely ruined my shot at my dream job, but I pull my laptop out of my tote.

"I'm going to help you."

"Thank you, but I'm sure you've got more important things to do," he says.

I don't have the heart to explain that this conversation will be the highlight of my evening.

Is that sad?

No, of course not. I'm in my zone!

"This *is* important, Matthew." I pull up one of my presentation deck templates and look over at him. "Show me what you got."

The bar fills with laughter and loud conversation. We sit

together for a few hours as the crowd changes from sordid day drinkers to the Midtown happy-hour set.

The two glasses of wine have finally gotten to me, and the blaring noise is causing a pounding in the front of my head. Outside, the blue sky is starting to dim.

I reorganize the remainder of Plastech's marketing presentation and send it to Matthew.

During our talk, I completely overhauled their mission statement, and I tailored their fundraising goals to help continue the work they're already focused on. Matthew has a vast knowledge of venture capital firms and more traditional fundraising methods, but Plastech hasn't tried to raise money through individual donors and philanthropic family offices. The changes I made will help them with that.

"It's all about how you present the information," I explain. "Plastech can really make a change. You just have to show that to your investors."

"This is incredible!"

"Look it over with your team, but you should be in good shape."

"Thank you so much, Avery. I owe you one."

"No need." I smile. "I'm happy to help."

Matthew beams at me, seemingly mesmerized by the information I provided on the inner workings of fundraising. He tips back his drink and reaches into his back pocket for his wallet.

"I know you're waiting for ORO," he says, extending a business card with his full name and phone number, "but if you're ever interested, Plastech would love to have you on board."

I hesitate before I take the card from him. I'm not be ready to give up on ORO just yet, but a new connection never hurts.

"Good luck," I tell him.

I CLIMB the last steps to my fourth-floor walk-up and deeply reconsider Lily's claim that the glute workout would be worth the hike when we agreed to rent this place.

I kicked off my pumps two floors below out of sheer exhaustion, resolving to carry them instead.

The blister on my foot throbs.

My head spins vigorously from a lack of oxygen as I jam my keys into the front door. This thing never opens on the first try. After a few minutes of wrestling with the doorknob, I finally stumble into my apartment.

Lily and I moved here in February, securing an incredible deal on the two-bedroom on the Upper East Side. Despite its somewhat petite size, it's a mansion compared to the tiny studio apartment we shared for two years when we first moved to New York City. Our new place has a large chef's kitchen, where I occasionally stress bake. The street that houses our brownstone is close enough to Central Park for my morning runs and near Lily's job at the Mademoiselle.

An oversized thrifted couch sits in the middle of the room next to a vintage teak coffee table. A collection of plants lines the windowsills and decorates the media unit which supports our small television in the corner. On the beige wall hangs one of my dad's photographs. A large ocean expanse with a pair of dolphins on the horizon. They're one of the few creatures in the wild that mate for life.

Huh, maybe that's me and Lily—platonic mates for life.

Our bedrooms are on either side of the apartment, lending some privacy to a fairly small space. Not that I need much privacy. I spend most nights here on my own.

My tote collapses onto the hardwood floors, and I strip off Molly's blouse. My stomach rumbles with hunger, so I glance around the kitchen. A medium-sized white box with a bow sits on the counter.

That wasn't here this morning.

On top of the neatly wrapped box rests a small note card.

Congrats on acing your interview! Sorry I had to pick up a shift at the bar - Love, Lily.

I sigh.

Lily and I were going to rewatch our favorite sitcom over a pint of ice cream tonight.

I open the box to reveal half a dozen perfectly decorated apology cupcakes in shades of blue and green to match ORO's colors. Warmth works its way into my tight chest. I try to smile and ignore the sad feeling of missing my friend.

It's fine.

I can't be upset with Lily. Of course, work must come first. I pick up one of my consolation prizes and bite into the fluffy cake and thick buttercream frosting.

Avery: 3 | Bad Luck: 1

Lily still deserves an award for being the best friend of the century. I make a mental note that if I get the job at ORO, I'll use the first paycheck to buy her that fluffy black purse she's been eyeing.

I sweep the box of cupcakes into my arms and carry it over to the couch. I take another bite and stare at my phone, willing it to ring with good news. Maybe Joanna will call me tomorrow with a generous job offer. We'll chat the way a mentee and a mentor chat, bonding over how seasick the trek to Antarctica made us and how my fundraising strategy will take ORO to a new level.

But even if it's terrible news, I hope it's Joanna who makes the call so I can tell her how much her work has meant to me. Or maybe Molly. Honestly, anyone would be better than the heartless suit.

Chapter 3
Luca

"OH, NO, NO, NO, NO." A PANICKED VOICE ECHOES INTO MY corner office, breaking my concentration on the latest project reports.

The clock reads 6:00 a.m.

Who on earth is in the office at this hour?

I roll back from my desk and leave my office to walk through the corridors toward the noise. The yelps cease, but they seem to have originated from the opposite side of our floor. I could return to my desk, but what if someone's hurt?

My parents taught me to always lend a helping hand.

Thirty-one years later, I may not enjoy it, but I can't seem to curb the kind instinct.

The early morning sun lights the laboratories, and I search for the source of the disruption, but nothing looks out of the ordinary.

There's no way I imagined the whole thing.

I slink my way past the weighted door to the research wing. The area is eerily quiet except for a faint scratching noise.

There better not be any rats in here.

I pick up a metal contraption from one of the large steel desks cluttered with piles of overflowing folders.

Protection first.

My eyes land on a small shoe peeking out from behind a steel cabinet.

Okay. Most definitely *not* a rat.

I can see the headlines now: *Woman slain at ORO—new chief operating officer only suspect.*

I lower my voice. "Hello?"

Another piercing scream erupts at my question. The sound is so violent that I screech back in response.

Audibly screech.

A scientist whips her head up from behind the cabinet. "Oh, it's just you, Mr. Navarro—"

Am I that frightening?

I walk closer to Dr. Hana Claremont, one of ORO's premier researchers. Her lab coat drapes over her shoulders, covering a pair of animal-print pajama bottoms.

Because why else would someone wear pants with cats painted on them if they *weren't* pajamas?

She's grasping at scattered books and loose papers on the ground before her.

"*Luca,*" I remind her. I don't clarify that people constantly slightly mispronounce my last name. It's easier this way.

"Right, yes, Mr. Nav—" Her eyes fall to the floor and quickly return to me. "Luca."

"Is everything alright?"

"Yes, thank you. I just learned that I, maybe, need to start lifting more weights at the gym." She finally stands, and her eyes dart to the device in my hand. "Why are you holding a utility clamp?"

The metal still rests in my palm. "Never mind."

I set it down.

"Sorry." A nervous laugh escapes her.

I should have stayed at my desk. Nothing's wrong, and this silly ordeal will set me back at least ten minutes today.

Fine. I'll just cancel my fifteen-minute lunch to catch up on the missed period of productivity. It's not the first time.

At least when I missed lunches at Douglas & Draper, I could do it from the privacy of an office with actual walls *not* made of glass. The luxury of going an entire day without unwanted run-ins or even a conversation brings a subtle smile to my face.

It was wonderful.

"So, you're not hurt?" I confirm. "That scream was over nothing?"

She lets out a loud gasp. "The books are not *nothing.*"

Is she serious? That's the most unreasonable thing I've ever heard.

But the past couple of weeks have proven that many things at ORO skirt the line of unreasonable, from the attire to the terrible regard for punctuality. I hook my fingers into the knot of my tie and adjust its position around my neck.

I'm the only one who takes my work seriously, and dresses appropriately. I understand that success starts with your wardrobe. With enough persistence, I'm sure I can convince the rest of the staff to think the same.

Dr. Claremont kneels down again and sweeps the books and files into a neat pile in front of her.

"Let me give you a hand." My suit creases as I bend down to collect the research materials from the white-tiled floor.

To fill the silence, Dr. Claremont shares details about the robotics project she's working on. I tune out her excitement about robots swimming in a pool.

I'm not sure what's exciting about that, but everyone at ORO passionately and collectively advocates for innovations that could support their shared dream.

It's what drew me to pick up ORO as my first pro-bono client when I started at D&D. The work I did for ORO was impactful

and meaningful. It reminded me of the environmental extracur-
riculars I did in college, so I continued taking on their cases over
the years.

The board was impressed with how detail-oriented and effi-
cient I was, and they offered me the position of chief operating
officer. But when the board approached me, I'd just been made a
partner at D&D and wasn't going to throw away my hard work
there.

That changed after I was assigned to the Shift Industries
case.

A year after ORO's first offer, the COO position was still
vacant. Apparently, the last two people had quit within a few
months because of the workload. I figured the board must have
been desperate when they immediately hired me and didn't
consider my connection to the Shift Industries case a problem.

The career change was supposed to help my guilt. But it
hadn't so far.

"Thank you for your help," Dr. Claremont says. She climbs
to her feet, half the books cradled in her arms.

"You're welcome." I set the pile I gathered on the table next
to me.

Dr. Claremont's mouth parts as if hesitating with her
following words. I should leave.

"Did you do anything fun over the weekend?" she asks.

I sigh. *There it is.*

The most useless and intrusive question a colleague can ask
another colleague. A superior, in this scenario. Why must people
always turn work into their social playground?

"Not really," I insist dryly, hoping she won't pry any
further.

"That can't be true. New York is practically a theme park for
single men like you."

Single men like me?

There's no way she knows anything. I haven't divulged the

slightest hint of my relationship status, or lack thereof, to anyone at ORO.

"That's a personal matter I do not wish to discuss, Dr. Claremont." I turn on my heel and dash my way out of the room.

"Well, that confirms my hypothesis and earns me twenty bucks," she says under her breath, likely hoping I couldn't hear her from my corner of the laboratory.

What's with people whispering around me lately?

"Good luck on your work trip." The annoyance is now apparent in my voice.

"Please don't take my questioning the wrong way. Most of us have worked here for years. We're simply curious about our new boss."

I don't grant her a response. Instead, I exit the lab and walk back to my office. At least I can cross one item off my to-do list —check on the research teams—and make a note to never return to the laboratories in the future.

———

Bing.

The reminder for my meeting with Joanna flashes on my computer.

Hopefully, she's in a good mood today.

I grab the contract for the new development position off my desk.

Avery Soko may disregard punctuality, but that suggests she'll fit in at ORO perfectly. She thoughtfully researched her ideas—precisely what the company needs now—and she can stand her ground with me, unlike many others here.

On the brief journey to Joanna's office, I glance at the neatly framed articles on the walls, illustrating the many decades she has been the pioneer of change in the conservation space. Her accolades always rouse a sense of purpose in me.

Joanna sits in her signature blue velour chair and sees me walking toward her office. The stillness of her body mimics a marble statue. It's as if she's so lost in her thoughts that she manages to stare right past you.

I rush my way inside.

Smack!

My flesh collides with cold, hard glass. The nearly transparent entryway and the rest of the walls shake.

These fucking glass doors.

I brush off the crash and gather myself quickly.

Joanna doesn't acknowledge my intimate meeting with the glass, a great indicator that this meeting will be exactly like our other curt encounters. I force myself inside and rub the bump most likely forming on my forehead.

"Look who finally decided to show up!" Joanna's piercing blue eyes meet mine before snapping back to her computer. "Call Ms. Soko and inform her that we will not be proceeding with her candidacy."

Not proceeding with her candidacy? I clench the offer letter.

"Why not?" A pang of irritation dances through me. "Ms. Soko is the best candidate we've met in weeks."

Apart from the occasional spur of impatience, Avery Soko was an exceptional candidate. Her edge reminded me of a lesson *Papi* taught me when I became a lawyer: People reveal their most significant character flaws under pressure.

"She's way too young," Joanna says.

I let out an exasperated sigh. "I'm going to need a better reason."

"I don't want a child with too many untested ideas and not enough life experience managing relationships with our investors."

"Were you not at that interview yesterday? Did you even look at her resume? Avery has more than—"

"Make something up, Luca. My decision is final." Joanna

takes a loud slurp from her pungent green smoothie, and her features contort in disgust.

I'm beginning to understand why the last two COOs quit. Joanna is insufferable.

Does everyone else see it too? Or is it just me who thinks she's disagreeable and wretched?

But it's nothing I can't handle; I'm equally ruthless.

"Joanna, I was hired to make decisions that move *your* organization forward. I know we all want ORO to grow, so I implore you to trust my judgment."

"I've already decided for us." Her icy hand reaches over to mine and gives it a reassuring squeeze. I flinch at the unexpected contact, baffled at the invasion of space. "As for the *board* hiring you, I've already explained it was against my better judgment. ORO doesn't need a COO when it has me."

I roll my neck, not nearly ready to move on.

Being ignored and belittled by partners at my law firm was the norm, but I'd assumed working with Joanna Benbart would be different.

I repeat the mantra I've been replaying in my head since my first day at ORO: *Coming here wasn't a mistake.*

I didn't make the youngest partner at my firm by rolling over when things got tough.

I'm here to make a change for myself, for the world—an opportunity to heal my guilty conscience.

Joanna may be mad that I'm here, but I will be on the right side of history for once.

"Joanna, I was brought on to help handle the workload, which includes hiring new people. We need to acquire new projects and bring in adequate funding for the ones we already have, and Avery can help us with that."

Joanna laughs. "Luca, I appreciate your interest in *my* ORO, but my decision is final."

"It would be better to have an exp—"

Joanna's phone rings, and she quickly picks it up. "Hello, yes. I won't be able to make that appointment anymore. Hold on."

She waves me out of the room without looking in my direction.

BACK IN MY OFFICE, I toss the hiring contract in the recycling bin, then unsuccessfully scavenge my email inbox for Avery's contact details.

My entire body is humming with annoyance. There's no use in procrastinating the inevitable.

I yank open my desk drawer and search through the loose pages.

Jackpot.

An elegant header reads *Avery Soko*.

I scan her resume again, and something in the lower right corner catches my attention. Underneath the *Interests* heading reads *joined expeditions on all seven continents*.

That's impressive.

Why didn't I notice this initially?

I should've asked her about it.

My past billable hours kept me attached to my phone and computer during the sporadic trips to visit my family in California over the holidays. My brother, Nico, on the other hand, has been all over the world. Maybe even matching the extent of Avery's wanderlust.

Magna cum laude undergrad, hiked all mountain ranges in New England, First Prize Banana Bread at the Vermont State Fair.

I realize I spent more time assessing her fundraising strategy than learning anything about the person we interviewed.

The ridiculous factoids unexpectedly make my lips curl.

These portions of a resume are ordinarily coated in useless details, but Avery's list is rather intriguing.

My eyes move to the contact information printed below her name. My pulse quickens when I punch the numbers into my phone.

Am I nervous?

"You got Ave," says a cheery voice on the other end of the line. A disruptive series of voices clouds the background.

I glance down at my phone, confirming I dialed the correct number. "I'm looking for Avery Soko."

"Yep, this *is* Avery Soko."

The memory of her wrestling with the printer while she attempted to make copies of her presentation figures returns. She wasn't afraid to snap at me, so hopefully, this goes smoothly.

"Hello, Ms. Soko, this is Luca Navarro calling from the Oceanic Research Organization. Do you have a couple of minutes to chat?"

A loud slam suddenly echoes. *Where is she?* Is that a closing door?

"Hi, Mr. Navarro! It's great to hear from you."

"I wanted to thank you for coming in yesterday, and I'll cut straight to the chase. We've decided not to move forward with your candidacy." My tone carries the most indifference I can muster for such an unfortunate situation.

A long silence resonates from the other end of the line. Which quickly morphs into a painfully awkward pause. Ignoring the golden rule of power in any unpleasant exchange—not being the first to break the silence—I clear my throat.

"Ms. Soko?"

"Yes." A tone of annoyance suddenly hinders her voice. "Could I request some feedback on the interview? I thought my presentation went very well."

"The interview committee, unfortunately, disagrees with you, Ms. Soko."

"Of course, and I respect your decision. However, for the sake of my future career endeavors, I'd like to know if there's room for improvement."

I shift in my seat, trying to think of an excuse.

"Your presentation was not quite up to par." My teeth grit at the lie dancing on my tongue. The words come out too easily, too slimy. I cringe. "And I didn't appreciate being accosted by the printer," I add, trying to brush away the lie with another lie.

I regret the words as they swarm in a rushed whisper from me. I survived years of legal debates riddled with meticulous arguments, yet after a brief conversation with this woman, I'm suddenly defensive.

"Excuse me?" she retorts without hesitation. The weight of the disaster I created unfolds before me. "Mr. Navarro, you shut the elevator door in my face when you saw I was headed straight for you."

"I don't interrupt my schedule by holding doors for frantic strangers."

She scoffs. "Any feedback that has to do with my presentation?"

My foot taps with impatience as I lean forward in my chair, pinning my arms to my desk.

"I'll be frank with you. At the Oceanic Research Organization, we place a high value on timeliness, and your disruptive tardiness is not something we can overlook."

"Look, I apologize for my lateness—"

"Ms. Soko, you really need to learn to handle rejection better. We will not be moving forward with your candidacy. Thanks again for your time. All the best."

I slam my phone into the reclaimed maple-wood desk, the subtle plea in her voice still echoing in my ears.

Chapter 4
Avery

LEARN TO HANDLE REJECTION BETTER.

It should be a crime for handsome men, especially those with fine suits and pointed glares, to make life-changing decisions for hardworking women.

Weeks of researching fundraising strategies for companies in New York, memorizing the inner workings of ORO's fundraising gaps, pouring hours into public tax filings, and reviewing existing projects. All for nothing.

Years of tailoring my background. *Years* of work in conservation and protecting our environment, and my career was left in the hands of a man who flushed it down the toilet.

But I handle rejection like I do everything else in my life, with poise and grace. Even if my grace mirrored the likes of a discombobulated deer this time.

The call replays in my head like an incessant melody. Who needs a backup plan for their wildest dreams?

Me. I guess.

I roll over, and the crumbs coating my three-day-old pajamas tumble onto the couch, adding to my pit of despair.

I need a plan. Not leaving my apartment ever again is *not* a plan.

The front door rattles before flinging open, and Lily rushes in. Exhaustion is apparent all over her face. Lily decided that her first foray into college life would start at one of the city universities here in New York. When we first met in North Carolina, she worked to save money, not wanting to take on any student loans. I commend her ability to take a few gap years and not feel pressure to go to college right after high school. Now, she is going through general education courses while figuring out what her career may look like in the future.

A pang of guilt knocks at my chest. I spent the entire weekend sulking while she worked her ass off between lectures and bartending on the Upper East Side.

"Wow, Ave. This is a new low for you." She glances around the apartment, which is a dreary reflection of me—a *huge mess.*

"Sorry, Lil."

"Now that I see you've been lying here all weekend, I wish you didn't cancel on me Friday night. I could've cheered you up!"

Lily tried to convince me to join her at the Mademoiselle for a movie-themed costume night, but I was too busy steeping in my sadness.

Regret fills my chest. "I think my midlife crisis is setting in."

"Oh, please, a quarter-life crisis at most," Lily says. "But I've never known you to feel sorry for yourself. The Ave I know is a strong and hardworking badass."

I smile with an overwhelming sense of admiration for my best friend. She never fails to check me, even when I fall into infrequent spells of feeling overwhelmed.

Lily always ensures I can get back on my feet and continue my goals.

"Thanks. I just—I wanted Joanna's mentorship."

"You've already achieved so much *without* Joanna!"

I peel my stiff body away from the couch and look at the perfect imprint I left on the cushions.

"I guess so." I walk to the kitchen for another snack to fill the dull ache inside me.

"You got this, Ave!" Lily throws one of her hands at me in exasperation. She always makes a habit of speaking with her hands, arms, and legs. "Last month, you single-handedly organized rebuilding the community garden in our neighborhood."

"That's true." I sigh.

"You spend your weekends convincing locals to keep it from closing!" she reminds me. "You're literally the only person that can get people excited over zucchini."

"Hey, it's more than just vegetables! The local kids plant flowers there too."

She raises her brow at me as though her point was made. "When was the last time you went on a run?"

More guilt returns. I've been neglecting the one good habit I've managed to work into my schedule. Running has saved me through some of the best and worst of times. And right now, it's most definitely one of the bad times.

"Wednesday morning." My muscles crave a sense of purpose after four days of laying around.

"Ave!"

"Lily!" I counter, and a smile breaks across her face. "Look, I know. I need to get myself together but let me process this!"

"You're not processing. You're wallowing. Please do the dishes, and then we can make some food together that doesn't come deep-fried once I'm done showering." She leaves me in my mess.

"I want something deep-fried."

"Same!" she yells down the hall. "But we're going to eat greens so we both can wake up tomorrow and be productive. I need to study, and you need to go on a run."

I abandon my search for a snack and attack the pile of dirty dishes sitting in the sink.

With Lily gone, *his* words of rejection creep back into my thoughts.

I bet he *enjoyed* turning me down. I should've taken the opportunity in the copy room to rip the smug grin off his striking face.

If an organization like ORO would even hire such a galling, fretful, and obnoxious human being, do I even want a job there?

Of course I do.

Hundreds of Luca Navarros could charge at me, and I would fight them all off for the opportunity to work there.

Lily emerges from her room with her slick black hair wrapped in a towel above her head. She wears a black crop top with devil horns that match her bright-red pajama bottoms. Her full chest always makes me a bit envious. Where I'm long and slim, Lily is petite and curvy. Attention easily strays to her, and who could blame her admirers? Lily's gorgeous.

I set another clean dish on the drying rack. "I'm almost done."

"There's my Ave." She comes into our kitchen, grabs a sizable chef's knife, and lays it on top of a cutting board. Next, she pulls ingredients out of the fridge.

I groan at the sight of the vegetables. "Is this new health obsession part of your nutrition course?"

"I dropped that last semester," she says. Lily's constantly changing her major. "Enough about my classes. How are you *truly* feeling?"

"I'm spectacular," I say with false overconfidence. "But that Navarro is a jerk!"

I set the last of the dishes to dry on the rack and sit on the barstool at our kitchen island.

"That's the guy who called, right?"

I sigh. "Yes, I swear the interview was fine. On the call, he couldn't point out one flaw in my pitch. I don't know what happened."

Maybe I misread the entire situation.

"I hate him," Lily declares.

"Me too."

She prepares a salad and catches me up on her busy weekend of bar fights and a random hookup. Apparently, an old fling of hers rolled into town and gave her a ride in his new car. *A lot* of rides.

"You're scandalous, Lily." The weight in my chest finally lifts a little at the welcome distraction of my friend's life.

"And you're jealous that I'm actually getting laid."

I hate that there's truth to her words. She knows I don't date. But that never stops her from jabbing at me, hoping she'll change my mind. The last thing I need right now is the stress of caring about someone else.

I slump in my seat. "You're right."

"Wow. No comeback?" She sits down in front of me and scoops a healthy serving of olives into our bowls. "You must be really hurting, Ave."

I exhale once more. My stomach welcomes the savory smell of the meal Lily sets on the counter. I love that we always share food.

"What about that guy…" Lily considers me as she takes a bite of her meal. "Michael?"

"Matthew?"

"Yes, that one!" She taps my bowl with her fork. "Didn't you revamp his entire business plan and fundraising pitch?"

"I mean, I helped tweak a few things."

"ORO did a number on you if you're sitting here doubting yourself."

I take a bite of the annoyingly healthy meal in front of me. "Plastech has no capital. I'd be surprised if they could afford to support another person on their team."

"Don't assume, Ave. Call him. He gave you his card for a reason."

It does seem more compelling than going back to the Adams family. Maybe I can lead Plastech's funding responsibilities since the team is so small. Plus, when have I ever turned down a challenge? Even one that desperately requires a complete overhaul?

My real goal is to impact our world, and I can do that without ORO.

I jerk out of my daze. "You're right. I'll call them tomorrow!"

"I know I'm right"—she gives me that pleased grin I love—"but you should do it now."

"Lily, it's eight thirty-seven on a Sunday."

"Your point?" She curls her eyebrow in a challenge. "You just said they may not exist tomorrow."

We refuse to break eye contact.

We're both too stubborn for our own good. If one of us doesn't snap the tense silence soon, we'll end up in another nightlong staring contest. The last time this happened, Lily borrowed one of my bags and accidentally left it at her one-night stand's house. It was the purse I'd spent my first real paycheck on, so I wasn't going to let her off that easily. We immediately fell into one of our stare-offs until Lily finally conceded.

We made the trip to the hookup's home and knocked on his door for two hours. The guy finally believed we weren't there for a revenge threesome and returned my bag. When we got home, Lily called out of work, and we spent the rest of the time icing our burning eyeballs.

After sweeping the last bite of food off my plate and into my mouth, I swivel off the stool. I make my way toward my tote—sprawled by our front door since I came home from my interview—and rummage through the random clutter before coming across the business card Matthew gave me.

Here goes nothing.

Chapter 5
Luca

"WE'LL GIVE EVERYONE TWO MORE MINUTES TO JOIN US, AND then we'll get started." My pen taps the conference table incessantly.

Gathered today are three of ORO's department heads. There should be five of them here, but I have yet to fix the punctuality problem—one of the agenda items I plan on discussing today.

"Luca, what's the rush?" Jamie, the head of technology, chortles. It's hard to take him seriously when his wardrobe consists of linen pants and loose button-downs. "Are you billing us by the minute, or will you just round up to the hour for this meeting?"

"Depends. If you're the one covering the bill, it'll have to be pro-bono." My eyes don't lift from the agenda, but my skin prickles in irritation.

The lawyer jokes are never in short supply from him, but knowing he wouldn't be able to afford my old rates makes my lips curl at the edges. I would prefer he was afraid of me like the rest of the staff seems to be.

They all return to silence, and I refuse to wait another second for anyone else to show up.

I clear my throat. "Let's begin."

Initially, I scheduled these meetings to help me find my bearings here, but the department heads have made excuses for not attending or don't participate at all. It's proven quite difficult for them to respect the structure I'm trying to implement.

Jamie speaks up again. "We've been operating fine without these prying check-ins. We should vote to end them."

"Well, if you can get all the heads in one room to vote, I might entertain the idea. Until then, we continue these meetings."

How do people show up to work every day but not genuinely care about simple company rules? Can people seriously get things done if they're not always here?

Highly unlikely.

I turn to face Chelsea, the head of finance. "Now, Chelsea, did you finish putting together the list of projects that secured the most support last year?"

Chelsea slowly looks around the round table, a pleading look in her eyes. For weeks, she's been pushing aside my requests for our financial data.

"Well?" My patience is wearing thin.

"As I've already explained, Jo handles all that. She's single-handedly been running this company for years." Chelsea fidgets with the string of her hoodie. "I'm here to ensure we comply with federal guidelines, not to put together balance sheets."

One month into working here and I'm still struggling to understand precisely *how* ORO manages its finances.

Every staff member I've spoken with has said the same thing. Jo handles it. Jo takes care of that.

There's no way they've all been coming to work and doing nothing for years while Joanna runs the ship.

Irritation burns through me. "It's your job to ensure we're in a place of fiscal stability."

"ORO has always been stable."

The rest of the department heads nod.

Their unquestioning trust in Joanna would be commendable if it weren't directly making my job harder.

We chew through existing projects and anticipated year-end impact targets for the next grueling hour. The only plan we can agree on is that each department head will do a deep dive into their extensive backlog of leads that slipped through the cracks.

Funnily enough, I got the idea from Ms. Soko during her interview last week. She recommended exhausting every existing ORO contact before targeting new investors.

Her voice echoes in my head. *Occasionally people need to be reminded why they cared in the first place.*

That's exactly what we'll do.

We wrap up, and I walk to my desk to send an email to an old colleague of mine, Kora Noble. She left Douglas & Draper to join a consulting firm. I need a scrutinizing eye with no affiliations to ORO to perform an unbiased analysis of our historical financials, which have been difficult for me to get my hands on. Even if Joanna has been running ORO for years, a single person shouldn't be in charge of such an essential aspect of the business without oversight.

Despite my team's intent on sticking their heads in the sand, I need to be aware of any shortfalls.

Failure is not an option. I refuse to crawl back to my old job.

The senior partners at my firm all laughed when I left, taking bets on how quickly I would return, begging for my partnership to be reinstated.

No one should ever bet against me.

THE NOODLE RESTAURANT Raku is nestled inconspicuously between a bodega and a laundromat. I make my way inside, where waiters bustle from table to table, carrying large, steaming bowls that fill the air with a salty tinge.

A quick scan across the people occupying the wooden tables confirms what I already expected. Nico is not here yet. The concept of time has never entirely made sense to my little brother, who prefers living life in the present instead of by the hour.

Come to think of it, he would make a perfect addition to ORO's band of tardy employees.

I pull out my phone and type.

LUCA

> If you bail on this double date, your life will officially become a living hell.

I send the text message and idle by the hostess stand like some loiterer. My patience teeters on the edge when worry flashes over me.

Nico probably lost track of time while coding, or maybe his train was delayed, but I haven't heard from him since this morning.

My brother has an annoying habit of not keeping his phone charged. It's led me to answer random numbers, even suspected spam calls. When Nico lived abroad, his sporadic calls were usually during loud parties or on the back of a motorcycle. As his older brother I can't help but to worry about him.

But right now, that concern is getting on my nerves because he's late after bothering me for weeks with the same incessant plea: *You haven't been on a date with anyone in years! YOU. ARE. GOING.*

The restaurant door opens again, and Nico waltzes in sporting his signature grin, his curly chestnut hair neatly arranged on his head. A cream-colored button-down stretches across his body where a graphic T-shirt would typically be.

This date must be important.

The similarities between us are undeniable; it's like staring into the reflection of my younger self.

My younger self before my face creased due to the stress of working and endless months with little sleep.

"Luca. This is a date, not a work meeting." Nico tugs at my jacket before pulling me into a hug.

"Don't be ridiculous. I'd never take a meeting here."

"Right."

I look at him again and realize the shirt he's wearing is mine. Before I can confront him, he flashes another of his signature Nico smiles at a nearby waitress, who blushes in response. She rushes to grab a set of menus and walks us to a table next to the bar. Nico gives her a split-second wink, and the red color on her cheeks deepens.

Is that all it takes to make people compliant?

The idea of forcing a smile through every interaction makes me cringe, but it works for Nico.

"You're wearing my shirt."

Nico looks at the button-down and then back up at me. "Am I?"

"If you spill anything, you'll have to replace it with a new one."

"Why would I spill anything?" He chuckles.

A bold question from my brother, who often borrows my clothing without permission, only to return it with numerous stains.

Living with my kid brother was never part of my plan. As more time passes with us living under the same roof, the familiar annoyance I had for his neatness, or lack thereof, when we were children returns. His bath towels always find their way around my apartment, drying on doorknobs and coat hook handles instead of in the bathroom. The socks he shucks off at random places are like an invasive species: once you put away one pair, another one comes to replace it. I love having him around, but existing in my own space is becoming a challenge.

"You have me for another fifty-four minutes," I say, feeling more annoyed than when I arrived.

"Loosen up. They'll be here soon." Neither of us looks at the menu, already sure of what we will order. "Besides, let's talk. I barely see you anymore."

Somewhere between Nico's first year of undergrad and three years of traveling abroad, he began working remotely at a Silicon Valley technology conglomerate, Viggle. A few months ago, he showed up at my Upper West Side apartment with an oversized backpack and laptop in hand. He told me he wanted to take a break from traveling but I think we both just missed each other.

After I fill him in on my day, the waitress returns to take our drink orders, and I request a premium bottle of sake and a round of beers.

"Did you talk to *Mami* today?"

"Todavía no. ¿Por qué?"

"She's been on my ass about why you haven't called her." Nico takes a sip of his beer as soon as the waitress sets it on the table.

"It's only been five days, and I told her I would be busy this week."

I love my parents, but I've been dropping the ball on our typically frequent calls. I massage the crease of stress from my forehead.

My brother shrugs. "You know how she is. She misses us."

Mami using my little brother to check in on me is a low blow. I have always been the one who made sure he was okay, not the other way around. My posture stiffens, and I run one of my palms over my clean-shaven face. The stubble is already returning from earlier.

"Aye, they're finally here!" Nico waves over two women standing behind a line of patrons waiting to be seated.

I look at the door, and a familiar shade of neat, golden-blonde hair catches my attention. My pulse quickens briefly. But when the owner turns around, the look I expect—Avery's determined stare—is instead a stranger's smile.

Our dates stand together. The contrast between their appearances is almost amusing. The taller woman is fresh-faced, and her bright smile complements the incredible detail of her physique. Her arms are easily the size of my calves, and I'm deeply interested in her workout routine. She towers over her friend, practically hiding her from view.

"She's the trainer?" I ask.

"Dude, she can squat my body weight. It's extraordinary." Where most men I know would cower at such an achievement, Nico's face lights with excitement.

The trainer's companion wears a skintight dress that leaves little to the imagination. It's something you would wear to a nightclub, at least from what I remember in college.

The thick strands of her blonde hair are tied in a messy ponytail. The two women make their way to us.

I wait for my body to conjure up some kind of reaction to them, but instead of an exhilarating rise, a familiar dormant feeling remains.

Fuck, when was the last time I felt a rush for someone?

Probably with Ms. Soko in the printer room last Thursday. But that likely was a result of a magnified case of annoyance.

My brother continues waving them over, already standing as they approach the table. I join him, getting to my feet.

"Mira, you look beautiful tonight." Nico's hand loosely wraps around his date's trim waist, pressing her into him as he places a small kiss on her cheek. The hue of Mira's flesh deepens, her smile splaying across her face. "This is my brother, Luca."

"This is Robyn." Mira's head inclines toward her friend before returning her attention to Nico. I reach my hand toward

Robyn and witness her face wither in disappointment as her eyes dart between my brother and me.

"Oh. Hi." Robyn cranes her neck to look up at me, the high pitch of her voice causing me to grind my teeth. "You're very tall."

Well, that's never been an issue before. "Indeed."

We get situated at the table. Nico pours a drink for Mira, and when he offers one to Robyn, her nose lifts to the ceiling in aversion. Before the date, Nico told me Mira and Robyn met at a sporting event after their dates stood them up. Shortly after, they vowed never to go on first dates alone. My eyes roll, thinking about their silly attempt to avoid the aftermath of rejection.

Our waitress returns to take our order and gives Nico another flirtatious smile, ignoring his hand tightly wrapped in his date's palm.

"Lychee martini. No lychee. And make it quick." Robyn uses her feeble fingers to snap at the waitress, who is rattling off the seasonal specials.

Nico is too busy memorizing every pore on his date's face to witness the impolite act.

I can hardly process the rude gesture. I give the waitress an apologetic expression, reminding myself to leave a very generous tip for her troubles.

When the waitress recollects herself, she manages to split Nico and Mira apart for long enough to get their orders. I don't want to entertain Robyn this evening, but my brother's laughter deters me. His evening shouldn't be cut short because of my unfortunate circumstances.

"So, Robyn, what do you do?"

"I own a used clothing boutique in Chelsea." Robyn smiles. Her attention drifts from me to the phone that rests on the table.

"You're a business owner. That's amazing." I toast her, then lift my cup of sake to my lips. Maybe I misjudged her. I take a deep breath and try to be more open-minded to my date.

"Yeah, my dad bought it for me so I could donate the clothes I already wore," she explains. "And all the new clothes I buy are just a write-off!"

I slam my leg into Nico's thigh under the table, just like we used to do when we were younger. That is the dumbest thing I've ever heard in my life. I shoot my brother a pleading look. My throat clears in an attempt to gain his recognition, but he ignores me, favoring Mira's attention instead.

Oh no, he doesn't.

Before I have the opportunity to whack him again, Robyn's nasally screech whips my focus back to her. "What about you?"

"I recently left my law career."

"Hmm." Her face wrinkles in disappointment. "Why?"

"Corporate law wasn't for me anymore."

"But it sounds so interesting!"

I struggle to believe her. "Not really. My dad suggested I would be good at corporate law."

Our waitress returns, setting Robyn's drink in front of her before piling an assortment of dishes on our table. The faster we eat, the quicker I can fulfill my end of the bargain and get out of here.

"Oh, your dad is a lawyer too?"

"Yes, but he does family law." I smile tightly, already revealing more than I want to. Robyn is one of the first strangers I've told about my career switch. "Anyway, it's done now. It was a great career for me, but things change."

"That's unfortunate." Robyn sighs.

I disagree with her sentiment.

I always was the lawyer Luca Navarro. *Papi* thought I would thrive in corporate law from the get-go, and I trusted his advice over my own instincts. I never bothered to explore other types of law, and after being worn out at Douglas & Draper, I was done with the career altogether. Except the rigid corporate mentality still is ingrained in me.

Some things mold to you, while others mold you. But now, I'm just Luca, overwhelmed, rattled, and overworked.

Okay, maybe I'm not that different.

"Sooo," Robyn drawls to Nico and me as we take our first bites of thick udon noodles coated in a spicy broth. "You don't strike me as native New Yorkers like me. Where did you grow up?"

"We're from California," Nico responds for both of us. "You can't tell from his gorgeous surfer bod?" He pats me on the shoulder and chuckles. I raise my eyebrows at him.

I have never surfed a day in my life.

"I love LA!" Robyn says in that high-pitched shriek that's caused a headache to form in my temples.

"There's more to California than Los Angeles," I tell her. "Nico and I are from the Bay Area."

"Oh." Robyn's small face pinches in disappointment. She seems annoyed, but a hint of a smile returns when a series of notifications appear on her screen.

The sound of her incoming messages triggers stiffness in my body. My fists clench with the desire to check my phone for emails.

"Let's do shots!" Nico chimes in, giving me a wink.

"You're not supposed to take shots of sake," Robyn says.

I sigh. "You won't get anywhere telling him what not to take shots of. He made me do a shot of wine the other night."

"It wasn't a shot of wine," Nico says. "It was an experiment."

"What was the experiment?" My brows furrow in confusion.

"To see if you'd listen to me."

I scoff.

"And did he?" Mira asks.

"Yes! He couldn't resist." My knee rams into his thigh again.

"It was the only way I could get you to let me get on with my work." I smile at him. "Speaking of which, you should pour those shots."

My brother laughs and grabs the sake carafe.

He fills four glasses, and Mira watches with fascination as one of her hands disappears below the table. I try not to think about what her hand finds under there, but the grin on my brother's face says plenty.

He and I grab our glasses and toast, "*Arriba, abajo, al centro, y adentro.*"

Mira follows suit and downs her drink, ignoring her insufferable friend's complaints. I can see why Nico likes Mira.

Robyn does not join us, pushing her drink aside and returning to poking at her bowl.

The rest of the meal is tolerable, with Nico doing most of the social heavy lifting. Despite Robyn's disagreeable attitude, my brother tries to ask her questions and patiently sits through her responses.

That's a gift Nico's always had, making someone feel important. It's similar to how Ms. Soko commanded attention during the interview. The collection of interests on her resume hasn't left my mind. If I saw her again, I'd ask about her expeditions or how she picked up on all of ORO's strategic pitfalls as an outsider to the organization. I would trade this ridiculous date for another conversation about a new fundraising strategy any day of the week.

I lift my head from my reflection in my bowl of noodles and watch Nico and Mira attempt to recreate the famous spaghetti scene from *Lady and the Tramp*. Robyn snaps photos of them after adjusting Mira's hair out of her face.

Yeah, my time is up.

I nudge Nico out of the seat next to me and smile at the ladies. "I have an early day tomorrow."

My brother excuses himself to walk me out.

"That wasn't so bad, huh?" Nico says, elbowing me.

"This was the first and last time I go on a double date with you."

Nico's laughter erupts, and I smile. "You know, you don't always have to judge people so harshly."

"If anyone was being judgmental, it was—"

"Alright, alright, I get it." Nico pulls me into a hug. "I'm gonna wingman for Robyn and then spend the rest of the night getting to know Mira."

"I have an early day tomorrow, so please don't bring the party back home." I pull my wallet out of the back pocket of my suit pants and pull out three crisp hundred-dollar bills.

"I got dinner, big bro."

"It's for the waitress." I hand over the money and pull my brother into another brief embrace.

Nico pats me on the back before he gives me a wink and turns to walk back into the restaurant.

"And, Nico, please be quiet when you get home," I chuckle.

Chapter 6
Avery

THE PLASTECH OFFICES ARE IN A COWORKING SPACE IN A downtown Manhattan high-rise. It's only a twenty-minute train ride from my apartment, making it a straightforward commute.

Well, maybe not as easy as the commute to ORO, but it'll have to do.

The space is cramped, with four plain white desks and a lone window facing out into the loud morning traffic. Fluorescent bulbs sting my eyes while the gentle whir from a nearby air purifier echoes through the room. The space is better than some of the crowded study rooms I've been confined to previously.

A tinge of regret festers in the pit of my stomach as I stare at the undecorated cement walls. The memories of intricate murals and cozy-looking velour chairs return to mind.

This isn't ORO, and that's okay!

I know that if I repeat the phrase enough, I'll start to believe it. At least, I hope I do.

At Lily's advice, I took a week to collect myself after the rejection. I was eager to throw myself back into work, keeping my mind from the pestering thoughts, but I knew I had to come to terms with the fact that I wouldn't get to work for Joanna.

Growing up, she was an idol for my dad and me. Maybe he'd still be proud of me for this unplanned next step. I just wish I could ask him.

I will become a woman *like* Joanna, even if I can't learn directly from her. Maybe in the future, if I can help Plastech get back on its feet, I could apply to ORO again.

Right now, however, I must come to terms with my new reality.

I, Avery Soko, am the head of operations and development at a conservation technology start-up.

I can't dwell on the fact that I'm the first-ever head of operations and development at this start-up and that it lacks substantial funding to survive for the next half a year.

"I know it's not much." Matthew hands me a piping-hot mug of coffee as a consolation.

I take it in both hands, savoring the delicious smell as it grazes my senses. The warmth is cozy in my palms. Coffee has a magical way of making everything better.

"As long as there's caffeine and a place to put my laptop, I'm good to go!" I respond.

"Trust me, lass, what we lack in interior design, we make up for with our winnin' personalities," Ollie jokes.

The mountainous Scotsman—whom I'm working on forgiving for drenching me in coffee on the day of my interview —flashes me a genuine smile. There's no room for resentment now, not only emotionally but literally. This office has reached its personnel capacity, and any pent-up frustration would shudder the walls. I'm afraid we'll all tumble down like a row of dominos if I move in the wrong direction.

I squeeze into my office chair beside him, moving carefully. I don't want to spill this new caffeine gift. Ollie beams at me when I finally settle in, and I match his toothy grin as my body meets the mesh fabric of my creaking office chair.

I try not to think about Lily's well-earned gloating session after Matthew answered my call on the first ring last Sunday evening. I was concerned that Plastech wouldn't take me on, but Matthew extended an offer five minutes into our conversation.

He was very transparent about their current cash flow issues and thoroughly explained what could happen if they went under. He answered every single one of my concerns and questions without hesitation.

Unlike that arrogant Luca Navarro, who refused to give me a plausible reason for not hiring me.

Although my new salary isn't even close to what I would've made at ORO, it's more than enough. It allows me to be *more than* comfortable, and I'll have no issues covering my share of the rent, but I may need to cut back on thrifting and toffee lattes. My mood sours at the expectant loss of my favorite things.

I'll just buy toffee syrup to keep at home!

Problem solved.

And on the bright side, I negotiated abundant vacation days with my offer.

I have three months of paid leave. *Three.*

I don't know why it seemed like a necessary perk. I haven't traveled the world in over five years, but I felt that itch of possibility. Maybe I'll be brave and change my mind.

If the Plastech team takes a trip to their cleaning site in Gaya Island, maybe I'll agree to go.

We spend the morning examining current project spending and pulling apart operational gaps. The platform is simple to understand—after Ollie explains it to me for the seventh time.

Plastech uses AI to capture debris in the ocean, separate fish from trash, and recycle the waste into pellets to sell.

However, my new team only has one operating machine that can perform the task and needs capital to expand. It's an incredible patented technology, but the process is costly unless scaled.

But that's where I come in.

Plastech's current funding struggles mean they need me on

their team as much as I need this job. A sense of responsibility surges through me for the work and my new team. I won't let them down.

A WEEK after my first day at Plastech, the team and I huddle over a slice of my homemade banana bread. I quickly learned that all three of my guys have appetites as big as mine. We've been bringing in different baked goods for our morning breakfast meetings for the past few days. Yesterday, Ollie brought in shortbread and Robert brought homemade croissants.

I hope we make a habit of it.

"So, I don't think I know the story of how you all met." I bite into my first slice of the loaf.

"It's a boring story," Matthew says. "We were on the same research team in undergrad at MIT. Spending all those hours together showed us that we worked well as a team, and things just made sense. We started hanging out more through our senior year. After graduation, we followed our own careers before finding ourselves in New York two years ago to start Plastech."

"It's amazing that you all stayed in touch."

It must be cool to start a business with people you've known for so long.

"You didn't even tell her the best part," Ollie bellows. "When we had to rescue you from the Charles River after you tried to collect the beer cans."

Matthew frowns. "Let's not take a walk down memory lane."

"Or, in your case, a swim down memory lane," Ollie says.

I squirm, not wanting to think about how a small tumble into the water could've turned into something dangerous. A prickle of anxiety tickles my throat, my heart quickly building pace against my rib cage.

Matthew notices the crease in my forehead. "Oh, don't worry, Avery. I was fine. I went in there to impress a girl."

"Turned out she'd found Mattie and his collection of beer cans a bit gross." Ollie breaks out into a laugh, and Matthew shrugs. Robert watches the exchange between his friends with a soft smile.

How could anyone find a person cleaning up a river unattractive?

After my third slice of banana bread, I take a few laps around the coworking space as my lazy form of exercise for the day before returning to my desk.

My run this morning was short-lived; the early summer heat insisted on slowing down my regular pace. I've been growing antsy in our four cramped walls, needing to move around or else I lose my focus. I should try to jog earlier in the mornings. I need the full extent of my runs to help me feel less restless from staring at my computer by the end of the day.

"Are you attending any of the upcoming events in the city?" I ask the group at large.

My screen fills with a list of fundraisers. I spent the week firming up every detail of our project models and how we should pitch to investors. The presentation is airtight, and I'm excited about the new funding we can start to secure.

I mapped out this strategy calendar for ORO, and I'm grateful I didn't destroy the research I put in during my dismal haze of rejection.

"Next Thursday, we're going to that Matthew Hall concert," Ollie explains nonchalantly, breadcrumbs decorating his pale chin.

A very unprofessional giggle escapes me. "No, I mean, have you signed up for any of the philanthropic events? The calendar is booming."

The three of them blink at me.

Alright, we'll start entirely from scratch in this department. I immediately dive in, ready to put together a plan.

"These galas can help foster industry connections," I elaborate. "There's no better way to introduce yourself to a bunch of wealthy people searching for a cause to support."

The air purifier hums in the background as I walk them through my calendar, intent on introducing Plastech to the world as soon as possible.

"Oh, here's something! The Ellington Gala is right around the corner, but getting a ticket would be impossible." I sigh and crack the joints in my fingers one by one. "These events sell out months in advance."

The Ellington Gala host is Willhelma Ellington, a New York City socialite who takes on all sorts of humanitarian ventures. This event is one of the most prestigious gatherings in the conservation space. I never had the opportunity to go in the past, but I've heard a lot about Ms. Ellington's theatrics. If we somehow get to attend, I have the perfect dress to wear for the occasion.

"Wait, even if we could get a spot, tables start at twenty-five thousand dollars!" Matthew's eyes open wide at the virtual gala invitation in front of him. "If you're okay with paycheck reductions next month, we could squeeze that into our budget."

I definitely don't want anyone to have to do that.

"Let me see…" I scroll through my contact list to see if I can call in a favor. No worthwhile industry connections grab my attention.

Then an idea appears.

"You know, I used to sneak into these things in grad school," I admit. "Maybe I can slip in with the waiters and quickly spark some interest *before* I get caught and carried away from the premises."

It's a secret I've only shared with Lily. Unlike many of my peers at Columbia, I don't come from a family with extensive fancy connections. My dad worked with prestigious people on his expeditions, but most didn't even bother to attend the funeral, so I had to start from scratch when I moved to New York.

When I wasn't organizing fundraising events for the Adams family during my master's program, I brainstormed other ways to stay ahead of the curve.

"Aye, lassie, good one." Ollie shoots up his large hand for a high five, and my palm meets his before his large frame relaxes into his seat.

I've been taking bets on how long it would take for that minuscule chair to crack beneath his weight. He's six foot five and built like a mountain. I don't know how he manages to sit all day long in a seat that looks like it's for a toddler when he's in it.

"Finally hired us an adventurous one, didn't you, Mattie?" says Ollie.

I laugh.

"No. We can't have you sneaking in." Matthew shakes his head, burying his face into his hands. "We'll think of another way."

The four of us spend the next hour searching for ways to get tickets to the gala when Robert's hushed voice finally cuts the tension in the room.

"My sister got back to me," he whispers. "She's actually on the gala committee."

"Wow, if you've texted your sister, Bobbie, you mean business." Ollie sends his fist onto his desk with excitement. The slam knocks over my glass of water.

I use my sleeve to clean it up. Two weeks of working here and the spills don't even bother me anymore; they're just a part of our day-to-day now. "Can you get us in?"

The three of us eye our savior.

"I could t-t-try, but—" Robert avoids our expectant gazes.

"Go make the call," Matthew says firmly. "If Ave thinks this is our way into fundraising, we need to get those seats."

Chapter 7
Luca

THE YELLOW CAB HALTS OUTSIDE THE AMERICAN MUSEUM OF Natural History. I shove a crisp hundred-dollar bill into the driver's hand, and he scrambles to provide me change.

"Keep it." I step out, slamming the door on him. The ride was worth the eighty-dollar tip. He didn't occupy me with nonsensical small talk and made sure I arrived sweat-free in my neatly pressed custom Savile Row tuxedo.

I turn to the stone building that demands attention with its presence. Despite the many times I've been here, the museum's magic still stuns me. I scale the steps and swallow my discomfort at the stark contrast between overdressed gala attendees and unhoused people sleeping on the stairs nearby.

The signs direct me toward the Milstein Family Hall of Ocean Life room for the Ellington Gala. These stuffy soirees were excruciating bores at my law firm. They were merely opportunities to kiss ass and schmooze with tipsy clients. Hopefully, none of my old colleagues or clients will be here.

Then maybe tonight will be different.

I want to make an excellent first impression. After all, it's my first event as COO.

I inhale a deep breath, preparing myself to talk to new investors tonight. I'm expected to know the ins and outs of my new organization.

I walk into the monumental space, and it spurs my appreciation for conservation. A brilliant emerald hue illuminates the room. I tilt my head toward the ceiling in awe of the life-sized replica of the endangered blue whale suspended above.

What if the cables break and it crushes everyone below it?

That would end the evening pretty quickly.

A plethora of circular tables covered with crisp white tablecloths and decorated with an assortment of ornate flowers occupy the space.

I weave my way through the maze, greeting a few familiar faces.

One of the many penguin-suit waiters passes by holding a tray of champagne flutes, and I swipe a glass for myself, leaving a tip. It will never fail to unsettle me how many wealthy people attend to these events, donate copious amounts of money to their causes, and simply refuse to tip the staff.

Scanning the room, I spot the ORO table near the stage. A small orchestra performs classical pieces to welcome the incoming crowd. My eyes land on Molly, our executive assistant, who aggressively waves me over with a warm smile, her laptop gripped to her chest as she stands beside her chair.

"Hey." The enthusiasm oozing from me is flimsy. "Hey, where's Joanna?" I ask, but Molly doesn't hear me.

"Hi, Luca!" Molly uses her free hand to point to my table setting.

Thankfully, my seat is next to hers, which provides me a reprieve for most of the evening. Molly is one of the few people at ORO who doesn't force me to adjust my leadership tactics to their lackadaisical style. I'm also confident she won't spend the evening talking my ear off with frivolous nonsense.

"Hi, Mr. Navarro," Chelsea says from the neighboring seat.

"This is my wife, Mandy." Beside ORO's head of finance sits an attractive brunette wearing a fitted orange blazer.

"Nice to meet you." I nod while scraping the heavy chair against the museum floor. I turn my seat to face away from Chelsea, hoping to avoid the pull for additional pleasantries and conversation.

I scan the table for Joanna, but don't find her. Other ORO staff members peer back at me with a few tight smiles before they return to their drinks and cocktails.

Molly clicks away at her phone screen.

"Where is Jo?" I repeat.

"Something came up," Molly admits, her lips thinning into a straight line.

"Elaborate." My patience is starting to wear thin with Joanna. It's one thing to be curt at work, but it's unacceptable for the CEO to miss fundraising events of this size and importance.

"I don't know." Molly shakes her head, and her voice travels to me in a whisper. "She texted me a few hours ago that she wasn't coming—"

Impatience gathers in me alongside concern for Joanna's attitude. My head turns to the entrance—hoping to see her walk through the doors of the grand hall—when I catch sight of someone far more interesting.

Avery Soko stands right by the door, flanked by three rumpled men in poorly fitting tuxedos.

A shimmering nude gown embraces her entire figure. The dress splits dangerously close to her hip, revealing the toned muscles in her legs.

A sudden dryness coats my throat.

This is not the same Avery we interviewed a little over three weeks ago.

She leans in to share something with the biggest of her companions. The hefty man with auburn hair looks as though he might burst out of his suit with any sudden movement.

After a quick exchange, the man starts howling with such zeal that his freckled skin flushes red. Then the group vanishes into the ballroom as swiftly as they appeared.

A tick in my jaw ruptures my prolonged stare.

Molly's voice draws me back to the conversation about the best ice cream places in the city, but I glance blankly at the ORO group. My attention is miles away from the debate about the best mint chocolate chip around.

"I have to go make the rounds." I spring out of my seat before setting off into the crowded room.

After twenty arduous minutes of flattering directors and explaining, in minimal detail, why I abandoned my law career to work for ORO, the bottom of my glass stares up at me.

Guess tonight isn't so different after all.

Navigating my way toward the bar, I spot Avery amid a group of people. Here's my chance to turn the evening around.

Her audience's eyes are transfixed on her as she presumably delivers the ending of an anecdote that's shortly followed by bubbling laughter. The same enthusiasm radiates from her as during her interview. Her captivating presence is partly why she would have been a great representative at these fundraisers. Avery's head tips back with a chuckle. The curve of her neck leads gently down her chest to a gown that seems coated in gems. The room's blue hues reflect off of every glistening inch of her.

She looks like some kind of ocean deity.

The sight of her easy movements sends a rush of blood beneath my belt.

I try to ignore the intrusive filthy thoughts. Even if I did have time to consider her as more than a potential colleague, there is no way a woman like that would be unattached.

But I find myself desperately wanting to join her conversation. I survey the faces of the people in the group. A familiar face belonging to Stanley Lewis, an old client of mine, grabs my attention.

I don't want to talk to anyone from my law career, but Avery's standing right among them. I have an unsettling need to find out what she's saying.

Stan is a perfect entrance. That is unless he brings up the Shift Industries case.

I make my way over to the group to catch Avery's story.

"And that's how I learned the hard way that you should never go snorkeling in a two-piece." Avery titters.

"She's marvelous, isn't she, darling?" The woman on Stan's arm looks to him and back to Avery, who smiles in response. "We must go snorkeling in the Great Barrier Reef!"

"You really must." Avery's cheerful tone changes slightly. "Just be sure you use reef-safe sunscreen because the coral bleaching has gotten worse over the years."

The group shifts uncomfortably at her truth, each face turning into a subtle frown. I can only focus on the fact that Avery Soko is spectacular, and she has impressive storytelling tactics.

A subtle yet brutal truth after an enticing story is the perfect way to spark people's interest. A closing statement like that could sway a jury.

I use the ebb in conversation to make my presence known.

"Stan! It's been a long time! How are you?" My voice musters as much enthusiasm as I can spare this evening.

I insert myself beside Avery and pat the back of the scrawny older man with half-moon glasses.

Her gentle scent lingers in the air, warm and inviting. Something about the fragrance reminds me of my summers at the beach.

Did she smell this good in the copy room?

"Luca!" Stanley's throaty voice scratches my eardrums. "I

haven't seen you since you worked on that leveraged buyout for us."

"Great to see you," I lie.

Avery returns to her conversation with the remainder of the group. I can't make out what she's saying over the noise.

"Congrats on the new gig!" Stan beams at me. "You've gone all 'greater good' on us, huh? A stark contrast to all those oil tycoons you built your career on."

Avery whips her head toward me at Stan's accusations. An unreadable expression scrunches her petite nose.

Well, at least that got her attention.

But seriously, tycoons? Guilt burns through me. It was one deeply regrettable case and a pivotal point in my career trajectory, and it will never stop haunting me.

I try to backtrack. "Someone's gotta save the world before you destroy it." The comment only causes Stan's body to fold with laughter. I try to steer the conversation away from myself. "Please introduce me to your…"

He finally acknowledges the spindly woman drooping off his arm. "Yes. Yes. Of course," Stan says. "This is my wife, Lina."

"Lina, so wonderful to meet you."

Lina's doe eyes flutter at my words. I'm glad to see that all those annoying hours of schmoozing kick in for me like muscle memory. Clearly, the misery inside of me isn't expressing itself in my features.

"And this is the wonderful Ave—" Stan begins.

"Hello, Ms. Soko." My shoulders sway toward her, and my burning stare meets the exquisite depth of her hazel eyes. Standing beside someone who takes up as much room as I do is thrilling. Without trying, it seems that Avery commands every gaze.

She inhales a sharp breath. Her piercing gaze narrows on me as it did before, and the corners of my lips pull into a grin.

Before she has an opportunity to respond, Stan interjects, "Splendid! You two already know each other?"

"We had the pleasure of meeting a while back," Avery says, a polite smile plastered across her face.

"Yes, if I recall correctly, Avery went out of her way to make callous remarks about my suit."

The thundering pools of her eyes attack me. A stubbornness invades her formerly loosened posture, straightening the long length of her spine even more.

"Oh, I'm sure that was well deserved," says Stan.

"You're mistaken." Avery looks at me, and her lip curls into a one-sided smirk. "I called you a heartless suit."

Lina snorts under her breath.

"Now, if you'll excuse me, I see an old colleague who will be absolutely devastated if I don't say hello." Avery makes haste to depart from the conversation.

A pang of irritation flames through me. *She's trying to avoid me.*

Lina chides, "Oh, don't leave us just yet!"

"It was such a pleasure to meet you all." Avery takes the wiry woman's hand and gives it a gentle squeeze. "I'll be in touch about the letter of recommendation for your niece."

What type of recommendation could she give a woman like Stan's wife, who probably has friends in higher places than Avery?

I try to recall her resume.

She worked as a philanthropist's assistant throughout grad school. Maybe that family is her connection?

Avery doesn't give me the impression that she's another socialite daughter or trust-fund kid, unlike Robyn from my double date.

How high do her familial connections actually go? And who is she to cringe at my past when she probably also has a few skeletons in her closet?

Avery gives everyone except for me a kind smile before departing, leaving a dull emptiness behind her with each determined step.

Stan returns to the conversation, but my eyes follow *her*.

I fake a laugh at another of Stan's poorly executed jokes, then excuse myself from the socialites.

I scour the crowd until Avery's cropped blonde locks catch my eye. Her body drapes over the bar, a relaxed set to her delicate shoulders. The curve of her back peeks through her lustrous dress. The parts of her skin not wrapped in the gleaming fabric appears soft.

How would she feel beneath my fingers?

I watch her stare and survey the room, an empty glass resting in her long fingers. My body draws closer to her, each footstep intent on bringing me near. When those vivid eyes finally land on me, they quickly roll into the back of her head.

Her peeved expression is growing on me more than I'd like to confess.

"Mr. Navarro." A coarseness drips from her words, but she makes no effort to look up at me.

"Let's start over." I wave the bartender over. "The job decision was a strategic move. No hard feelings. Please let me make it up to you by getting you a drink."

"Open bar," she remarks, then shifts her attention to the bartender. "I'll have a seltzer with lemon, please."

"And I'll have a 1942 on the rocks," I add to her order. She doesn't seem intent on making my apology easy. I steer the conversation away from the job rejection. "I've been wondering, Ms. Soko, did you really travel to all seven continents?"

She turns her face to me, and her eyes seem to fill with confusion.

"Or did you fib on your resume?" I clarify.

"No." She regards me. "I'm just surprised you asked."

I was able to take her aback; I smile at the accomplishment. "And why is that?"

Our drinks appear on the bar, and she thanks the bartender before taking a sip. I pull out a hundred-dollar bill and place it in the tip jar, leaving my drink on the bar. The bartender gives me a polite nod that I reciprocate before returning my attention to Avery, who seems to have watched the brief exchange the entire time.

"You've been thinking about me," she says plainly.

"Obviously." That came off more sarcastic than I intended.

Avery sets down her drink and crosses her arms in front of her chest in an unmistakably irritated stance, still facing me.

Why do I have to sound like such a fucking asshole?

I straighten the sleeves of my tuxedo jacket, searching my mind for a way to repair the situation, but Avery beats me to it.

"Humor me, Navarro. Did you decide to come tonight before or after my fundraising strategy highlighted this event?"

The bloom of her *r*'s drags behind her teeth.

Avery has me pinned.

I *did* scan the fundraising calendar in her presentation. I wanted new investor leads for ORO. I definitely can't divulge it now. I finally pick up my drink and take a long sip of the rich, straw-gold liquid.

"It was one of the best strategies we've seen in a while, but anyone with connections would be able to piece it together with enough free time."

"Excuse me? My hard work is much more than the relation-ships I worked tirelessly to cultivate. It's weeks of research, and —" She stops and turns away from me. "You know what, I don't have to explain anything to you. Especially after you sucked up to your old client dressed in a tux that probably costs my share of the rent."

Irritation raises my defenses. "Well, that's just wrong. *This* tuxedo"—I peer down at the luxurious fabric hugging my body—"is, probably, worth three months of your rent."

Growing up, I never spent a lot of time fretting over the way I dressed, but I quickly realized people at my law firm granted you a different type of attention when you donned expensive suits. Using the small fortune that was my first bonus, I replaced my off-the-rack suits and never looked back.

Now the woman I'm eager to impress tonight, as much as she dazzles me, refuses to see the person I want to become underneath my ornate wardrobe.

"Of course, a lawyer would see no problem with being that frivolous," she says sarcastically.

"*Retired* lawyer." I correct her. "And my past didn't stop ORO's board from making me the chief operating officer." That familiar undiluted guilt returns, and the muscles in my stomach clench.

I down the remainder of my drink and set it on the bar. The floral taste lingers on my lips.

"Either way, I'm glad I don't ever have to work with you." She stands rigid beside me but refuses to leave.

If she only knew how interested I am in revisiting the job proposition. But Joanna surpasses me in the hierarchy.

The charge building between us leaves no clear escape route. We stand in the heavy silence, watching the gala attendees swarm through the hall like ants.

Her scent melts into my senses again, that unique hint of ocean and sweetness causing my skin to flush.

An urgency arises in me to repair this petty spat between us. What person becomes this bent out of shape over a measly job rejection? It's not as though she'd be missing out on a substantial salary.

Let it go. Leave her alone for the evening.

But I want to fix this so we can start over and she can stop furrowing her brows at me.

"The way you handled yourself during the interview was impressive." I allow her this one truth.

"It doesn't matter now," she snaps.

"But you should really work on reining back your emotions." The words come out of me rushed, hurried, unnecessary.

Fuck, why'd I say that? *Why?*

"*What?*" she asks, drenched in exasperation.

I'm a fucking fool for continuing to play into Joanna's lie like an accomplice to a meaningless scheme.

I try to defuse. "You wanted feedback, and that is my honest feedback."

That was most definitely *not* my honest feedback, but I'm too caught up in this nonsense to stop.

There was not a single thing wrong with her emotions during her interview. Her passion for the job only made her a better candidate. Instead, I'm pulling out my cutthroat defenses for this battle between us. I shift uncomfortably.

"My *emotions* are present because I care about my work. Unlike you."

"You don't know a thing about me," I bite back.

"And I bet, I'm all the better for it."

Avery's small nose wrinkles again, and she folds the plump rosiness of her bottom lip into her teeth as though she's keeping another jab from escaping. A small lock of golden hair escapes her neat hairstyle, and I want to tuck it behind her ear before fisting the remainder of her tresses in my fingers.

I don't know why I'm desperately seeking her approval, but I can't seem to control myself.

"I think I could prove you wrong," I challenge.

She doesn't hesitate. "You'd fail trying."

"I don't give up that easily," I counter.

Her eyes meet mine in a combative stare. I work tirelessly to memorize each speck of honey swimming within them.

"Of course, how could I forget? Anyone who allies with oil tycoons must be belligerent."

So she did hear me earlier with Stan and thought the worst of me. I try to speak, but no words come out. She has me there, even if they weren't tycoons. Stan is such an asshole. I am and continue to be a combative prick.

A slight hint of a satisfied smile graces her face. "All out of things to say?"

My gaze follows her lips as she turns away from me.

Is the flare of her nostrils actually turning me on?

The room feels like it's a few degrees hotter. The desire to discover how her smart mouth would feel on mine overwhelms me. In a world where she is my employee, my direct charge, this kind of behavior would require a visit to a therapist. We stand on opposite sides of the same battlefield tonight, and I ache to discover where the confrontation will take us.

"Have dinner with me." The words pour out of me.

An expression of disgust contorts her gorgeous face, and her arms drop to her sides, those long fingers curling into fists. "What?"

"You. Me. Dinner. Isn't that clear enough?" My tone is annoyingly patronizing again, and I want to reel it back.

Avery's eyes anatomize each crease on my face as though her attention were on a captivating book. "I don't join strangers for dinner, Mr. Navarro." The rejection is much nicer than the *fuck off* I expected.

"I wouldn't call us strangers."

We stare at each other, and it's like another word readies itself in her throat, but there's a shift in the surrounding air.

One of Avery's oversized companions invades our sanctuary. His comically large bicep gives her shoulder a gentle nudge. He greets me with a toothy smile while the prod causes her to sway, and her fingertips sweep against the fabric of my trousers. A violent jolt fires through me as though I've been touched by a live wire.

"Ave, who's your friend?" the man questions in a deep, jovial voice.

Ave? Who is this guy? And why does *he* get to touch *her*?

Avery cringes, no doubt at the assumption that we could be friends.

Disappointment settles in my chest. We're barely acquaintances, but the disdain in her expression shallows my breathing.

I adjust the cuffs of my tuxedo jacket and then extend my palm in greeting.

"Ollie, this is Luca Navarro." Her hands run over the shimmering fabric of her dress. For a woman with so much to say about my tuxedo, her attire rivals mine. "He's the COO of ORO."

It's safe to assume this isn't the first time I've been mentioned to him, judging the widening of his eyes. My teeth grind against each other as another silent pang of guilt wrestles its way into me.

"*Oh.*" Ollie's meaty hand eventually meets mine in an unnecessarily aggressive handshake.

"It's a pleasure to meet you, Ollie." My grip on his hand loosens when I catch a glimpse of his kind eyes behind the tense glare he tries to give me. "Are you Avery's date?"

"We work together," Avery answers for him, "and I don't date. Ollie, I'll see you back at the table."

With a subtle nod, she points in the direction where her other two companions huddle together at a table. Avery reaches her free hand to his forearm, giving him a gentle squeeze.

Without a goodbye, she abandons us at the bar. Her words replay in my mind.

I don't date.

Chapter 8
Avery

My heels echo off the museum floor as I rush toward the far-back table Robert's sister secured for us. The evening is a success overall, except for the altercation with the heartless suit.

When I arrive at my seat, Matthew is chatting with Robert.

I can't wait to tell him about the verbal commitment I secured that will bring us $250,000 by the end of the month. It's not quite enough to keep funding the Gaya Island mission and continue testing our technology, but it'll help for now.

It's nice to be here tonight. I'm back in my element, surrounded by people. The strain in my neck unbinds.

Robert pulls out my chair, and I slide into the plush seat. I give him a warm smile that causes him to look awkwardly around before settling his eyes on the folded napkin on his lap.

Ollie is still standing beside Luca Navarro. Ollie's toothy grin is the size of a crescent moon, the opposite of how miserable he looked amongst the rest of the gala guests.

Luca. Navarro.

The way he scrutinized me, never shifting his chiseled face away from mine, put my sanity through the wringer. I can't recall the last time such an icy stare elicited a desire to remain in a verbal sparring match. I'm tempted to catch him off guard and figure out the exact reason he's here tonight—or even better, his intentions at ORO. I doubt he has some evil plan, but I'm struggling to paint the complete picture of who he is between the oil case, the fancy clothes, and that relentless attitude.

Something doesn't add up. I want to find out what it is.

Then there was the random question about my travels. I've never had someone ask me about the interests section of my resume. I'd hoped Joanna would notice that we shared the same accomplishment of traveling all seven continents. Instead, it was Luca who recognized my achievement.

Why would he think I lied?

My dad made sure I experienced the world entirely before I was tied down to my books and lecture halls at university. But I didn't have the chance to mention that he took me with him on photography expeditions during my interview.

The unsettling feeling in my belly refuses to fade.

What I said about Luca's law career may have been a bit harsh. But I was shocked by Mr. Lewis' mention of his oil cases. I felt betrayed. Betrayed about what, I don't really know.

The COO of ORO shouldn't be some ex-corporate lawyer tied to dirty oil. I realize the hypocrisy in my own thoughts. My reaction was likely blown out of proportion due to the guilt I felt for entertaining Mr. Lewis and his wife for as long as I did.

Luca may not be wrong. If ORO brought him on, then there must be a good reason for it.

There's also the fact that after we ordered our drinks, he generously tipped the bartender, whose tip jar is empty apart from some loose singles.

It was kind of attractive.

Okay. *Very* fucking attractive.

Especially when no one else at this gala has expressed their thanks in such a generous way. But he clearly only did that to show off.

Ollie pats Luca on the shoulder, causing Luca to shift briefly. Luca's impressive, lean-cut muscles make themselves known in his fine tuxedo. Somehow his stature doesn't diminish beside Ollie's ginormous frame.

How would the breadth of Luca's shoulders feel beneath my hands?

No. No. No.

I reach for Matthew's glass of red wine and down the remaining sip, drowning out the charge inside me.

My wandering imagination dissipates as Ollie turns around and walks toward me until he finally takes his seat beside Matthew.

"What took you so long?" I lean forward in my seat, failing to curb the snap in my voice.

Robert's eyes widen slightly at my tone, and I regret unsettling him with my outburst.

Matthew looks over at us while Ollie makes a great effort to create space for himself in the small banquet chair.

Matthew keeps his voice low. "What did you do?"

"Ain't done nothing, Matt!" Ollie chides. "Just being polite."

"He was chatting up the chief operating officer of ORO!" I say.

Robert lets out a slight wheeze.

"And?" Matthew urges us to elaborate.

"He's rather bonnie." Ollie beams at me, gently tucking a cloth napkin into his collar, "Maybe he fancies you."

The words fling me back into my chair. A whirlpool of emotions displaces me, and my skin pebbles.

"Why'd you say that?" Matthew runs his fingers through his messy hair and then replaces the empty glass I took from him with a fresh one that he swipes from a passing waiter.

Ollie shrugs.

I press my lips together, not wanting to speculate on Ollie's suggestion.

"Accurate inference, Ol," Robert mutters, carefully connecting his gaze from me to Luca across the ballroom. "The gentleman will not stop looking this way."

My cheeks burn.

"Alright," Matthew concludes, understanding the conversation has run its course. "That's enough."

Robert's observation stirs the rumble of curiosity within me, but I follow Matthew's lead to reroute the topic. "Can we talk about something else? Like the fact that I secured a funding commitment and a few serious leads warranting follow-ups."

"Already? You're incredible!" Matthew smiles.

I warm at the words. *I am incredible.* I don't know why I let myself forget it.

Ollie laughs. "He's right, lassie. No wonder that Navarro fella asked quite a few questions about you."

My fingers fidget with the shimmering fabric on my dress. "What did he say?" I ask, trying my best to remain calm.

"Just asked what you're doing at Plastech and if you like working with us. I told him, 'course you do."

But before I can interrogate Ollie further, the hall quiets as an elderly woman fights her way onto the bright podium. The hypnotizing blue glow of the gala coats each table as though we're all underwater. It's an incredible sight, even if I can't quite make out the stage from our seats.

The woman is quickly engulfed by staff members reaching for her hands as her legs climb the stairs. One of the staff members appears to pull the microphone away from her, but she holds steady.

"I don't need to be formally introduced," the woman mumbles loud enough for the microphone to pick up. "I'm the one and only Willa! The gala is hosted in my name!"

The room floods with anticipatory whispers as the guests' attention moves to the stage.

After a somewhat bumpy introduction involving an incoherent series of obscenities, two disgruntled assistants, and a screeching microphone feed, Willhelma Ellington stands ready to address us.

"I plan to make this short." Her stern voice booms throughout the room.

"Turn that down!" Willa yells again, this time at no one in particular. The guests share a quick laugh across the room. "Do you want to blow my eardrums out?"

I watch the stage and take another sip of the wine Matthew set in front of me.

"I'm announcing a competition." She adjusts her glasses. "*Of sorts.*"

The wave of murmurs spreads across the hall once more.

My stomach curdles.

A competition?

"Please give a round of applause for the Ellington Grant." The room obeys. "I'll be awarding five million dollars in funding to one company, small or large, to design and implement new technology that will advance conservation."

I stifle a gasp. Ollie's fork clatters onto his plate at the number.

Five million dollars?

My team's eyes connect, and I can almost see the thoughts turning in each of their heads. The silence in the ballroom envelops the crowd in a piercing silence.

"The rules are simple," Willa continues. "Most of you in attendance are companies that focus on bettering our planet. I implore you all to present an idea."

My pulse quickens as I clutch my silverware. I worry I'm denting it. I feel the vibration of Matthew's foot tapping synchronize with my heartbeat.

"To become eligible for the Ellington Grant, your proposals must meet the following requirements." A giant screen lights the space behind Willhelma, presenting the rules as she rattles them off to the crowd. "The idea must address and resolve areas of critical duress in our global environments. It must make use of sustainable methods to achieve its goals." She catches her breath before proceeding. "And the winning company assigned to the project must be willing to commit to the work for two years."

Our company's entire interface and motto are a shoo-in for this award.

This could be our saving grace!

"You'll have two weeks to submit a proposal for your idea. After I review each one over the next month, I'll select the company that will advance to the testing phase." Willa abandons her microphone and returns to her table.

A sprightly assistant takes over, offering more details about the competition.

I scan the room, mentally noting which tables are beginning their hushed conversations.

At the Oceanic Research Organization table, four people tap away on their phones under the white tablecloth. It seems ORO is planning to enter.

As though an organization of their size needs any more funding.

My curiosity betrays me when I notice Luca Navarro staring back at me. The corners of his lips quirk up as he raises his champagne flute to me in salute.

Game on.

Applause erupts in the ballroom, breaking our intense moment.

I turn to my team, and they all nod with contained excitement.

"Five million dollars can help us start scaling the platform," Robert says.

"Not only scaling, but we can finally finish the cleanup mission in Gaya Island," Ollie adds.

The understanding in his expression confirms he and I are on the same page.

Matthew pulls out his phone, likely clearing our schedules for tomorrow. I hide an eager smile.

"Guess our luck is turning around." Ollie clinks his glass to mine.

Chapter 9
Avery

A SWARM OF CARS INUNDATES THE ROAD IN FRONT OF THE American Museum of Natural History. The attendees of the gala flood the marble steps before gathering into the waiting vehicles.

I wait for an open cab at the top of the stairs. My body hums with anticipation at the proposal-structuring ideas coursing through my mind. While my team fled, itching to get out of their rented tuxedos, I chose to stay back after the evening concluded. I couldn't pass up the opportunity for some last-minute networking.

Two people exit the museum, their conversation traveling loudly.

"At least the food was decent this time, but that competition is complete bollocks," says a petite woman.

"Right? Did you see ORO was there? It doesn't matter what any of us do," says her taller companion, who wears a stunning blue gown. "If they're going to enter, they're guaranteed to win. They probably have countless projects to choose from."

Annoyance coats the back of my throat at the thought of ORO keeping people away from their dreams.

"Sorry to interrupt," I chime in. They stare back at me. "But smaller companies stand a chance, *even if* ORO is planning to enter."

Sure, they have enormous resources, a strategy and research team, a glamorous office, and Joanna Benbart.

The lofty woman stares back at me. "What? Do you work for ORO or something?"

A sting of hurt pierces my gut, but I ignore it. "No. I'm head of development at a start-up called Plastech. Our tech sorts trash from fish in ocean water," I say it proudly because, well, I am *very* proud of us.

"Cool, so you're tellin' us that we won't win 'ginst you either," says the shorter woman. "Our parasitic moss that naturally decomposes trash hasn't even left the testin' phase yet."

"What are you talking about? Parasitic moss sounds *so* cool." I try to convey my genuine excitement, but I fear that no matter how much my tone brightens, making moss sound sexy is difficult. "Think about it. The grant could support you through the testing phase. You must submit your proposal!"

I smile at my motivational speech.

Luca Navarro would probably tell this poor group not to enter. He probably wouldn't acknowledge them at all.

Unlike him, though, I'm not afraid of a bit of competition. Especially when winning could create a revolutionary impact on our planet.

"People just ain't carin' about the ocean anymore." The petite woman's shoulders sag in defeat.

"*We* care about the oceans. *Everyone* here cares." I gesture at the people on the stairs who work for companies like ours and the donors supporting them. "When the money runs out, we'll do exactly what we're doing now: find more people who care."

"True," the taller woman replies.

The ladies peer at each other; a familiar look of excitement fills their eyes.

"Plastech is lucky to have you." The shorter companion smiles at me.

"I know." My lips curve upward, and I hope that anything I say resonates with them enough to enter the competition.

The women leave our place on the stairs, and I go to the curb.

Luca Navarro is probably already on his way to the office to start on the grant proposal. Why else would he leave so quickly after the announcement?

His dinner proposition echoes in my head.

He has some nerve to assume I would ever want to spend an evening with a suit who ripped my dream job from my bare hands.

No amount of curiosity will convince me to join him. Nor will his striking, boyish grin.

Warmth pools in my belly.

No.

I don't have the capacity for dating.

My career comes first.

This means Plastech is my only priority right now, and I am determined to win the Ellington Grant—even if Luca's hand-somely arrogant smile lingers in the back of my mind.

My annoyance with him still refuses to budge. *Why am I letting him get under my skin?*

I pull out my phone and notice a missed call from Lily. She must be dying to hear all the gala details before her night shift at the bar. Dialing her number, I bring the phone to my ear and dig for loose cash in my clutch.

I notice the back of a taxi with a light on and a wide-open door. I hurry toward it, eager to snap it up for myself. My free hand grasps the train of my dress as I keep my attention on the sidewalk.

"This is Lily! If I gave you this number last night, it was to make sure you got home safe. *Not* because I was flirting with you!" her voice sings into my ear, making me laugh.

I begin leaving Lily a voicemail.

"The suit was here—" My lower half lands on something that very much feels like a person instead of a car seat.

My phone tumbles into my lap, and my hands settle on what I assume is a pair of pants beneath me, the sight of them almost camouflaged by the dark leather of the seat. I immediately reach for my phone.

Yep, those are undeniably legs.

I'm sitting on an actual person.

"I'm so sorry!" I yelp. I try to leap forward, but my head meets with the hard privacy panel.

The taxi driver turns to face me, his eyes widening in the front seat. *Is he not going to help?*

I try to pull myself out of the cab, leaning on the one leg connected to the pavement, but my dress fails me, the fabric pulling taut as it catches on something in the vehicle.

"Ave?" A deep voice tickles my ear.

Him.

I whip my head around.

Adrenaline pulses within me. My nose brushes against his, and our foreheads press together. I grip his shoulder for support, my other hand clasping the grab handle above the open car door.

So that's what his shoulder feels like?

The taste of a familiar woodsy smell tickles my lips. Undeniable heat surges between my thighs as his large hands firmly settle on my hips, steadying me in his lap. A hardness prods my leg. I try not to react to his very generous size.

A blaring horn snaps us out of our haze.

My eyes finally find his heavy intentional stare. "Only the people I'm close to get to call me *Ave.*"

"Well," he whispers against my neck. His callused fingers press deeper into my flesh. "What do you call this?"

A current of electricity runs through me from his touch.

That shock is from panic, right? It has to be. It can't be anything else.

"An accident."

"But you fell with such purpose," he says.

"I did not!" I try to scramble out of the cab, but the back seat is too small for our tall frames, and my body is practically trapped between him and the privacy panel.

"I bet you were looking for me, waiting to fall into my arms at my dinner invitation."

"You wish." I manage to gain control over one of my stuck limbs.

"I do," he exhales.

I finally wrestle myself out of the cab, but when my heels collide with the pavement, a tug of my dress sends me into the car door.

Great, it's still stuck.

"Let me help," he says, his eyes momentarily pausing on my lips before returning to my glare.

"I don't want *your* help." I angrily pull on the delicate fabric, and the sound of a large rip fills the air. "*Ugh!*"

Luca watches with an uncontained smile as the long slit of my gown rips up to midthigh, exposing my legs to the evening breeze.

"What on earth is so amusing about one of my favorite dresses being ripped to shreds?"

The smirk refuses to budge. "You'd react the same way if it was my tux stuck in this door."

"But, unlike your flashy tux, this is vintage!"

"Why does that matter?"

I let out another audible groan.

"Here." He starts pulling off his luxury jacket.

"I don't want favors from the competition!"

The statement ripples his forehead into a confused expression. "Competition?"

Of course, he has no idea what I'm talking about.

I clench my fists, trying to bite my tongue. "The Ellington Grant. Or is a five-million-dollar funding opportunity below ORO's threshold of importance?"

How can he be so nonchalant about this money?

"Look, just take this cab, okay?" He starts to exit the vehicle.

I stare back at him, unable to process the sudden kindness. The knot of his tie hangs loosely from him, offering glimpses of his veined neck, and a part of me wants to wrap my hand around the fabric and pull his face into mine.

To yell at him up close, of course.

"I'd rather walk." I press my heels into the street, wanting to get far away from him. If I walk home, it'll only be twenty minutes through the park.

Okay, in my stilettos, maybe thirty minutes.

I'll just find another cab. It can't be that difficult.

Luck is now in my favor. At the end of the block, another available car comes into view. I throw my hand in the air, flagging down my ride home. When it halts before me, I dip my head into the window, ensuring no one occupies the seat. I smile at the cab driver, who stares at me inquisitively.

"Just making sure no one's in here."

My body collides with the leather seat of the empty cab. I rattle off my address before I turn to look out the window. Then I try to rub his touch off my skin.

His words cling to my thoughts.

You've been thinking about me, obviously.

He meant to mock me, the condescension in his tone was unmistakable, but a part of me wonders if there was any truth behind his words. Why else would he be so adamant about dinner?

For two weeks, I tried to force him out of my mind, my existence plagued by his rejection call and the new career trajectory it had sent me on.

If Luca had hired me, I would've been the one who'd represented ORO this evening, brainstorming ideas for the grant with *his* team.

Maybe I would've even attended many events like this with him by my side.

That doesn't matter now. Plastech is my priority.

In sitting in traffic, I catch Luca Navarro standing beside my car. He watches me drive out of view.

Was he behind me the entire time?

Chapter 10
Luca

My eyes shoot open as the sun hits my face.

What's going on?

It's way too bright and loud for 5:00 a.m. I jerk out of bed and search for my phone on my nightstand. A loose charger sits in its place.

I rip the covers off my sweaty flesh. My heart thrashes in my rib cage.

What. Is. Happening?

I lift from my bed and slam my feet into the floor.

I planned my entire day to the minute. I can't afford to sleep in. I have way too much to do today.

Not a single person can possibly stay successful if they waste away their mornings by laying around.

Okay, what's on my to-do list? There's my daily morning run.

Maybe I can skip today?

My barber is at 7:00 a.m. on the dot, but judging by the sunlight, I probably missed it. My stomach churns at the thought of not giving Andrew proper notice. I need to call him at once. I run my fingers through my overgrown strands of hair, frustrated by the length.

I rip the blankets off my bed, but I still don't see my phone anywhere.

Where did I put it?

I need to go to the post office to mail my parents' anniversary gift. It's the last day I can ship it so it arrives on time.

The grocery store trip I can skip. I'll have to live without my protein bars this week. Nico keeps eating them despite the many times I've offered to buy him his own packs.

If I'd had all of this done before 9:00 a.m., I'd have had ample time to make it into the office and prepare for the Ellington Grant update meeting on Monday.

My heart thunders in my rib cage. It has been three days since Willa's announcement, and the team I was assigned to put together a proposal is experiencing technical difficulties that need to be resolved as soon as possible.

I also have that hour reserved for check-ins across ORO's international teams. Then, of course, there were a few investor calls I wanted to squeeze in this afternoon—all of which I will now need to push.

I walk into my bathroom and search the vanity. Still no phone.

Fuck.

I look out my bedroom window and see people filling the sidewalks. It must be past 7:00 a.m. Tension strains all over my body.

I rush out of the room, pushing the door hard. The handle strikes against my freshly repainted wall.

"Ahh."

Just another thing I'll need to fix. *Add it to my fucking to-do list!*

As I walk down the hall, my muscles feel heavy with sleep. Small clattering noises come from the kitchen.

Is Nico okay?

Is he home?

Did he have something to do with me sleeping in?

I barrel down the hall. My foot catches on something. I brace my palms against the wall to stop myself from tumbling. Another fucking cable. I was too distracted to notice the wire running from Nico's room into the kitchen. My irritation hits a peak when I see another pair of crumpled-up socks littering the end of the hallway.

I'm going to kill him!

I make it to the kitchen, and the unexpected smell of butter stirs an aching hunger in my stomach. Nico hums loudly to music playing blaring from his oversized headphones. He stands over the stovetop. The relaxing sway of his shoulders matches the melody; it's an absolute slap to the face.

Did I wake up in some sort of alternate universe? My brother is awake before me, and he's preparing breakfast. The clock on the stove reads three hours after I was supposed to start my morning.

I suck in a deep breath. Half of my day is gone already.

"Nico?" I shout to get his attention, working my way around the expansive island. The sink overflows with dishes.

This place was spotless before I went to bed last night. We have a dishwasher. Why does it look like eight people decided to have a bake-off here?

I inhale, trying to keep my calm.

His back remains toward me while he works at the stove. I clap my hand on his shoulder. Nico screeches like a bewildered cat at my touch.

"Look who's finally awake." He laughs off the reaction.

"Where is it?"

"What?" Nico plays coy, but I've witnessed this act since we were children. He's responsible for ruining my schedule. I just know it.

"My phone!" I erupt.

Nico turns to face me. "Luca, you've been working too much lately. We're all worried about you."

"Worried about *me*? I have actual work to do. Where is my phone?" I scan the counters for the device, shuffling things around with my sweaty palms.

What if someone from the board called me?

"Alright, alright, calm down." He flips a pancake on the griddle. "After *Mami* chatted with you yesterday, she called me and said you seemed more stressed than usual. We thought you could use the rest."

I'm the responsible one.

Our parents should not be concerning Nico with my well-being, especially when there's nothing to be concerned about. I'm his older brother. *I* take care of *him*.

"Don't tell me to calm down. I have a schedule. A carefully planned-out schedule. You've no right to decide when I should wake up!"

"Luca, it's a Friday!" Nico's voice booms through the kitchen. "Your first meeting isn't for another hour. I checked!"

"My phone."

He tries to hand me a plate of pancakes. "I was going to wake you up with breakfast."

"I don't want this." I push away the food. "Just tell me where you put my phone, so I can start my day."

"Eat breakfast with me, dude. You need to chill. You've been so anal lately. It's a real bummer."

"*A bummer*? A bummer is waking up three hours late to a messy fucking house and behind schedule. *¡No haces nada!*"

"Hey, I cleaned up last week!"

"*No mames.* You *hired* someone to clean up after you because you had a date coming over."

I haven't even brought someone to my place before.

"But it was clean! Luca, you can take one day off—"

"Just because you're careless doesn't mean you get to make my life a mess too."

He flinches at the statement. I regret the words immediately.

While I fit into the mold of academic success, Nico forwent college after two years to ride motorcycles in Indonesia and swim in the Black Sea. I don't understand his lifestyle; maybe I'm envious of how easily happiness seems to come to him.

"Luca, you haven't been sleeping or coming home in the evenings." There's a strain in his voice, and I hate that I'm the cause. Nico pulls my phone out of his pocket and hands it to me. "I just wanted to do something nice."

"Nice would've been cleaning up after yourself, not borrowing my stuff. Oh, and not taking my fucking phone."

I yank the device out of his hand and storm into my room, slamming the door behind me. An unsettling feeling coats my anger like hot gravel as I try to piece together how I will make up the lost hours of my morning. The first few weeks having Nico here were nice, but if he continues to pull these stunts, we won't be able to live together.

If I skip my run, I can get to the office by noon, but my body is too wound up with agitation.

I need to burn off some of this steam, or I'll spend the day unable to focus.

I throw on my black running polo and a pair of matching running shorts before I tie the laces of my new white sneakers. I hurry out of the apartment, ignoring Nico's apologies.

TOURISTS PACK the sidewalks and bikes race through traffic. After the mile-long sprint through Central Park, the uneasiness in my body begins to dissipate.

Unlike my runs at dawn, today the park buzzes with energy.

The sounds of barking dogs and endless conversation help keep my mind off my hectic morning.

My feet carry me onto the Reservoir's running path, and I find my usual rhythm along the body of water.

Guilt settles into me. I shouldn't have yelled at my brother.

He doesn't fit the structure that I exist in—a proud, determined workaholic. Something about the draining reality of my job helps me feel alive.

For Nico, that feeling materializes itself differently. He shares my hard work ethic, most notably on building back-end API systems with his peers, which he taught himself how to do, and earning a promotion in his first year at Viggle, but the idea of a schedule always makes him uneasy. I consciously try not to compare his path to the one I chose.

The last time I was this upset with Nico was probably when he was eighteen and lost his passport while traveling in Rome. Luckily, we both have US and Mexican passports. After hours of searching, I finally found the one he didn't take on his trip, and I flew out to find him. My flights were delayed, and I hadn't slept in two days by the time I landed.

He was partying at some rooftop bar near the Vatican. It took me three hours to get him back to the hotel room. Once I got there, exhaustion took over, and I fell asleep instantly. Thirteen hours later, I awoke to a written note from Nico.

Gotta live in the moment, thanks for the passport, big bro!

He left me alone in Rome for backstage passes to a music festival in Berlin. On the flight home, I almost ground my teeth to dust with my anger.

I didn't speak to him for a week until he showed up at my apartment in Berkeley with a bottle of whiskey and those signature puppy dog eyes. I forgave him on the spot.

Like I always do.

Maybe he's right about me working too much.

The workload at ORO is starting to mimic my early years at

the law firm, and the stress of my position is growing more detrimental.

And now I took it out on the only person in the world who tolerates me daily—my little brother.

For weeks, I've dropped hints about how I miss eating breakfast with him, and Nico finally took charge, even if his approach drastically differs from mine.

I would have put something on the calendar, a tangible commitment to spend time together. But the thought of him sitting in that empty apartment right now, alone and with the heavy weight of my words over him, makes me feel sick.

Go back!

I change direction, pushing the final mile home.

I zone out as muscle memory pounds the rubber of my sneakers against the concrete. People from every place in the world crowd the path. New York is a city of strangers looking to make their mark. It was one of the reasons I chose to pursue my law career here. It's somehow both tiny and sprawling, and right now is one of those times the city feels comically small.

Running in my opposite direction is a familiar face.

It can't be.

Avery Soko's flushed body is barreling toward me. Her attention is sharply focused, and I can hear music blaring from her headphones, even from the considerable distance between us.

She keeps a steady rhythm in her disheveled running shoes. They look like they'll fall apart. Damp strands of her blonde hair cling to her skin. An oversized UNC-Chapel Hill T-shirt drapes over her body, the mascot dancing with each of her movements.

Avery passes me, oblivious to the people around her.

Our last unplanned run-in ended with her storming away from me. I should probably just keep going.

But I can't fucking help myself.

I whip around, sprinting after her. My legs threaten to give out on me, but I keep a steady pace behind her.

She's become a stain on my thoughts. A piece of lint that refuses to leave the fabric of my mind. I've caught myself veering toward her on more than one frustrating occasion.

I need to spend more time around her, pick her brain and watch her take each of my pointed words in stride. Now that we're competing for the same grant, I think I've lost my shot at a smooth relationship with her.

It's okay, though. If she wants a rival, a rival she will get.

I jog behind her, keeping my distance. I can't help but steady my eyes on how her round ass shakes in those bright-green running shorts.

My mouth waters at the image of her drenched shirt clinging to her tight waist. That familiar scent of her body lingers behind her, and I savor every whiff. The blood rushing to my compression shorts forces the fabric to tighten around me.

Am I seriously getting hard right now? In public, in broad daylight?

I fill my head with the faces of passersby in an effort to remove my reaction to Avery from my body.

I pick up my pace again until I match her stride. We're perfectly in sync. Our feet pound in rhythm next to each other. Until she notices me. Avery's beautiful face turns straight once more before quickly meeting my eyes. I'm grinning. A shock of recognition causes her eyebrows to furrow into what is becoming my favorite position.

She glares at me before picking up speed. I force myself to keep up.

Damn, she is fast.

Avery removes one of her earphones, clutching it in her fist. "Why are you following me?"

"I didn't realize you owned this running trail."

"It's my side of the park." Her lungs heave with a labored breath. "I run here every day."

I relish the morsel of information she reveals. We are more alike than I thought.

My brows quirk in amusement at her eye roll. "*Your* side of the park?"

"Yes, Navarro," she yells. "Run somewhere else!"

"Why?" I tease. "Running right here is *so* much more fun."

"Only for one of us."

We take a few more strides before her body halts abruptly. My feet take me a few steps ahead before slowing to a stop. Avery bends over, picking something up from the ground.

"What are you doing?" I call out to her, jogging back to where she's veering off the running path.

"Trash in the park is an atrocity." She holds up a half-empty water bottle and heads toward a nearby recycling bin before discarding the bottle inside.

"You know, there are conservancy crews in the park to help keep it clean."

Avery returns to the path, and I follow her, our brief walk turning into a jog. I'm entertaining this encounter for too long, especially since it might cause me to miss a meeting with one of ORO's international teams, but there's a pestering need brewing inside me. *Stay beside her. Talk to her. Don't let her run off again.*

"Of course, I know that, but it could blow over into the Reservoir, and no one's going to jump in and fish it out." She glares at me, beads of sweat pooling at her temples. She looks so pretty, if not more stunning, as she did the night of the gala, all dolled up in her stunning gown.

I must stare at her too long because she mistakes my fascination for scrutiny. "What? Are you afraid of getting a little dirty?"

I smirk while shooting out both my palms in front of me. "These hands are very good at getting dirty."

She rolls her eyes and picks up her pace.

I sprint after her, trying to recall the last time I picked up trash since moving to the city. It's a moot point to try and pick up *one* piece of trash because too many people live here for it to stay clean.

Mami would scold me if she heard me talk like that. Once a month, she would drive our family to the cold beaches of Northern California. We would build giant fortresses of sand and then after we would sift through the kelp and seaweed that had washed up on the shore. Old bottles and plastic bags would be intertwined within their slimy leaves.

My favorite part was when Nico and I raced to find the most oversized kelp stems, using them for intricate sword fights to defend the sandy castles.

The pungent smell of salt water clung to us until we got home and rinsed away the day. I smile at the memory. Those wonderful days in my childhood inspired the club I created to clean up the Santa Cruz beaches as an undergrad. The busy weekends brought in waves of tourists who treated the beach like their own trash can. We spent hours digging debris out of the sand before cooling off in the water at sunset.

But New York City is different from a glistening, pristine beach.

Right?

Stepping on a glass bottle while walking on the beach is much worse than just hearing the crunch of a water bottle under your foot during an early morning run.

Is it?

I glance over at her and realize how careless I have become since moving to the city.

Is working at ORO enough?

My tumbling thoughts distract me from how long we've been running together. It's comforting to have a companion keeping pace beside you. I look at Avery again, but she returns my warm gaze with an irritated stare.

"Don't you have something better to do than follow me around the park?"

"No," I lie, trying to ignore the apology I'd planned to give Nico and the to-do list that is getting pushed further and further behind.

"Well, there's a bench around that bend if you're getting tired."

"If you need a seat, I know you found my lap quite comfortable."

The memory of her full hips unexpectedly landing on me the night of the gala makes me wish I wore more loose-fitting shorts.

Get it together.

"You've been misinformed."

I catch up to her, and our eyes lock, electrifying the sweltering heat around us. The gorgeous determination on her face reveals itself as if a stage curtain had opened. She runs ahead, and I race up to her, the both of us trying to outrun the other.

After a few minutes of her finally outpacing me, I stop trying to run in front of her. "Are you enjoying this game we've created as much as I am?"

"No game," she pants. "There is *only* the competition."

"Right, the competition. You failed to mention your obsessively competitive nature as a flaw during the interview."

"I just know what I want. And right now, there is nothing I want more than to win the grant."

Her tenacity is so fucking sexy that it manages to splatter another smile across my face. "Well, it seems you'd want to win the rights to *my side* of the park."

"You mean *my* side," she says.

"How about this? The first person to reach the streetlight at the far exit of the Reservoir gets to keep their running path." I gesture with my head at the lone black light post about half a mile ahead of us.

Avery smiles and does not hesitate before she takes off in a sprint.

Oh no, she doesn't!

I take off after her, ignoring the screaming muscles in my legs. The blistering heat is intolerable, but I swallow the humid air and push on.

This need to win her over *must* stem from our disappointing run-in at the gala. To prove that the negative impression she has of me is wrong.

Right?

Why do I even care what she thinks?

But here I am, chasing after her like a fool.

We pass the first bend, the streetlight now clearly in our view. Avery leads; her pace is quicker than mine. Those lean legs carry her effortlessly across the pavement.

A random movement in my peripheral distracts me. I keep moving forward, but I turn my head and see a plastic bag dancing frantically around a grassy patch. I try to ignore it, but the thrashing movements become more distracting, like a cartoon ghost skipping on the bright-green lawn.

It's probably just a pigeon. New York City's sky rats have a knack for getting stuck inside random places.

Avery must not have seen it, too intent on beating me to our finish line, but a piercing squawk comes from the bag. Indecision tumbles inside of me, and I can't seem to ignore the helpless bird fighting to break free. I veer off the running path and slow my pace as I approach the grassy area, solidifying my loss against Avery.

I approach the trapped pigeon, trying to keep my footsteps light. The bag gains a few inches off the ground, and the crinkling sound of plastic mixes with the bird's cries.

Squatting down, I reach forward, and my fingers pinch the bag to rip it off the helpless creature. The small gray bird stumbles around in the fresh air before taking flight, each flap of its wings a tad disoriented. I ball the bag into my fist and turn my head, searching for Avery.

The bright blonde of her hair makes itself apparent as her feet carry her past the streetlight. She turns, a glowing smile plastered across her face, and my body fills with a warm excitement where I expected to feel disappointment.

If my loss means she's happy, I'll concede it.

We lock eyes for a quick moment, I salute her win, and she sticks out her tongue in response before running off the Reservoir path out of sight. I straighten, steadying my tired legs before attempting to catch up to her.

Smack!

A scalding pain thrashes into the side of my face.

"Ouch!" I exclaim and rub the tingling in my cheek.

My eyes drop to the ground where a wet, bright-green tennis ball rests near my sneakers. I look ahead once more, but I only have a second before I'm pummeled back into the grass by three large animals.

One of the heavy beasts steps on my chest, pulling a heavy breath out of my lungs. I fling my arms up across my face, protecting myself from the paws scratching at my skin.

"Ow!" I yelp again.

The dogs dig at me, searching for the tennis ball that's now wedged between the ground and my back. I struggle to pull myself away from the tangle of furry limbs and fluffy tails batting at my face.

A sudden wetness attacks my ankles and my cheeks. I pull my hands away from my eyes and come face-to-face with two smaller dogs vigorously licking the sweat off my body.

"Oh my gosh. I'm sorry. Ziggy, Nellie, Mia, come here." A young woman appears over me. Her words come out between her pants as she wrestles the large dogs off me. The leashes for the two small dogs are in her free hand. "They saw a squirrel, and all took off at once. This new belt leash broke, and then some kid threw a ball and—"

"It's fine." I wave away the dog walker's helping hand and spring up to my feet. My body is already aching from the impact. I still clutch the plastic bag and look down at my new sneakers, now covered with grass and dog drool.

Gross.

I try to get my bearings, my head peering toward the streetlight in search of the source of my distraction.

That woman will be the end of me.

NICO IS GONE when I finally find my way home covered in small injuries.

I grab my phone and text him an apology.

LUCA

> Sorry I'm an ass. At least I'm still your favorite brother.

A few seconds later, his reply appears on my screen.

NICO

> u mean least favorite brother

I smile at his text, thankful that our fights never last long.

The aggravation of this wasteful morning worms itself back into me. My run-in with Avery further screwed up my meticulous plans for today, which certainly didn't include getting mauled by a pack of dogs. She obviously saw that, but probably not my heroic pigeon-saving mission.

I wrestle my laptop out of my bag and jump on the call with ORO's international staff while simultaneously changing the Ellington Grant meeting from Monday to today, so we can spend the weekend working.

I assigned Jamie, Molly, and Dr. Claremont, who are all seemingly capable of handling a few robotic fleets of trash collectors. However, two days ago, Dr. Claremont was concerned they were still having issues with the robots switching between salt water and fresh water. I need an urgent update on the progress of that problem.

I can hear Avery's voice echoing in my head. *There is only the competition.*

That is surely the case now.

Our run-in at the park sparked an urgency, an excitement even, that I hadn't yet felt at ORO. Finally, an adversary who could challenge me.

Yet the run failed to reset my tense nerves, instead leaving me unsettled in other ways and with tiny bruises in the shapes of paw prints.

I pass the expanse of my closet and walk into the bathroom, aching for cool water on my skin. I turn on the faucet, hoping for the icy shower to wash away the strain brewing in me. I scrub dirt off my legs as loose grass floats down the drain.

My palms connect with the tiled wall, and I soak my face in the frozen stream, but it does not cool the flame coursing through me.

The frustration rips at me from within. I'm desperate to escape the building tension. I reach for the shower handle, changing the temperature until heat pours over me.

Maybe it's been too long since I've been with someone.

I try to recall what it's like, the distracting feeling of warmth beneath me. But the thoughts are replaced with *her*.

Avery Soko is the first woman to pique my interest in years. The memory of her gorgeous scowl sends a thrilling jolt through me. My teeth grind at the greedy need to hear her breathe my name.

My name that keeps twisting her tongue over every rolling *r*.

I want to run my fingers over those beautiful lips and teach her mouth how to say it over and over again, without fail.

The images of her drenched skin during the run and her body in the shimmering gown flash behind my closed eyelids. Each fleeting memory of her causes blood to swell in my dick, which aches for release.

The hot steam permeates the room as I picture Avery's palms running all over my body, helping me work the tension out. The length of her delicate fingers would wrap around my hard cock, teasing me with every long stroke. My touch is a disappointing replacement for the way her hands might feel around me.

I crave to feel the rocking of her hips onto my length like when we sat pressed together in the car, the fullness of her thighs unknowingly teasing me. What I would give right now to just smell her again.

Fuck.

I feel so fucking wrong for fisting my cock to the mere memory of her. But the desperation of my climax has completely taken control. I clench my jaw as one of my hands slams into the tile again.

Each stroke grows more hurried, unsteady. My orgasm builds at the base of my spine, begging for the inevitable crash.

I can only imagine how soft Avery would feel in my hands. Her lean muscles writhing against my touch.

Is she just as stubborn in bed as she's been in the few moments we've had together?

The image of those hazel-green eyes rolling back into her head boils the remaining tension in my body. How fucking badly I want to see her do the same exact motion, but from the pleasure I could give her and not from her annoyance with me.

I rim my cock, which has never been this hard with need, until the image of her beautiful smile fills my head, finally tipping me over the edge.

Chapter 11
Avery

"AND THEN I DUMPED THE LAWN CLIPPINGS BACK ONTO HER property." My mother's voice drones through the speaker phone. I have spent the past twenty minutes listening to all the passive-aggressive neighborhood drama she's involved in.

As she continues to ramble, I make the call more productive by folding laundry I neglected for weeks.

I called her this morning to update her about my new position at Plastech and share some details about the Ellington Grant competition. I wanted some kind of congratulations from her or an assurance that I was doing a good job.

When my dad passed away, the connection between us became instantly strained. Our calls grew sparse in the first year, and our interest in each other's lives seemed to wane.

At least, my mother's interest in my life has not made itself apparent; she never visits me in the city. But I suppose I haven't felt ready to return home since the funeral.

I try to suppress the budding exasperation within me.

My temper is a critical flaw, I'm aware. It's not cute being an angry woman who grinds her teeth or tosses around anxiety like an aggressive tennis match. But it's safe and easy. Barely anyone gets to see this side of me, only Lily and Mom, and maybe that's for the best.

A dull ache inside me remains. I wish the only remaining connection to my father would help me relive his memory.

I just want her to assure me that Dad would have been proud of me, even if my career at ORO didn't go to plan. I've been able to achieve so much on my own, and I wish she could enjoy it with me.

Instead, she's talking about lawn clippings. *Or was it the neighbor's lawn clippings?* I'm not entirely sure anymore.

I pick up one of my running shirts, still damp from sweat even though I wore it two days ago. The bright-red lettering has faded into a pale purple. *Riptide Runners Club.*

My fundraising shirt collection is one of my favorite parts of my wardrobe. As much as I adore my beautiful, thrifted clothes and designer vintage pieces, it's these T-shirts that are some of my prized possessions.

Riptide Runners was a walkathon I joined last year. We meet every quarter and walk the Hudson River Greenway to raise funding for city schools transitioning to sustainable study materials.

I toss it into the laundry bin and reach for the blouse I wore last night. The beige cuff is covered in red wine. I throw it into the pile of dirty clothes.

Ollie.

We submitted our proposal for the Ellington Grant on Friday morning. It was a relatively easy feat as I'd already revamped our marketing presentation and worked with Matthew to create an implementation schedule for our trash-identifying AI.

It turns out the Plastech team loves to party. *A lot.*

We decided to celebrate with dinner. Dinner turned into "just one more drink." And that drink turned into a private karaoke room somewhere downtown. To my surprise, Robert's singing voice has an uncanny resemblance to D'Angelo's. For a man of so few words, he worked the crowd as though he were a natural-born performer. The muscles in my face hurt from the perpetual smile I wore last night.

My mother's dry cough brings my attention back to our phone call.

"I'm sorry, Mom, what were you saying?"

"I got a new coffee table at an antique show."

"Another one?" A pang of concern stings my chest.

My mother's hobbies since my dad died have constantly changed. Last month, she picked up rollerblading, but it was hard on her knees. Her new obsession has been collecting antiques, and each new piece replaces something in my childhood home.

"It's lovely. I drove an hour to get it."

"You know the flight from Burlington to New York is only an hour, and I'd be happy to pay for your ticket."

"Avery." She hesitates, sensing the pleading in my tone.

I know we all cope with loss in different ways, but my mom's reclusion saddens me each time we talk. I want her to enjoy life again, the way she used to when Dad was around. We all used to travel together and take adventures in our little camper van as a family. I wish we could return to that.

I can barely recall the last time I got on a plane. Maybe for that trip to Australia in freshman year? I frown at the lapse in time.

"There are a lot of great antique stores in the city!" I suggest. "Trust me, I would much prefer to come home to Vermont and have you show me your favorite places, but I can't take time off work right now."

"Maybe soon," she says.

"The anniversary of Dad's death is coming up—"

"Ave, please."

There's that familiar sadness in her voice that breaks something inside of me. It feels like we're both walking through the dark when we talk about him. Our hands desperately reach for each other, but we never find the familiarity in our touch like we used to.

But I shrug it off, keeping my thoughts away from the sadness festering in me. I refuse to force her to see me. If the best thing we can do is enjoy these brief phone calls, then that's what it will be. I have too much to celebrate in my life right now, with or without my mother doing it with me.

"It's fine." I sigh.

"I love you." Her voice is soft again.

I twirl the watch around on my wrist, remembering the day it arrived in the mail with a note from my mom.

Now you and Dad match. Love, Mom.

"I love you too. We'll chat soon."

I throw my phone onto the bed. A huge inhale unwinds the knot in my chest. I know there's nothing I can do to change her. She's not suddenly going to wake up and be the mother she was when Dad was still around. But she *is* my mother, so I'll keep making whatever effort I can without hurting myself too much.

I can only control what's right in front of me.

I repeat it over and over. The mantra has kept my head clear since he passed away.

I grab another item of clothing from my barely dwindling laundry pile. The carcass of the dress I wore the night of the gala rests in my hands. It was a vintage Atelier Versace gown that probably belonged to a fabulous woman who would never allow it to get shredded to pieces.

Not that I was to blame.

Unfortunate things happen to people all the time. But each time I'm around Luca, my world slightly tips on its axis—so maybe it's his fault.

I fold the dress with great care, holding the cinched waist when my mind immediately wanders to the way *his* hands felt through the sheer fabric.

No. No. No.

I force myself to focus on the dull task of cleaning.

I will not succumb to curiosity. That's all it is. *Pure, unadulterated curiosity.*

Luca is simply difficult for me to read. Between our biting exchanges and his sudden appearances in my life, I don't know if we can spend time together without me wanting to defeat him somehow.

Even if I wanted to know how the rough feel of his hands would explore more of me?

My fantasy quickly betrays me when a shiver coats my spine. I wipe away the phantom feel of his breath from my cheek.

I need to get out of this house. The laundry is not going to grow legs and walk out of here if I leave it for another day.

I pull on a pair of loose jeans and a clean T-shirt from the unfolded pile and slide into my thrifted kitten heels.

I need a distraction.

"I swear I'm fine," I tell Lily. I pop another salty potato chip into my mouth. "I just needed to get out of the apartment."

The dim chandeliers in the bar light the classy space. The decorations mimic a speakeasy, and all the employees wear wool boiler hats and thick velvet aprons. Except the smartly dressed servers are missing today. Lily's coworkers all decided to call out sick, leaving her in charge.

To brighten her day, I came with lunch from her favorite deli for us to share.

We devour our sandwiches over the bar, and only three other regulars sit at a nearby table.

"Well, you came to the right place," Lily says, her mouth stuffed with turkey.

"Am I a masochist? I know Mom's not going to just wake up

one day and come to the city. Why do I keep trying to change her?"

But I do know. I just couldn't bring myself to admit I wanted her back in my life.

"You care too much," she says. "But it's my favorite flaw of yours."

I warm with her words. Sometimes the people who are meant to love you forget how to, and you wander through life alone. That ache of loneliness simply dulls to resemble a fading bruise. Thankfully, I have Lily to fill that void. I stretch my arms over the bar and pull my best friend into a huge hug.

"I know," I say as she returns my embrace.

We take a few more bites of food, then Lily cleans up our lunch.

"I don't want this to come off the wrong way, but why is it so empty in here?" I ask.

The bar is not usually packed on Sunday afternoons, but no one has come in since we started our lunch an hour ago.

"I may have flipped the We're Closed sign when you went to wash your hands." She smirks.

"Lily!" I leap off my stool, but she pins my arm to the mahogany bar.

"I needed some quiet time to study for an exam!"

"Isn't your boss going to kill you?"

"She's roasting on a beach in Cabo with her new boyfriend," Lily explains. "Besides, an hour isn't going to hurt anyone."

Lily's approach to work-life balance has always fascinated me. We both dedicate ourselves fully to any job. Yet Lily knows that at the end of the day, a job is just a job. I can't quite wrap my mind around going through life without my career guiding the way.

"I wish we were on a beach in Cabo." I laugh.

"Me too!" Lily exclaims. "My midterms have been draining

me, and the bar has been short-staffed lately. I can't remember when I felt relaxed or spent the afternoon getting my hair done."

That was true. I couldn't recall a time recently when either of us got to enjoy a spa day. Lily and I used to spend one day a week slathering our bodies in fragrant lotions and trying different face masks while we recreated dishes from our favorite restaurants. We'd pull homemade pasta and fail gloriously at assembling pies. Instead, we've both been so focused on our responsibilities lately that we haven't made any time for each other or ourselves.

"Can I do anything to help?" I offer.

"You can tell me about that weird-looking toy boat you bought home with you Friday."

The vessel is a model replica of the Ellington Foundation's new sustainable electric boat. It was sent as an invitation to all the companies who attended the Ellington Gala. The replica was inscribed with the date and time for the official unveiling celebration. I spent fifteen minutes examining the beautiful white vessel through the glass, really trying to understand how they made it. The guys thought I should take it home since I was fascinated by its logistics.

"That *toy* boat is the replica of the first-ever fully functional solar-powered—"

"In normal people's terms!"

"It's an over-the-top party invitation."

"You go to so many fun events that I'm considering switching my major again."

Lily has changed her major so many times in the last three years, a new subject always catching her attention.

I'm amazed at how well Lily manages her income, especially when she made the impressive decision to save up for her tuition before applying to college. Even now, as she takes more and more classes, Lily manages to never be strapped for cash.

Instead, she assures me her finances are never a cause for worry, so I don't worry.

"You're welcome to come as my plus-one."

"Please, I learned my lesson after you took me to that sustainability conference at Columbia." Lily was disappointed that we spent the day actually attending electric vehicle policy sessions and not mingling with hot scientists.

"This is different."

"You're right." Lily takes a bite of the last pickle. "I don't want to be a third wheel with you and that hot ocean lawyer there."

"Retired lawyer," I correct her. "Luca Navarro is the frustrating chief operating officer of—"

"The Oceanic Research Organization," she completes in a taunting voice. "I'm sure he wants to work out some of his *frustrations* with you after you won your little race in the park."

My cheeks burn hot. "How many times do I have to tell you that I'm not interested in his games?"

"Until I finally believe you." She gives me an immoral grin.

Someone interrupts us by knocking loudly at the door, attempting to enter. Lily sighs and reluctantly makes her way over to let the patron in.

My mind returns to Luca again, as it has been for the past few days after our bet by the Reservoir.

Something very strange happened after he suggested we race for my side of the park. About halfway to our stopping point, Luca ran off the path. I figured he was forfeiting, probably too tired to keep up. When I tried to spot him behind me, he was pulling a plastic bag off a pigeon.

An actual pigeon.

The sight stirred an irrational wave of arousal in me. I was really losing my head if a bird rescue sent a needy sensation through my body.

It was probably the uncharacteristically hot morning and lack of water that sent my heartbeat quickening above my regular running rhythm, definitely *not* the way his muscular arms ripped at the bag like some kind of heroic warrior.

Either way, I won that round of our bet, and I get to run on my side of the park in peace.

Avery: 1 | Luca: 0

My antsy curiosity causes me to pull out my phone and type *Luca Navarro* into the internet search bar.

It's research, I assure myself. After all, ORO is now the obstacle between Plastech and the grant.

I read through news articles covering his corporate law cases, struggling to wrap my mind around his career shift.

One of the articles has a photo attached. It depicts a tanner and more youthful version of Luca surrounded by a group of people on a sun-soaked beach. Each of them holds overflowing trash bags.

I read the caption.

University of Santa Cruz's Trash Titans, an environmental cleanup group, founded by Luca Navarro.

I scoff. He probably needed another accolade on his graduation transcript.

The article details the club's various cleanup missions in Santa Cruz. There is a small blurb on him toward the end.

Luca Navarro started cleaning up Northern California beaches at a young age. The practice remained with him throughout high school, leading him to open the first environmental club at Santa Cruz.

Interesting. So he does know how to get his hands dirty.
How would those dirty hands feel on my skin?

Hold up.

My game must be off if the first thought I have about him doing a good deed is *feel me up, you rich, sexy trash man.*

So, his pristine exterior actually deviates from what I assume are his luxury comforts and a corner office.

My eyes find their way back to the picture. There's Luca, surrounded by a horde of smiling faces, hugging a bag of trash like it's his proudest achievement. It's hard to miss him. He towers over everyone, almost a head taller than his companions. I scan the detailed build of his bare torso.

Is that what's hiding in those ridiculous suits, or has he changed since graduating?

His sculpted abs are clear, even in the pixelated picture.

I bring the phone close to my eyes.

"What are you doing?" Lily snatches the phone from underneath my nose. Her eyes widen at the evidence on my screen. "Is this the elusive Luca Navarro?" Lily lets out a loud yelp.

"No, it's just research for the upcoming event." I rip my phone out of her grip.

She laughs. "*Sure.*"

"The more I know about Navarro, the greater advantage I have over him!"

"You didn't tell me he looked like an underwear model for Calvin Klein."

My eyes roll as I release an exaggerated sigh.

"I'm sure he would love to see you make that face." Lily giggles like a child.

"Lily!" I throw a napkin at her, and she dodges it, her laugh filling the bar.

"If you hook up with him on the boat, you can finally say you had your *Titanic* moment."

"If you're referring to the part in *Titanic* where Rose lets Jack drown, then you are correct."

"Don't deflect." Lily pours a large soda and sets it on the bar. "I've been telling you for weeks that you need to get laid."

"No relationships until I'm where I want to be in my career!" I remind her again.

There has been a long track record of incredibly successful *single* women—Joanna Benbart being one of them. The distraction of a partner would only weigh me down. I have too much to achieve before I can care about a significant other.

"But you can't deprive your body of this hot, trash-loving executive!"

I can and I will. Even if a part of me is curious to see if that six-pack stuck around.

I crumple another napkin in my fist and throw it at her. "No distractions."

"Just let yourself have a taste of something with no strings attached."

"When have I ever been a casual person?" I laugh. "I don't want a random fling with a stranger!"

Casual is not my strong suit. My entire life has been dedicated to one cause: creating a lasting impact on the world. It was a promise I made to myself and to my dad as a kid, and it has never wavered.

If anything, I'm wildly monogamous, committed to one thing, and I'm simply not interested in allowing a stranger to take advantage of that.

Lily tries again. "He's not a random fling!"

"You know what happened the few times I listened to your advice and tried to date."

Lily leans her arms on the bar. "Yes, yes. It's a waste of time but I think you've just never picked someone who matched your speed."

I sigh. "I think I'm doomed to choose between working on my dreams and being with the person who needs my attention."

I wasn't going to put my career on hold for evenings filled with dinner dates that would lead to mediocre sex.

No, really. Why do some of the men in the city approach a woman with the confidence of a raging bull, but when it comes to getting down to business, they act like lambs?

"That can't be the case with Luca. He likes all the same stuff as you! Running, the ocean, recycling!" Lily takes my hand in hers and gives it a squeeze. "He even looks fit enough to go on a hike, and maybe you can finally get back to doing that with someone."

"But I have *you*," I explain. "And you've never forced me to choose between our time together and my job."

For that, I'll always remain fiercely loyal to her for understanding what was important to me.

"That's true, but I can't exactly be the one to fuck you, Ave." She laughs. "But Luca—"

I interrupt her. "*Lily*!"

"He's already seen you all hot and sweaty on your run. It'll be just like that, but you'll both be very nake—"

"Stop." I whip my head around, ensuring no one was eavesdropping on our conversation.

"No, you stop! You need to get all that tension out of your body before it turns into one of your frustrated tantrums and you're snapping at me for borrowing your clothes."

"That was once," I counter. "And you ripped one of my skirts to pieces."

"How many times do I have to tell you? It wasn't me who ruined it. It was Yevgeni," she corrects me. "And I replaced your skirt immediately."

"Okay." I sigh.

Lily shoots me a pointed glare. "You can't keep deflecting!"

"I'm *perfectly* fine."

Yet the way my thighs clench under the bar tells a different story.

Chapter 12
Avery

WHY ARE BOATS ALWAYS NAMED AFTER WOMEN?
The dock before me is flecked with miniature yachts, all with names that probably belonged to past lovers or second wives. I imagine that a first wife doesn't get a boat; she gets the headache that comes with a workaholic husband.

When I can afford to buy myself an opulent representation of my successes, I vow to name it after a man. Maybe Alfred? Sebastian? Or better yet, I'll buy the boat and name it after Luca Navarro, just to sink it.

How's that for handling rejection better?

Alright, still a bit sour.

Ahead, a short purple carpet has been rolled out in front of the vessel hosting tonight's celebration for Willhelma Ellington's new sustainable electric innovation. The monstrous ivory-colored boat is the size of a pirate ship. Its ginormous deck and the balconies on the lower levels are already crowded with people. Beneath, the Hudson River glimmers like a swarm of lantern fish hiding in its dark waters.

A name is displayed proudly in large letters on the hull. *Willhelma.*

Now that is a power move, I can get behind.

I check in with the elegantly dressed greeting party and climb the ramp onto the anchored prize of human achievement. Solar panels run along the deck floor, capturing the rest of the afternoon sun. A flurry of guests decorates the space, all dressed in a rainbow of summer pastels.

Now, where is the spectacular Ms. Ellington?

Certainly, after her grand entrance at the gala, Willa will arrive like a sudden crackle of thunder.

I scan the deck for familiar faces, but none of the groups pique my curiosity.

A group gathered around a small cocktail table catches my eye, their conversation appearing stale by their bored expressions. A perfect opening for me to stir up some noise about Plastech while I await a private opportunity to make an impression on Willa.

I head over to them and introduce myself. After befriending a wildlife biologist named Amil and his partner, Lucy, I leave to locate some much-needed snacks.

The Plastech team was impressed with the investor leads I collected at the gala, but I can't say the same will come from this over-the-top affair.

My eyes make their way around the deck, but there is still no sign of Ms. Ellington.

Or Luca Navarro.

A brief flash of disappointment curdles in my chest like sour milk, but I brush it off. Luca not being here is one less obstacle to endure this evening.

Hunger builds in my stomach, so I walk toward a waiter carrying a platter of bruschetta.

Why do I always forget to eat before coming to these things?

I swipe a few pieces of the toasted bread and find a quiet part of the boat to finish my meal. I savor the deep sunset reflecting off skyscrapers. Shades of purple, pink, and orange light up a cloudless sky.

The fabric of my dress tickles my skin in the gentle breeze, and I grow restless. I've been walking around this boat for a half hour. If Ms. Ellington is not planning to attend, leaving is probably the best option. I can head home early and catch up on some much-needed rest.

I pull out my phone and load up a taxi request, already feeling that blissful relief of taking off my heels and exchanging my slip dress for a pair of cozy pajamas. Then, I browse the menu from a pizza place near my apartment. I finish my order for an extra-cheese pie and begin to make my way off the boat.

Upon turning the corner of the helm, I collide with an incredibly large mass.

"Ouch!"

My chin tilts up to meet the person's eyes, an apology resting on my tongue, but *his* brown eyes pour into mine, halting my breathing.

Luca.

His dark chestnut hair is unusually disheveled from the breeze, an overgrown curl hangs freely onto his forehead. I have an unhealthy urge to reach out and mess up the longer strands even more.

"Not this again."

"See something you like?" His deep voice stretches over me like the thick summer humidity.

My sanity returns as I take a step back, the short distance forcing me to keep my neck tilted to meet his face.

Once again, he wears one of his ridiculous suits tailored to show off his muscular figure. The crisp collar of his white shirt is slightly unbuttoned, revealing a delicate chain resting on his collarbones. His typical dark suit has been replaced with a sandy-beige linen, and he's not wearing a tie. It softens his tightly wound appearance and makes him look unusually rugged.

"Did you forget one of those suffocating ties at home?"

Luca's lips curve into one of his signature smirks. The smugness I expect is replaced with an expression so welcoming it leaves me on edge.

"You don't like the look?"

"Suits never impress me," I lie.

Well, it used not to be a lie. The handsome linen suit covering Luca's broad shoulders is beginning to change my opinion on the matter.

Save your curiosity, Avery! Keep your eyes on the prize.

"And what does impress you, Ave?"

"It's Avery," I scold him, shaking off the melting feel of my name in his mouth. "Enjoy your night, Mr. Navarro."

I abruptly turn, itching to slide into the cab, waiting to carry me home to my large pizza.

"It'll be a very enjoyable part of my evening watching you try and get off this boat."

"I'll be leaving the same way I got on." I sashay away, savoring the satisfaction of abandoning him.

But I peer back at him and catch his drilling stare. I wish my poise didn't fail me. It would've been much cooler if I didn't look back.

Luca calls out to me. "Then I hope you packed a swimsuit because we're undocking."

"What? No. We're anchored." My eyes dart to the two deckhands rolling up the ramp from the dock.

What are they doing?

"I know you're smarter than that," he chides, and I push away the familiarity he tries to place on me.

"Then stop messing with me." I walk to the rail and lean over, watching the dock move away from us.

"Did you really think Ms. Ellington would host a soiree to celebrate her new boat and not give us a test drive around the Hudson?"

The pointed question prompts me to flare my nostrils as my lips form a tight line.

A part of me thought we would remain docked. Once the sun sets, the boat will simply not have enough power to keep propelling forward. Unless the energy is being stored somewhere in the hull?

What an outstanding yet highly annoying technological advancement.

A sudden rocking of the boat cements my nightmare into reality.

My balance collapses under the motion, and I reach out for something to stabilize me.

That *something* is Luca's muscular arm.

He wraps his warm hand around my fingers, steadying me, and heat works its way through me.

"I don't need your help." My hand rips away from his in an instant.

"I know." The words carried sincerity. "But *you* were the one who reached for *me*."

I blow out an annoyed breath. "What am I going to do now?"

"The offer to go for a swim with me still stands."

Fantastic.

I'm trapped on a boat with the heartless suit, no Willa in sight, while my poor cheesy pizza grows cold.

"If your running is anything like your swimming," I say, "I hate to break it to you, but that suit will not make a sufficient life jacket."

Luca chuckles, and the sound brings an involuntary smile to my face. I wipe it away quickly and return my attention to the crowd.

"Why are you even here?" I ask. "You looked miserable at the gala."

"Have you been keeping an eye on me?"

He doesn't give up, does he?

"No," I lie.

"All things considered, that evening had a surprisingly pleasant ending."

"Maybe for one of us," I lie again.

I bite my lip at the memory of his hands steadying my waist as a growing bulge made itself known through his trousers. There was no way that was all *him*.

Right?

What am I even thinking about right now? This suit is my adversary.

"This laid-back crowd just doesn't seem like your speed." My fingers fix a strap on my dress. "A *busy* guy like you."

I catch Luca watching the movement intently, his black pupils swallowing the brown of his eyes.

"You're not wrong. But unfortunately, I don't have someone to take over the nuisance of attending these things at ORO."

"And whose fault is that?" I snap. The bite in my words comes off harsher than I intended.

The truth is that since I've been devoting my time to Plastech these past couple of weeks, ORO hasn't monopolized my every free thought. The future I designed for myself, which I thought I wanted, has been diluted by being on a team that needs me.

"What is this obsession with ORO?"

"I don't want to try and explain something you wouldn't understand."

"Try me." The words are an undeniable provocation.

"Joanna's career inspired a lot of my own professional choices," I explain, unsure why the words leave me with such ease.

"How so?" There's genuine curiosity in his features.

"When I was younger, my dad would take me to see Joanna in action, and it stuck with me."

"Is that it?"

Of course, he would assume it was as simple as that. As

though Joanna's legacy had nothing to do with it. Like ORO's impact isn't a good enough reason.

Does he even understand how important environmental work is?

"Obviously not."

"Are you close with your dad?" Luca asks, and I hate that I want to answer his intrusive question.

I don't talk about my dad to anyone except for Lily, and when I try to speak to my mother, she titters around the topic like it's a poisonous substance, ready to destroy her all over again.

I decide to change the conversation, not wanting to give him an advantage over me by oversharing the delicate details of my past. "You know, now that you're stuck on this crowded boat all night, you might actually have to make conversation with people."

"I'm talking to you right now."

"Let's be clear, you and your overpriced suit are being tolerated as I come to terms with being trapped here."

"You talk about my suits so frequently, it's almost as if you're obsessed with them, contrary to your statement earlier."

Can he let me get the last word for once?

I don't think I've ever met someone who attempts to parry every interaction—well, besides myself. Something about his persistence, so much like my own, makes my blood heat.

Does he talk so much to everyone?

"You're insufferable."

"And yet we still stand here, suffering." His hands slide into his trousers as he gives me a boyish shrug.

Is he flirting?

"Oh please, you couldn't even convince five people to tolerate you enough that they'd hand over their business cards by the end of the night."

"Is that a bet?" he says, intrigue filling his eyes. I suddenly notice how thick his lashes are, perfectly lining the brown around his irises.

"Yes. Whoever gets five business cards first wins."

"What do I get when I win?" The confidence in his voice makes me want to rise to the challenge even more.

"When *I* win, I get your suit."

His eyes widen, and I realize how incredibly wrong that sounded. Even though part of me wants to see what's underneath one of those stuffy jackets.

"Seems like *I* would be the one winning."

"That's not what I meant!" I snap at him.

"And what *did* you mean?"

"Forget the suit! I don't want anything to do with it."

My cheeks burn at his words, and I take a deep breath to recollect myself. Why does he make it so difficult to talk sometimes? I'm better than this.

He speaks first. "How about when I win, you join me for a drink after we get off this boat?"

Yes. The yearning in my body immediately betrays me.

No. There will be absolutely, definitely no drinks with the suit.

Drinks can lead to all sorts of *things*. Potentially very large, bulging, and protruding things. I most definitely do not have time to explore exactly what those *things* are.

No casual flings, no relationships, and absolutely no drinks.

"I don't want you to spend your oil money on me, Navarro," I snap at him, but the words leave me without conviction.

Why am I this upset with him?

"All my *oil* money, as you're so obsessed with calling it, went right back to the families impacted by the spill," he bites out as though the words have been festering inside of him. "What happened still haunts me every fucking day."

"Huh?"

"I gave the money back. Every single cent."

I stagger back, the delicate heels of my stilettos shaking slightly beneath my feet.

Luca's fingers rub the frustrated crease out of his forehead.

Something inside me wants to comfort him. I don't quite know why, but my hand reaches for the one hanging at his side.

"Look, I didn't mean—" I say quietly, but he pulls himself from my fingers.

"I have a bet to win," he reminds me, the pained expression gone from his face. "Have you picked a prize?"

If this is how he wants to play it, then fine. I gather myself. "No drinks. No suits. Winning against you will be enough."

Luca tilts his head toward me. I take the nod as an acceptance of our wager and make my way to the side of the boat farthest from him, but not before I grab a flute of champagne.

Chapter 13
Luca

AVERY IS AN EXPERT AT COAXING THE STUBBORN ARROGANCE out of me. It's like she revels in the smart-ass tongue my parents said would get me in trouble one day.

The guilt for snapping at her still lingers, but I couldn't let her believe whatever falsehood of me she created. At least now it's out in the open.

I didn't set out to work that case. Shift Industries was a long-term client at Douglas & Draper, and the owner of Shift was a close family friend of a senior partner.

The case was a standard acquisition. Shift wanted to buy a solar project development company that owned ten thousand acres of land.

A case for a client of this caliber was typically managed by the senior partners. They all knew it would be a hundred-hour-per-week case for two months, and I figured it was the perfect opportunity to prove my commitment to the firm.

I was excited to be working on such a prestigious deal so quickly after making partner. The negotiations took a couple of weeks, but I wrapped the case in our client's favor. The bonus I received for helping Shift Industries was half my annual salary. I was on top of the fucking world.

A couple months after the case concluded, Shift announced they'd discovered oil deposits on the land I'd helped them acquire. Apparently, they'd ripped the solar projects to shreds and chose to drill on the property instead.

I didn't think much of it, but a couple of months after their announcement, an oil spill occurred.

I still feel responsible for the severe damage it caused to the local river and small fishing community. It was the first time I questioned whether law was right for me.

When the news broke, I donated the entire half-a-million-dollar bonus I'd received from the case to the cleanup efforts. But something inside of me shattered. My ability to tolerate long hours, the hostile bosses, and the drain on my life came crashing down all at once.

For the first time in my career, I'd actively contributed to hurting people. I'd fucked up, and I knew I had to make a change.

Avery may not truly understand or even forgive the part I'd played in the situation, and I don't blame her. She's been on the better side of history her entire career. But I hope she can see past my failure.

I search for her among the crowd of people.

A glowing smile caresses her face each time someone catches her attention. I envy how carefree she seems, as though this bet we've agreed to comes as easily to her as breathing.

Avery tucks her short blonde hair behind her ears, exposing the curve of her neck. The sage color of her dress complements her eyes.

Right now, all I can focus on is the desire to pluck her away from the group she's with and find out her answer to my earlier question.

What impresses you, Avery? Because I would do it in an instant, over and over.

I return to the man in front of me who's rattling on about his company's new donation-matching program for his employees.

I need to concentrate on my goal. My opponent is so confident that she can win a bet against me. I can't wait to prove her wrong.

I swap information with the man and promise him a personal introduction to ORO's impact report, gaining a potential new investor and a business card in return.

One down, four to go.

As the next hour progresses, I find myself actually enjoying the strings of conversation I join. Each new group of people I speak with helps cement my decision to leave my law career behind. The different projects and organizations I'm learning about tonight are intent on creating a sustainable future for the planet.

After I collect three more business cards, I make my way to a group I haven't seen Avery speak to yet. She's still lost in conversation, the lean shape of her legs occasionally peeking out of her dress.

As if she senses me watching her, Avery looks back toward my side of the boat. The annoyed wrinkle on her nose is so subtle, I have an urge to smile.

The people around me barely notice my arrival. They're deeply engrossed in a conversation about a new sustainable protein-packed alternative to almond creamer.

Why can't people just drink their coffee without all the extras?

My mind wanders back to work, and uneasiness creeps into me. It's been a month since I hired Kora Noble to investigate ORO, and I have yet to hear anything conclusive.

Each time I've approached Joanna, seeking more information and providing organizational suggestions that could propel our conservation efforts into the future, she is, ironically, resistant to change. She ignored me this entire week, making up frivolous excuses like taking her dog to the groomer and tending to the garden at the Benbart oceanside mansion.

From the corner of my eye, I see Avery sauntering toward me.

Ready to concede, I'm sure of it.

The group surrounding me dissolved sometime during my flurry of thoughts. I'm left standing alone to soak in the sway of Avery's hips. Her elegant hand holds a stack of business cards that she uses to fan herself dramatically. She walks like a predator stalking its prey. Each movement is laced with deliberate confidence.

It's so fucking sexy.

I try to shift my eyes away from her movements and count the cards, but I'm distracted by her sudden closeness.

Avery pauses in front of me. The urge to grab her and breathe her in causes an unbearable tension in my body. My hand grips my empty drink.

She leans in, her mouth only a few inches away from my ear. My breath shallows. If I slightly turn my face, our lips will indeed meet. I resist the urge to find out if she tastes as sweet as an ocean breeze.

"It looks like you need these."

Avery drops the stack of cards into my glass, then strolls off.

Every fiber of my being aches after her as she makes toward the front of the boat, leaving me lusting for her warmth.

I pull the business cards out of my glass and count eight.

Atta girl.

A proud smile spills across my face and fails to falter when I walk over to the bar.

"A Paloma and a glass of champagne, please."

The bartender smiles as they hand me my order. I leave a fifty and allow my feet to carry me to Avery.

She stands at the bow of the boat, her face raised toward the sky.

When I near, Avery's arms wrap around her shoulders, and she shivers in the cold breeze.

I offer the champagne. "This should warm you up."

She twirls around, her eyes scanning me. "Are you here to congratulate me on my win?"

"What other reason is there?" I ask.

"I'm sure you could come up with something."

She takes the champagne from my hand, our fingers brushing. The touch is so brief, it leaves me hungry for more.

I pull the business cards out of my pocket before handing the neat stack over to her. "Congratulations, Ms. Soko."

A genuine smile kisses her face, and I watch the way her pink lips light up her features. She uses her palm to push the cards back toward me.

"I already saved these on my phone."

I bet she did.

"Well, you never know if you've missed one."

Avery stares at the cards, seemingly deliberating. "I would never miss one."

"Then consider the cards your trophy for this evening, especially since you were so adamant in denying yourself the suit off my body."

"I didn't say that." Her nose wrinkles.

"Sure."

She snatches the cards and tucks them into her purse.

The waves carry us on the river. She leans against the boat's railing and throws her head back toward the deep purple sky. The position intimately displays her body. I dream of discovering what's hiding under that dress as the sage-colored silk teases a display of her curves.

She takes a slow sip of the champagne, her lipstick imprinting on the rim of the glass. The cold hardens her nipples, and a tremble runs through her. Avery's priority may be the competition, but I can't stop looking at her long enough to focus.

I place my drink on a nearby table and shrug off my suit jacket. "Take this so you don't freeze before we make it back to land."

"I don't need—"

"You can keep fighting me."

"I'm not—"

"Just don't be cold while you're doing it." I drape my jacket over her shoulders.

That unyielding reluctance remains on her face as she drowns in beige fabric.

"Admit it." I raise my drink to her. "That's much better."

"The only thing I'm willing to admit is that I would win every competition against you," she says proudly.

"I don't doubt that."

"Would you stop?"

"Stop?" My forehead wrinkles in confusion.

"The pleasantries," Avery says with a frown. "You can cut the nice act. Willa is going to pick a winner within the next three weeks so there's no need for us to keep *this* up."

"What?"

She glares at me. "Whatever it is you're doing right now."

"This isn't an act." I take my drink into my hand and take a sip.

"Of course, it isn't."

That familiar frustration widens her eyes. After she takes a deep breath, her lips press together. Did I finally manage to render her speechless?

"It isn't," I repeat firmly.

She shifts in my suit jacket. I wish I were the one wrapped around her. *Am I jealous of my own clothes?*

She finally says, "Either way, I know you're trying to distract me."

"After the way you walked into me, it would be the second time this evening that *you're* caught off guard by *me*."

"Well, I wasn't caught off guard during our race."

As expected, she isn't going to make this easy. "You mean our silly run on your side of the park?"

Why did I have to come off so abrasive? It was one of the most fun runs I've had in years.

"Could you remind me who won that? Oh right, it was me."

"Is everything a competition to you?"

"With you?" Her eyes fix on me. "Yes."

I take a step toward her, my body ignoring the rational thought that screams, *Keep away!*

I ask, "And have you always been such a sore winner?"

The mixture of her perfume and her skin dries my tongue. I shorten the distance between us until her round eyes drill into mine. Her stare traces the full extent of my body.

The beautiful flecks of honey and green in her eyes are radiant in the setting sun, making my cock lengthen in my trousers, aching to discover her warmth.

Avery doesn't pull away, but her hand firmly grips the railing. "I've never enjoyed winning against someone so much."

The boat suddenly ricochets off a huge wave. My body crashes into Avery's, the impact emptying the contents of our drinks onto our clothes.

The front of her dress and the lapels of my jacket are soaked in the sticky liquor. There goes my custom Italian linen blazer.

"Why? Why? Why?" Each question cuts from her like a knife.

"Let me help you clean that up."

"It's not your problem to solve. I got it." Her voice is riddled with the heat of aggravation.

Avery speeds away from me. I feel the emptiness of her presence instantly. It's becoming my least favorite thing, having her vanish in front of me.

She makes her way into the deep hull of the boat, trying to conceal the revealing stain molding the dress to her skin. I follow close behind her, using my body as a shield against curious stares. I'm not going to encourage anyone to see her lose her composure. I know how seriously she takes these things. Besides, I've seen enough prying eyes peruse what I wish were mine. The spill on her dress only reveals her more.

The boat's lower level leads to the captain's quarters and an expansive private balcony. Avery hurries down the spiral stair-case until she finds a floor absent of people so that we can clean up the mess we've made. A few cushioned sofas decorate the small deck, surrounded by small tables made of driftwood.

"Sit down, I'll find something to remedy this."

"No, I can take care of it." She closes her eyes, clearly trying to compose herself.

"I'm helping," I say, my voice uncompromising.

Avery's eyes open in surprise.

I gently wrap my hand around her wrist and walk her to a seat. "I'll be right back."

"Why is it that when I'm around you, my clothes are always drenched?"

"Is that why you had an outfit change before your inter-view?" I begin piecing together the reason behind her shrunken blouse that day.

The corners of her lips curl toward the floor, and she gives me a slow nod. I immediately regret the comment I made about her clothes.

"I promise, next time you're wet around me, I'll make sure it's because of something you'll enjoy."

She glares at me. "What are you going to do? Take me swimming?"

I let out a chuckle. Without warning, her hard exterior cracks before me. Avery's laugh joins mine, and it's a sound I want to replay endlessly.

Once our laughing fit fades, I instruct her to stay where she is.

This balcony seems empty of prying eyes, but I wrap my blazer tighter around her. My hands are dying to trail the body underneath her layers of clothes.

I return with a stack of plush white towels from the private suite restroom. Avery sits in the same place I left her, her hair whipping in the evening wind. She's even more breathtaking when she's flustered, her immaculate features not diminished by the small dent to her composure.

What would she look like if she were undone because of me?

"You should blot." I hand her a towel, focusing on her eyes and not the now-transparent material of her fine silk dress.

"Did your girlfriend teach you that?" she asks.

The question lands between us unexpectedly.

"I've been single since graduating from law school."

"Well, that makes two of us." Avery sighs and wads the towel in her palm. "I mean, since graduating. Obviously, I'm not a lawyer."

"I gathered that."

She begins to press the towel into the fabric while I stand frozen, willing my gaze away from her supple breasts and trim waist.

"It's not working!" Avery says, pulling her dress into her palms and wringing out the alcohol. The material gathers high on her thigh.

I'm a fucking asshole staring at her as though I were a teenager attracted to a woman for the first time.

I stand over her and reach out my hand.

"Enough of your help, Navarro." Her wild eyes wreck me, and the slight jumble of my name in her mouth finally sets me off.

"You know, you've been pronouncing my name wrong," I finally admit, distracting her from her irritation.

"Oh, and you thought it was fitting to tell me this right now?" The sarcasm is thick in her voice as her hands point to her drenched dress.

"It's Navarro." I roll the *r*'s emphatically. "Not Navaroe."

She stares at me, the realization contorting her features into an unreadable expression. "Navarro."

I shake my head; the roll of her *r*'s still hides behind those plush lips.

"Navarro."

She repeats it again. Okay, maybe it didn't bother me that much. Especially not when the sound of my name raises my pulse.

"Not quite," I say.

"Teach me."

"When you let me clean up this mess," I say, my hand massaging a clean towel into her hip, trying to dry the fabric of her dress.

"Fine."

"First, you need to say the letters *t* and *d;* feel the way your tongue hits the back of your teeth."

Her head tilts to one side.

"Do that until you can trill your tongue against your teeth."

"You can't be serious." She looks at me in disbelief.

I kneel before her as she leans back on the cushions, giving herself more leverage to blot the dress. I extend my right arm to the back of the sofa, shielding Avery's body with mine as we continue to work the fabric.

Euphoria washes over me at the feel of her warmth. Her knees part slightly, grazing the inside of my thigh. My cock throbs at the touch.

"Just try it," I urge.

"Fine." She takes a deep inhale before carefully repeating the letters out loud, opening her mouth and stacking her lips into a perfectly round shape. She tries to vibrate her tongue, but only an exhale of air escapes between her teeth.

"Your lips need to be closer. Like this." I press mine together and demonstrate.

Avery tries again, pushed by her relentless determination, until she finally sounds a vibration.

"Good." I nod. "Just like that."

Her gorgeous smile appears, celebrating the achievement. *Would she be this receptive to other lessons I want to teach her?*

"Now repeat after me," I say. "Trust."

"*Trust.*"

"Rough."

"*Rough.*" She does not hesitate, the word leaving her like a confession.

The thick heat of need suffocates the air around us.

"Do you feel the way your tongue moves when it lands on the *r*?"

"Yes."

"Now, when you roll your tongue, add the movement we practiced."

Avery watches me intently as I display the motion. She imitates me until her lips move in a perfect rhythm.

"Now add it all together." Her eyes watch me intently. "Repeat after me. *Cariño.*" I accentuate the *r* to emphasize where the roll of her tongue should sit.

"What does that mean?" She eyes me suspiciously.

"Repeat first, ask questions later."

"Tell me."

"Later." I smile.

She glowers.

"Go on."

"*Cariño.*" She says it over and over.

My gaze is glued to her mouth, and when I look up, she meets my eyes with the same intensity.

"A little wider." I reach my thumb to her, the pad of my finger gently pulling her bottom lip.

Avery's chest rises and falls slowly as a tempest erupts behind her eyes. The corners of her mouth lift in a slight smile as her stare falls to my lips. The wetness of her tongue finds my thumb, where she teases the skin with a tiny lick.

"Now that's very distracting—"

"Do you always have something to say?" she breathes, not pulling away from me.

Kiss her, you fool!

"Only when you're so keen on talking back." I stretch the moment between us like hot taffy.

"Oh, just kiss me, Navarro."

This is either going to be the best or worst decision I make in my life but I don't falter.

My mouth crashes into hers. The weeks of aching to feel her in my arms pour into the kiss.

I am ruined.

Fuck.

I savor the way our tongues greedily explore each other, the hungry strokes becoming more vigorous. I drown in the tart sweetness of her.

Avery pulls away. Her eyes search my face, the pools of hazel almost black. My pulse quickens at the pause. We stare at each other. My lips are already sore from the fiery caress of her teeth. All the heated blood coursing through my veins has traveled to my dick.

"I've thought about this for weeks, Avery." I run my palms over the warm flesh of her cheeks.

"Weeks?" She smiles at me underneath her dark lashes and wraps her hands around my neck, pulling me back in.

Our lips fuse together. Her tender skin against the roughness of my fingers sends me into a further carnal need. Her moans echo into me.

It's a sound so fucking beautiful, it will be my life's goal to rouse it with each opportunity she gives me.

Her long legs part, inviting me in, and I wrap them around my waist as I stand and lift her off the sofa. Her warmth is now only separated from me by a few layers of fabric.

For the first time, I understand Avery. *This suit is fucking ridiculous.*

Avery claws at the skin under my shirt, the metal of her watch cold against my skin. Even in this heated frenzy, we're competing again. Each touch is selfish, full of pent-up hunger.

I try to find my footing as she wrestles in my arms until we finally slam against the wall behind us. The New York City skyline is now the only spectator to our overflowing desire.

"Avery," I breathe.

"Navarro," she says against me.

Avery's hips grind into me, and I take pleasure in the fact that she can feel my arousal rousing beneath her. My fingers ache to explore the wetness I know is pooling between her thighs. Instead, I cup her face, hoping nothing will rip us from this kiss.

I need more.

My left hand finds the curve of her hip, and I trail my fingers up the thin fabric of her dress. I graze over her stiff nipples, and a soft whimper escapes her. With each new sensation, her moans grow louder and louder, causing me to fall deeper into the now.

I move my teeth to the skin of her neck, savoring every taste I can get, before returning to her swollen lips. As we collapse into each other, I can't tell whether we've been standing here for a minute or an hour.

I'm swimming in Avery Soko. My being merely collapses before her. I relish in each fucking second of it.

Loud static erupts above us. We break away. A familiar voice booms over the intercom.

"Can everyone please join me on deck?" Willa Ellington destroys whatever reality we accidentally fell into.

My stare reconnects with Avery, and she wiggles her way down my body, already readjusting the fallen straps of her dress. The charge behind her eyes is entirely extinguished. She stands in front of me and thrusts my jacket into my chest.

"This never happened." Her voice is so cold, it threatens to freeze me. Her footsteps faintly echo up the stairs to the boat's upper level.

Whatever this summons is for, it better be fucking worth it.

Chapter 14
Avery

As I emerge onto the crowded deck, nightfall has overtaken the city. I weave through the guests, trying to distract myself, but my mind is still absorbed with *him*.

When did I let myself to become this distracted?

My first mistake was allowing Luca Navarro—or should I say Nava-*rr*-o—to drape his jacket over my shivering skin. His rich, musky aroma still consumes my every sense, reminding me of the damp forest earth during my hikes across the northeast. My body betrays me as it hums with desire from his recent touch.

Our kiss—if you can even call the way we devoured each other something as simple as a *kiss*—prevented me from meeting Willa tonight.

I snap back to the present like a piece of worn elastic, forcing myself to focus on our hostess.

Onstage, Ms. Ellington is draped in a glistening black gown, making the rest of the guests look severely underdressed.

"I'm not getting any younger, so I'll get started," she says into the microphone.

Luca appears beside me, his looming presence blocking my view of the stage.

Why is he standing right in front of me?

"I can't see Willa!" I peer out from behind his broad shoulder.

Whose shoulders need to be this large?

He looks back at me. "You're not missing that much."

"You don't get to decide that." I break from him and walk further into the crowd to escape him.

He joins me. "Where are you going?"

"Stop following me," I bite. I'm so wound up right now between the kiss and the sudden interruption.

"No."

"Then don't stand so close!" I whisper to avoid calling attention to our spat.

This man is intolerable.

"I'm not going to let you stand here alone like that," he says behind me.

My eyes widen. I stop and turn back to face him. "Like what?"

"Your dress is ruined, Avery."

I really didn't need a reminder!

I whip away from him and walk a few more paces toward the stage until I can't go any further. Luca stands only a couple of people behind me. I can almost feel his stare on the back of my head.

I've been trying to process what he said about the oil money in the brief moments we spent apart this evening. How he helped the people impacted. Part of me, somewhere deep down, wants to believe him. Maybe I simply misjudged him in my unpleasant feelings about the ORO rejection, which at this point doesn't even sting as much as I expect it to.

I even regret the comments I made about his appearance. It isn't like me to make assumptions about others based on how they carry themselves, and Luca shouldn't be any different. His exterior, clad in fine fabrics and accompanied by piercing glares, has done little to paint the full picture of the man underneath the suit.

"Thank you all for giving me a reason to wear my new gown," Willa announces, and the crowd applauds for her. She has the energy of a rock star. "I never set out to own a boat. My father had one, and he loved it more than his children." She doesn't let the awkward silence linger. "But the Ellington Foundation continues to support projects that make lasting change *and* help me heal my inner child.

"My boat, *Willhelma*, is fully powered by renewable energy." Applause from the crowd erupts once more. "Yes. I know. Isn't it wonderful? Now only if I could power this body through renewable energy—that would solve most of my problems."

A few scattered laughs spread across the deck.

"I cannot wait a second longer!" she says. "Tonight, I will be announcing the results of the Ellington Grant. I know it's two weeks early, but the decision was easy. I've found the perfect match for my funding."

What? But my team isn't here. I need to call Matthew.

"Will the representative from ORO join me on stage?" Willa's voice booms again.

Understanding washes over me. The Oceanic Research Organization will receive the grant. I look back at Luca, and the bragging stare I expect from him is missing from his handsome face.

My head begins to pound as the air fills with clapping again. I may have won our silly bet, but Luca won the real prize.

Avery: 2 | Luca: 1

Luca leaves his place in the crowd and saunters to near the stage, remaining at the bottom of the podium. I watch him adjust the upturned collar of his shirt. He's donning his soaked blazer once more.

Is he going to wear that thing onstage?

My own dress is still damp, the silk fabric sticking to my flesh. The feel of it sends a chill down my spine as the summer breeze picks up.

Luca climbs to the podium, towering over Willa.

"Good-looking men like you sure didn't work in conservation back in my day," she squawks and gives his hands a squeeze.

The traitorous hands that were wrapped around my breasts only minutes ago.

My heart drops into my stomach at the memory. I'm going to be sick.

Willa highlights the impact ORO's robot fleet will be able to make in decreasing the amount of trash flowing into the ocean. Of course Luca would try to turn his college club into a little army of robots. He knows what he's doing, and I have to concede on that. I just wonder if they'll have *Trash Titans* inscribed on them.

I take a swig of the champagne I nabbed on the way over, trying to tune out the excitement from the crowd.

This grant would have been a huge opportunity for my team to pad our dwindling finances.

This is not the end. Plastech will find another way to remain afloat.

My eyes find Luca again. His stiff posture occupies most of the small stage. I search myself for a speck of happiness for him and the organization that was once my priority. It's hidden some place within me because I know the grant would be used somewhere good, especially if Willa chose their proposal.

"Also, because projects under the Ellington Foundation are exemplary, I have chosen a second recipient to join us up here."

The entire deck goes deathly silent, and my thoughts race. *There's still hope.*

After what feels like an eternity, Willa says, "Is there a representative from Plastech that can join us?"

I stand cemented to the deck. Luca's eyes scan the crowd, probably searching for me.

"Did she just say Plastech?" I ask the person standing next to me, and they confirm with a curt nod.

I need to call Matthew as soon as possible.

The crowd parts as I make my way through the sea of people, willing my feet to step one in front of the other. I climb onto the stage and stand beside the man whose taste I can still feel on my tongue.

"They look like movie stars together, don't they?" Willa says. "Already drenched with excitement!" She signals to the damp spots on our outfits. She turns to smile at the crowd. "All my great ideas share the same philosophy: teamwork."

"Teamwork?" A devilish grin splatters itself across Luca's face.

I struggle to understand where this is going. Are we splitting the prize money?

"After reviewing all the proposals, I decided ORO and Plastech have a complementary garbage-elimination strategy. My foundation's analysis shows if these two projects merge, they have the potential to eliminate the Pacific trash vortex three years after deployment. That is one point six million square kilometers of garbage *gone*."

She claps her hands, and the crowd goes wild.

"Wait," I say, the situation rattling my brain. "We're combining the projects?"

"You'll be working together as a unit to create a much better project!" she explains.

"But how are we supposed to *work together*?"

"Within four months, you must find a way to combine Plastech's AI and ORO's robots and put them through sufficient testing for deployment in the Pacific Ocean. Once you present your final execution strategy, you'll have access to five million dollars to scale the collaboration."

"The money is not divided equally between us?"

"The funding will only be used for *my* idea." Willa smirks.

"What if we can't combine the projects?" I ask.

"Oh, you've got bite!" A smile pulls across her face, creasing her laugh lines from the years of a seemingly beautiful life. Her expression sends a tinge of annoyance into me. "Then neither of your companies receives the funding for this project, and you can't split the profit from the recycled materials your robots will produce during the testing."

"No profit? Will we be able to negotiate the terms of how we are going to split the recycling profit?" Luca finally decides to join the dialogue.

Of course, he's only thinking about the money.

"Yes, you can negotiate the profits from the recycled materials as your companies see fit.," Willa says. "It is estimated to bring in ten million dollars a year in profit. That should be enough motivation to work together."

"Together?" I echo, picturing it.

I grapple with the new information attacking my thoughts.

Work *with* ORO?

I itch to pull my phone out of my purse and explain the situation to my team at Plastech.

My rib cage constricts as I try to catch a steadying breath. Luca stands beside me, unmoving.

I finally connect my gaze with his, and the darkness still lingering in his stare devours me.

Flashes of his lips exploring my body appear behind my eyes, and the dampness between my legs makes itself known. I know the way his large hands can caress my body. I know the reaction he could elicit from me without even trying.

I struggle to stay steady in the wave of confusion.

No. *No.*

But who won? I'm determined to get to the bottom of this.

Did ORO have the better project? Does this make us even? How are we supposed to compete now? The questions coat my thoughts like honey.

I scratch the memory of that kiss from my mind. It did not happen. And it will most certainly never happen again.

Luca Navarro will not be the distraction keeping me from my career, even if he had a hand in steering me away from ORO in the first place. I recalculate our wins since we both take the prize in this round.

Avery: 3 | Luca: 1

My focus is going to be supporting Plastech through this debacle in whatever way I can.

If we must work together, whatever briefly erupted between us is officially extinguished. Now that I got him out of my system, I refuse to be distracted by him and his silly bets. No matter how much my body is screaming for his touch again.

Chapter 15
Luca

A BURST OF LAUGHTER FILLS THE OFFICE AS I MAKE MY WAY OFF the elevator.

Avery stands over Molly's shoulders, their eyes intently watching the computer screen at the front desk. Avery blushes, and she tips her head back. My eyes wander to her low-cut blouse that shows off her flushed chest. My mind drifts back to her soft lips on mine.

Remain professional. You can do this.

Plastech has successfully transitioned to working in the ORO offices after Willa forced the combination of our projects. The Monday following the announcement on the boat, Plastech moved into our offices. It took them one afternoon to pack the things from their coworking space and settle into ORO's facilities.

I have to give Willa credit: the teams seem to be excited about how our ideas can seamlessly work together. Our original project complements Plastech's innovative technology, but the real draw is the earnings potential.

The CEO of Plastech, Matthew Hudson, and I agreed that the best way to work together would be for his team to set up shop here. Undoubtedly, ORO has better research and technological facilities than their coworking space. Matthew explained that the rent cost hindered their current spending capabilities. Now they can take advantage of our resources without wasting money. There also is the added benefit of seeing Avery every day.

I walk toward the front desk, where Molly and Avery are still laughing. It seems like they have become fast friends.

It doesn't really surprise me. Molly is an ideal employee. At least she has never given me a reason to think otherwise. Molly is the only person at ORO, well, apart from Avery, who has proven to respect how I work. The rest of the staff is still resisting my organization tactics, but the two of them seem to have no issue with my desire for frequent check-ins and clear communication.

Even yesterday, Molly shared her concern about the front desk assistant who resigned. She was afraid that hiring someone new would cause more strain on my schedule. I appreciated her concern even if I had to waste my morning reading through a backlog of resumes to find a quick replacement.

By the time the afternoon had rolled around and I was prepared to set up interviews with the new candidates, Avery already helped Molly divide some of the urgent tasks between all the assistants so nothing would fall through the cracks.

Avery has only been here a week and is already making my life easier. Even if she tries to keep her distance.

"Luca, you've got to see this!" Molly says, finally spotting me walking over to them. Tears, probably happy tears, stream down her cheeks. "We've seen it like a million times!"

"What's up?"

"It's not going to make sense if we just explain it to you. Come here."

I watch Avery as her focus remains on the screen. The rosy tint of her lips is covered by a bright shade of red today.

I want to press the pad of my thumb to her mouth again, and

stain my fingertip with the lipstick. The thoughts of our kiss return, and I shift uncomfortably at the blood traveling below my belt.

Not now.

"Look who finally decided to show up." Avery shoots me a sly smirk when I approach the desk.

This is only the second time she has beaten me to the office this week.

"Waiting for me?" I ask. Before she can come up with another snarky remark, I step behind Molly. My body is content to be only a few inches from Avery. "Show me what has you disrupting what could be a productive morning."

"You don't have to take the fun out of *everything*," Molly says. Then she presses Play.

Avery leans into the screen, giggling at the moving images of animals doing…

I'm not exactly sure what?

My eyes move to Avery, who had wildly strong opinions on joining the office. She claimed that working together in such proximity would destroy the soul of our projects.

Whatever that means.

I'm sure the real destruction she fears is us falling into each other's arms again. We decided on the boat that we should keep our relationship professional. Avery declared that her dedication to the project doesn't need any distraction, but it's done little to stop our somewhat frequent run-ins.

I, on the other hand, welcome the way my attention shifts to her.

Even when the memory of her lips has kept my fist wrapped around my dick every single evening since, I can't seem to keep my mind off her.

But I did learn that Avery shares my affinity for playing by the rules.

I spent the night after kissing her parsing through ORO's

ridiculously long employee handbook only to find that there are no rules about dating clients, colleagues, or contractors if neither party is directly above the other in the hierarchy. Even then, exceptions can be made.

A faint whiff of her scent sends a skipping stone of need through me at the memory of her hot mouth on mine. I want to drop to my knees right now and worship her on this desk. I salivate at the thought of running my tongue along the warm place that ground against me on the boat.

I really need to fucking stop.

This woman is all-consuming and painfully frustrating.

The video abruptly ends, and Molly is the only one still laughing.

Avery regards my still features. "Of course you don't have a funny bone in your body.

"Wouldn't you like to—" I try to retort, but Molly interrupts me.

"Luca, I found out Ave only lives a couple of blocks away from me, so we started a new running challenge this morning!"

That nickname again. The one *I* have not been allowed to call her.

"Interesting."

"No, what's interesting is Ave being able to convince *me* to go on a run," Molly says. "I hate running!"

Ave. Ave. Ave.

Avery merely shrugs. "You just had to find your rhythm."

The memory of her running beside me returns. I flinch at the thought of the paw-shaped bruises that lined my body for a few days after.

"And did you know there are showers in the gym downstairs?" Molly informs me. "Life changing!"

"I did, in fact, know about the showers." I turn to Avery. "I hope you're not letting Molly borrow those running shoes that look like they've been put into the shredder?"

Her scolding stare is catastrophic and so fucking beautiful. "Are you upset you haven't found a way to run in your suits yet?"

I check to make sure Molly is still facing her screen. Then I lean into Avery and let the words out in a whisper. "Another mention of my suits. You must really love them."

"I would *love* to wrap that tie around your neck and pull."

The brief warmth of her breath sends such a strong surge of butterflies through me that I almost feel giddy. I try not to think of how much time I've spent focused on nothing but her.

"I can show you quite a few uses for my ties that I know you would enjoy."

Avery steps back, her icy glare failing to hide the interest brewing inside her.

Molly turns to face the both of us. "What are you guys whispering about back here?"

I smile. "I was just telling Avery that I've been running on your side of the park. Every. Morning."

"That's cheating!" she scoffs. "I won that race."

"Am I missing something here?" Molly finally turns to face us. "Have you two been running together?"

"We've run into each other *accidentally*," Avery corrects her.

"Maybe Luca can join our running group," Molly says. "The ORO Runners."

"No," Avery says quickly.

"I don't know what's going on between you two, but I am here for it," Molly teases.

"Nothing is going on," Avery bites back.

The harshness in her tone unintentionally cuts deep. She seems repulsed at the idea of there being something—anything—between us. But the night on the boat was more than a fit of passion. I want to spend more time talking to her, watching her counter everything I say like a game of chess. I want more.

"Whatever you say," Molly replies.

"And she says nothing is going on," I say calmly, pulling my bag over my shoulder. "Molly, please send me the latest updates on the Ocean Tidy project."

"I already sent them to you this morning," Avery brags.

"Great." I leave them to their mindless entertainment. "We'll get something on the calendar to review the notes." I turn to walk down the hall.

"Already asked Molly to schedule it," Avery says.

Naturally, Avery took care of everything already. I have a feeling she's going to continue to keep me on the edge.

Chapter 16
Luca

THE SUN SPILLS INTO MY OFFICE AS I SCAN KORA NOBLE'S latest reports. She just sent over her initial financial health assessment. It's been a month and a half since I contracted her, and her findings are still inconclusive. In her email, she says she still has the entire backlog of prior funding data to review.

If she hasn't found anything that should be a good sign, right?

A brief tightness returns to my chest.

As my thoughts start to spiral, a loud screeching noise from the dreaded communal kitchen disrupts me.

Why is this office so fucking loud? Did Joanna not invest in soundproofing?

I head down the hall to check on the commotion.

Plastech has seamlessly integrated with the team I assigned to the Ocean Tidy project. Avery, especially, seems to be thriving in the new dynamic. During her first week here, I caught the end of a presentation she was giving, her energy matching that optimistic confidence she brought to her interview. It reconfirmed the decision Matthew and I made to appoint Avery as the spokesperson for the team. Her ability to articulate the combined idea is remarkable.

I can't wait to see what else she will accomplish during her time here.

I turn the corner to the kitchen and there *she* stands.

"What on earth are you doing?" My scream is barely audible over the noise.

Avery's hips are wedged into the counter while her arms press into a machine I can only assume is an ancient coffee grinder.

She's wearing jeans today, the denim wrapped firmly around her curves. It's making me reconsider my previous opinion on casual clothes at the office, not that I would ever wear jeans to work. But when Avery does it, I can make an exception.

The noise ceases. I clear my throat and alert her of my presence. "Are you always so loud this early in the morning?"

For the second week in a row, our unspoken competition of arriving first to the office persists. She is ahead by one, but I clearly won this morning, arriving before the sun even rose.

"And good morning to you, Mr. Navarro."

I hide a smile at how the *r*'s roll off her tongue more easily.

I'm so fucked.

"You've been practicing."

Her eyes meet mine. "*Maybe.*"

"I think you have been." My throat dries at the idea.

"I don't give up on a challenge."

Avery's hair is pulled into a high ponytail today, drawing my attention to her nape. I flex my fingers at the phantom feel of how her soft skin feels in my hands.

"I bet you don't," I whisper under my breath.

"Hmm?" she asks.

Did she hear the deliberate provocation from me?

Her eyes scan my face. "Nice scruff."

What?

My hand shoots up to my jaw, and my fingers rub against the coarse stubble. I knew there was something I had missed when I rushed out of my apartment this morning.

Naturally, she doesn't hesitate for a chance to point out my imperfections.

I try to play it off. "I'm trying something new."

"It looks good." She smiles, but I brush off her teasing.

I join Avery, watching her scoop coffee out of the oversized grinder and into a reusable mesh filter. I hope that thing has been cleaned.

Her brows quirk when her head tilts to one side. She regards me before she changes the topic. "Can I just say, I'm so glad I didn't get the job here? If I knew the coffee would be this horrid, I would have never applied in the first place."

"Why did you *really* apply to work here? Apart from Joanna."

Avery pulls a kettle from her tote bag—*an actual kettle*—before drowning out the brief silence between us with the tap. "I care about the environment."

"Why?"

She huffs. "Are you looking for a reason to steal?"

"I know why I'm here."

"Well, it's most definitely not because of the coffee." Avery skirts away from the conversation again.

What fuels her?

"I always get mine from down the street." I press my free arm onto the kitchen counter.

"I'm sure more people would like better coffee at the office."

"Do you have any recommendations?"

She hesitates, seeming unsure if my question is genuine. "There's a very cool coffee machine called the Grinder 9000." Her face lights up. "It has flavor attachments and over twenty latte options!"

"Interesting name."

Avery glares at me. "Making coffee yourself is better than buying it out. Did you know cafes often use cups that have a plastic lining?"

I bring my portable mug into view. "I don't use them."

"*Of course.*"

"The employee handbook discourages disposables."

"You should make the effort because you care," she says, cleaning up the spilled coffee grounds as her brew steeps. "Not because it's in some rule book."

"I do care, and just like you, I *also* care about the rules."

She cracks the knuckles of her slim fingers as she sighs. "You care because you've been told to."

"Actually, I was raised to care about the environment." Our emphasis on the word *care* grows with every jab. "But you find it so easy to assume the worst in me."

"I do not," she says.

Avery's long legs effortlessly carry her across the small kitchen. She leans the back of her head against the wall, her fingers spinning the watch around her wrist. She pretends the steeping coffee is more fascinating than our conversation.

"Tell me two good things you think about me," I challenge.

"Huh?"

"Apart from your obsession with my suits."

Her stare briefly rolls upward, and my own needy frustration returns.

How many times does she have to do that before she realizes it rouses something within me?

"Two nice assumptions, Avery."

She hesitates, and my heart quickens with the fear that she won't confess to one single thing.

Then her mischievous stare meets mine.

"You have a soft spot for pigeons."

My eyebrows crease in confusion. I watch her wicked grin and try to piece together the meaning behind her words.

It finally hits me.

"You saw me in the park! Does that mean you left me to be mauled by a pack of dogs?"

"What? No." She giggles. "I would've paid to maul you myself."

I like the sound of that.

I tip my head forward in provocation. My body relaxes against the counter, one foot crossing over the other. The sound of her laughter quickly stops, and her full lips part.

"I misspoke."

"I definitely wouldn't charge you to—"

She interrupts me. "Ugh! You're so annoying. I regret missing those dogs attack you!"

I give her a side-eye. "Right."

"But I'm glad you're okay." Her cheeks turn the color of cranberry juice. "I know puppies can be vicious."

"They were the size of beasts!" I exclaim, and she laughs.

We haven't had this long a stretch of privacy since our kiss over two weeks ago. The lack of interruption is welcome.

"Alright, anything that doesn't have to do with my heroic rescue?" I contend.

Avery's eyes run up my body from my loafers to my face. She considers me before replying, "I think it's your turn. Do you have something nice to say about me?"

Instead of responding with the truth—you're brilliant, gorgeous, delightfully headstrong, and my list of nice things I think about you is ever growing—I keep my answer ambiguous. "I can't just pick one."

She gawps at me from across the kitchen and fails to produce one of her signature witty remarks to retaliate.

I break the small silence between us. "Do I get another one?"

"You're very persistent."

"That's not an assumption. It's a fact."

She sighs and tips her head back against the wall. "Your snooty attitude is exactly why I never compliment you out loud."

I blink at her.

She's wanted to compliment me before?

"So I've been meaning to ask," Avery says, steering the conversation away from her admission. "Does Joanna work in another office? I rarely see her here."

"CEOs tend to have a packed schedule." I keep it brief. The last thing I want is to risk sharing my own negative views about Joanna. Avery looks up to her, so it may upset her to know Joanna isn't all that great.

"Huh, I was hoping to take advantage of being here and get a chance to learn from her."

"Jo's very busy."

Avery shrugs then pulls an ivory mug from the kitchen cabinet. *Trash Titans* is printed on the side in bold teal letters.

"Why'd you pick that one?" I say.

She looks down at the mug, and I can almost make out the hint of a smile on her face. "This? Oh, the colors are my favorite."

I can't tell if she's messing with me or if she actually doesn't know.

"It's *my* mug."

"I had no idea." The now evident smirk on her face leads me to believe she knows the exact origins of my trash cleanup crew mug.

Avery returns to the counter and pours her coffee into the ceramic. I walk to the fridge and pull out a carton of oat milk, placing it beside her.

She looks at the offering. "What's that for?"

"I thought that's how you take your coffee."

"I do." Avery eyes me scrupulously before unscrewing the cap and splashing the liquid into my mug. The sight sends a warmth between my shoulder blades, and I reach up to rub the back of my neck.

I watch her return the carton to the fridge, collect her mug that she presses to her lips with a smile, and move around the kitchen out of arm's reach.

The gentle bounce of her short ponytail follows her around the room. And I have an unprofessional urge to wrap it around my palm and pull her face toward mine, once more prying eager moans from her lips.

I'm on the verge of breaking our agreement to ignore that our kiss never happened.

"What?" she asks.

My attention snaps back to her. The gentle curves of her brows are pinched together. "Nothing."

"Why do you have that look on your face?"

I smirk. "I can't just enjoy you, Ms. Soko?"

She stares at me for a moment. The ice between us is beginning to thaw.

"You should probably spend less time enjoying messing with me," she says, obviously mistaking my brief pause for another game, "and more time focusing on getting the team to actually like you."

"They do like me," I say, hiding the defensive tinge in my tone.

She scoffs. "When you actually manage to leave that corner office of yours, your own employees run away from you."

I'm not that bad. Am I?

"Hey, Luca, Avery! There you are." Matthew interrupts us, and the familiar frigid air returns to the room. "Join us for this meeting if you have time."

"Yes, we'll meet you there," I say.

"I'll be done in a minute." Avery's coffee steams in her hands.

Matthew walks out of the room.

I refuse to concede to her claim. I'm certain the Ocean Tidy team likes me. They're the only group whose recurring meetings I don't dread. And *not* just because Avery happens to be present. "Well, I can make someone on our team so excited that they'd jump out of their seat. You can't dislike someone if they make you happy!"

The words cause her to pause, and I'm not sure what she's considering. Avery finally breaks the brief silence. "The only way you'd get someone out of their seat is by running down the halls, yelling that there's a fire."

Well, that makes no sense. "I'd just pull the fire alarm."

She rolls her eyes at me.

"I bet I can get at least one person to hop to their feet from joy within the first ten minutes of our meeting."

"That's *easy*," she says. "I'd be able to do that in three minutes."

"So, you should have no issue agreeing to the bet."

Avery regards me. "What do I win this time?"

"New running shoes?"

"What's wrong with the ones I have?"

"Is that a serious question?"

The corners of her mouth slightly turn to the ground, and I regret that my words came off so harshly. I'm only concerned that her worn sneakers are going to cause some kind of injury.

If only I could trade my lawyer's tongue for something— anything—kinder, I would do it right now.

"I just meant that they're awful."

Her frown turns into a glare.

"Awful ankle support." I fail at clarifying my meaning.

Get it together, Luca.

She's never going to reconsider nullifying our agreement if I keep acting like such an asshole.

"I want to burn one of your ties," Avery deadpans.

"Seriously?" I ask, but she makes no effort to barter. "Fine, but if I win, you tell me another nice thing you've thought about me."

"Three minutes. One person jumping out of their seat from excitement."

"It's on." I turn and exit the kitchen.

How hard can it be to get these people excited? Last week, they interrupted a meeting to cheer on a sports team that made it into a championship. This is the first time I regret not keeping up with sports. I take my phone out of my pocket and search the headlines for anything to jog my memory, but nothing sticks out. Maybe I should call Nico and ask him for help.

I enter the large conference room we're using as a shared office for the time being. It's spacious enough for both my team and Plastech to work here together. Desks line the floor-to-ceiling windows, and a conference table and seating area were put together in the center of the room.

Avery suggested that giving everyone access to daylight would be more productive, and she wasn't wrong. I've even caught the team watching the sunset together.

"Hey, guys," I say.

Everyone's head turns to me, their faces painted with puzzled expressions.

Okay, not the reaction I expected. Maybe I am a little cold.

Dr. Claremont—or Hana, as she insists on me calling her—stands beside a seated Ollie. They're practically the same height when he's in his chair. Her voice is rushed, reciting information while he types away on his keyboard.

Robert and Jamie, the technology gurus, are quietly staring at the data displayed on their computers, large over-ear headphones decorating their heads. The pair is incredibly smart, and with Robert around, Jamie has toned down his snarky comments.

Matthew sits at the head of the conference room table. I actually like Matthew; we share the same determined and hard-working qualities that do not come easily to many leaders.

I glance at the time on one of the computers. A minute has passed, and I haven't made one of them smile.

Okay.

Focus.

Where would Avery sit?

I walk over to the seating area decorated with blue velour seats. Everyone seems to love these chairs, so I resolve to ignore my typical place at the conference table and join this painfully informal hangout spot.

I run my hands down my royal-blue suit, straightening the creases. The last time I sat in one of these plushy things, the blue fuzz transferred to my custom Alexander Amosu suit. It took several trips to the dry cleaner to remove the lint. It was very fucking annoying.

I sit down. The crackle of static fills the air, and my body begins to slide on the soft fabric. I plant my hands firmly on either side of my legs to try and steady myself, but I continue to slip off the velour seat.

Time is ticking.

"So, did you all watch the baseball match last night?" I ask.

Ollie is the only one to respond. "You mean, the game? Since when are you keeping up with sports?"

I brace my heels against the floor. My impeccable wool suit continues to glide on the chair. I can feel my spine condense into a half circle.

"Luca, are you alright?" Hana calls over. "What are you doing over there?"

Okay, no more sitting.

I pop up off the chair. A trail of electricity dances on my fingertips.

Where is Avery? Did she decide to forfeit this round?

"I have an announcement." My voice booms through the room.

Everyone looks over at me, and I try to come up with something exciting to share with them.

"We're getting a new printer this week. You'll be happy to know it uses one hundred percent compostable paper."

That's the best I could come up with?

"Mr. Navarro, I do not want this to come off the wrong way." Robert's quiet voice makes itself known. "But most paper is compostable."

"Hope you didn't pay extra for that!" Ollie chimes in.

I sigh. "I meant the paper *and* the printer are all made from recycled materials."

The room settles into a brief silence. This is not successful. I figured they would be excited about the sustainable option.

"Good morning! I brought banana bread." Avery's voice comes from the doorway, and the sound of her heels echoes against the floor.

I don't have enough time to turn and face her before Ollie is running out of his seat, taking the plate out of her hands. A thick slice of the baked good is already on its way to his mouth. Avery places a piece of banana bread on a napkin she brought with her, then walks to where I'm standing.

"I had one minute left. This is cheating," I say in a low whisper, not ready to concede. There's no way I was going to win, but she couldn't have known that.

"Don't be a sore loser," she smiles. "Have a slice." She holds it out to me.

The bread sits there, a looming midday sugar crash waiting to happen.

It's worth it. She's offering it to me.

I reach out to her. The tips of our fingers brush, and a charged spark transfers between us.

"Ow!" Avery yelps. She jerks her arm back, but I manage to grab the banana bread before it falls to the floor.

My heart sinks immediately at the way she rips from my touch so forcefully.

"Those damn chairs." I try to play it off, but I'm already itching to touch her again.

"It's fine," she says.

"Sorry."

The swirl of her hazel eyes draws a line from my face to the almost crumpled banana bread in my fist. "Are you just going to stare at it? Because I'll take my peace offering back."

"No, no." I yank my hands back defensively.

I peel the napkin away from the cake and bring a piece to my mouth. Immediately, my taste buds light with hints of spices, cinnamon, and nutmeg. The sweetness is more subtle than typical banana bread, each bite growing more delectable. It tastes as though it were pulled out of the oven minutes ago. The home-made flavors bring a smile to my face.

"Did you make this?" I ask.

"Yes."

"It's delicious." I beam at her.

Avery returns my smile and makes her way back to Ollie. They dole out slices to the rest of the team.

Since Plastech's very first week at the ORO offices, I've noticed each member of their team bring in treats for the Ocean Tidy crew. I figured it was merely a habit they brought over from their coworking space, and I avoided partaking in the sugary morning rush, not wanting to start my day off like a spoiled toddler, stuffing myself with sweets.

But now, I watch our team swarm around Avery like bees protecting their queen. Each of their faces lit with happiness at her considerate gesture, and praise for her baking skills fills the room.

This time, instead of corralling their attention back to the meeting, I join them.

Chapter 17
Avery

THE TWO BLUEBERRY MUFFINS CURRENTLY SWIMMING IN THE PIT of my stomach are about to project themselves onto the seashell floor. Luca brought three dozen of these fluffy baked goods from the same place I visited a few days ago. He's trying to use treats to win over the team and the remainder of the ORO staff.

It may be working.

The muffins seemed like a perfect way to start the day—right until now.

At least I'm ahead and on a winning streak, despite Luca's refusal to admit I'm right.

Avery: 4 | Luca: 1

The crowd of nervous butterflies within me has morphed into angry mockingbirds screeching into my chest. I take a deep breath to steady myself, then tap my knuckles lightly against the glass door.

"What?" a hoarse voice snaps.

My palms grease the handle and I enter Joanna Benbart's lavish office. Each transparent wall is lined with free-standing shelves crammed to the brim with awards and photographs. A stunning view of Central Park is revealed by the windows. I peek over and try to find my daily running path in the distance.

The one and only Joanna Benbart is perched on her large chair, her stare locked on her computer screen. I glance down at my clothes.

Perfect. No spills or stains will be joining me for this impromptu meeting.

"Hi, Ms. Benbart. It's so nice to see you again. Do you have a minute?" The words rush out of me in a hurried request. I'm sure all she heard was *Benartseeyouagainhaveaminute.*

Snap out of it, Avery.

She's just another person.

Don't think about her as the woman you idolized your entire life.

My features contort into a tight knot.

The confidence I wore like a badge of honor during my interview has vanished, replaced with more nerves weaseling into my chest.

I'm not going to tally up the number of times in the past month—*eleven*—that I made an excuse to walk by this part of the ORO offices, waiting for the opportunity to catch Joanna alone and explain my admiration for her work. Her schedule has been impossible to predict, and most days she's barely at the office.

But today is my lucky day! An opportunity to redo my first impression.

I'm not expecting much, just a little career advice or a word of encouragement would be great.

Hi. Hello. Huge fan! Happy to be here again! Our combined project is going smoothly. Any chance you're looking to take a mentee under your wing?

And done.

I force myself farther into the room, holding my head high.

As I approach Joanna's desk, I notice her creased features still resemble the younger woman whose shining face is captured in news articles around the office. Her long, gray hair is tied back into a braid.

She doesn't glance up at me, and a pang of guilt for disturbing her without an appointment sets in.

It's fine. Yes, Luca said she was busy only a few days ago, but I'm not going to let him dictate my decisions. This will just be a quick hello.

"Who are you?" She regards me briefly before interest seems to fizzle out of her blue eyes.

"Avery Soko. You interviewed me for a developmental role two months ago."

My body hums with excitement. I stare at her, unable to form any other sentences.

This is the woman who organized marches against fracking. Who lived in the Gulf of Mexico after the biggest oil spill in years. She was one of the few activists who showed up to help instead of just condemning the tragedy.

"Hello?" Joanna bites.

I snap out of my daze. "I never had the opportunity to thank you for how much you've inspired me and my career."

My ambitious little Ave, my dad said to me as we left an environmental protest in New York City led by Joanna. *You'll do big things in this world. Just like her!*

Now I'm here!

Our shared universe of promises to change the world together. I'm not going to let him or myself down.

"I thought I told Luca not to hire you?"

My face falls.

Told Luca what? I must have misheard her.

"What did you—"

"Why are you here if you were specifically told not to be?"

"I'm here because I work at Plastech," I remind her. "Our

teams are collaborating on the Ocean Tidy project for the Ellington Grant." My knees wobble like the late-summer breeze outside.

"Right, the Ellington Grant." She scoffs. "Willa and her petty little games, always making her philanthropy into a roulette."

I stand in silence, my words now lost for a completely different reason.

"Well, are you just going to stand there?" She clears her throat. "Or are you going to get back to work, Ava?"

"Avery."

"Yes. *Avery.*"

"Um. I just—" I take a deep breath.

I can save this, maybe I just threw her off a little. "I just wanted to ask you what it was like when you were arrested during the first Earth Day prote—"

"I don't have time to reminisce today. *Please* see yourself out."

Pressure collects in my chest. I couldn't have heard her right. Her rude tone must be a figment of my imagination.

Maybe she hasn't had her coffee?

Joanna waves her hand to me, signaling me to leave.

Dad would never forgive me if I gave up right now. I need her to just hear me out!

"Look, if you can give me a second—"

"You really need to learn to handle rejection better." Jo's voice is like venom.

A sting of hurt reverberates through me, knocking the wind from my torso. Immediately, I'm transported to when Luca called me to deliver the news that I was not suitable for my dream job.

"I—"

"Molly?" Joanna yells over me.

Her voice rips through my shock.

"Molly!" She smashes the button on her phone's intercom, and I immediately take that as my cue to leave.

My body rips itself from that horrid office, and then I crash against a wall down the hallway. Anger stings my eyes, but I refuse to cry.

The decades I spent idolizing Joanna, for what? For everything to crumble in front of me, like sand slipping through my fingers. There's no way that is the same woman I modeled my life after.

That indifferent shell.

The sleepless nights, the long hours, and the emptiness in my chest suddenly hit me all at once. I shut my eyes, forcing them tighter until the stars behind my lids finally wipe away the tragic scene in her office.

"Are you taking a nap?" Luca's deep, rich voice brings me back to this reality.

I refuse to meet his stare, but I can sense his presence all around me, and even with my eyes closed, I can feel the intensity of his gaze.

"Avery?" he says.

I'm afraid that if I open my eyes, he'll tower over me, and I'll shatter into pieces before him like I haven't with anyone but Lily. The kiss we shared on the boat was already a terrible mistake; I crossed the professional line I must navigate. But something about Luca seeing me right now, spiraling, terrifies me. As though he would finally win the upper hand over me.

A desperate feeling chews away at every cell in my body. Fighting to escape.

I need to be alone right now.

The nearest bathroom is only a few steps away, and I break in that direction. But Luca's fingers circle my wrist, cementing me to the floor.

"What's wrong?"

"I'm fine, Luca."

I swat his touch from me, not wanting him close. Joanna's words reopened a wound, and the familiar sting of rejection returns. I thought I was over not getting the job at ORO, but the memory cuts deep right now.

I look back into Luca's concerned eyes.

I don't want to relive that terrible phone call. I don't want to fall apart in front of him.

Right now, I just need to be alone. I'm good alone. *Perfectly fine* being alone.

I walk away.

"I know you better than that by now." His steps follow me.

"This isn't another game." Just a few more paces.

"Avery, talk to me."

My heart skips at the way he says my name so urgently, but I rip open the bathroom door, leaving Luca in the hallway, and make for the sink. There's a hammering in my chest as the raging drum of anxiety bursts into me.

Breathe in. Breathe out.

The tension in my chest begins to calm but my enamel grinds together.

I open the faucet, and the sound drowns out my thoughts. My hands tremble under the cool, running tap.

Why did I just barge into Jo's office like that?

The creak of the door draws me away from the spiraling thoughts.

Molly's kind eyes appear. "Ave?"

I turn away from the faucet and face her. She pulls a few napkins out of a nearby dispenser and dries the dampness on my hands.

"Do you want to tell me what's wrong?" Her voice is soft.

I heave a sigh, and tension eases briefly in my sore rib cage. "I promise, everything's okay."

She gives me a warm hug, and I enjoy her embrace before we pull apart.

"I don't want to overstep, but judging by Jo's outburst, did she say something to you?"

I nod reluctantly.

"Right," Molly says sincerely. "Look, this isn't going to make you feel that much better, but I promise, it's not personal."

"Thank you."

"Jo didn't get to where she is without being a bit…" Molly pauses. "The work we do here isn't always easy."

That is true. There have been so many times when I looked at the state of the world and doubted I could ever make a positive change. Countless times when my dad's death or the never-ending workload would diminish my spirits.

However, that never stopped me from trying.

"I know you're right. But I looked up to Joanna. I just—I wanted her to understand that."

"Ave, oh, she understands," she says, trying to reassure me. "I've worked with Jo for so many years. There are good days and bad ones."

I straighten my spine and pull together a smile.

"Just remember, we're all trying to complete this project within four months." Molly pulls stray hair out of my face and widens the set of her shoulders. "We need to play as hard as we've been working!"

She's right. Everyone needs a release.

"What about we all go for drinks at that new rooftop bar on Forty-Fifth?" Molly suggests.

"We should do a girls' night there. That place has a strict dress code. The guys would hate it if we took them some place they had to wear a blazer. Maybe we should do something more relaxed."

"Right. This really is your specialty, Ave."

"We need a team-building event!" I say.

It's true. I need to get back into being around people outside of the office. I've been so lost in the haze of my computer screen, presentations, and Luca's distracting presence around the office.

I cringe at how easily I almost fell apart in front of him.

I need to create some space. I've been too friendly. The little bets and challenges are obviously making me lose my mind. I bring my fingers to my temples and massage the strain away. I'm not going to veer away from what's important: my career.

Not because of Joanna and most definitely not because of Luca.

I just need a night to cut loose and reset.

Molly jumps in. "ORO went bowling last year. It was so fun!"

As much as I would love to take out my frustration by throwing around some balls, I don't want to ruin the manicure I finally got with Lily a few days ago. I rattle my brain and try to pull out some ideas.

"I know! We can go to Trivia!"

"I love trivia!" Molly chimes in.

"My roommate hosts a weekly game at the Mademoiselle, and it's always a fun crowd."

Lily and Molly would get along so well.

"Okay, I love that place. Everyone is dressed so freaking cute!" Molly says. "As long as they have dancing after trivia, you can count me in."

"Let's do it."

Chapter 18
Luca

THE MADEMOISELLE IS HIDDEN IN PLAIN SIGHT ON A BUSTLING Upper East Side street. The twenty minutes I spend walking around searching for its creaking mahogany doors almost causes me to faint from heat stroke.

Late summers in New York City have a way of suffocating you. Between the weather and my overflowing to-do list at ORO, my chest is in a constant state of constriction.

I enter the modern-day speakeasy, and it takes me only a few seconds to find *her*.

The bright blonde of her hair peeks out through the group of people she's standing with. They all laugh around a large table under the dim light of the bar's chandeliers. It's one of the things that makes it easy to fall for her, Avery smiling, surrounded by people.

She seems happy.

I hesitate at the door. I could still leave. I have a ton of errands to catch up on. And she did make it pretty clear she didn't want me here when she left me off the invitation for tonight's team-building event. If it weren't for Molly sending it to me, I would still be at the office working on those errands.

No. I have a purpose tonight.

Avery has been avoiding me since her eruption outside Joanna's office on Monday. Maybe she's done playing whatever game started between us, no longer pushing the boundary of our working relationship.

I miss her daily quips, but she's made a great effort to avoid me for two days straight.

A dull ache rests in my chest. All the progress I thought we made seems like it's been wiped away.

It can't be though. Just this morning, even in the haze of her avoidance, Avery spoke up for me after one of Jamie's biting remarks. I caught them in the kitchen yesterday, Avery complaining that the coffee tasted like a pile of cement. Jamie had the great idea to compare the way I carried myself to the aforementioned cement, but Avery didn't laugh. Instead, she said, "Cement isn't that bad. It makes a good foundation."

Her whisper traveled into the hallway where I stood, away from view.

Whether Avery intended to make the brief distinction, I'm not sure. But I'll take it. I *would* be a good foundation. Especially since we're on the same team.

Why won't she let me prove that to her?

Regardless of what happened in Joanna's office, I need to mend this recent divide between us.

But what kind of asshole crashes a trivia night? This asshole.

My fingers rake through my hair, pulling the strands away from my face. It's going to be a long night.

I skirt around patrons until I stand behind Avery and my colleagues. "I'd love to know how you intended to play with an odd number of people tonight."

I'm a fucking jerk. I couldn't just say hello?

Each of them spin around at the sound of my voice.

My eyes settle on the only person I care about tonight. Hers are wild with surprise. My favorite expression. I've been learning that I have a lot of those.

There's the eye roll. The smiles she hides. And, obviously, her determined stare.

"Why are you here?" Avery turns to Molly, who won't meet her stare.

"This is a team-building event, isn't it? Last time I checked, we're all meant to be on the same team. Besides, you may not know this about me, but I can be the life of the party."

Ollie shifts to the side, making room for me inside of their circle.

"Maybe at a funeral," Avery retorts.

A woman appears at my side, standing in the most outrageous outfit I have ever seen. A wooly cap is placed above her sleek, ebony hair. The collar of her frilly blouse splays across her shoulders, and she dons a burgundy velvet apron. The entire ensemble makes her look like a pirate and a person from the Roaring Twenties had a baby. Her head meets the top of Avery's shoulder. From Avery's couple of mentions of her personal life, she must be her roommate.

"Hi, you must be Lily." I give her a polite smile. Avery's eyes dart to me.

"Lily Rodin, Avery's better half." She laughs and extends her hand. I give it a brief shake. "You work with this rowdy crew here?"

"Yes. I'm Luca Navarro. It's nice to meet you."

"Luca?" A quizzical note laces in her voice. Lily turns to Avery as a seemingly devious smile stretches across her features. This is not the first time my name has come up between them.

I bite the inside of my cheek, suppressing a smirk.

Avery's face whisks from me to her roommate.

"Listen, friend, if you're playing with us, you ought to join us for a drink." Ollie's immense hand squeezes my shoulder, his eyes already somewhat glazed over.

"No amount of liquor can relax the suited statue," Avery says.

"Ave's in the mood to quarrel tonight." Ollie beams and gives her a grand smile. "Hope you're on my team, lass."

Avery fidgets with her hands. It's like anxiety has trapped itself inside her body. Her usual air of confidence and my favorite affable demeanor are gone. I want to help her relieve whatever seems to be festering. I'll give her the green light to take her anger out on me. Especially if it'll bring her back to me.

It's just one night. I can loosen up for *her*.

"Ollie," I say, "I'll take the coldest beer on tap."

Our friendly giant departs, leaving me with the rest of the rowdy crew. Lily watches me intently, an overexcited grin refusing to leave her face.

"So, did my invitation get lost?" I ask Avery.

"No." She turns away from me.

"Huh, well, I'm hoping to get a crash course on this team-building thing tonight. Not sure if you noticed, but I tend to be competitive by nature."

Her roommate watches us intently.

"Of course, I noticed," Avery bites. "That's why a friendly game of trivia won't help your case. You need an entire personality overhaul."

"So, we've finally gone from strangers to *friendly*?" I smirk.

Her hazel eyes roll into the back of her head. "That's not what I meant." She huffs.

Lily notices the shift in the air. "Alright. Seems like you both need a way to work out this"—Lily looks between us—"*energy*." She walks over to a collection of small whiteboards and pulls two from the stack. "You'll be the captains."

"Lil–"

"No arguing, Avery. *I'm* the trivia goddess." Lily places a whiteboard with a detachable black marker in front of each of us.

"Fine." Avery grabs her board and glances at me. Her

pointed expression conveys that she's ready to drag me across the bar floor.

Let the games begin. Again.

Ollie returns with a round of drinks, and we take a few minutes to split up the teams. I wanted to be on Avery's team tonight, but maybe the competition will bring us closer together. Like it has in the past.

In the grand scheme of things, my team is pretty tough. I have two tolerable brainiacs in Robert and Hana, plus the friendly Scotsman. Ollie's been a welcome amusement for the office, always cracking jokes and including everyone, even me.

The different trivia groups disperse among the small high-top tables all clustered together at the front of the bar. A group of college students joins to my left, but the *real* competition is to my right. The cramped space allows me to stand close enough to Avery that the back of my hand could caress her skin. As if she can sense the heat of my desire, she turns her back to me and leans over her table to whisper strategy with her group.

"Welcome everyone to Trivia at the Mademoiselle." Lily's voice booms through the bar.

We all face the makeshift stage Lily is standing on, and everyone raises their glass to toast the beginning of the game.

Avery whips her head around to give me one last glance. I smile, raising the lip of my bottle to her.

Her beautiful mouth forms the words *game on* amid the sound of clinking. The competitive excitement is plain in her features.

Exactly the look I was hoping for.

Lily walks us through the very uncomplicated nuances of bar trivia. There's a total of eleven questions, which we will answer on our handheld whiteboards within thirty seconds.

"The winning group gets to be included on the hall-of-fame wall." As Lily ends her speech, the lights point to a giant collage of Polaroids decorating the back of the bar. Hundreds of pictures contain strangers laughing or having fun within the Mademoiselle.

"Now every group needs to pick a name!" Lily instructs.

Ollie grabs the whiteboard out of my hands. "I may not be the quickest to answer, but I always pick the best names."

I groan. "No, please. Last time we let you pick a name, you convinced us Ocean Tidy was cool."

"First of all, Ocean Tidy is *still* cool, and second, it'll be better than Team One or whatever boring name you'd pick."

No use arguing. I take a sip of my drink.

I'm sure that whatever he's scribbling will at least be witty and full of zeal.

Ollie holds up the board.

"Welcome, Sea Men," Lily announces, writing our team's name on the scoreboard.

"Ol," Robert murmurs to his friend, "I don't think that's inspiring the reaction you wanted it to."

"What, Robbie?" Ollie says. He gestures at the team. "We're protecting the sea, and we're men!"

Hana clears her throat.

"Well, apart from Hana. Sorry, lass, didn't think that one through, did I?"

Our table collectively lets out a sigh.

"We're the Sea Men. C'mon, guys! Sea Men." Ollie begins to coax us into an unreciprocated chant. "Sea Men!"

I glance over at Avery, whose team is holding back laughter at Ollie's wildly inappropriate words. Her mouth curls into a smirk, mischief flashing on her face as she slowly lifts her board, revealing her group's name.

Trash Titans.

"It's such a creative name." She winks. "Don't you think, Navarro?"

My cheeks rise. Every second of her teasing is one step

closer for us to return to our normal. It's nice to see her happy, even if it is at my expense.

Avery's lean, smooth arms lift high above her head, showing the whiteboard to Lily. The arch of her back deepens, leaving those full hips on display for me to see. My dick stirs beneath the tight grip of my pants, and I shift uncomfortably in my seat.

I can't be fucking thinking about this right now.

Avery turns around and scoffs. I knew she picked that mug for a reason. She looked me up. I try to hold back another smile.

I wish I'd picked a cooler name than Trash Titans. But Sea Men is much, *much* worse.

A few more group names are added to the scoreboard as the bar packs with more people. My group's name is neatly scribbled in between the *Trash Titans* and *Clam Bake*—which turns out to be the group of college students sitting to our left, all laughing their asses off at the puns.

I readjust myself in the seat, ready to get started.

"First question." Lily's voice captures the attention of the bar. "In one calendar year, how many deaths involve an elevator?"

The obvious grin on Lily's face is hard to miss. She gives Avery a huge wink before Lily's dark eyes land on me and squint with aversion.

That settles my earlier suspicion. Avery definitely carried my name home with her. I imagine the stories that may have spilled from her beautiful lips. Hopefully good ones.

"Well, ain't that quite morbid to begin with?" Ollie bellows, and my attention wavers from thoughts of the woman sitting only a few inches from me.

"Around thirty," Hana says, holding the whiteboard in her hands. "It should be the elevators *and* escalators because those are grouped together in the death report."

"Um, how do you know that, lass?"

"I like true crime." She shrugs.

"Remind me never to piss off Hana," I say.

But the laughter I expect from the group grows into a stiff silence when Hana shoots me a glare. Robert subtly moves his head disapprovingly.

Tough crowd.

Clam Bake must also like true crime facts because they were the only other group that received points for this round.

"Of course, your group would get that question right." Avery scoffs, her body bending back into the air between us. The curve of her voluptuous behind almost presses into the top of my thighs.

"Interesting that your roommate would pick an elevator question to start with," I point out. "Are you sure this game isn't rigged?"

"Stop fraternizing with the competition, Luca." Ollie grabs me away from Avery and wedges himself between us.

Competition.

That word keeps attaching itself to her and me, stoking the lit embers between us.

The next six rounds drag out. Most of the questions are nearly impossible to guess, but luckily, our team has Robert and Hana, who are walking human encyclopedias. I knew they are brilliant, and yet each right answer leaves me impressed.

The scoreboard reads:

Trivia Swift |||
Trash Titans |||
The Sea Men ||||
Clam Bake ||
Stay at Homies ||
Quiz Kings |||
Good Girls ||||

"I'm getting another water," Avery says to our two teams after Lily calls for a small intermission. "Does anybody want one?"

Most people nod in response.

"I'll help." I stand and follow her to the freestanding jug of water.

I wince at its sight. When was the last time this has been sufficiently disinfected?

"Oh, I'm sorry, I didn't know you recently discovered an ability to help others," she whispers, but I brush it off easily. I know she knows differently. I've proven such to her on numerous occasions. Her defenses are just back up, and I'll patiently wait out their storm.

What did Joanna say to her?

The question forms on the tip of my tongue, but I don't want to ruin this.

Instead, I say, "Only when it comes to you."

"Right." She sighs.

"Your roommate seems cool." I try to take advantage of the few private moments we have together. "Did you meet her in the city?"

"Lily's my best friend," Avery says. "We met in North Carolina during my senior year. We both wanted to live here, so we moved after my dad died."

Oh. Did she tell me that before?

Her face scrunches. No, I think she didn't mean to tell me.

"I had no idea, I'm sorry."

"Don't apologize." Her eyes meet mine, and her words come out in an unusual stutter. "I-I don't know why I even said that. I wasn't trying to…"

"Thank you for telling me." I try to smile.

There's a vacant expression in her beautiful eyes, an unsettling contrast to the brightness I'm used to seeing there. I want to fix whatever is causing her to feel like this. Now seems like the worst time to grow silent at her confession, but all I want to do is pull her into my arms and hold her close. For now, I try to accept whatever piece of her she's willing to give me and go at her pace.

"Let me get this." I pull the glasses from her hands and begin filling them.

No pushback? The corners of my mouth fall toward the floor.

I study her. Tension seems to run through her, and she fidgets with the metal clasp of her watch.

"So, what's our bet?" I gently swipe my thumb across her wrist, causing her to snap back to this reality.

"Hmm?" Our eyes meet.

"What are we betting this time?"

She grabs an empty glass to fill. "No more games."

"Oh, is it because you aren't ready to lose another bet?"

"I've won all our bets!" Fire returns to her eyes.

"I think you're going to have to remind me." I persist with the need to distract her.

She hands me another full glass of water. "I'm not in the mood."

"I see." I fake an exaggerated sigh and bring my lips to her ear. "Did I draw all the fun out of you on the boat?"

When I pull back, I see her cheeks turn as crimson as a glass of merlot.

"We agreed to not talk about that," she snaps.

"I would like to renegotiate the terms of our agreement."

"No."

"Yes."

Avery drops what she's doing, plants her hands on her hips, and turns to face me. "What do you want, Navarro?"

You.

"If my group wins trivia," I offer, "I get to kiss you again."

Avery's eyes widen, and her brows shoot up. She considers me.

If she agrees to our little side bet, I'll know that I haven't fully lost whatever this is between us.

Those beautiful eyes close in on me, and one corner of her mouth lifts slightly. "And *when* my team wins, you can never kiss me again."

I will not lose. The stakes are too high.

"Deal." I gather four of the full water glasses and hightail it back to my group before she has a chance to change her mind.

These past few days have been torturous without her. I won't collect on my winnings if she doesn't want me to, but a part of me hopes that she craves my lips as much as I hunger for hers.

When she returns to her table, Avery strategically places herself away from me, using her group to create space between us.

Lily resumes the game, the questions spanning a multitude of pop culture references. The Sea Men only guess one of the three correctly, while the other groups rack up multiple points.

"After ten rounds"—Lily turns to her scoreboard—"the Trash Titans are in first place with seven points. And in a close second, we have a tie between Good Girls and The Sea Men. Both with six points."

Avery's group erupts with celebration. They all seem to be really enjoying themselves.

"Now for the final question," Lily says to the room. "Name the student responsible for placing the UNC Rams mascot in the National Mascot Hall of Fame five years ago?"

"What in the bloody hell?" Ollie asks.

"I don't think I know this one," Robert admits reluctantly.

On the stage, Lily is leaning against the scoreboard, practically keeled over from laughter as confusion plagues the room. I peek over at Avery, who is sending her roommate a death glare I have only seen directed toward me. It conveys a very unsubtle *fuck you.*

Fifteen seconds left.

Think, Luca. Think. I can't lose this. My palms sweat, and I try to shallow my breathing.

Wait.

When I ran into Avery running on *her* side of the park, she was sporting that baggy college shirt. Her shirt would ride up slightly each time her foot met the ground, making her thighs shake. My dick stirs.

Not now.

Focus.

Five seconds left.

What was on that shirt? An image of a ram flashes into my mind.

It *must* be her.

I rip the board out of Ollie's hands and slam the tip of the marker onto it.

Three.

Two.

I frantically raise up the board. No one else has an answer displayed.

"Avery Soko is correct." Lily reads the name off my board, struggling to catch her breath between her fits of laughter. "Congratulations, Sea Men."

My adversary stares at me, her mouth gaping wide.

"Lily, what the fuck?" Avery glares at her roommate.

Molly playfully backhands Avery's shoulder. "Why didn't you write your name down?"

"I…" Avery stutters. "It's embarrassing, okay? I didn't think anyone would know such a *ridiculously* specific fact!"

Lily's laughter refuses to let up, her hands gripping the back of a nearby chair as she wheezes.

I wipe sweat from my brow. This game elicits the same feeling as running a mile.

"You're telling me you dressed up as this ram?" Ollie points his phone in her face.

The screen displays a comically large furry ram with over-sized spiraled horns attached to its head. A light-blue jersey covers the animal's chest. The mascot's large eyes are furrowed into a cross expression, similar to the one Avery wears on her face right now.

"Technically, it's named Rameses," she counters. "It was fun! Leave me alone!"

"Okay, okay, sorry, Ave." Ollie puts away his phone. "I just couldn't pass it up."

Lily finally composes herself to conclude the game. "We have a tie between the Trash Titans and Sea Men! Which means it's time for the lightning round!"

The rest of the bar cheers while The Clam Bake team yell their disappointment at the stage. Their group is immediately tamed by a waiter offering them a round of shots.

Now that's a pacifying tactic I wish I could try at the office.

"The lightning round has three questions." Lily walks over to us and replaces our whiteboards with small service bells that you might find in a hotel lobby. "The first group to ring gets to answer. If they don't get it right, the other team has a chance to steal the win. Since I knew you would be coming tonight, I put together some ocean-themed questions." Lily winks at us and walks back to the stage. "Ready?"

We all nod.

"What makes up the biggest percent of plastic in the ocean?" Lily shoots.

Bing!

"Fishing nets." Avery's hand is still on the bell. Her delicate brows crinkle into an indestructible focus.

"Correct." Lily nods.

That's my girl.

I shouldn't root for her to win, but seeing Avery light up again may be worth losing the bet.

Ah, who am I kidding? I want to kiss her so fucking badly.

The questioning continues. "How long is the lifespan of the *Turritopsis dohrnii*?"

"*Turritopsis dohrnii*?" Robert looks at Hana.

My hand slams on the bell.

"Trick question—it doesn't have a life span because it's immortal." I thank the elective oceanography class I took while in undergrad.

"That can't be right!" Avery says.

"That is correct!" Lily flips to the final question in her hands. "Next point wins."

Avery and I hover over our bells. She avoids making eye contact with me, but I can't help noticing the flush spreading across the nape of her neck. The silence in the bar is piercing as we anticipate our next question.

I would lose every single bet I've ever made to win this one.

"The final question is…"

The pounding in my chest quickens.

"Seagrass captures carbon up to how many times faster than tropical rainforests?"

I hesitate.

Ollie grabs the bell from me, a chime emanating from the pounding of his palm. Avery hits her bell a millisecond after Ollie.

"Thirty-five times faster." Ollie grins.

Is that right?

I look from Lily to Avery. Avery's hands push against the table, her stool scraping on the ground as she lets out a sigh.

"That's *correct*! The Sea Men win! Y'all are some strong swimmers!"

The room erupts in applause, and before I can react, Ollie wraps his arms around me and lifts me off the ground, swinging me from side to side as though I weigh nothing.

A bright flash fills the room. I watch Lily pull a Polaroid out of her camera and walk to the black wall before pinning the developing photograph on it.

The second the soles of my loafers finally touch the ground, I spot Avery throwing back a shot with Molly.

And when Avery pounds the shot glass down, she stares right at me.

Chapter 19
Avery

Avery: 4 | Luca: 2

MY GLASS COLLIDES WITH THE MAHOGANY BAR.

I lost. I *lost.*

Did I purposely sabotage myself? I could've easily won. I'm going to get Lily back for that mascot question.

I should've written my name, but I didn't want to give Luca any ammunition. How did he even know something so specific? I bet he's been scouring the internet for ridiculous dirt he could use on me in his games.

Those wretched, distracting, addicting games.

Agh!

The new bartender sets a new drink in front of me. He's been serving up a novel mixture of cocktails with lush flavors of passion fruit and strawberry. I take a sip of the red drink. It's like a spin on a pineapple sangria, so deliciously sweet, and it's absolutely helping me mull over all the emotions brewing inside me.

The glow of the chandeliers ripples across the space, and a small disco ball reflects sparkles of light from the ceiling. Lily had the barkeeps clear the high-top tables out of the center of the room, creating a makeshift dance floor in the crowded bar.

The music pulses loudly.

I should join the people dancing and burn off whatever is coursing through me.

Or at least avoid Luca so he can't claim his prize.

A kiss.

Maybe he'll take a plea of temporary insanity and let me off with a warning. Or will those hands pull me closer to him until his hot, filthy mouth collides with mine, forcing me to pay the debt?

I violently suck in a breath. My body shivers at the thought. Do I have a fever?

What. Am. I. Thinking?

For the first time in a few days, my veins are filled with something other than anxiety. And even though my knees are unsteady at my need for him, I can't kiss him. It'll just complicate my already muddled feelings about Joanna and my job.

He's only here to get a rise out of me. Probably to pry about the Joanna encounter the other day. Hasn't he gotten the hint that I don't want to talk to him about it? What would I even say?

Hey, Luca, the woman I looked up to my entire fucking life hates me.

I clench the drink in my hand. I didn't realize how much I've been ignoring my feelings about the initial job rejection. It's like a dull bruise refusing to heal.

And now, after this whole *thing* with Jo, it feels fresh again. *Learn how to handle rejection* must be the ORO catchphrase or something.

Also, why did I have to mention my dad?

My head spins a little. The four drinks must be finally catching up to me.

Good. I need to get out of my head.

Molly unglues herself from her stool. "Ave, let's dance!"

Her typically neat curls splay across her shoulders. I need to remember to ask her to manage my own unruly waves.

"I don't know, Molly." I sigh. Maybe I just want to wallow here with my fruity drinks.

I turn my head to face the dance floor. The Clam Bake team dances while Ollie laughs around them, his body bopping clunkily to the music. They all have smiles plastered on their faces.

Unlike me, the rest of my team is taking the loss in stride. Venomous envy grows in me for the relaxation in their movements. I want to remember a time I wasn't consumed by my overwhelming workload or disappointment.

"It'll be fun!" Molly tries again.

I'd probably be stiff on the dance floor. But not as stiff as Luca.

Okay. Not thinking about Luca's stiff anything right now.

The last time I allowed myself to go dancing must have been a few months ago when Lily dragged me out of the apartment for an impromptu 70s disco party. Nowadays, neither of us has the time for a girls' night where we can put on the glamorous dresses we keep thrifting and cut loose from our exhausting weeks.

"Come on! I'll teach you how to salsa. One, two, three, four." Molly counts under her breath as she steps toward me, throwing her hands above her head and swaying her hips offbeat as she performs her dance.

"You're a pro!" I smile at Molly.

"Trust me, Ave, you *have* to come with me to my next class!" Molly reaches her arms toward me, urging me off the chair. "The one I've been taking has *so* many hot single guys."

I flinch. Luca is beside me.

When did he arrive?

"Tell me more about these dance classes," he says. His voice drips with arrogant pride.

I don't want to deal with him right now. I sit up straighter, refusing to recoil in his presence. That bet between us should've never been made.

"Luca! You can dance with me," Molly says. "I started taking salsa lessons. I go with this girl from my gym. You can tell a lot about a man based on how they dance."

A flick of annoyance runs through me. No one should be dancing with Luca.

"That's definitely one way." Luca licks his lips.

Molly ignores the hidden meaning in his words. "I've wanted to invite you, Luca, but I don't think you'd go! Sometimes, I'm not sure if you're able to have fun."

She gives Luca a teasing smile, but he remains quiet.

Why isn't he rubbing his victory in my face? I nudge away the prickling question sitting on my lips.

"Sometimes?" The sweetness of my fruity drink still coats my tongue. "More like all the time. He's incapable of fun."

The warmth of the alcohol soothes the pent-up tension in my body.

I take another sip. My strain is ready to snap. I know the man standing beside me would be more than willing to unravel me, but I refuse to remind my body how easily he can uncoil the knots inside of me. I don't want it to become something I crave in the future.

Luca finally says, "You always underestimate me."

"Don't kid yourself, Navarro, dancing would wrinkle that suit."

He steps closer, only a couple of inches between us. "If my clothes bother you so much, all you have to do is ask, and I'll let you take them off me."

The image of the Trash Titans photo flashes in my head, tempting me.

"It's those ties that bother me, they seem to be cutting the oxygen to your head."

Luca grins that annoyingly heat-stirring, grin. "Ties. Suits. I'll give it all to you."

"No." I slam my glass against the wooden bar, the contents spilling onto my fingers. Instinctively, I press my tongue to the sticky liquid coating my skin.

A rush of heat meets my side, and I look up at Luca's pitch-black eyes devouring me. I pull my fingers slowly from my lips, savoring the way his stare refuses to waver. The tight muscles in his jaw tick.

I need to get away from him.

I lean over the bar. "Put something else on?" I yell at Lily, who is swarmed by patrons. "I wanna dance!"

She nods, ignoring her customers, and walks over to the speakers before changing the music to something more my speed.

The bass of the song causes the floor to tremble, and more people make their way to the dance floor. The alcohol in my system takes over, each cell in my body thrumming. I need to move, to be touched, to release.

"Let's go, Molly." I stretch out my arms toward her hands, and she leads me into a dance. Molly abandons her relentless salsa step and gives in to the rhythm of the drums. My body writhes to the music, each beat rolling my hips.

A yip of excitement pours out of her, making us both laugh.

The air in the bar swells with heat from the moving bodies. I'm not sure how much time has passed when Matthew joins us with another round of colorful drinks. We down them as we all keep tempo with the music.

Sweat beads on my face. The weight inside of me evaporates through my skin. My team's expressions are lit up with excitement, probably from not having to spend another evening poring over work.

We needed a night like this.

The only person I can't find on the dance floor is Luca. He probably left the second he was done tormenting me.

I scan the bar and find him sitting in the exact spot I left him. The length of one of his muscular legs stretches out before him while his other foot rests on my stool.

Why is he still here?

His stare targets me.

My neck rolls in the opposite direction, certain that any annoyance in my expression will be lost in the dim lighting.

I try to keep my attention on my hips swaying to the new song filling the bar. But my curiosity gets the best of me, and I turn back to find Luca through the crowd.

He finally stands, allowing my eyes to trail the full extent of his body.

Luca shrugs off his jacket, revealing one of his annoyingly creaseless white shirts that stretches over his firm chest.

A familiar lust erupts through me, causing my already sweat-coated thighs to press together while I dip low on the dance floor, my body returning to the tempo.

Luca's tongue smooths across his lips, and his large hands reach for his tie. Gradually pulling the knot apart, he is deliberate with each movement and plays it out in slow motion as if time has ceased to exist around us. The silky forest-green fabric now hangs undone on the ledge of the bar.

The fire between us roars, the flame too dangerous for me to leave unattended, like a burning candle in a wooden house. His striptease causes my palms to clam up. I run my hands down the front of my body, smoothing my skirt over my legs.

A change in the music's tempo finally snaps me out of the trance, and I look around to see if anyone else is witnessing Luca's unusually salacious behavior. But when my eyes search for my team, I realize they've left me to sway on my own. I struggle to find them among the entangled bouncing bodies. Nervous, I move around on the floor, losing myself in the crowd.

I catch sight of Molly and Matthew pressed together in a dance. I don't want to interrupt whatever is happening between them, but I should ask her about the sudden connection tomorrow.

Ollie is still cocooned in the younger bodies around him, but he gives me a wave before picking up one of the women beside him and twirling her around. Her yelp is lost over the loud bass.

Hana, Robert, and Jamie sit idly at the bar, locked in an intense conversation.

My eyes again find Luca, who smiles at the return of my attention. I can't piece together the shift in him, but he oozes a different type of confidence than I'm used to. The bitter glimmer of his arrogance is replaced with something more *intentional*. More controlled. Like chaos encased in glass.

The core of my body burns with anticipation as my interest refuses to budge, and I continue watching him. There's no way he's going to come dance.

Luca unbuttons the cuffs of his shirt and neatly rolls the sleeves up to his elbows, displaying his muscular forearms corded with thick veins. It's the most intoxicating yet simple motion, and I clench my jaw.

I cannot watch any more of this.

I throw my face toward the ceiling, trying to get lost in the rhythm and the lights.

The song changes to something I don't recognize, but the heavy bass pulsates in my blood. I try to find the reason for the sudden shift in music. When I finally find Lily at the speaker, her face sports a giant grin as Luca finishes saying something to her over the bar.

Adrenaline rips through me when Luca's attention returns to me, his stare attacking my movements as he begins walking toward me. Those perfectly sculpted forearms are at his sides, and I sink my teeth into my bottom lip, maintaining my composure.

How are his forearms that sexy?

I shift around on the dance floor, trying to find an escape, but the moving bodies trap me where I sway. My eyes bounce to Luca, and his predatory gaze freezes the air in my lungs.

He closes the space between us. His fingers gently glide across the skin of my arm, and my entire body ignites.

The movement is exhilarating and leaves me craving more. I can no longer tell if the drinks are responsible for the heat in my blood or if it's him.

"What do you want?" I manage to say.

"To dance with you." I barely hear him over the blasting music.

"Oh yeah, like you know how to da—" But before I can finish, his warm hands are on my hips. My body tenses at the sudden contact, and I want so desperately to dissolve under his callused hands.

"Is this okay?" he breathes into my ear.

Yes. More than okay. So much more than just okay. But what if someone looks at us right now?

The hands of ORO's chief operating officer are all over my body. I look around the bar. I don't want to give anyone the impression that there's something between us.

"They don't care, Avery," Luca says as though he's reading my mind again. He uses his fingers to tilt my chin back to his face.

I want to plunge into those devouring eyes. *Or do I want to run away?*

"I've never danced like this." I go to step back, but his grip tightens on my waist, pressing his body into mine.

"Then let me lead."

"No." I try to convince myself.

"Let me."

I search myself for another wave of reluctance, but I simply don't have it in me to fight the safe feeling of his familiar embrace. The proposition may be tainted with an overwhelming amount of risk. Yet the rhythm of the music picks up, and my intoxicated body eases under his hold.

I stare into his sultry gaze and open my mouth to say something, but words fail me. He shakes his head, urging me to stop, a plea for us to share this moment.

"Just trust me."

I do.

The creases around his eyes relax, reminding me of when we were alone on the boat.

I let his hands and feet guide me to the rising tempo, my sensibilities completely escaping me. The space between us vanishes as if the bar were suddenly empty and no one else existed.

"I like this song," I manage to say.

"I picked it out just for you."

I release into him when his fingers latch around my wrist and spin me around. I never would've imagined that we'd move together so easily. For the time I've known him, our conversations have been laced with a current. Right now, I'm finally reshaping the puzzle that has been us, fitting together the pieces. I can feel the heat seeping from his chest against my back. My hips cannot help but grind into Luca.

I feel *all* of him. I want—no, I need—*all* of him.

"You're doing so good," he whispers.

A heavy anchor drops into my belly, obliterating the hesitant tension in my body.

Our sweat mingles, and Luca pulls me even closer, controlling my movements with ease. Every inch of my exposed skin is wrapped around his warmth. We are two souls lost in each other's needs. The nerves in my body thrum under his touch.

For the first time in a long time, I don't have anything to say to him. I simply want to fall deeper into our dance.

"It could be like this all the time, Ave." he breathes into my neck, and I smile at the words. The way he says my favorite version of my name.

My name.

No. No.

He isn't allowed to use that name.

What am I thinking?

I whirl around, escaping his tantalizing clutch. Sweat covers the creases of his shirt, displaying every muscular line on his chest.

Was it this hot when we came in here? I can feel my own skin coated in sticky dampness.

I push out of his grasp and rip my body from the dance floor toward Lily, who is making drinks behind the bar, to collect my things from her safekeeping.

"I need some air," I yell to her over the music. "I'll see you at home."

I grab my purse and jet out the door.

The thick humidity outside hits me like a ton of bricks. My hand digs through my purse, and I stumble as I pull out my phone.

How much did I have to drink?

"What are you doing?" That voice. That hypnotizing, unforgettable, rich voice comes from behind me.

I walk away from Luca, my heels stabbing at the pavement. I finally stop at the light post illuminating the street.

"Getting away from you!" My back leans against the cool metal, steadying my spinning head. When did the ground decide to warp into unsteady waters? I can feel a slosh of acid in my stomach; the drinks are finally bubbling to my throat.

"*Why*? Can you just stop?" He stands a few feet from me, his shoulders ironed into an overbearing—alright, more like protective—stance.

"I'm going to say something I don't mean, Navarro, please.

Leave me alone." I press my palms to my eyes, trying to rub the severe dryness.

"No." He hovers above me. I hate that there's a wash of concern in his eyes. "I'm not going anywhere because your temper doesn't bother me. Nothing you can say or do will make me leave. I can take it."

The words make me feel like I've been dropped into an unhinged rollercoaster with no seatbelt.

Why do I have to easily fall into this bottomless pit of anger? *Why?*

"We were having fun." His voice comes again, gentler this time.

"No, we weren't," I lie. "That was incredibly *unprofessional.*"

"There are no rules against us dating," he says, but I refuse to concede. He just wants to collect on his bet.

"I'm not going to throw away all my hard work. For what? For this?" My hands throw themselves between us. "For Joanna to use *this* as another reason I don't belong at ORO?"

"What did she say to you?" An icy coolness now radiates from him.

"Nothing."

He steps forward, his body so much closer to mine now. I want to lean into him. Fuck the competition. Fuck the rivalry.

Fuck. Me. Luca.

I shake the words from my head.

"Whatever *this* is," he says, "it's not going to affect either of our jobs."

At his words, something profound in me fractures like each of my bones has splintered in my limp body. It all rushes back to me in a vile tsunami. The way my knees trembled in Joanna's office and the tears I cried when falling asleep after Luca's rejection phone call. I catapult into the all-too-familiar anger and dejection that live somewhere within me.

I feel utterly pathetic.

"Of course, you'd know that. Is there an ORO handbook on your phone?" I say defensively. My hands begin to shake. "Did you review all your precious rules before you made your bet, so you could claim your kiss without guilt?"

Luca pulls away from me, an unexpected hurt lacing his features. "You've had too much to drink tonight."

Panicked laughter escapes me. "Are you keeping track?"

He runs his tongue over his molars, closing his eyes as though he has a terrible toothache. "You've had five since I started counting."

My eyes bulge at his admission.

"I'm taking you home, Avery."

"Home?" I question. "The bet was just a kiss, Navarro."

A fit of venomous anger returns to invade me. Slithering through my body and morphing into something rotten.

He stretches his right arm onto the light post, towering over me. My breathing shallows in my chest, and I smell the alcohol mingling between us.

Luca's lips brush over my neck, and I arch toward his warm touch. He finally nears my ear.

"Let's get one thing straight." His voice spills into me. "When I kiss you again, you'll remember every single fucking second of it."

I gasp, but he continues, his free hand steadying me.

"I promise that each one of your moans, your breaths, will pour out of you willingly. Because I know you want me as much as I *need* you."

I lean my face toward his, my lips parting at the sight of his mouth only a few inches away. But he steps back, leaving me in the cold aftermath of the fire between us. My body needs him, and he chooses to deny me.

"I'm making sure you get home safe. Now. Get. In. The. Cab."

I turn toward the street, not realizing a car I don't remember ordering is patiently waiting for our tussle to end.

"I don't want to go home!" My heel slams into the pavement. "Because when I wake up tomorrow, I'll have to drag my sorry self into that ridiculous office where I'll be reminded of Joanna with every step."

"Tell me what happened with her." Luca's voice is sterner than I've ever heard it before.

"Stop pretending you don't know! I hate ORO, I hate Joanna, and I hate—"

"Avery, don't say something I know you're going to regret." His voice drops another octave.

I catch the hostility that was ready to topple out of me. I'm thankful for the interruption.

"You really need to handle rejection better." My throat feels raw. "Sound familiar?"

The thunder crackling within me pulls me toward sobriety. After years of doing the right thing, making the best decisions, and then ending up where I am now—I was bound to break.

But I don't want it to be in front of him.

Lily's my only rock. She's the only one who has been allowed to see me like this.

The anger inside of me is so familiar to when my dad died. It was then that Lily cemented herself to me, refusing to leave my side. I tried to pull apart our friendship by getting mad at her and snapping at every chance I got. Instead of fighting back, Lily simply didn't leave. She missed class for a week to avoid leaving me alone. She dragged me out on walks when I could barely feel my legs.

She's the only person who hasn't left me. Yet, Luca stands here, refusing to budge at my outburst.

I'm not ready to figure out what it would mean for another person to stick by my side while I fall apart. I want to focus on my career and wait until the fulfillment I always expected to come from my job to fully settle in. It'll come. I know it.

Luca drags me from my apoplectic spiral. "We'll talk about this in the morning."

"No!" I yell, the final wave of anger escaping me. "Luca Navarro and his ridiculous suit always dishing out commands. Why are you *really* here?"

"You want the truth, Avery?" Luca bites back at me. "I wanted to hire you from the second you opened that wretched, beautiful mouth of yours during the interview."

I stagger back at his confession.

His eyes relax slightly, and the stressed creases on his face begin to smooth. "And when Joanna told me I couldn't hire you, I should've pushed harder, not fallen under her thumb like a coward. But even though I'm sorry for denying you the job you wanted, I don't regret it."

Luca hesitates, and I feel the gates within me closing before his eyes.

He doesn't regret not hiring me?

"I spent weeks wondering where I went wrong." My throat is strained. "I dedicated the better part of my adult life working toward the opportunity at ORO. How could you?"

"I didn't agree with her decision," he barks. "But I'm happier to have you as my equal and my teammate than as another employee."

I'm too focused on Joanna to even process his last words. "What was her decision?"

Another pause as he puts together a response.

"She thought you were too young," Luca finally admits. "Full of ideas, not life experience."

I cringe. Age has never been something I felt insecure about, even when I was the youngest person in the room throughout my career. It gave me an edge, more ideas, and a different perspective.

"I drew up the paperwork to hire you the next day, but—"

"You did?"

"Of course, what don't you understand?" I finally notice the pained expression on his face. "You're fucking brilliant, Avery. You make me want to be a better person with your relentless optimism."

The words soothe whatever was building inside of me until the alcohol swirling through my veins begins pulling me into another haze. My feet wobble in my heels, and I falter.

Luca gently reaches his hand toward me, and I walk to him, wrapping my fingers in his soothing touch. I feel a strange wave of calm settle through me, a sudden steadying of the ground. Luca didn't recoil from me or abandon me in my anger; he pushed through, recklessly climbing my walls. Refusing to leave me standing on my own.

"Avery, please get in the car." His rich voice is heavy with demand.

I finally agree, and he carefully guides me into the back seat, his free hand covering the top of my head as I stumble through the door. I allow myself to succumb to the fact that maybe I'm not actually immune to his commands.

And maybe I'm okay with that.

Chapter 20
Luca

"I AGREE WITH YOU, LUCA," MATTHEW SAYS. "OUR complementary technology will make a bigger impact than our individual projects."

We sit in my office, Matthew's laptop propped open on my desk, his hair in its usual disheveled mess on his head.

"It seems Willa knew what she was doing," I say. "I hope the technical difficulties on my end won't risk the overall success of Ocean Tidy."

Worry returns. Each of our teams managed to resolve the gaps in Plastech's AI technology within the first two weeks of working together. But ORO's machinery is still underperforming in salt water. Hana explained that the salt coats the gears of the robots, causing them to deteriorate, but the research scientists are still testing out alternatives.

"It's not just for ORO to resolve. We're here as a team."

"I appreciate you saying that, Matthew."

"And I know my team is grateful for all you've done for us this past month. Especially hooking us up with those new computers."

"Don't even think about it." I chuckle. "After Ollie spilled water on Hana's keyboard, I figured the entire team needed an upgrade."

He gives me a kind smile. I've been receiving a lot of those since Plastech joined the office, and it's been a welcome gesture.

I return to the negotiations at hand.

"The merger proposal will outline that we'll build additional Ocean Tidy robots with our profit so that we can reinvigorate Plastech's previous projects together. It's important that we impact small communities that need us urgently."

This is the stipulation I proposed in the merger contract. My own conscience urges me to make amends for the Shift Industries fiasco. I may have returned every cent I earned from giving them the opportunity to destroy people's livelihoods. But it wasn't enough.

I refuse to sit idly by while more communities need protection from the likes of them.

Matthew nods. "I couldn't have said it better myself. We hope to return to Gaya Island soon with the money Avery brought in prior to the Ocean Tidy project. We just need to finalize the final build on the robots."

The mention of her name makes my lips curve. Every day I know her, she never fails to impress me.

Over the past few hours, we've finished outlining how Plastech can become a permanent part of the Oceanic Research Organization. We've wrestled with how our teams are going to split the proceeds from the Ocean Tidy project *if* Willa approves the grant. The best solution is to come together under one entity, allowing profit to be split across the areas with the most urgent needs.

Matthew doesn't seem to mind becoming another roster in ORO's collection of innovations, explaining that selling the technology was always part of his plan. Plus, the merger plans don't alter Plastech's day-to-day operations. If we receive the grant and go ahead with the absorption, their team will receive a generous bump in their paychecks.

As for the work we'll continue to do together, our teams will remain focused on Ocean Tidy after its launch. Also, I'll be around Avery every day.

"Let me know Joanna's thoughts on the matter." Matthew types away on his keyboard.

I plan on presenting the merger for Jo's review followed by the board's approval later this week.

"Certainly," I assure him. "Just remember, we have to keep this under wraps until the board approves. They tend to control the way information gets dispersed across the org."

"Done." He shifts his chair back, gathers his things in his arms, and nods.

We shake on our potential new future.

Any man as dedicated to his team and ideas as Matthew will always have my admiration. There hasn't been a single time in our working relationship that made me doubt our decision to merge.

My office door finally shuts, and I release a deep exhale.

I check my emails to see if Avery has sent around any updates to the Ocean Tidy team today, but just as Matthew explained when he walked into the office, it seems she's taking the day off.

I rap my fingers on my desk.

Avery's brief explosion last night stirred something inside me. Her attempts to push me away did nothing to dent my need to be around her.

I'm glad that by the time we made it to her apartment, she appeared sober enough to make her way inside. I ached to walk her upstairs. To tuck her into bed safely. But she insisted she was okay. Avery pointed to the top floor and told me she would wave when she got inside her place. I ran up the fare until her beautiful face appeared in the window.

I need to talk to her.

But first, I need to discuss with Joanna how she speaks to people around this office.

At my old law firm, I never got involved when the partners yelled at the staff, but this is Avery. This is *my* team. Everyone here is my colleague. Joanna can't treat people with such disdain anymore.

Ping!

The familiar sound of my never-ending notifications populates the room, distracting me. I open it.

An email from Kora fills the screen. I take a minute to scan the contents, not believing the message. I read it again. And again.

This can't be right.

There's a massive discrepancy between the financial statements Joanna has been providing to the board and the reconciled numbers Kora put together.

I hit Print on her email and begin to read the highlights of her findings. Things haven't added up for a long fucking time.

How could anyone miss this?

"What the actual fuck?" I pour the entirety of my strength into hitting the desk.

I didn't take the plunge, give up my law career, and commit myself to saving this planet's oceans to end up without a job in six months.

The oil spill case has already tried to destroy my conscience. I can't be involved with or held responsible for fraudulent activity.

Joanna's months of secrecy, lies, and distance start to make sense. The bitter tinge of betrayal settles in and my spine locks straight. This work I've been doing here has meant more to me with each passing day. I'm not going to let Joanna's lies take it away from me.

I grab the papers and rip open my office door.

ORO employees scramble out of my way. Each step of my leather-soled oxfords echoes through the hallways.

I burst into Joanna's office. "We need to talk."

Joanna's ruthless stare lands on me, wrath across her features that likely mimics mine.

"I'm going to call you right back," she says to someone on her phone before hanging up the call. "What the hell is wrong with you, Luca?" Joanna stands from her chair. "You can't burst into my office when I'm busy."

"You've been busy for the entire time I've been here." I throw Kora's reports on her desk. "You told everyone not to worry that ORO had money. Well, Joanna, the balance sheet shows we have no fucking money!"

The dark circles lining Joanna's eyes are deeply set, making it seem that she hasn't had the luxury of restful sleep in years.

"I don't have time for this." Her eyes flit to the documents atop her already overflowing desk. "The nerve of you to barge in here and—"

"The financial statements you showed the board are full of shit." I do not yield. "The cash flow you falsely said we have is tied up in an escrow account for a live project, and the actual funds we have available will only cover our operating expenses for the next six months before we have to start firing people."

Indignation gnaws away at my composure. My hands clench at my sides. My stomach flips violently, and tightness overtakes my chest. I'm fucking suffocating.

"How dare you?" Joanna yells back, the veins in her neck flaring. "ORO is my company! I built it from the ground! I pulled it into existence with the sheer force of my will. I alone know what's right, Luca."

"No, *Jo*. You don't get to dismiss me again."

I pace in front of her desk. How dare she try to sweep this under the rug.

"You're barely here, you disrespect *our* employees, and

you're committing fraud! Have you forgotten I'm the chief operating officer of this organization?"

Joanna stands in stiff silence. For all her recent faults, I cannot help but scan the awards and honors that clutter her shelves.

Bitter resentment lingers on my palate as my regard for Joanna breaks apart. "I'm providing you the courtesy of bringing this to you first before I go to the board, out of the remaining speck of respect I have for what you've committed to this company."

"You don't underst—"

"*You* no longer deserve the confidence of this organization."

My voice finally steadies, finding ease in the facts. I will not fail to do the right thing this time. I will not fuck that up. ORO is Joanna's legacy, but saving it from imploding will be mine.

"Are you done?" Joanna finally takes a seat. "Why don't you sit down so we can discuss this like civilized adults instead of creating a scene for the entire office?"

A group of people has gathered around Molly's desk, watching us. They catch my stare and scurry away. These fucking walls need to be soundproofed.

I lower my voice. "I'm not interested in listening to you talk your way out of this." I turn to walk out of her office. "My decision has been made."

"I built this organization into one of the highest-regarded agencies of conservation in the world. It was me protesting on the steps of the Capitol while my peers went to prom. I spent years and years of my life dedicated to this cause.

"I tapped every single one of my father's connections behind his back and refused to take his private equity money. I fundraised for change and forced projects that could make a lasting impact into existence. Do you know what all that work and sacrifice amounted to, Luca?"

I pause at the door, wanting to know the answer. "*What?*"

"Absolutely fucking nothing. The world's worse off than when I started, and all I'm left with is the loneliness that haunts me each grueling night. While the weight of *this*"—her hands shoot out before her—"draining exhaustion crushes me. Giving up my life, my desire for a family, and my friendships means all this is mine. Not the board's. Not yours. You think bursting in here will do what? Save this *precious* Earth?"

The cynicism wears on her words.

"Sorry to break it to you, Luca, but if I can't fix this, there's no way in hell that an insipid lawyer like yourself could."

No. She doesn't get to dictate what I can or can't control. Not this time.

She has all the money, all the connections in the world, and she lost control. She lost sight of what is important.

"How could you let it get so bad?" I finally ask her.

She seems resigned. "I dug my claws into every dollar that came in and out. But things advanced too quickly, and ORO grew too fast. I couldn't trust anyone to keep up with the pace. I know the flow of my organization better than anyone."

I'm unsure if she's trying to convince me, herself, or both. Another wave of irritation invades me. She didn't do any of this work alone. Instead, she has the nerve to take credit for everything ORO has accomplished during its existence. Joanna may be the face of this organization, the ideas, the motivation, but what about all the staff?

It's not like Joanna is even around to watch over the day-to-day flow of things. It's not like she travels to visit existing projects.

Annoyance flares in me at her selfish views. I've spent over a quarter organizing her operational mishaps and getting teams to stay accountable for their work; I'm rebuilding an entire infrastructure, for fuck's sake. Yet she sits here, clamoring on about doing everything herself.

"And I know what you're thinking," she continues. "That

this would've all been different if I didn't decide to climb this impossible mountain alone. But you're wrong. I didn't fail because of my own doing. *I* failed because no one fucking cares. Because no matter how much you can get the little guy to do, companies like the ones you used to represent will strip away years of progress."

The truth spills out between us, tugging at the silent guilt I've been carrying around.

Joanna's posture is strong, but there is only rage in her shattered gaze. The woman before me fought her entire life for one thing, and that backbreaking effort is breaking her.

She's so concerned with the impact she makes, the overall macro goal of her dreams, that she forgot people do care. Everyone here cares. I fucking care.

"I understand, Jo, but despite all that, I still need to inform the board."

It's the right thing to do, so I can handle this disaster she's brought crashing down upon us.

"You can tell the board," she says, "but they will remove both of us *immediately*. Then will come the immediate dismantling of *my* organization. The board believes in prosperity, and between the pretty penny it cost to hire you and the active maintenance cost of our many projects, it would be cheaper to sell ORO for parts than to put it back together."

That can't be true.

"Don't make this about me, Joanna." My fingers massage my temples. "The bones of this company are the people who work here. If the board clips funding, hundreds of people will lose their jobs. Their livelihoods."

"The board does *not* care."

How can a company focused on conservation not care about the people whose lives they impact? Is it always about the bottom dollar?

My spine stiffens, and remorse seeps into me. "You should have told me. I could've helped you repair this much sooner."

"No," she bites. "People simply do not care anymore."

"They do, Joanna," I say. "Every single person here, including me, dedicated themselves to you. Trusted *you*."

"And none of you could actually help."

We stare at each other. The words hang in the air.

How dare she blame us for her failures. She hasn't attended one meeting about the Ocean Tidy project. She wanted nothing to do with it or anyone on the team.

We don't need her.

A resolution begins to form on my tongue. I finally make my way to stand opposite her, and my hands lean on her desk.

"This is what will need to happen," I begin. "Starting the second I leave your office, you'll pack your things and go on a leave of absence. Maybe the distance will help you realize the impact we've been creating here is real. Not just the work *you've* done but the work *we've* all put in."

Joanna's head swings immediately, but I raise my palm to silence her.

"I'll take over your meetings. Secure the Ellington Grant. The Ocean Tidy project we're working on with Plastech is revolutionary, and the funds it will generate can keep us afloat while I figure out a way to keep all our programs alive."

It'll work. It has to work. There are too many people counting on me now.

"And why do you think I'm willing to hand over the reins of my company to *you*?"

I stare at her blankly. "Because, Joanna, you have no other choice if you want the legacy you built to survive."

She doesn't care about money or the environment. She cares about her legacy. She may have given up hope, but a small part of her must want to leave her company on a good note.

Joanna grows quiet, considering me. Her eyes intently assess me as though this is the first time she has seen me. A barely noticeable flash of what I can only assume is relief washes over her face.

"You're only going to plummet ORO deeper into the ground."

"One thing you should have taken the time to learn about me, Jo, is that I do not fail."

Chapter 21
Luca

FOR THE FIRST TIME IN YEARS, I TOOK THE DAY OFF FROM WORK. After Joanna's implosion yesterday, I needed some time to think through my next steps.

Or at least try to.

Plus, how could I have gone in today and looked everyone in the face when their jobs are at stake?

I continue to pace my apartment.

Everything's riding on the Ocean Tidy grant being awarded. Once the grant is allocated, then the merger with Plastech can go through, and that will at least sustain our existing projects.

But that's *if* the board approves. What if Plastech pulls out? We have such spotty streams of revenue, and ORO's business model relies on our investors to help support the projects at hand.

Why hasn't that damn saltwater problem been fixed yet?

I need to check in with Hana again and create a backup plan.

I pull out my phone and try to type out a to-do list. Task items pour out of me, but with each new line, my chest constricts with more panic. My breath grows hurried. Spots of light poke at my vision.

This isn't helping. I abandon my phone and make my way

into the bathroom to shower. The warm water does little to calm my nerves. I dress, then slump my body into the cool sheets. Good decisions are never made in a panic.

Maybe I can sleep it off? I lie down, struggling to find a comfortable position to alleviate my stress.

There is no use in any of this!

I find my phone between the sheets, antsy to escape this unease, and resolve to text Nico. If there's one person who knows how to take a step back and relax, it's him.

But he's at some kind of company retreat in Maine. It better not be one of those ridiculous no-phone places.

I type a message and delete it. What the fuck am I even going to ask him?

Stop overthinking. I type out the message and hit Send.

LUCA

> Hey. Help me relax.

I roll my eyes in shame. How pathetic. I'm a grown man asking his kid brother for advice on how to relax. But desperate times call for desperate measures.

A second later, a message comes in.

NICO

> really?

LUCA

> Yes.

NICO

> have u tried getting laid

Is he serious?

A memory of Avery dancing against me floods my head. Right now, I don't need to get laid. But I do want her so fucking desperately.

LUCA

That's not how the long game works.

I miss being alone with *her*.

But she's working through whatever she needs to and is keeping me at a distance. I don't even know if she showed up to work today. It would be fruitful to unpack everything that's gone down with Joanna with someone who understands my disdain for her. I hope the explanation I gave Avery about Joanna's decision to not hire her helped settle some of the resentment she carried. I'd figured she was over the entire thing, but after seeing Joanna in her vexed element, I can easily understand how the burn of rejection flared within Avery again.

I rise from my bed, trying to keep my mind off of everything that's tightening the disquieting knot in the cavity of my chest. *It can't be that hard.*

Just stop.

Stop.

My eyes lift to the open laptop on my nightstand. The screen displays the merger proposal for ORO and Plastech.

My heartbeat quickens at my new responsibilities, and my stomach cramps with acid.

Did I make a big fucking mistake?

It doesn't matter now. I can't go back.

Joanna emailed the board a transfer of responsibility as soon as I left her office, citing that her leave was effective immediately and will go on indefinitely.

I look back at my phone, still desperate for a solution to the stress building inside of me. I try Nico one last time.

LUCA

Actual advice, please.

I throw myself back into the pillows and await Nico's next message.

NICO

k i usually stretch when i'm stressed. do some
yoga, it'll even keep u limber for when u
accept my earlier suggestion ;)

Yoga?

But I hate stretching. Running is the way I blow off steam.
The rush of my legs pounding against the ground is enough to
help me unwind.

Isn't yoga just like a long cooldown? I always skip the posi-
tions, preferring to get on with my day instead of spending
fifteen minutes contorting my limbs in different directions.

Whose legs even need to go behind their head?

Except my run did nothing to relieve the tension inside of me
today. It's been less and less of a helpful activity lately, especially since Avery's been on my mind.

A minute later, a link comes in with another message from
Nico.

NICO

here, try this. my yoga mat is somewhere in
my room.

u can borrow it if u can find it

LUCA

Seriously?

NICO

just try it

LUCA

Fine.

I get up to trek to Nico's room. Another message
chimes in.

NICO

this flow is a good warm up for any sexu-

I throw my phone away before reading the rest of Nico's message.

Why's he so obsessed with my sex life? It hasn't been that long since I've been with someone!

After scouring his messy room for his yoga mat, I finally find it hidden under a pile of laundry. I set up in the living room, rolling the navy-blue rubber into the empty space beside the windows.

When was the last time I sat on the floor?

It's actually quite spacious. I have plenty of room on either side of the makeshift practice space for my six-four frame to spread out.

The morning sun warms my skin. I grab my phone to check the name of the video before pulling up the yoga routine on my TV. The instructor's studio is full of plants. A slender woman sits on her floor, a black-and-gray speckled dog joining her.

Am I meant to have a dog for this?

She starts speaking in a calming voice, instructing me to get into a seated position. She guides me through slow movements, and they do little to help my mind, which is still drifting to ORO.

I give it five minutes then inhale.

My stiff limbs ache in frustration as I plant my hands and feet on the ground and push into a downward-facing dog position. My hamstrings and calves scream with tension, and I have to keep my knees bent. Blood rushes to my head, and I get deeper into the stretch, pulling my rigid muscles. Maybe I really should do this more after my runs.

How many more breaths is she going to tell me to take?

Inhale.

My muscles loosen. The heat of the extended position raises my temperature. A cool bead of sweat runs down my forehead. My entire focus is on the pull of my shoulders and the release of my neck. A small wave of release floods through me. This actually feels kind of nice.

Maybe Nico was right.

The remaining twenty minutes go by quickly, and we leave the practice in some kind of starfish position on the mat. The instructor says it's supposed to help me meditate, but all it's doing is making me realize I need to vacuum my floors. The silence resumes, and my mind is already finding its way to my earlier worries.

I take another deep breath.

I can do this. Just focus on your breath.

My phone rings, breaking the agonizing silence.

Ah, a diversion.

I pick up my phone and press it to my ear.

"If it isn't the prodigal son," *Papi*'s jovial voice from the other line.

"Hey, *Papi*, what's going on?"

I get off the yoga mat and make my way to the kitchen.

"You first, Luca," he laughs. "And after I can reprimand you for ignoring our calls for a week."

"It's just work."

"It's always *just* work. Now, tell me. I can hear that something's wrong."

Either Nico texted him or he can still read me like a book from three thousand miles away. Growing up, he could sniff out a lie before we even thought of one. It was the one downside of growing up with a hyper-aware lawyer.

Nico and I never had the chance to get away with anything, so we both learned to argue in different ways. Nico became nonchalant, and I became headstrong.

Papi has always helped me work through the mess inside my head, peeling apart each of my thoughts and finding a reason for them.

I'm glad he called.

"It's about ORO." I realize I want his perspective on my situation. "Can I request attorney-client privilege given the sensitivity of my current situation?"

I joke slightly, but he is a renowned partner at his own law firm and the only person I would trust with what I'm about to explain to him.

"My retainer is twenty thousand dollars right now."

I appreciate his attempt to try and lighten the mood. "I'll be sure to include the check with my next Christmas card."

He chuckles, and that heartwarming sound nips away at the anxiety in my chest. When the small talk halts, I take it as my cue to begin.

"The short of it is that ORO's in trouble. It's running out of money and has been for quite some time," I say. "If the media gets the information that one of the most important conservation organizations is going under, the CEO's reputation, and ultimately my own, will be at stake."

"Okay." He considers. "Is there something more important at play than a media frenzy?"

"Yes." I pause, struggling to articulate the problem. "Entire conservation efforts will go under with ORO. The people who rely on me will lose the paychecks that feed their families. Life-changing projects that are helping communities all around the world will no longer have funding."

What I also don't say is that the woman I am falling for will find out her team won't be able to contribute their piece to protecting the planet and that I was the one responsible for it. Pain rips at my chest. I would fail so many people, including myself.

"What makes you think you have to do this alone?"

"I'm the only one who knows," I explain. "And if I can't fix it, it'll be like D&D again. The damage this could cause—"

"Luca, stop beating yourself up over what happened at D&D. There's no way you could've known that corporation was lying about branching into solar energy. *No fue tu culpa.*"

"I just feel like whatever I try and do isn't going to be enough." I slouch on the kitchen counter, disappointment coating my tongue.

"*Mijo*, you have to put it behind you. You've committed to ORO now. If you're going to take on the challenge of saving it, don't do it to atone for sins you didn't commit. Most definitely, don't take this on alone."

Heavy silence hangs on the line as I process his words.

For the first time in my career, I feel like I'm a part of something more significant and meaningful. I want to save ORO. Not because it is the right thing to do but because I finally feel a sense of purpose. And now that everything's out in the open, I understand what needs to be done. I can do this. I know I can.

"Do you regret becoming a lawyer?" I never asked him if he was happy in his career because he never talked about wanting to do anything else.

"Never," *Papi* says. "I get to spend my time arguing with people for a living, but when I get home, I don't let that agitation from the office follow me. *¿Y tú?*"

"I don't think so."

"Then do you regret leaving law for ORO?"

"No," I say truthfully. "But it'll be a lot of work."

"When has that stopped you?"

I let that settle in, but his voice comes from a distance. "*Mami's* taking the phone."

"Sounds like you're still working too much," she says.

There goes that attorney-client privilege I was promised. I should've wired him the money when the call began, not that it would have stopped her from listening.

"You know me. I never slow down."

"*Y por eso no estás casado,*" she chuckles.

"*Mami...*"

"It would just be so nice if you could finally find someone to bring home. The house is very lonely on the weekends with all you kids gone. *Tal vez si tuviera algunos nietos.*"

"*Mami!*"

"Oh, I know, *job, job, job.* I don't know why you think having a career means you can't have a girlfriend. Look at us! For thirty-five years, we've managed our busy schedules, and we're all the better for it."

She runs her own thriving architect firm and has put in many early mornings and late nights.

My parent's relationship sets unrealistic expectations for a joyful marriage. They're two sides of the same coin. Each moment they share is approached with passion and tenderness.

I'm not quite sure why the words leave my lips, but I finally admit, "I actually met someone."

Chapter 22
Avery

I SHRUG MY CARDIGAN OFF MY SHOULDERS WHILE OLLIE AND I make our way down the street, on the search for the new arepa truck rumored to have been posted up a few blocks away from the ORO offices. The streets are littered with professionals rushing around during their lunch hour.

"Do you ever miss the coworking space?" I ponder.

"Not really, I've been enjoying the new offices," Ollie says. "Luca's been making sure all of our favorite snacks get restocked!"

"Yeah." I sigh. But the mention of Luca sends a wave of embarrassment through me. I can still remember my uncharacteristically vulnerable outburst in front of him from almost ten days ago. I haven't seen him around the office in so long. The lack of resolution between us has started to bring me a pang of distress.

Ollie turns to me. "Why the big sigh, Ave?"

"I just miss the job I was hired to do," I admit. "You know, the meaningful parts of being a head of development. Not just spending all my time in front of a laptop, translating data into something Willa's team will understand."

The previously unspoken words are finally untangled, and a lightness enters my being since I can share some of the thoughts I've been grappling with for weeks.

Ollie muses, "Yeah, I getcha. We've been inside so much that I've begun to turn translucent from a lack of sun."

I chuckle. "I think I'm just having a hard time."

"I hope only because of how committed we are to making Ocean Tidy the best it can be." Ollie gives me a gentle nudge. "Not because of us lads, 'cause now that you're on the team, we're not gonna let you leave."

I smile, and that familiar warmth returns to my chest. Ollie is like the big brother I always wanted.

"I promise it's not you guys *or* the rest of the Ocean Tidy team." My eyes stay glued on the pavement. "I'm just struggling to feel like what I'm contributing is enough."

"I hear you. Honestly, I'm not even sure I know the extent of what you're doing on a day-to-day basis."

I laugh. "Yeah, that's what worries me. Like, does my small contribution with the presentation actually make an impact?"

I try to ignore the anxiety that consumes me.

"Certainly, you're making an impact, Ave!" Ollie stops me.

"I guess."

"No *guesses*." Ollie beams. "The money you've fundraised already got us one of the new fancy robots we designed. We're goin' back to Gaya Island in a few months because of you!"

"That's true, but—" I'm excited about the release, but something feels like it's missing.

"Stop trying to undercut your feelings. We appreciate you on the team even if we knew Plastech wasn't your first choice."

"No, Ollie, it's not that," I say. "I always had this idea of what working at ORO would look like, and now that we're here, I'm realizing the role I gained is not how I pictured myself enacting change."

We continue our walk, and the blood coursing through my

legs feels exquisite. I've been neglecting going outside during the day and clearing my head like I used to at Plastech. The fresh air feels so calming, and I resolve to bring back my routine afternoon walks.

"What did you hope it would look like?"

"I want to be out of that stuffy office," I admit. "I miss the rush of convincing someone to care about something bigger than themselves. I kind of hoped I'd get to learn from Jo, but that didn't pan out. I don't think I want to work behind a desk for the rest of my life."

I briefly explained what happened with Joanna to my team, though I omitted the details of her harsh words and my subsequent downward spiral.

I debated not telling them about it at all, but Matthew kept questioning why I've avoided that part of the office. I had to give them something.

They knew how badly I wanted to work at ORO, so their attempts to comfort me, which involved coffee runs and shared eye rolls at the mention of her name, made me feel better.

Robert, who typically avoids all confrontation, designed a digital version of Joanna so that I could throw wads of virtual paper at her in a game titled *Ave Destroyer*. I love it.

Lesson learned: don't meet your idols.

Another lesson learned: my team is amazing.

"I get it," Ollie tells me. "I went through the same thing in my own career. When I graduated from uni, I worked at a prestigious finance job in the city. They forced me into a suit, sat me in a windowless office, and asked me to stop making jokes at work. You know how much I like jokes, Ave. But I did it. And every meeting the branch manager would tell me, 'Be serious, Oliver.' And I listened. I molded myself into the reality they created for me."

I've never heard this story before. My Ollie was only ever

Ollie, our head of logistics, the person who can make everyone smile during the worst of days.

"I thought the crushing misery in my soul was normal, part of the job. I had my *dream* job, after all, in my *dream* city." He pauses, and I squeeze his arm, urging him to continue. "When people asked me where I worked, I bragged about my important career. My important company. It never occurred to me that most people didn't understand the fourteen-hour days or the way I misinterpreted *work hard, play hard*. I spent my nights decompressing alone at some dodgy pub."

"Ol, I had no idea," I say.

"No need for sympathy, lass." He smiles one of those irreplaceable grins. "One day, Matthew came to town and told me about his idea, wanting me to join him. I told him no."

"Really?"

Ollie nods. "I convinced myself that I couldn't give up everything I worked toward. I was following the plan I spent years cultivating."

I understand his sentiment so much. I've been grappling with understanding my own purpose. I associated my value and worth with ORO and how proud my dad would have been of me for working at Jo's company.

But, in the end, I'm happiest doing what I am good at—not working in the most prestigious place. It doesn't matter for whom or why, I simply want to make people believe there's so much we can do for the world if we all band together.

"So, what happened next, Ol?"

"I walked into the office one day and got called a worthless screwup before I had a chance to have my first sip of coffee. Apparently, I forgot to reply all on a database configuration email."

Ouch. I want to yell at the person who dared disrespect Ollie for something so menial.

"I quit on the spot. Called Mattie right after handing in my resignation, and Plastech came to life. If it weren't for him, I woulda been lost in the shell I was becoming. What I'm telling you, lass, is that deep down, you know what you want."

I consider his words and how similar of an impact Matthew has had on both of our lives. Appreciation for my wonderful team comes back to me.

I need to let go of the expectations about where I was supposed to be and what I was supposed to be doing. It's been easier to bury myself in my goals, relentlessly focusing on my career as a way to keep my dad's memory alive. Still, I hope he would be proud of me despite my current circumstances. After all, the promise I silently made to my dad has nothing to do with *where* I work but how I can live a meaningful life.

It was easy to create all these rules for myself after he passed or to briefly flounder in my own anger. Mom's hesitation to partake in my life didn't make it easier when I needed to seek out confirmation that I was doing the right thing.

But it's time to let go. Let go of the shattering temper within me and the misguided belief about my own happiness.

The Ocean Tidy project still has a few more months of work. and then I can speak to Matthew about going back to what I love to do: fundraising instead of spending hours formatting slide decks. The five million from Willa is going to be spent on global scale implementation. We're still going to need funding to support our smaller impact projects!

I can do that.

"Thank you for sharing with me, Ollie." I wrap my arms around him, barely fitting half of his body in my embrace.

"Don't go telling people I'm all mushy now." He chuckles.

"I won't." I smile at him. "Anyways, we only have a few more weeks at ORO before we can try to find our own office space!"

"Don't remind me! My gut and my arse love it here too

much. The snacks and the chairs at ORO are something else," Ollie says. "Do you think Luca would care if I stole four of those lush velour chairs?"

"With the amount of time he's been out of the office, I doubt he'd even notice."

I've tried to figure out how to approach Luca and clear the air after my eruption outside the Mademoiselle, but Luca's presence has been scarce this entire week. I'm glad I got it all out in the open, but I wonder if it will cause him to pull away from me. My heart quickens with anticipation of the meeting he's supposed to be at today. The one where I'll be presenting.

Will he even show up?

I straighten out my favorite tailored lavender dress that I may or may not have pulled out for the occasion. It's always been one of those pieces in my closet that makes me feel like I can conquer anything when I wear it.

Here I come.

THE MUSIC of coffee beans grinding serenades the entire floor as Ollie and I return from lunch. Our noses follow the smell into the kitchen, where Luca stands, shaking hands with another gentleman in a pristine all-white suit. The man finishes polishing the bright new espresso machine taking over most of the counter, then leaves.

My heart stops at the sight of Luca. Those large, veined hands were on me a few days ago.

Have hands always been this sexy?

I cringe a little at the memory of yelling at him in the street after trivia. I try to pull myself together and put on a brave face. The next time we're alone, I'll just apologize, and we can return to our friendly bets like nothing's changed.

Upon closer inspection, it's not just any espresso machine but the state-of-the-art Grinder 9000. This monstrosity has a ten-month-long waiting list and a price tag that could pay a year's rent on a house in my hometown. The machine has unlimited syrup attachments and is able to concoct over twenty espresso drinks with a multitude of flavors.

I want to scream with glee.

"What's going on?" I can barely contain the genuine excitement exploding out of me at the thought of unlimited lattes.

Luca's eyes find mine, and a smile splits across his face. One of those radiating, rare smiles that make me feel simultaneously relaxed and full of anticipation.

I stand beside him. Our bodies' unreleased electricity from trivia night still hangs heavy between us.

"I've heard rumors that the coffee at ORO is intolerable," Luca says nonchalantly, "but since you seem to know more about this contraption than I do, please explain why it took me two weeks to get this thing here—*after* calling in some favors."

My chest warms, but I try not to get ahead of myself.

There's no way he bought a coffee machine *just* for me. There are plenty of other coffee enthusiasts in this office who will make great use of this magical apparatus.

But he deserves a point, nonetheless. Okay, maybe two.

Avery: 4 | Luca: 4

I inspect every fob and button on the machine, reading through all the different options on the screen.

When Luca hands me a bag of ethically sourced coffee beans, the smell of citrus and earth blankets my senses. I fill up the grinder, giddy with anticipation, and try for one moment of normalcy between us.

I've missed him.

What?

No.

The excitement for the machine must have made me too giddy.

Ollie runs his finger over the sparkling stainless steel. "I may have to start drinking coffee again just so I can use this thing."

I read off every flavor of syrup imaginable on the freshly stocked shelf above the machine.

My eyes finally land on mint. "Who puts mint in their coffee?"

"I wasn't sure which one you liked the most, so I bought them all," Luca replies.

I gasp.

Which flavor *I* like the most? He bought. Every. Flavor?

I almost pinch myself, but I snap out of it when Ollie clears his throat. Luca's eyes shift from my heated face to my companion.

"Excuse me, I meant I wasn't sure which flavors the office would be most partial to." Luca gives me a wink, and my insides melt like an ice cream cone on a blistering summer day.

Who's this gorgeous man smiling and winking at me? What has he done to the pain in the ass I've grown accustomed to?

"I'm going to alert everyone of this extraordinary new addition to the team." Ollie walks out of the kitchen, leaving Luca and me with the office's new toy.

I try to ignore the urge to wrap my arms around him in gratitude. I refrain from touching him by focusing on the syrup names I've managed to read through twice already.

"Which one is your favorite?" Luca pulls *his* mug out of the dishwasher.

"Toffee, but caramel is a close second."

Luca leans around me as he pumps one squirt of the toffee sweetener into his mug. "Is that enough?"

"More."

The corded arm hidden beneath his ebony suit jacket injects another serving of toffee syrup into the mug. My mouth waters at the motion, and his darkened stare watches me. I trace my eyes over his shoulders and up to his lips.

Don't think about him pumping anything, Avery.

"Is that good for you?"

"Very." I gulp.

"Are you ready for your presentation in a few hours? How are the charts showing the objectives of the first launch coming along?"

Work? How is he thinking about work when I am thinking about—

Snap out of it.

Last week when I presented, those were the slides that needed the most help. The fact he remembers makes my lips spread into a smile. "It's coming along. I still need to work on the layout of the extraction numbers, but Ollie is helping me with that."

"Well, if you want someone else to look at it, you can send it to me before our meeting." He smiles.

Is this another one of his tricks?

"Do you just want a sneak peek at my slides so you can figure out which ones to dissect in front of the team again?" The last time he reviewed my notes, he picked me apart at our group meeting, citing that I should be able to answer every question under pressure. I did so flawlessly, but it still sucked.

"I want to help."

I watch him as he places his mug under the spout of the machine and presses a combination of buttons. A double shot of espresso pours out of the machine, mixing in with foamed oat milk.

"I promise," he says again.

He hasn't once brought up my drunken outburst or my

comments about Jo or the fact I lost our trivia bet. And now a coffee machine I mentioned weeks ago shows up.

I don't think that is a coincidence. I should just apologize now.

"Luca, look—" I try to gather the right words just as the machine finishes preparing the concoction.

Luca presses the mug to his lips and sips. His bottomless dark gaze flashes at me with intent, and I watch, my jaw slacking in expectation.

"For you." He hands me the mug.

"Hey!" I squirm and scrunch up my face. "I thought that was for me." But I do sort of, kind of want to taste him.

"It's just a sip."

My arms fold in front of me. *I want my own luscious coffee!*

"Besides, I wanted a taste of what you were about to taste like."

That does it. I am entirely speechless.

Is he reading my mind?

I gape at him, my heartbeat humming loudly. His stare travels across my face and then lands right on my lips. Luca stares penetratingly, and my thoughts beg for him to lift me onto this counter right now so I can give him a taste.

You're at the office. Pull yourself together!

But his words from a few days ago pull me from reality. *There are no rules about us dating.*

Is that what we would become? People who date?

The mug still hangs in the air between us, *Trash Titans* clearly displayed in bold lettering.

"Well, isn't that your mug?" I ask.

"I will always share—"

"The new coffee machine created a mob!" Ollie's voice reverberates through the hall as a trail of people follows him into the kitchen.

I am grateful for the interruption—otherwise my mouth

would've skipped right from the mug and straight onto Luca's. I pull the hot steam of caffeine from his hands, our fingers brushing, and tilt the latte to my lips.

"Guys, not only did Mr. Navarro get us this new coffee machine, he offered to make everyone their first cup all by himself," I announce.

He glares at me.

"I never—" Luca scans my face and resigns his argument with a sigh. "*Fine.*"

A line forms in front of the machine, people already shouting orders at him. Instead of leaving people to figure out the contraption on their own, Luca begins preparing the first order.

After completing the fifth latte, Luca drapes his stark-black jacket over a nearby chair. His light-blue button-down looks as though it has been perfectly sewn onto his body, highlighting every bend of his robust shoulders.

He looks over at me—the sharpness of his jaw accentuating a faint smirk on his enchanting features—and I can't help but relish in this private glance between us.

Is he enjoying this?

I would've never imagined the heartless suit who plagued my existence only a few months ago would be caught dead mingling with his coworkers. My heart swells with pride.

I search the cabinets for an empty jar before finally finding the ideal one.

"Don't forget to leave the COO his tips!" I giggle and walk around the kitchen, collecting contributions.

Ollie pulls a five-dollar bill out of his wallet and walks over to Luca before putting the crisp bill into the pocket of Luca's trousers. Ollie whispers something to him, and the deep set of Luca's brows suddenly clap into a taught line. He looks as though he is about to shred my friend to pieces. But before I can intervene, Luca bursts with laughter, pulling Ollie into a friendly

—well, I'm sure the half hug is friendly by Luca's standards —embrace.

Plastech and ORO employees mingle around the kitchen as we all load up on caffeine. Whatever nerves remain in my belly dissipate as I take a deep inhale, savoring the moment I want to last forever.

Chapter 23
Luca

I FINALLY MANAGE TO BREAK MY STRAINED EYES FROM THE bright screens in front of me.

9:00 p.m.

I sigh.

Another lengthy night since Joanna left a little over a week ago. It's the only time I can dedicate to my actual workload as the chief operating officer *without* juggling CEO-level responsibilities. Taking over Joanna's strategy calls and introducing myself to our extensive list of high-profile investors is proving to be time-consuming. I would've been able to finish earlier if I hadn't spent a few hours moonlighting as the new office barista.

Sleep better come tonight.

I unknot my tie, pull it from my neck, then throw it in my bag before disconnecting my laptop. I make a mental list of the emails I still need to send. But my mind is intent on remaining on Avery.

The joyful look on her face when she saw that absurd coffee machine is permanently ingrained in my memory. It was worth every cent.

I wasn't able to justify the fifty thousand dollars as an office improvement expense, so I just bought it with my own paycheck.

Avery could ask me to roast coffee beans by hand, and I would simply ask her for how long.

The sweet latte put the familiar pep back in her step, and she objectively crushed her presentation during our brief one-on-one today. I beamed with pride at her flawless articulation of the Ocean Tidy project's progress. There's no way Willa will find a flaw in our proposal. At least I hope she won't.

There's something about Avery's confidence and brilliant mind that sends an unrivaled delight through me.

I didn't see her in over a week, and I found myself missing her. The way she scrunches her nose when she doesn't like something or the laugh she makes when she tells a joke.

My computer pings, but I ignore it, closing my laptop before I walk out of my office. My phone follows with a buzz, indicating another email came in.

Who could be emailing me at this hour?

I pull out my phone, and two notifications appear on my screen from Avery.

My mouth breaks out into a full-on grin.

Avery Soko: *Are you still at the office?*

Avery Soko: *It's okay if you're not. I know it's Friday night.*

I try to figure out the best way to respond to her auspicious question.

Luca Navarro: *Just heading out. Did you need something?*

Alright, that's casual enough. I stare at the screen, refreshing my inbox every second.

Maybe asking her if she needed something didn't translate

correctly. I'm overthinking a simple message with an unforgivable level of intensity.

> **Avery Soko:** *I'm trapped in the conference room. Can you please unlock the door? I can't find my key.*

I hurry down the hall, and I type a new email.

> **Luca Navarro:** *You're asking for my help. Has the earth flipped on its axis?*

The office is drenched in darkness, each bulb turned off hours ago, except for the ambient glow of the surrounding high rises. I catch sight of the small light down the hall.

> **Avery Soko:** *Forget it, I'll try the front desk again.*

Inside the conference room, Avery's face is dimly lit by the light of her computer. I swipe my key card and pull open the door.

"Is this how you come up with your witty remarks?" I ask. "Alone in complete darkness?"

"I had my headphones in when the janitor was locking up," she explains. "But if you're going to rub it in, I would rather sleep here until the morning."

I laugh at the silly suggestion. "Go get your stuff. I've had a long day sweating over artificially sweetened lattes."

I hold the door open for her.

She gasps. "Lend yourself some more credit, Navarro. Most of the syrups you got are naturally sweetened! I'm just surprised you splurged on the good stuff. Besides, you looked like you were having so much fun." Avery walks past me, and I breathe in her scent, which never fails to remind me of the beaches back home. "And you made a whopping thirty bucks!"

"I'll use it to replace your toffee syrup when it runs out by the end of the week." I follow her down the hall before stopping to flip on the lights.

A cascading fluorescent glow illuminates Avery's beautiful face. The hazel of her eyes leans toward brown today, and I love how the colors change slightly each time I stare into them. Her lavender summer dress makes her look like she's being hugged by the sunset. The small size of her shoulders makes me want to pull her underneath my arm.

The heels she's wearing today make her legs look like they stretch for miles. She's somehow the perfect height beside me. Tall enough that her lips could meet mine with a brief tilt of her head.

"You know, your favorite cafe down the street has an open position if this whole COO thing doesn't work out for you." She chuckles before disappearing into her office to grab her stuff.

"Yeah." I try to laugh with her.

The harsh reality is that I may need to brainstorm some career alternatives if saving ORO doesn't work out. The only thing I'm sure of is that corporate law is not going to tempt me back into its ravenous jaws.

I try not to focus on the fact that I don't have a backup plan. For the first time in my life, I don't have a Plan B. Or, frankly, a clear Plan A. I have no clue what would happen if ORO fails.

I try to bring my brother's words back to my mind. *This may be good for you. Take some time off and travel, figure it out.*

Maybe I could take Avery somewhere?

"Hey, so can I talk to you?" She walks back into view, hesitating in the doorway. The corners of her full lips collapse slightly, and it causes my jaw to clench.

"What's wrong?" Worry creeps over me. I take a few steps toward her, our bodies now surrounded by the doorframe.

"About trivia night." Her eyes dart down. "I just want to say I'm sorry for how I acted."

"You don't have to—"

"Yes, I do. I was upset at Joanna, and I took that out on you. I've spiraled too easily into my anger since my dad passed away. Nobody's seen me like that in a long time, and I'm a little embarrassed."

"Avery, you have nothing to be embarrassed about."

A ripple of empathy runs through me. Each time Avery has shared something about her father, she clams up. I feel desperate to pull her into my arms and soothe the worry constricting inside her. But it's not my place to yank the pain out of her. When she's ready, I hope she will want to share what happened with me. Truly, the way Joanna got under my own skin makes me understand how Avery could feel such fury with her. I have yet to receive the full picture of what was said, but her words and disappointment only 'confirm what I already presumed. Joanna hurt Avery.

I'm going to make sure no one disrespects her ever again.

It takes all my willpower not to reach over and cup her pink cheek with the palm of my hand.

I never want Avery to feel uncomfortable when talking to me. I want to see all of her. The good. The bad.

Her gaze meets mine, and I break into a smile, which she returns at once. This smile is my favorite look of hers—well, besides all that eye rolling, the stares, the curious curl of her brows. Who am I kidding? Her looks have always been and always will be my fucking favorite.

"Okay, thank you. I'm happy to clear the air and get back to normal." She turns around and shuts the office door. "Wait, what are you doing here so late?"

Avery leans against the glass office door, and I mimic her stance. We ignore the fact that we're here at this time of night. She doesn't seem to desire a walk toward the elevators right now, and I'm thankful for it.

"I'm always here at this time."

"Yes, but this is later than usual. Actually, you've been busy all week or staying behind into the night. Is it because of Jo's leave?"

I'm not exactly sure what I should tell her.

ORO may have to close. Joanna practically drove us into the ground.

Avery's too perceptive and stubborn for her own good. She eyes me expectantly, those long arms crossing over her chest in anticipation.

I shrug off her question, despite the urge to confide in her. "You never told me exactly why you were mad at Jo."

"Honestly, it really wasn't her fault. I mean, I know she's your boss, so I don't want to speak poorly of her."

I nod for her to continue.

Avery's feet cross in front of her. "When I tried to talk to her, she seemed nothing like the person I grew up idolizing, and it was a bit of a letdown. Also, she was just really fucking rude."

I laugh at her bluntness. "I've come to learn the same thing over the past couple of months."

I try to defuse her uneasiness, but my frustration with Joanna refuses to budge. If Jo had hired Avery, I'd have someone to turn to and maybe help me get ORO out of this financial mess.

That curious look returns to her eyes. "What do you mean?"

"Jo's proven to be a little difficult to work with, that's all." I sigh.

"What's wrong? Are you having to pick up her work?" Her brows furrow, and worry spreads across her face.

She's so quick to be concerned, and it's one of the things I've grown to respect about her.

Avery will attack a piece of bad news and demand it be fixed. No matter the size of the issue. She's somehow managed to befriend most of the people at ORO, not just the Ocean Tidy team, and I'll catch her helping around the office, always eager to resolve any problem at hand.

I scan the halls, confirming that we are alone. When I see the rest of the floor is empty, I turn back to her.

"This has to stay between us."

She nods. "Of course."

"ORO's dealing with some funding gaps. It's nothing I can't fix, but I'm having to put in some extra time figuring out how to get us back on track."

I chose my words very carefully, not wanting to escalate her worry about the situation, but a hesitation still sits inside of me. I know we've only worked together for a month, but she seems like the only one that can both understand me and help me. She looks up at me with worry in her features. I can trust her to not speak about this with anyone. *Right?*

"That's…" Her eyes grow wide, I'm not quite sure with what. I shouldn't have said anything.

"It's fine, I got it covered. We should head out. It's getting late." I straighten and turn to leave.

Her hand grabs firmly at my forearm before I start walking. I turn to face her. I could stay right here forever, in the darkness of the glass walls around us.

"Let me help." Her voice is stern, focused.

"You really don't—"

"Look, I don't want to overstep, but I've been feeling so restless trapped at my desk while we continue working on Ocean Tidy. I promise I know ORO like the back of my hand. I've poured hours into building out different strategies and lanes for funding. I can help you."

My heart swells at the familiar sparkle returning to her eyes, the waves of possibility already playing out in that brain of hers. Her hand hasn't dropped from my arm at all, and I want to reach for it, closing my fingers around hers.

"You already have so much going on with Ocean Tidy."

She cranes her neck back, her brows pinched together. "Are you doubting that I can help?"

"Not even a little bit, but this isn't your responsibility."

"My responsibility has always been creating an impact. If ORO's having financial issues, that means they can't make the changes they need to. It would be wrong of me to sit idly by and let you figure this out on your own." She gives me a soft smile, and every neuron in my brain is telling me to kiss her.

"Thank you, Avery."

"Besides, I'm so sick of designing graphs all day. I promise, it's a selfish request. I want to fundraise, meet people, and convince them that we're doing something good!" She winks at me.

Yep. That does it. I so very fucking badly need to kiss her right now.

"I'd be remiss to deny you." I join her laugh.

The tangled wires in my rib cage finally unbind. The weight I've been carrying around evaporates off my shoulders, hanging in the air around us.

Avery watches me, and I take what feels like my first deep breath in days.

"I'll do some research, and we can talk about my ideas over one of your famous lattes, Mr. Navarro. Now, let's go. It's way later than regular work hours." She winks and drops her hand from my forearm. I miss her touch already.

Avery makes her way down the hallway, and I follow, my eyes focused on the way her hair sweeps against her shoulders. She turns to face me and gives me another smile before walking ahead. I already feel lighter at the confession.

"I can't thank you enough," I say. But all I want to do is drop to my knees before her in gratitude. This woman didn't even hesitate when she realized something was wrong.

I've been engulfed in my own stress for days, trying to figure out how to take care of this on my own, but here she was, the lifeline I needed the entire time.

"I'm happy to help."

We arrive at the elevator, and I press the button to call the car up to our floor. I enjoy our silence. When the car arrives, I step inside and press the button for the first floor. When Avery steps on, one of her heels catches in the crevice between the floor and the elevator. Her body tumbles into mine, and I catch her by her soft shoulders.

"Ahh, that's the second time I've gotten stuck in these heels." Avery uses me for support while she pulls her leg out of the gap. Her exasperated eyes meet mine, and I become very aware of how much of her body is wrapped in my arms.

"I thought you missed falling into my arms," I say, trying to distract myself from her intoxicating proximity.

"Maybe you just missed catching me." She pulls out of my grip and moves to stand beside me.

"Mhmm." I raise my eyebrows at her.

The doors close, and the car begins its very lengthy descent.

I've always hated how long these elevators take to get up and down from the lobby. But right now, I wish time would get stuck and we could be trapped here instead.

"You know, you never collected," she says, avoiding my gaze.

"What?" I feign confusion.

She rolls her eyes, and a smile breaks out on her face. One of her hands travels up to her face, and she runs a finger along her lip. My dick stirs at the memory of my thumb tracing over her mouth on the boat.

"Never mind." She looks from me and back to the door.

I need to taste her again. An uncontrollable need begins to thunder in my veins.

Not a single day has passed since our first kiss that I've neglected to remember how she felt. Every single morning, I've pushed myself longer and harder during my runs, trying to force the craving for her kiss out of my body.

It hasn't worked.

I turn toward her and caress the outside of her jaw with my hand. Her face returns to mine, the flesh of her skin blooming pink.

"Do you want me to kiss you, Avery?"

I need to kiss you, Ave.

"No," she whispers.

That must be her new favorite word for me. There's a twinge of defiance in the mixture of bronze and hazel of her eyes as she observes me. I lean down, my forehead only a short space from touching hers. Avery's lashes flutter closed, and her chin lifts toward me. My own mouth parts, mimicking hers, and I inch my way closer to her, hovering right beside her.

My body is screaming at me to shatter the distance between us.

Kiss her. Kiss her!

I breathe on her parted lips. "Liar."

Her face tenses with bewilderment. I don't let her pull away, my fingers tilting her jaw slightly, and I press my mouth gently to her soft, burning cheek.

The elevator doors swing open. I can feel every cell in my body groan in protest that our time here is cut short.

But the promise I made her remains. Avery doesn't deserve a rushed moment. When I taste her again, I want all of her, every second.

Chapter 24
Avery

THIS IS MOST DEFINITELY NOT HOW I PLANNED TO SPEND MY Sunday night, sitting atop a never-ending pile of clutter. That kiss—or I should say *almost* kiss—in the elevator has left my body feeling restless.

Get it together, Ave.

I try to snap my focus back to the task at hand: finding more investor leads.

My calendar for the next two weeks is packed to the brim with investor leads and introductions. The first of which is tomorrow morning with Foster and Deborah Adams.

Last time we saw each other was at my graduation. I'm excited to find out if they took that expedition I helped put together for them in Japan.

The Adamses know almost every affluent family in the city. They're like the oldest of the old money in New York, their connections spanning across every humanitarian area of focus and people in really, really high places.

In their retirement, they've decided to play matchmaker between other wealthy families and various charities, organizations, and individual start-ups around the city. From the clients of theirs I remember, I've been able to put together a list of potentially interested parties and will ask them for an introduction. I'm positive they'll want to help.

My passion for fundraising thrums under my skin. I have missed being in this world.

I feel somewhat strange that Joanna's recent disappearance has landed me in the place I've wanted to be since the beginning: helping fundraise for ORO. But without her leave, I wouldn't have gotten this opportunity.

A part of me is happy she's not around even though a pang of guilt slides through me. My dad wouldn't want me to lack compassion for her. I just wonder how she could just abandon everything on Luca's shoulders.

What happened to her?

I sigh, focusing on the mess before me.

Random receipts, bobby pins, a spilled tube of sunscreen, an embarrassing amount of half-finished lip balms—really, who needs four lip balms?—and colorful sticky notes covered with unintelligible messages are splayed before me.

It's humbling to see the museum of your existence laid out on the floor like this before it ends up in a neatly organized pile. If I were to disappear and leave behind my room as it is right now, the only thing someone would be able to deduce is that Avery Soko is a mess.

I need to find more exciting ways to entertain myself other than work and binge-watching television with Lily.

Right now, however, I simply can't think of anything other than this disaster that has slowly been swallowing my room whole. So I'm choosing to organize my things instead of catching up on some much-needed rest before tomorrow's meeting…

Or thinking about a certain elevator ride.

That darn elevator.

I throw a few old receipts into the recycle pile and reward myself with some chocolate I picked up on my way home.

I learned early on that if I don't make cleaning a game, it simply will not get done.

One item to the waste pile. One chocolate for me.

My watch reads two o'clock when I finally start going through the contents of my evening clutches. I reach for the little gold clam bag I wore on the night of the boat soiree when I almost let Luca Navarro take me right there on the deck, despite the people above us.

The way he confided in me a few days ago brings a smile to my face.

The entire time I've worked at the ORO offices, I haven't once caught him asking anyone for help. Instead, he keeps piling and piling more work onto himself.

It's not that big of a deal that he told me about OROs issues, I'm obviously the most qualified person on our team.

But I'm happy that he wanted to tell me.

Just me.

Luca continues to prove me wrong about my initial judgment of him.

The heartless suit who interviewed me and delivered the crushing news of my job rejection doesn't resemble the man I've been getting to know over the last couple of months.

When I share ideas that seem unattainable, Luca doesn't back down from the challenge of making them a reality. Each time our team hits a logistical wall, Luca finds the time to help us resolve it. His presence on the project is not overbearing, and I know he's been essential to moving us forward. I hope I can be as helpful in getting ORO back on its feet.

Over the past few days, we've been sending emails back and forth about the new strategy. Some of them have been bordering on flirty. At least I think so?

Luca actually used a smiley face to tell me I was doing a good job.

Luca Navarro: Good job. :)

If that's not Luca flirting, I really don't know what is.

Whenever we've found ourselves alone, my body has betrayed me. I struggle to understand what happens to my common sense when I'm around him.

I repeat the thing I've been trying to convince myself of for weeks: *Luca Navarro is my coworker. Nothing more.*

But the thoughts just don't ring true anymore.

Does that rule that I put on myself—no relationships until I'm where I want to be in my career—all those years ago still matter?

Questions flood my mind, and I try to brush them off, turning back to the task at hand.

I unclasp my clutch before emptying it into my lap. A collection of business cards spills out before me.

I gather up my paper trophies, rolling the cards through my fingers, happy to see my winnings again. I pick out a few that could make for soft leads for ORO to secure funding from.

Luca's rich voice worms itself into my consciousness from the night on the boat over a month ago. *What if you forget one?*

Why does he always ignite my need to prove him wrong?

I pull out my phone and rotate the cards to match their owners to my contacts. All are accounted for.

Ha!

When I flip over the stack, a neat scribble catches my eye.

"Call me when you're ready to raise the stakes," I read out loud to the emptiness in my room. The writing is followed by a collection of digits.

My lungs fill with a sharp gasp, and I flip over the card. Luca Navarro's name is typed on the other side in a clean, bold font.

The phone number on the back does not match the one below his work email.

Of course.

I can't escape him. Luca's infecting my thoughts like ivy in a garden. Vining his way into the depths of my being so heavily that I'm not sure I could get rid of him even if I dug for hours.

"Navarro," I say out loud, his name tickling my tongue.

I could have used this number instead of emailing him. I bring my hand up to my cheek, touching the faint outline of where his lips caressed my skin.

But, really, on the cheek?

I pretty much had a sign above my head that said *KISS ME ON THE MOUTH, YOU GORGEOUS ANNOYING MAN.*

I rub the card through my fingers, my eyes closing as the memory of the way his large thumb traced the shape of my lips while he taught me how to say his name on the boat heats my blood.

I press the card to my lips, wanting to taste him.

What is happening?

I spring to my feet, abandoning the tainted card on the floor. It's cursed. It must be.

What am I, a teenager making out with a poster of her favorite celebrity?

There's no other explanation for why a sane woman just makes out with a business card. Alone in her apartment. Dressed in her T-shirt from junior-year summer camp.

I am losing. My. Fucking. Mind.

I shoot into bed, then slam my fingers on the bedside lamp switch. I'm simply delusional from lack of sleep. I ignore the tingling sensations consuming my body and instead try to force myself to sleep.

Sleep. Sleep. Sleep.

It's not working.

The warmth causes every molecule within me to thrum.

The recollection of Luca's mouth only inches from mine causes goose bumps to run up my legs. I knead my hands at my skin, trying to rid my body of these overwhelming feelings. The way the sweetness of his breath tickled my lips when I reached for him longingly. His hands on my body at the Mademoiselle, guiding my hips into him. Then it's the image of his taut, muscular body shirtless with his beach cleanup crew.

Of course I'm thinking about Trash Titans right now.

Is that picture permanently ingrained in my brain?

Fuck.

My sheets tangle between my limbs until I turn to my side, my eyes landing on the drawer of my bedside table.

My *devices* better be charged.

Chapter 25
Luca

OVER THE PAST MONTH, AVERY'S BEEN IN MY OFFICE EVERY FREE hour to discuss her fundraising strategy with me. She has already secured a million dollars in funding through the philanthropic family she used to work for, and various other connections in her repertoire. I've been able to sleep better, knowing that ORO will be okay.

I regret ever assuming that the old job was just a fluffy title to pad her resume. It gave her a lot of meaningful connections and taught her about what these wealthy humanitarians actually care about.

I was a real fucking jerk when I met her. But I realize now that I haven't even thought about my old job in a while. The impending guilt from the Shift Industries case and my past as a lawyer haven't had time to return in the throes of all my new work.

I'm better for it.

Avery set up meetings with every possible lead in the greater East Coast region. She doesn't even understand the extent of how much she's helping me and everyone at ORO. I can't imagine doing this alone anymore.

She's been staying later, and I've been leaving earlier just to spend more time together.

I leave my office, and my lips curve up when I see the hallway is illuminated with light.

Most nights, I wait by the elevator bank, hoping she's still here.

I reach for the call button, and the brightness down the hall dims. It's like she can anticipate me staying back for her.

She appears, a jacket tucked below the purse hanging off her arm. Today, she wore a simple black dress that hugs her thighs. Her hips sway with each step toward me. She's breathtaking. I want to pull her into my arms right here and let our bodies sway together to the rhythm of our breathing.

"How did that meeting with Dax go?" She stands so close to that our shoulders almost touch and I feel sunshine flood through my soul.

"It went really well, thanks again," I say, and she nods.

The elevator bell dings, and we get on.

"All things considered, we've managed to work pretty well together," I note.

Her eyes meet mine, and then her stomach lets out a loud growl.

She breaks into one of her heartwarming laughs. "Sorry, the only thing I had today was the latte you made me and the snacks Molly has gotten into the habit of bringing me."

I smile. I've been enjoying making her sweet lattes for our daily meetings.

But I despise that needless apology with a passion. "Please never apologize for existing."

She laughs again, but my comment wasn't a joke.

I turn to face her. "We're going to get dinner."

"Outside these office walls? Scandalous," Avery says as the elevator doors reveal a brightly lit lobby. We step off.

"You're hungry and I am hungry," I counter. "Let me feed you."

I hold back the real reason I want to get dinner with her.

We haven't spent any time together outside of the office since trivia night, and our conversations mostly focus on work and a side bet we have going about what snack Ollie will bring to the daily team meeting. I cherish the fact that our ongoing games continue to bring us closer.

And right now, I crave her familiarity outside these glass walls.

"Are you trying to trick me into a date?" Her hazel eyes are a deep green today, and they meet me in a dare.

Yes, for the past three months.

"If that's what you want, then just say so."

She rolls her eyes, but her expression sets into a delicate smile. "Let's go."

I take her delicate palm in mine, giving her no time to change her mind.

Outside, I hail a cab, and we slide into the back seat. My knee gently bumps into hers, and although she reclaims possession of her hand, our legs are still touching as the car carries us uptown.

I turn to face her, trying to find the best way to start a conversation that won't involve a jab, but my loss for words grants our driver the ideal opportunity to reveal his life story during the ride.

Avery is captivated by Mikhail, asking the man all sorts of questions about his life. My hands dig into the leather of the seat, my tongue trapped between my teeth. I want Avery to return her attention to me, but I can't help admiring her genuine interest in Mikhail's family dynamics for the remainder of the cab ride.

"Tell Yara good luck on her exam, Mikhail!" Avery grins, slamming the door as we exit at our destination.

"Do you always talk to your cabbies?"

"Yes," she says, as though the act were as simple as breathing. "What, are you one of those weirdos who just sits there in silence?"

I open my mouth to respond, but she interrupts me.

"A food truck?"

The truck stands on East One-Hundred-Eleventh Street. A string of lights coils around a nearby tree, lighting the small ordering counter. The sidewalk transforms into a crescendo of music and laughter from the locals throwing block parties in the warm weather.

"Not just any food truck—La Vaquita. It's quite literally the only place in New York with food that reminds me of home."

"I'm so excited!" She smiles.

Instinctively, I take her hand in my again. The motion is no longer tentative. Her palm feels clammy against my skin, and her fingers tense for a moment. When her face tilts up to mine, her lips are pursed as though she's ready to scold me again.

"Are you nervous?" I murmur in her ear.

"No." She removes her hand from mine and wipes it on the fabric of her black dress. "It's very humid."

Fuck, why did I say that?

Avery turns away from me and walks toward the menu scribbled out on an oversized chalkboard. The heavy, hot air adds waves to her hair. The cropped blonde tresses weave themselves into delicate, wispy swirls as small beads of sweat gather on her forehead.

She studies the menu beneath the radiance of the string lights, her skin gleaming and her foot tapping to the rhythm of the reggaeton blasting from someone's car speakers.

"Would you stop staring at me like that and tell me what's good here?" she snaps at me, the rosy bud of her lips lifted in a half smirk.

"I'll order for us both."

"Okay, but how do you—"

"I know."

"What do you mean, *you know?*" A quizzical expression colors her features.

I want to gently take her by those slender shoulders and shake her for not realizing how much I notice everything about her.

"I pay attention," I explain.

"Okay..." Her gaze briefly trails to the bustling activity on the street.

It feels good that she trusts me.

My first few months in New York, I tried over fifty restaurants trying to find the best food. When I found La Vaquita, I came here every week for months.

We approach the ordering window, and I spot my favorite cook, Miguel.

"Aye, Miguel. ¿Cómo estás?"

"Ooooh, Luca. ¿Quién es la señorita?" His eyes bounce between me and Avery.

"Es mi futura novia."

He laughs. *"¿Y ella lo sabe?"*

"Pendejo," I joke.

"No te creas. ¿Qué les puedo dar?"

"Dame cuatro tacos de nopales, una torta de pollo asado, y dos mulitas de rajas. Ah, y una horchata, por favor."

"¿Si, y para la señorita? Tal vez una cerveza, para que te pueda soportar." Miguel looks over at Avery and gives her one of his friendly grins. This is what I get for finally bringing a woman here.

"Miguel—"

Avery surprises me and chimes in, *"No, gracias. Un agua, por favor."*

Does she know Spanish? Or is she learning Spanish for me?

I finish my conversation with Miguel and pay for our feast. Avery makes her way to the side of the truck and grabs us a few napkins. I'm giddy in anticipation of seeing Avery's face as she tries some of my favorite foods.

"I didn't know you could speak Spanish," I say.

"If by 'speak' you mean I can say the most elementary phrases?" she taunts. "*Agua* and *una cerveza* were some of the first lessons in Spanish basics."

The clumsy pronunciations rolling off her tongue flood my heart with warmth.

My parents would love her for trying.

"Any particular reason you've been learning Spanish recently?"

Avery turns to me, a wicked look in her eyes. "Figured I can learn how to tease you in more than one language."

My lips curve up. I'm glad she's learning.

"We'll have to see how good of a student you've been later."

My heart darts with the hope that there may be a later.

"I'm a very good student," she says confidently.

The scattered assortment of tables and chairs are all occupied by other patrons, but Avery finds an empty curb and gestures for me to join her, which I do. She sits upright on the pavement with her ankles crossed in front of her. Her short black dress hugs her waist, the seams slightly stretch around her thighs.

We sit together for a few quiet moments. Avery enjoys watching the people around us, and I cannot keep my eyes off her.

Miguel shouts my name, pulling me off the curb to collect our meal. On my way back to our intimate street corner, I spot a free chair and drag it over with my foot for Avery.

"Here, I grabbed you a seat," I say, placing the chair in front of her, but she instantly springs to her feet, helping gather up the overflowing cartons of food in my hands.

"Thank you!" She swiftly unfolds one of the napkins onto the chair and places the food on the seat. "Now we have a table."

I sit back down beside her and watch her peek through the

assortment in front of us. The delight beaming from her makes me feel like I'm about to try my favorite dishes again for the first time.

"Why did you order so much?" She exclaims, opening each of the boxes and picking up a mulita. "Tell me what everything is! *This* looks like a mini-quesadilla."

"Trust me, we might go back for more."

Avery sinks her teeth in. "This is so good!"

She takes another bite and executes her signature eye roll, which is even more impeccable when it's filled with pleasure instead of annoyance.

I want to be the reason behind the happy little moans escaping with each mouthful she takes.

"What's inside that one?" She points to one of the tacos, still chewing.

"*Nopales* or cactus." I bite the delicious taco as she watches. "It's not really common at restaurants and it's hard to find a spot that prepares them well. But Miguel is one of the most talented chefs."

"What do they do with the thorns?"

"He probably eats them." I laugh, and she joins before sinking my teeth back into the nopal taco.

"Oh my god...that is so, so good." She draws out each word, and now I want to take her right here on this street.

What's the charge for public indecency nowadays? A jail term of up to ninety days, probation for a year, and a fine? Might be worth it.

Avery takes a bite of the torta before settling back to the rest of her mulita.

"The food here is out of this world. But this right here is my favorite drink." I pick up the white paper cup and take a sip. The sweetness of cinnamon rushes across my taste buds. "My mom would only make it on special occasions. My brother and I always overindulged and made ourselves sick."

I hand her the cup, and she brings the liquid to her lips.

"Okay, I love this." That word sounds so exquisite coming from her. "I didn't take you for someone who enjoys something this sweet."

She hands the cup back to me, and I take another swish, savoring the ease she feels at sharing the same drink with me.

I grin. "I will always make an exception for something this delicious."

"You surprise me more and more each day."

Joy suffuses through me. "There's a lot of things you don't know about me."

"Like what?"

"Well, you already know I'm competitive and that, occasionally, I like the taste of something sweet."

Avery smiles and her cheeks flush a deeper red, a heat permeating from her that isn't just from the blistering air outside. "Only occasionally?"

"More and more lately," I admit.

She nods. "What else?"

I take another loud slurp of horchata. "You'll just have to wait and see."

Chapter 26
Avery

"I'm about to burst!" I lean back on the pavement, tipping my face to the dark sky.

Now that my hunger has been satiated, I can feel the brief dizzy spell I felt in the cab finally subside.

Unless the lightheadedness has something to do with the way Luca's body leans into mine.

I return my gaze to Luca sitting beside me, his relaxed face watching the few couples dancing under the city lights. Is he remembering how our bodies moved together as we danced at the Mademoiselle like I am? The memory of him pressed into me causes my mouth to dry.

I smile at this unusually candid moment displaying his ruggedly handsome features. The fold of his shirt cuffs is unkempt, and I have the urge to reach over and fix them.

We watch each other for a period that could span an eternity. The city around us seems suddenly, piercingly quiet.

That happens so often when I'm around him.

Luca takes another sip of horchata. A small drop of the sweet liquid drips from his lip, and he languidly licks it away. The nagging need between my thighs doubles at the sight.

The tense moments from the past few weeks of being around each other are on the verge of culminating. The way he so easily wrapped his palms around my fingers made my heart skip a beat.

Now, the ecstasy of witnessing the lick of his lips is streaking through me like a fallen star. I want to leap into his arms and cover his neck in kisses.

I'm losing my fucking mind.

A loud siren slams cold reality back to my senses.

For the past couple of weeks, my fundraising efforts have been in full swing. Between figuring out ways to help ORO and focusing on Ocean Tidy, Luca and I have spent our time doing nothing else.

But right now, his ridiculously bright smile, which he has gotten into the habit of flashing whenever he catches my attention on him for too long, is a welcome distraction.

"I'll be right back." He suddenly gets to his feet, but before he steps away from me, he leans down. "Are you good to hang here while I grab something for us from the truck?"

"Yes, of course," I say.

A small prickle of annoyance tickles me at his overprotective gesture. I'm not used to someone actively looking out for me. I've gotten used to taking care of myself, and giving up even a bit of that independence is uncomfortable. But something about Luca's actions during our time together and his genuine tone, not intended to patronize or make me feel feeble, puts me at ease again.

Luca walks over to the truck, glancing over one of his broad shoulders a couple of times to check on me, before leaning over the order counter. Luca's laughter erupts, and when he makes his way over to me with a small box, the remains of a laugh still trace his features.

"Tres leches." He reveals the contents of the box, giving me a wink.

"Three?" I say, racking my brain for the words I learned in the Spanish basics book I picked up a few weeks ago.

"Milks," he says.

He dips a spoon into the dessert and then brings the spongy texture to his lips before it disappears behind his teeth. I watch him intently, each second slowing again.

"Want some?" Luca dives the spoon back into the airy cake.

"Yes," I mumble under my breath. My heartbeat pounds in my ears.

"Cake." He hovers the dessert in front of me. "Do you want some cake?"

"Yes," I say. "Cake."

His brows quirk up in response as though he's expecting something else to materialize from me, and my ability to keep it together falters. The points of my face burn red again.

I wrap my mouth around the spoon, and the sweet flavors explode on my taste buds.

It's funny how all the resentment I carried for him has dissipated over the last couple months. One moment, this overpowering man is making me want to pull out my hair, and the next I want him to fist the strands for me.

Deep breath.

I rummage in my mind for something—anything—to say. "I've never had such a delicious wet cake before."

Wet cake?

Why did that sound so sexual?

Has my vocabulary gone completely into the wind?

"I'm glad I could feed you your first *wet* cake." Luca rakes his hand through his hair then spoons the last bite toward me.

I open my mouth, and his tongue slowly traces the bottom of his lip at the sight.

The knowledge of how good he tastes sparks up each hair on my body and my spine goes rigid.

A shiver creeps down my spine as our time alone on the boat finds its way back into my consciousness.

"Are you cold?" he asks. My skin pebbles. "I can call you a cab home."

I definitely don't want to cut the night short. My tongue is still antsy to find his again after the unfulfilling almost kiss in the elevator. I pause for a moment.

"I live only a couple of blocks south of here."

Luca towers over me, taking my bag in his hand. "I'll walk you."

———

WE STROLL BESIDE EACH OTHER, our conversations veering off work and on to more details of our lives. The colors of his life begin to fill in the shape of the man next to me as I take the long way home, walking us along Fifth Avenue with the malevolent rustling of the trees in Central Park above us. A heaviness forms in the air from the growing shift in weather.

I finally break the lengthy silence. "Are you going to tell me how you found out that last trivia question? The mascot one?"

I know that even if you dig around online, there's no mention of who was in the mascot suit.

"I remembered the shirt you were wearing."

"What shirt?"

"The shirt you were running in," Luca says. "When you abandoned me to those dogs."

"I didn't see, or I would have helped!" My voice is suddenly raised.

Luca laughs, and I join him.

"I'll concede," I say. "But I can barely remember what I wore yesterday, let alone weeks ago. How did *you* remember?"

"How many more examples will it take for you to realize I remember everything about you?" he says. My heartbeat quickens. "Every ordinary and extraordinary piece of you, Avery, has a home within me."

The words slam into me like a cannonball into a cement wall.

I don't have a chance to respond to him when a crackle of thunder rips the air, the boom echoing through the plethora of buildings lining the park.

"Did you know it was supposed to rain?" I call over the ear-piercing rumble.

"It'll probably stop soon."

As if the universe hears the challenge from Luca, another droplet lands on top of my head, and before I can fully register the situation, the sound of violent rain fills the air.

"Run!" I yell.

I take off, not waiting to find out if Luca will follow me. My apartment is still too far away from this far Uptown, and I regret the white lie I told him about living only a couple of blocks away.

I weave into the park, the rain drenching my jacket. I run toward the bridge I pass during my jogs to take cover from the storm.

The downpour continues to soak my clothes. My wet strands of hair stick to my skin. The dampness of the earth envelops my senses, while the heat from the pavement radiates up my legs.

I feel the rush of life come back to me, the vibration of my muscles bringing me out of my emotional swell. Running has been my companion during some of my lowest moments. Keeping myself focused on a destination makes me feel like I was meant to be going in that direction all along. These past few weeks have helped me find my purpose again.

I hear Luca beside me. Saturated beads pelt against my skin.

For the first time in years, I feel the warm familiarity of the woman I was before senior year in college.

Overjoyed. Willful. Utterly free.

Except now, I've changed and begun to steady myself in who I am becoming. I know I'm all the better for it.

Time stands still again. I slow my pace, turning my face to the sky, letting the heavy rain massage my cheeks. I spread my arms, my palms catching small pools of water. Laughter erupts from me.

Luca takes one of my wet hands in his and spins me on the damp gravel. He looks so *beautiful*.

Is that even the right word?

His overgrown strands of hair stick to his face. The smile he wears illuminates every part of his features. My favorite brown of his eyes is lit up by the dim streetlights around us.

"You've made life so interesting these past few weeks," he shouts over the rain.

"You too."

My heart thrums with more than the adrenaline of the run. More than the building understanding that Luca's somehow so much like me. Determined and strong.

We run and dance in the pouring rain, our laughter swallowed up by the thunder.

He spins me again, and the twirl brings the bridge into view. I lock eyes with Luca, a devious grin revealing my plan.

"Race you there!" I yell and take off before he can reply. Our footsteps beat against the wet cement.

"You better hurry up." Luca takes the lead.

Oh no, he doesn't!

My lungs feel as though they are being torn to shreds, but I refuse to give up. I urge my pinched toes and sore legs into a quicker sprint.

Luca twists his head around and smiles at the gain I'm attaining on him, and he pushes ahead.

"So, what do I get when I wi—" Before I can finish shouting through the noise of the rain, the side of my left ankle crashes into the ground, and I stumble over a deep puddle. The pain is already beginning to throb, but I push through, determined to reach the finish line.

Luca misses my epic battle with gravity, and when he finally takes cover below the bridge, his strong arms stretch into the air.

"Did I win?" he calls out over the boom of thunder.

The smile on his face is one I've never seen before, and it warms the very blood in my veins.

"Only because I let you win!" I yell back at him, slowing into a jog when pain shoots up my hurt leg. I fell only about a hundred meters away from the dry shelter.

"Avery?" He sprints over to me. "What happened? Are you hurt?"

He puts his arm around my shoulders and, in a sudden motion, scoops me up under the knees as though I were weightless. My hand grasps the material of his shirt. Rain continues to pummel us as he walks back under the stone overpass.

"Are you feeling guilty about that little victory dance while I made friends with the ground?" I tease with a hint of sarcasm, my giggles sneaking out of me.

"You really fell?" Luca's serious voice crashes into me.

"I rolled my left ankle," I admit. "I'm perfectly fine."

"You didn't exaggerate a dramatic collapse so I would have to carry you the rest of the way?" His fingers wiggle beneath my arm, and the tickling feeling sends me into a fit of writhing laughter.

"Put me down! Put me down!" I scream through each howl of my snickering. The acute pulsing in my ankle has dulled.

"No." He smiles down at me. "This is my prize for winning."

"What? An injured woman?" I crane into his chest, now exposed by the wet fabric of his shirt.

"*No.*" He pulls me near his lips. "I get to hold you close again."

The streetlights flicker on and off.

"I'm really not hurt though." There's only a dull ache. Nothing a little ice won't fix.

"We are almost there and then I will set you down."

I groan in fake protest. I've been missing out if this is what it's like to be carried. No one's ever picked me up with such ease or been tall and strong enough to carry me around like I'm weightless.

"You know, no one's ever picked me up so easily before."

"Why not?"

"I'm tall."

"Why does that matter? It's their loss."

Luca moves easily to our dry safe haven. My pulse quickens. Okay, it's official I want to be carried everywhere.

We make it to a patch of asphalt.

"That wasn't so bad now was it?" He smiles, one of those tempting smiles, and sets my body on the balmy pavement.

I adjust my legs in my new seat, stretching them out on the ground before me, but I don't want to loosen my arms from around his neck. Holding onto him is like wrapping your hands around a steaming cup of coffee first thing in the morning. There is a comfort to it that is truly irreplaceable.

I sulk from the release of his embrace around my torso. "It was nice. You have really big shoulders."

"You like big things, Avery?"

"Yes."

Wait. Did I say that out loud?

He chuckles. "*Good.*"

Luca kneels before my bruised ankle. The backs of his fingers run up my calves, assessing for any other damage, and I urgently want those warm hands to find their way up my thighs to the wetness pooling in my lace panties.

"I didn't mean, I just—" My lungs heave a sharp inhale from his touch. The feel of him caressing me catapults a shiver from the base of my spine and into my clavicle like a struck high striker at a carnival.

"Is that okay?" He begins to massage my knee as his other hand brushes the damp strands of hair out of my eyes.

I nod.

"I'm only going to check if it's swollen, alright?" Luca asks.

I nod again.

Luca undoes the strap of my ballet flat, and his warm fingers considerately rub around my left ankle. The sensation is so pleasant that a moan escapes me. The sound cuts through the heavy rain and echoes under the bridge, causing him to stiffen completely.

"Are you alright?" he asks.

"Yep. It's fine," I say, clearing my throat.

"It looks like a small bruise." He smiles, and the warm color of his irises is now filled with that familiar pool of darkness. Luca takes my hands into his, folding my fingers between his palms. "I'm sorry to break it to you, but I guess you're not as athletic as you were in your mascot days, *cariño*."

I can't help but smile at the nickname.

Darling.

His *cariño*.

"Hey! I'm very athletic." I playfully smack his arm again.

He snickers like a naughty toddler. That boyish grin sticks to his face. "I bet you are."

"Well, maybe I fell on purpose to make it up to you for *all* the times I've won our bets."

His face grows serious, and he traces the pads of my fingers with his.

Did I say something wrong?

We sit for a moment, neither of us able to form words while we listen to the droplets dancing on the pavement, our breaths exchanging the same air. The smell of his musky cologne blends with the damp asphalt, and I lick my lips, wanting a taste.

My rationality wavers as I lean into the brief space separating us.

"Avery, this game between us can probably come to an end," he whispers only a few inches from my mouth.

My spine claps against the brick, and a rampant trembling fills my heart. "What game?"

"*Our* games, competitions, bets," Luca explains. "These excuses we've fabricated to be close to each other."

I can't even argue back because he's right. The games *aren't* harmless play to pass the time; they *aren't* simply my competitive side being roused around him.

Each time we're at each other's throats, I feel a thrill I haven't felt before. When I lose, I know he'll start another game with me. And each time I win, he's eager to take on more challenges. The act of outdoing each other has become one of my favorite parts of the past couple of months.

Luca finally speaks. "Why are you denying that there's something here?"

"I'm not—" I hesitate. "I'm just... I'm not ready to get close to someone. I'm not where I want to be in my life."

"Where do you want to be?"

I frown. "I've always put my career first, and there's just so much I thought I'd accomplish on my own before someone one like you came along."

"Whatever you'd want, Avery, we could do it together."

I've relied on myself for so long. Apart from Lily, no one has ever wanted to push me to be the best I can be and share my wins.

Until Luca.

He never fails to show me that he cares in my worst moments and in my best.

"I don't know how to navigate something serious."

His eyes scan my face. "Then, for now, let's just pretend *this* is one of our games."

"I thought you wanted to stop?"

"The only thing I truly want is you," he says.

I sit here, simply staring at him. The rain is barely falling now.

"I need to kiss you again, Avery."

"Ave."

"Ave," he repeats, savoring the name in his mouth as though it's candy melting on his tongue.

His large hand palms my shoulders, pressing my back into the damp concrete wall until his fingers finally reach my neck. The pad of his thumb glides along my jaw, lifting my face closer to his. Our eyes meet and I feel the months of apprehension dissipate from my body and morph into certainty.

I close the inches between us, and time stops in the mingling of senses when I finally meet his earthy taste. A wildfire only he knows how to claim from me reignites.

"I don't think I'll ever get enough of you," he whispers.

My heart skips a beat. Or two. Or maybe it was three?

The hunger from our first kiss returns, and our tongues explore each other with a depthless lust. His strong arm cradles me, settling my body in his lap as he replaces my seat on the pavement. I wrap my legs around him and immediately notice the stiffness now settled between my thighs.

We barely have a chance to come up for air when I release a groan. My need for him begins to peak, and I finger the buttons of his shirt, desperate to feel more of him.

The scraping of bike tires on the gravel wakes us from our trance.

Why are we cursed with these wretched interruptions?

We break away from each other, the silence of the paused rain filling my ears. My body aches for more.

"Let's go home." Luca stands, picking me up off the ground again, and I am enveloped in his embrace.

"You really don't have to carry me," I say, steadying my

voice and ignoring the desire to pull him back onto the ground and tear at this shirt.

"Will you ever stop trying to fight me?"

"I doubt it," I admit.

He smiles. "Good."

"I've been quite harsh at times, haven't I?" I hide in his chest.

"If I can put it behind me, so can you, Ave."

"Alright, let's call it water under the bridge."

He stills, and I push back to meet his gaze. Another bout of laughter explodes from him, vibrating the entirety of my body. I join him with an uncontrollable giggle.

"Let's get some ice on this ankle." He begins walking, tucking me closer to him.

"I live on Sixty-Fifth Street and—"

"Did you forget I've taken care of you once before?"

I rattle my brain for the memory. "Wait, so you knew I lived over sixty blocks away?"

He nods, causing me to blush. "I would walk all of New York with you, Ave." That dark stare digs into me once more before he raises his brow. "Now, we can finally discuss why you live above a bodega."

"So I never run out of snacks."

Chapter 27
Luca

"The second your lease is up, I'm finding you an apartment with an elevator." I ascend another flight of stairs.

Her roommate better not be home right now because the twenty minutes of her squirming and laughing in my arms have caused my pulsing cock to tent beneath the damp fabric of my pants.

"Let me guess, you live in some fancy building with a doorman and useless amenities like a basketball court."

"It's a pool, actually."

Her eyes widen with surprise, and I smile.

"I told you that you didn't have to carry me all the way up the stairs."

"I want to." My body courses with the strain of her weight and the desire not to set her down as we finally arrive at the fourth floor. My muscles refuse to concede to the exhaustion of the day.

"Okay, but you're going to have to let me go so I can open my door."

I finally allow her to detach herself from my grasp, and she digs through her purse.

If I were a truly selfish man, I'd take another taste from her in this cramped hallway. Then I would press her back against one of these walls and strip every piece of damp clothing off her skin.

I tower in front of her, and Avery's eyes meet mine in an entrancing stare. Luscious blonde waves sit in a messy crown above her head. Her tight black dress sticks to the dainty slope of her collarbones.

I lean down and whisper into her neck. "I think I've learned to dislike my suits as much as you do."

"Why?" Her voice returns to that precious taunting sound.

I guide my hands to her waist. "It's one of the things getting in the way of me making you mine."

She smiles in response. "That can be easily rectified."

Who am I kidding? I am a selfish man.

I move one of my hands to her face and reconnect our lips like two opposite poles of a set of magnets. Our kiss sends us crashing against her front door.

A metal sound echoes from the ground below, interrupting us. We break away. A bead of sweat rolls down my face, and I inhale deeply into her neck.

She smells like a storm waiting to wreak havoc. My body hums with the need to let her.

Control yourself.

"The keys," she says into the small space between us.

I bend down to grab them. When I stand, I leave a trail of soft kisses up her body.

Finally, I reach her mouth and look down at my goddess drenched from the thundering summer rain.

"Avery, you're the most beautiful woman I've ever seen."

Our hearts beat loudly in the silent hallway.

"You're not too bad yourself." She winks and steals the keys from my fingers, turning around to unlock her door. She stabs at her lock a few times, but the damn thing appears to be stuck.

"Jam it in," I whisper impatiently.

She peers at me under her dark lashes. "Hey, it just needs a little warm-up."

"Don't worry, I know all about warming up," I assure her, and her cheeks flush even more.

"*Oh.*"

When she steps inside her apartment, I wrap my arms around her and lift her from the ground. I walk us toward her couch.

No roommate in sight.

I lower her onto the couch and prop her ankle under a pillow.

"Don't move." I walk to the freezer, pull out some ice cubes, then roll them into a clean towel. I peek to see Avery's leg hasn't left the position I put it in.

So, she can comply with at least *some* of the things I ask of her. I walk back to her and place the ice pack on her ankle. She shivers.

"You're so good at doing what you're told," I tease.

Her breath shallows, and she tilts her hazel eyes up at my frame, devouring every inch of me. She pauses on the bulge in my pants. I smile at the way her eyes widen.

"Don't get used to it," she says. Her pink tongue reveals itself between her lips in a teasing gesture. She doesn't cower at the scrutiny of my gaze. Every single word is a challenge tempting us to take it one step further.

"How's your ankle?"

"It's perfectly fine," she says.

Avery strikes me as the kind of person who would still laugh with an open wound in her chest.

Her couch gives under my weight as I sit down. Avery adjusts her hips, and the pillows around her hug the curves of her delectable body.

"It's scorching in here," Avery finally murmurs into the growing silence.

I unfold the towel and pluck an ice cube from the pile. I gently put the ice directly on her ankle.

"Is that better?"

"I think so," she says before turning slightly to hide her smile into a pillow.

Seeing this woman, who is so full of fire, act timid right now is making my cock swell.

I massage the skin of her leg with the melting ice. The gentle graze of my fingers on her flesh stirs a carnal hunger.

I feel like a ravenous bear emerging from its den after a long, lonely winter. Every part of me wants to gorge myself on her.

Avery's hips squirm deeper into the cushions. I work my way farther up her leg, carefully sliding her tight dress up to reveal her toned thighs.

Our eyes don't break away from each other.

"If your ankle is fine, I guess I can put the ice away?" I go to stand, but Avery hooks her foot onto my lap and forces me back down beside her.

"Actually, it's starting to hurt again." She flutters her lashes at me.

I pick another piece of ice from the towel and return to massaging the hot flesh of her thighs. I forage for the moment Avery stills in anticipation, but she's the one who shifts the hem of her dress even higher.

"You want me to make it hurt less, *cariño*?"

She nods in response.

Fuck.

Her hips buck again, and it takes all of my strength to hold off on consuming her right this second.

"I bet you're as wet as your clothes right now," I whisper, yearning to feel the heat between her legs that must be warming with each teasing swipe of my fingers on her thighs.

She sucks in a breath. "I am, Luca."

I tense my entire body at the soft sound of my name coming from her.

"Don't forget to breathe, Ave," I say, my voice saturated with demand.

She complies.

"Such a good girl you are, *when* you actually listen to me."

The words rouse something in her because in a blink, Avery shoots up from her seat beside me and hooks her long legs across my waist. She fuses our mouths, and I drink from the bitter and sweet taste of her. My fingers latch on to her waist, and I guide the need between her legs against my cock. My lungs constrict at the pressure of her straddling me.

I palm her breasts and commit to memory which of my exploring touches elicits a loud moan from her. I compel myself to rip away from the sweet taste of her lips to cover her neck and chest in kisses, then sink my teeth into one of the stiff nipples peeking through the fabric of her dress.

"Can I taste you, Ave?" I say, now massaging one peak as my mouth presses against the other breast.

A demanding moan escapes her. I fist her hair, dragging her desperate eyes to me. Sweat coats the flushed skin of her face. I tilt my head close enough to feel her breath on my skin.

"Can I?" I ask again.

"*Yes.*" She looks up at me.

"Yes, what? I've never known you to be at a loss for words."

"*Yes*, I want you to taste me." Her voice comes out raw, demanding in a way I haven't heard before.

Music to my fucking ears.

I wrap my free arm around her exposed ass, hoisting her up on my body. The short skirt of her dress bands around her waist. Her bare flesh is only slightly covered by the lace of this pathetic excuse for panties.

Has she been wearing this underneath her clothes at the office this entire time?

I stand and return her to the cushions.

Avery is pliable under my touch, and I fucking love the way she relaxes into my guiding movements like when we danced together.

I take her hips and gently turn her on all fours. Avery's hands and knees rest firmly on the cushions. I descend behind her and kneel. The sight of her curvaceous ass only inches from my face forces an aching throb into my cock.

I want the wetness dripping from the lace. I want to drag it slowly around my aching length.

I kiss on her damp panties. "Do you want me to taste you here?"

"Please," she breathes.

One of her hands stretches behind her, searching for me.

I lock our fingers together and use the thumb of my free hand to swipe the damp, lacy fabric.

A pleading groan echoes through the room.

"Have you thought about the way I could worship this beautiful pussy?"

Avery's body arches deeper into me, answering my question. The length of her spine is splayed out before me as her hips lift higher into the air.

I laugh into the heat of her. "Such a demanding girl you are."

"You keep teasing me!"

My fingers hook around the useless lace that's keeping her glistening slit away from me. I savor the sight of this electric woman unraveling before me.

I want to take her right now. She leans forward into the back of the couch, spreading herself wider for me to see.

She's absolutely fucking perfect.

Every exposed, amorous inch of her.

My most primal desires wreck me. The months of self-imposed torture I endured, picturing this moment.

Yet my imagination didn't do the slightest justice to the reality of being with her.

I raise my chest and slide one of my arms under her belly, anchoring her body to me. I caress her neck with my lips, then strip the rain-doused dress over her head, leaving behind a delicate silky bra.

"So fucking exquisite," I whisper.

I take her hands and rest them on the couch. Her weight shifts forward, her hips lifting into the air.

"Hang on." I plant kisses on each inch of her exposed spine and then make my way down to her entrance.

My fingers return to massaging her breasts over the soft fabric as my gaze confronts her swollen center dripping before me once more. My cock throbs at the sight.

"Luca…" She whimpers, her hips thrash into me and her cunt begs for my attention.

My name again?

It's the final straw.

I fill my lungs with her fragrance and my tongue spreads onto her slit. A loud moan escapes Avery's throat, and I smile into her. The way her body lights up at my touch is euphoric.

I meet every roll of her hips with my tongue. Each wet stroke glides over her clit and teases her soaked entrance. The silk wetness of her pussy drips down my chin, coating my unshaven skin. I want to drown in her.

I continue to taunt her with different speeds, learning quickly that slow, deliberate laps of my tongue make her throw a needy tantrum.

I've never been with a woman who required so much of me as she rode my mouth. I'm obsessed with every fucking minute of it.

She tastes so good. Like somehow, somewhere, Avery was crafted just for me.

My cock struggles with violent throbs, mimicking the strokes of my tongue.

Adrenaline rips through me. I pull one of my hands away from her body and unbuckle the metal clasp of my leather belt. My fingers fumble with the zipper. I pull my trousers from my waist and step out of them, not letting my tongue break contact with Avery's swollen clit.

I rub my painful erection through my boxer briefs. My precum already coats the cotton fabric. The desire to feel Avery beneath my hands returns. I'm too intoxicated by her pleasure to not focus solely on her.

"Do you like riding my face, Ave?"

"Yes…" The rocking of her body against me becomes more brutal. "I need more…"

"That's my girl."

I finally pull my tongue from her and hook my hand around the front of her hip. My fingers replace the same rhythm on her clit. I lift off my knees, my tongue gathering the sweat pooled in the curve of her neck. Her glossed-over gaze targets me. I spent way too much fucking time away from her dreamy eyes.

I continue to tower over her, the fingers of my other hand pulling her face to me. "Tell me exactly what you need."

Her mouth closes on mine, and I allow myself to get drunk on our languid kiss.

"I need more of *you*, Luca," she breathes into my mouth. "I want to look at you."

The request echoes within the depths of my soul. How could I ever deny this headstrong woman anything her tender heart desires?

She has wholly soaked my hand, and I ache to feel her convulsing around my fingers.

I guide her to settle onto her back, her spine against the cushions.

Avery is on display before me, her eyes watching my movements in anticipation. A wicked grin splits across her flushed face when her gaze lands on my cock tenting my boxer briefs.

I reach for one of the many throw pillows littering the floor. "Lift your hips, my gorgeous girl."

She does as she's told, and it feels like I've just discovered a superpower.

I plant another kiss on her forehead, then descend to the needy center awaiting me.

The new position exposes me to the full extent of her pleasure, her eyes lost behind an intoxicated haze. The glowing flush on her skin is replaced with a cherry red, matching the stain of lipstick still clinging to her lips.

A new obsession occupies my being. I want to pour everything I have into her. Destroy every door, shatter every wall between us.

There's a concentration on her face as she watches my tongue work her clit, my palms mapping each inch of her perfect breasts.

I break my mouth away from her and return my fingers to her clit, circling the swell steadily.

"I want to feel *you*." Her hands grip the cushion as her eyes search for my throbbing erection.

I could spill over right now, just from her words.

Patience.

"Not yet, Ave."

I slide two of my free fingers inside her, and she immediately tenses around me. I lick my lips. Avery's taste is still on my tongue, lush and sweet.

I bring myself to her and whisper, "I want you to come around my fingers."

In response, she convulses around me. Every hot inch of her glides over me as he continues to spill out into my palm.

"Can you do that for me?" I demand.

Avery arches her back. The corner of my mouth turns up, and

I curl my fingers inside of her. Each thrust of my hand is quicker, deeper.

"Yes, yes, yes," she pants with each thrash. "I want to come."

"Remember this, Ave," I say, adding another finger into her, and she groans at the fullness. Each movement's soaked and filthy sound pierces through her lustful gasps.

I connect my forehead with hers, and we lock stares.

"Whatever you ask of me, I will give you," I promise. Her moans form into screams of pleasure. "Over, and over, and over again."

Avery finally shatters in my hands. Her body is restless beneath me, and it only intensifies the throbbing pulse in my cock. All I hear are her addicting whimpers and our synchronized breathing.

The tension in her limbs softens, sending her marvelous figure collapsing onto the cushions. When her convulsions seize, I withdraw my fingers from her.

"You're everything."

"Mmm." She smiles and murmurs something unintelligible under her breath.

I kiss the damp skin of her face, then pull one of the knitted throw blankets off the side of the couch. I drape it over her body, planting another kiss on her forehead. I take a step back, but Avery's fingers wrap around my hand, and my heart skips a beat at her touch.

"I'll be right back," I say.

I walk over to the kitchen, flip the tap on, and peek in her cabinets, searching for a glass.

"To your right, top shelf," Avery whispers from directly behind me.

I knew her compliant streak wouldn't last long.

I rotate my body to fill the glass with cold water. Her hands eagerly explore my body from behind. It's divine, being touched by her. Avery unfastens each button apart until my shirt hangs open, and she pulls the fabric off my shoulders.

I face her, replacing the material in her hands with the glass. "Drink."

She hesitates but brings the water to her lips. Once she's done, I gently cradle her face, planting the edges of my mouth onto hers. The delicate feel of her against me is like a lullaby pulling me into a heavy sleep.

Her hands return to gentle strokes down my chest. Then her eyes spot my bulging erection, and those long fingers trace the outline in my boxers.

"What about you?"

"When I get to have you, Avery, it'll be because you're begging for me."

Her eyes light up with amusement, and she curls her bottom lip, which is plumper than the top one, beneath the firm clench of her teeth.

"Just so you know, I don't beg."

"We'll see about that." I plant a tender kiss on her nose, like a butterfly landing gently on their favorite flower, and her mischievous stare is replaced with a resounding yawn.

My drowsy lioness.

I lift her into my arms again, and she easily wraps her limbs around me.

"It's the first door," she whispers.

I carry her into the bedroom and settle her on the covers.

"Luca?" Her voice is so gentle, the nuzzle of her forehead warming every inch of my insides. I slump into the bed beside her, pulling the colorful sheets over our bare flesh.

"Hmm?"

"This may be my favorite game."

I smile at the words and pull her closer to me. "Mine too."

Chapter 28
Avery

Luca Navarro is in my bed.

Avery: 1 | Luca: 1

I've long lost count of the scorecard I used to keep. But right now, I think we both deserve a point on equal footing.

I gently lift one of the seahorse-printed sheets wrapped around his large body and peek underneath.

A *naked* Luca Navarro is in my bed.

Avery: 2 | Luca: 1

Roaring heat works its way into my cheeks.

I guess that six-pack from college never went away.

Luca's arm reaches from under our shared covers, searching the bed for my body. I gently roll out from his seeking range, careful to not wake him from his deep slumber. I scoop up his abandoned shirt, pull on a pair of clean panties, and tiptoe my way into the living room.

I'm so glad I managed to keep my room clean since my last decluttering session.

Soreness still pillages my muscles after last night as I pull the oversized button-down over my body. Brief flashes of our unquenchable hunger replay in my head.

My body has never, ever been so gently dismantled and carefully put back together like that. He allowed me the freedom to let go beneath his touch, tethered to him as my safety net. Luca ripped waves of pleasure from my body as though they all belonged to him.

I stumble into the kitchen, but the feeling of his hands imprinted on my body follows me. The small bruise on my sore ankle is only a little tender from the night before. I fill the tall glass of water Luca gave me last night and chug the refreshingly cool liquid.

Lily's door is ajar, hanging in the same place it was last night, and I am thankful I didn't have to experience her confusing the delighted screams emanating from the apartment for a vicious murder.

My throat still burns from my loud cries.

A compelling urge to do something nice for Luca warms within me. I search my cabinets for a bag of coffee beans, but my luck runs short. Lily must have finished the bag yesterday.

I'm typically skilled in the kitchen, so I type *horchata recipe* into my phone's search bar and pull up a plethora of results. I scroll through each of them, searching for one that doesn't require the rice to be soaked overnight.

Okay, so this, most definitely, will not taste like the one we had last night.

Hopefully, he'll appreciate my attempt, especially since the drink made him so happy yesterday.

I do my best to collect most of the ingredients I *do* have and pull out the trusty blender I got from an estate sale three years ago.

The sweet smells of cinnamon and vanilla fill the kitchen. I try to substitute the soaked rice for the instant grain sitting in my pantry and replace the recipe's indication for evaporated milk with the remaining carton of oat milk in my fridge.

Okay.

Nerves settle in my chest.

This certainly won't be right.

But I cling on to my wish that this amateur version might be *sort of* not the worst thing in the world.

Before turning on the blender, I peek my head back into my room. Luca is sprawled out on my bed, making the queen-sized mattress look minuscule beneath his large body. My pillow is tucked below his shoulder. The messy sprawl of his hair warms me.

I could easily get used to seeing him like this.

I close the door behind me and hesitate when I return to the kitchen, not wanting to wake him. But the pang of hunger in my stomach is making me antsy for some sustenance.

It can't be that loud.

I press the button, and the ingredients begin to pulverize before my eyes.

Luca rips my bedroom door open and bursts into the living room. His face is priceless with bulging eyes and furrowed brows. My seahorse-printed sheet tied around his waist follows behind him.

Of course he came over when my very uncool bedsheets were on the bed.

My eyes widen at his erection so vividly on display. He catches me trailing down the deep V of his abs. His lips curl into a smile as he wraps another layer of the fabric around himself.

"What are you doing?" The sleepy texture of his voice quickens my heartbeat.

"Have you never been taught the words *good morning*?" I yell above the noise of the blender.

How long are the ingredients meant to be combined?

One of Luca's long arms stretches above him in a yawn before he leans against the tall rise of my kitchen island. "That's quite an alarm clock."

I expect there to be the familiar pause of awkwardness that comes after spending a night with someone, but it never comes. Instead, Luca towers in my kitchen, wearing my bedsheets, like this is any other weekend morning. As though he belongs here.

"A little noise never hurt anyone before," I tease, turning to the thrashing blender behind me, but I'm too slow.

Luca wraps himself around me, pulling my face close to his bare chest. "Quite the opposite."

The heat of his body is my favorite new feeling as my senses welcome him, the rich earthy scent of his skin causing my mouth to parch. The depth of his brown eyes reminds me so much of home, a comfortable feeling settles in my bones. Luca's gaze lands on me, and a smile splits across his handsome features. Without thinking, I lift to him, and our lips lock in a familiar embrace.

I don't think I've ever enjoyed kissing this much before.

"You taste even better this morning." The deep sound of his voice ripples within me, awakening the storm he let beat against him last night.

"Even if I haven't brushed my teeth?" I blush, peeling away from him.

Luca smiles and plants another kiss on me. "Even if you had no teeth to brush."

"That would've been good last night," I say. My fingers reach over to the curve of his lips, and I trace a faint bite mark. "Sorry about that."

He guides my fingers into his hand once more and gives them an affectionate squeeze. "I'm not afraid of some battle scars."

I want him to take me against this kitchen counter with a fist in my hair and prove how well I can take the hardness hiding under that sheet.

"Ave?" He pulls me from my daydream.

"Hmm?" I meet his tender gaze.

"I like your shirt."

I peer at his button-down swallowing me whole.

Before I can respond, the uncontrollable splutter of my blender pulls my attention from him. The small device crashes wildly against the kitchen counter. I shut it off, and silence returns to my apartment.

Luca takes a seat at one of the stools lining our small island. I pour the creamy liquid through a strainer and into a clean glass. There's only enough for one serving, so I hope the recent desire to share drinks hasn't left him.

I turn to place my attempt at horchata on the kitchen island. Luca is engrossed between the pages of one of the romance novellas Lily keeps stacked on the counter, his grin peeking from behind the sexy cover of a muscular man holding a wrench. The title spells out *The Loose Screw*.

I really hope he's not reading one of the intricate sex scenes that Lily described to me only a few days ago.

He notices me watching him and lets out a chuckle. "I should take this home with me. It has some very creative uses for a showerhead I'll need to test out."

"Keep it. Lily keeps bringing home duplicates," I say, pushing the drink in front of him. "We have so many Zoe Mona novellas. I'm sure we could start a revolution with them."

Luca nods firmly and puts *The Loose Screw* back on the counter.

Turning back to me, he looks from the drink to my grin. "Now, what's this?"

"Something I really hope you're going to like," I say.

Baking skills don't fail me now!

"You've managed to pour me a glass of you?" He leans his

forearms onto the counter, those gorgeous, veiny forearms that will be the death of me, pulling his upper half over the island.

"Have you always had a way with words?"

"Yes, I'm glad you've finally noticed." His face nears mine. He softly kisses me. A ridiculously happy grin tugs at my face.

Is this what it would feel like to be around him all the time?

He sits back down and takes a huge gulp from the glass. Luca's throat bobs as he swallows. A tight smile lines his face, and he hands the glass back to me, nodding.

After a few beats of silence, I ask, "So, how is it?"

"*So* good."

Enthusiasm thrums through me. I take the glass, my lips pressing to where his were just moments ago, and sip the concoction. The thick, starchy substance coats my tongue, the burn of cinnamon and granules of sugar ruining my palate.

This is fucking awful.

I flip over to the sink, running the faucet on my tongue, trying to wash away the grainy texture from my mouth. Luca's laughter booms through the kitchen at my catastrophic failure, and I shoot him a glare.

"Can I ask what exactly you attempted to make?"

"Horchata," I confess. The mixture tasted nothing like the delicious drink we shared last night.

"*Why?*"

My cheeks flame with embarrassment. "I wanted to do something for you that would make you smile like yesterday. Ugh! I shouldn't have tried to wing a recipe you're familiar with."

"I appreciate that you wanted to do something nice for me. Next time, I'll teach you the real recipe and we can prepare it together." He chuckles lightheartedly. "Also, Horchata is not typically a breakfast drink."

"I'm sorry." My shoulders slump in defeat. "Why didn't you just spit it out?"

"You just looked so ravishing, standing there with your

happy grin." He wraps his large hands around mine. "Be honest." His voice is commanding. "Did you need a sugary refill after all the fun last night?"

My heartbeat pulses loudly in my veins. "In case you've already forgotten, I made it for you."

"Everything that was made for me is already here." Luca guides me to him from across the counter. "Besides, I don't think I'll ever get tired of you doing something nice for me even if your typically praised cooking skills failed you tragically this time."

He smiles. Luca's thick, muscular legs part when he pulls me into his embrace again.

"I didn't realize you were such a big softie." I tease.

"Only with you," he says plainly, as though the truth doesn't surprise him.

His palms cup my cheeks, and his lips press to mine. His shaggy scruff pleasantly tickles my skin. The temperature in my kitchen begins to swell.

No matter how many times I kiss this stunning man, it feels unnervingly familiar yet like the first time.

There will eventually come the last time, too. I try not to think about it.

Instead, I drift into him while my body reacts to his touch. The aching tenderness returns between my thighs.

A loud throat-clearing fills the room, and the front door clicks closed. I instinctively pull myself from his grip, taking a step back.

"Lily?"

My best friend comes into view. An uncontrollable cheeky grin is cemented on her face.

I glance at Luca, who is sitting on a dainty stool wearing nothing but a toga of my sheets. I am dressed in his crinkled shirt from yesterday. My eyes try to communicate an urgent message to him: *DO NOT SAY ANYTHING. DO NOT SAY ANYTHING.*

"Nice to see you again, Lily." Luca breaks the awkward silence and rises to his feet, the seahorse-printed sheet held firmly in his hand.

"I'm glad Avery finally brought home a replacement for her vibrator." Lily gives me an exaggerated wink.

"Vibrator?" Luca turns to me, a wicked grin across his face.

What is happening?

"It's pink with rainbow sparkles." Lily dashes into her room, and I could disown her right here.

My palms envelop my heated face.

Luca walks past me and makes his way to the fridge. "I didn't take you for someone who likes sparkles."

I roll my eyes. "What are you doing?"

His toothy smile peeks up from behind the door. "I need to feed some energy back into you."

He pulls out a stick of butter and a half-empty can of peaches from my attempt at a cobbler a month ago.

My face scrunches at the combination.

"Did someone rob you of your groceries?"

"I don't really have the time to shop, cook, or plan for meals when I spend most evenings at the office with you," I admit.

"Understandable." He puts the items back into the fridge. "But since we have to eat something, let's go to my place. I'll make you breakfast."

My heart collapses into my stomach. The offer is so simple. Normal. Breakfast at his place. As though we've been rotating weekends together for months.

"Is your brother going to be there?"

Does he even want me to meet his brother?

"He's out of town. But if you want, we can get dinner with him next week."

I smile. Luca wants me to meet his family. He's spoken so highly of Nico that I can't wait to meet him.

"I'd like that." I walk back into my room, and Luca follows.

"But before we go, you *must* tell me. Does your apartment have a temperature-controlled room dedicated to your suits? I don't want to be surprised."

"Obviously it does." A hint of sarcasm ripples off him, causing me to laugh, and his palm lands softly on my ass in a firm but gentle smack. "We can have something similar made for your living room. Otherwise, I won't be able to leave my clothes here."

I snicker at the ridiculous suggestion, though glistening happiness multiplies through me at the thought of his things occupying my apartment.

THE WALK across town to Luca's apartment turned into a mini-workout as we trudged through the persistent early autumn heat. My shirt clings to me when we enter the expanse of his home. We take off our shoes, and Luca stacks them neatly by the door while I make my way around the space.

The corner unit is lined with floor-to-ceiling windows. A plush gray couch sits in the middle of the living room, facing downtown New York. I imagined his space feeling cold. In reality, art clings to the walls. There are bookshelves filled with souvenirs and picture frames. He even has throw pillows.

The kitchen is breathtaking. The space is marvelously large and adorned with stunning granite countertops *and* a stove with *six* burners.

How fancy!

"It's beautiful here." I turn to face him, and he watches me trace my fingers over his things.

"It's definitely the best it's ever looked now that you're here."

My fingers knot together. "Is it alright if I take a quick shower? The walk over here was hotter than I expected."

"You don't have to ask." Luca nudges his head down the hall, and I follow him past the two other rooms until I step into his large bedroom.

There's a king-sized bed with crisp, white sheets tucked neatly into the mattress. Two wooden A small collection of shelves on one of the walls displays an assortment of books and photographs.

I follow Luca through his closet that leads to the bathroom. He stops at a large dresser and pulls out a fluffy towel, nicer than some of the fancy hotel towels I've seen in my day. He hands it to me, and we continue our journey into a spotless bathroom with a soaking tub. A massive, giant, full-sized tub. The bathtub in my apartment can barely fit my body if I fold my legs to my chest. This is something else!

"You take baths?" I say, eyeing the assortment of soaps lining the walls.

"Rarely." He switches on the hot water, and it begins spilling into the porcelain tub. "But you might enjoy it after last night."

"I definitely will."

Luca touches his lips to the crown of my head. "I'm going to make us something to eat."

Five minutes later, he returns with a bowl of strawberries and grapes before leaving me to soak in the fragrant bubbles.

A hot bath and a gorgeous man feeding me. *Does it get any better than this?*

"If you leave me alone in here, I'll go through your stuff," I call out.

"I wouldn't have expected any less." He stops at the door and smiles. "I have a collection of tees for you in my closet, and all my dirty secrets, similar to yours, are in my bedside drawer."

"You own an actual T-shirt?" I laugh.

"I won't spoil the surprise." He walks out of the bathroom.

I strip and get in the tub, then lose track of time soaking in the warm bubbles. Luca's aromatic soaps tickle my senses as I massage each of my sore limbs in the warm water, replicating his touch on my skin.

I exit the bath, wrap myself in the plush towel, and put on the pair of underwear I was wearing. My clothes are too damp, so I hunt for a clean tee to replace mine.

I return to the walk-in closet. Now that I'm alone, I realize that this space is the size of my bedroom. My mouth drops open as I take in the floor-to-ceiling windows overlooking the city. *This is a dream.*

A truly impressive collection of suits hangs from the racks on the right side of the wall, all in differing neutral shades. I am mystified at how many are here, I can barely count them all. The neatly embroidered tags have names I've never heard of before: Alexander Amosu, Dormeuil, Savile Row. I try to remember them so I can look them up later.

Beside the suits, his neatly pressed button-downs are draped over hangers. Followed by a backlit wall of ties.

Yes.

An actual wall of ties.

There must be hundreds of ties here. I reach over to touch them, and delicate silk wraps around my fingers.

So that's what one of these things feels like.

What would it feel like to have Luca wrapping one of these ties around my skin?

A rush stirs inside of me.

I stroll over to the wall of drawers stacked neatly beside the racks. The opposite wall is mostly desolate, with only a couple of shirts hanging there.

This is the cleanest closet I've ever seen. My closet is lucky it can shut right now and isn't pouring out all over my room. The fact that my bedroom was clean-*ish* when he spent the night is a miracle.

Maybe he can organize my closet. Then I would always be able to find what I want to wear. But I like a little bit of clutter.

I have the sneaking urge to rearrange everything, just to see if it would get under his skin. Finding my way beneath that rocky exterior has been one of my favorite parts of the past few months.

After sufficiently snooping through his drawers, I finally find the very small collection of T-shirts. With the holidays coming up, I will definitely buy Luca a hefty stack of tees. I pull the softest one from the drawer, the faded logo putting a smile on my face. *Trash Titans.*

I leave the closet to make a stop at the drawer of dirty little secrets.

My bare thighs meet Luca's cool sheets, and I want to crawl into his bed right now, dissolve into the smell of him. I pull open the right bedside drawer and rummage through it. Disappointment settles over me at the false advertisement—there's nothing juicy in here.

One tube of hand cream, one phone charger, and a couple of loose sticky notes. I pick up one of the papers and peer at the miniature doodle on it.

I flip it over and see a date written on the back. It's the first week Plastech started working at the ORO offices.

This is from months ago.

I stare at it, cemented into the confines of my own skin. My fingers trace the blunt edges of the paper as an anchor collapses into me.

Heavy, solid, familiar.

My breathing catches between my steady inhales. I feel as though I'm encased in marble, unable to move.

Luca has been collecting pieces of me before I could even accept being around him. Before I let myself unravel my stubbornness and discover what it's like for us to settle into the same side of a fight.

I'm anxious to find my way back into Luca's arms.

I unwrap the towel on my head as I walk back to the bathroom. Freeing my dried waves onto my shoulders, I return the towel to a hook hanging off the bathroom door, then peer around his closet one last time. My attention snags on a stack of brightly colored boxes nestled in the corner by the dresser. They sit unusually out of place in the neatness.

Why didn't I notice these before?

I struggle with my urge to peek inside them.

You've snooped enough already!

No secret dungeons, no robotic suits dangling from racks, no relics of past girlfriends.

But the elegant decoration of one of the packages draws my attention. I bend down, my hands pulling the boxes out of the nook.

A barricade quickly builds around my feelings as I inspect the garments. My heart leaps from the pit in my stomach, now thrumming wildly in my chest.

I peek into each box and pull out different pairs of stretchy shorts and leggings and a few training tops in a variety of pastel colors. A small box contains what appear to be scrunchies, the silky material burning in my hands.

What the fuck is this?

I stack the boxes in a fury then gather up every single piece of the vile evidence. What kind of inconsiderate jerk keeps women's clothes in their apartment when bringing another woman home?

I storm into Luca Navarro's annoyingly neat kitchen. *Why does it need to be this spotless anyway?*

My feet pummel into the floor until I come up behind him, tossing the clothes and boxes onto the counter beside the point-lessly large stovetop. My gaze immediately betrays me when it scans across his naked torso and lands on the very, um, sizeable bulge in his gray sweatpants.

Seriously? That's what he's wearing when I'm about to tear his head off. What the fuck does he even have in there?

I want to yell in frustration.

"You've returned from your snooping." Luca peers down at me with a grin before his attention returns to the hot pan.

Oh, how I want to grab that pan right by the handle and whack him right here.

"Why is there an abundance of women's clothing in your room?" A prickling rips up my spine as I wait for him to answer. My foot taps wildly on the white tile.

He chuckles. "If that's what you call an abundance, then we're going to have to have a serious talk—"

"Answer me." This was not a time for his incessant teasing.

"About the clothes…" Luca turns off the stove, pulling the pan off the heat to face me.

I shift my weight from one leg to the other. The roaring in my chest plummets into an avalanche.

Okay.

Fuck!

Okay.

No damage done.

I could try to believe that.

Just a game we're playing. Our silly, little games.

"I've had my eye on someone for a little while," Luca says slowly, his eyes flickering toward the clothes and back to me.

His face is unreadable.

Is that a shred of guilt on his insufferably attractive features?

"And she's fucking extraordinary."

The pan feels so close right now as my fingers roll into fists.

Inhale. Exhale.

Inhale. Exhale.

"But now that—"

I cut him off, unable to bear the next words coming from his mouth. "If you're just going to—"

One of Luca's fingers finds itself on my lips, and I bite it. He doesn't even yelp. A hint of a dimple curves into his smiling cheeks, which does nothing to dull the panic bubbling within me. My teeth reluctantly unclench around his finger, and he returns his hand to the assortment of boxes.

"But now that she's here, I finally get to tell her she's a running hazard."

My neck cranes back and my brows furrow into a pointed pinch. Luca unwraps one of the packages I didn't have a chance to open, revealing a shiny pair of brand-new white running shoes that match the ones he wears, in my size.

"What?" I say.

"I'm not a fan of dismantled sneakers." He kneels, then takes one of my feet into his large palm and slides the cushioned sneaker onto it. The padded mesh fits perfectly.

"I do warn you, though, this woman of mine just revealed a bit of a jealous side." He smiles. He leans down to slide on the other shoe. His hands on my leg jolt me back to last night.

I wiggle my toes inside my new sneakers.

Luca straightens, and his lips kiss each heated point of my flesh: my cheeks, my nose, my lips. I want to give in to the warmth each affectionate touch elicits, the way it heats something beneath my belly, but I don't falter.

"How did you know I'd find them here?" There's *no way* he got these specifically for me. Even if the shoes *are* my size.

"I didn't. You're the first woman I've ever brought home. But over the past couple of weeks that we've worked together, each time I purchased something for myself, I couldn't help but think about you and your uncharacteristically poor athletic fashion sense."

The first woman he ever brought home? The past couple of weeks?

He smiles.

"There's no one else but you, Ave." An overwhelming wave of emotions washes through me, and I want to reach out and curl myself into his embrace.

Instead, my fist meets his muscular chest.

I feel ridiculous. Luca spent weeks taunting and teasing me as though his sole purpose in life was to get under my skin. Instead, he's been chipping away at my hard exterior.

"Ow!" Luca feigns injury but keeps grinning. "What was that for?"

Luca takes a few hits without the slightest dent in his posture before he wraps his hands around my waist and throws me over his shoulder.

Why does he have to be the frustratingly strong, handsome, annoying affliction that causes my head to spin on my shoulders?

Ah!

"Stop messing with me!" I shout.

"*Never.*" His palm meets my ass, and I yip. The short sting of my flesh turns warm. The heat between my thighs returns beneath the wave of panic.

Blood rushes to my head as I hang upside down. I kick my feet into the air, beating my fists on his backside.

"Is this what it's going to be like with you? A temper that needs constant taming?" His voice comes from above me. His other arm has my new workout clothes. He carries me toward the bedroom.

"Yes. Now, put me down!" I yelp, my annoyance turning into a fit of laughter.

Luca carries me into his closet and sets me down in front of the empty racks opposite his suits.

"Luca?" I hesitate for a second.

"Hmm?" Luca faces me, and an unsettling need runs through me for him, who is now folding the running gear and setting it into an empty drawer.

"Just in case you were wondering, there hasn't been anyone but you also…"

His body rotates toward mine, and he kisses me. I smile on his tender lips, feeling so unbelievably happy.

"Now your things finally have a place in our closet instead of those boxes." He says it so casually that I don't think *he* even heard what left his lips.

"*Our* closet?" I say, trying to play off the way my heart steadies at his words.

"Yes," Luca says.

The confidence in his tone straightens my spine.

Simply yes.

No consideration. No explanation.

The space we occupy is suddenly mine.

Ours.

"You're convinced that I plan on coming back?" I bait him, trying to remove the serious tone from his teasing voice. My own emotions are still trying to resist his intentions. Not because I don't want him but because I want him too much.

"Yes," he says as though it were obvious. "You can do what- ever you want in here."

The hardwood floors suddenly feel like the moving deck of a ship.

Is this what trust feels like? Simply waking up one day and

realizing the person you wanted to throw off a cliff would jump with you? I want to feel a release with him, and something wild inside of me begs to be tamed.

"Then, can I do this?" I drag the words out slowly. I knock the new sneakers off my feet and toss them into a messy bundle on *my* side of the closet.

"If that's how you like to store your things." Luca has long abandoned the folding. Instead, he stands there, watching my every move. "Then yes."

There is a familiar challenge in his voice, causing my common sense to surrender to the promise of something reckless brewing between us.

I pull a piece of clothing from the drawer and drop it on the floor. "What about this?"

"I told you, Ave." His voice deepens with each word. I reach out to touch him, and he caresses my fingers with his mouth. Electricity crackles in my navel. "Everything in here is for you to do with as you please."

"Everything?" My lips curl at the offer I was previously hesitant to accept.

I never truly explored my own greedy fantasies, knowing no man would be a match for my raw desires. But with Luca, I want to experience what it would be like to collapse into him, surrendering every carnal part of me.

"What do you want, Ave?"

I know with every molecule of my being that I can ask Luca to rearrange the ground beneath my feet and he wouldn't hesitate to do it. So I don't hesitate to tell him the truth.

"You."

Chapter 29
Luca

A<small>VERY</small> <small>CONTINUES</small> <small>TO</small> <small>WREAK</small> <small>HAVOC</small> <small>ON</small> <small>HER</small> <small>SIDE</small> <small>OF</small> <small>THE</small> closet, a toothy grin across her features. Her mischievous eyes bring a smile to my own face. Normally, I'd be losing my fucking mind right now seeing the mess littering the floor.

But there is something far more interesting in my closet than the disarray.

I look at the woman I want to make mine as she moves those irresistible bare legs toward my wall of ties.

"Avery." My voice is low with warning like I've never heard it before.

"Luca," she challenges, then gathers a handful of my ties in her palm.

"Don't even fucking think about it."

But she's already dragging them off the wall in droves.

In an instant, I rip Avery from the ground and lift her body into my arms. Her laugh trails off, and I take the opportunity to adjust her thighs around my waist, her arms grabbing my shoulders.

She feels pliable in my hands. Exhilaration pounds through me, and the hazel of her eyes matches my anticipation. I feel on top of the fucking world watching this woman wait on my next move.

"I like it when you misbehave," I say, carrying her out of the closet and into the bedroom. "But I'm going to *truly* love making you obey."

At the words, Avery's lips meet mine, and our tongues return to their dance. My length throbs aggressively as I carry her to our bed. I gently settle her on the sheets. Her release yesterday isn't going to compare to the way she's about to come around my cock.

Avery doesn't wait to impatiently kneel before me on the mattress.

My fucking perfect goddess.

She could bring me over the edge right now with her stare. That current of arousal returns in another tempestuous wave. Her eager fingers reach for my sweatpants.

I intertwine our fingers. "Do you trust me?"

She laughs, her hand wriggling out of my grip, and makes for my waistband again.

"Avery?" My voice is stern.

She lets out a growl before her palm begins to stroke the fabric around my pulsating erection. I press the thickness against her hands. But once her fingers start tugging at the material, I take a step back.

"I trust you," she finally says, a scowl painted on her picturesque face.

The preciousness of those words sends fire through me. I'm almost willing to succumb to her and give her every last inch of me. But I shake my head and rein in some of my control, wanting to savor every tense second of this moment.

Her eyes roll into her head in frustration, and I relish the expression. Avery is needy, needy for me, and there's never been a demand I was so eager to satisfy.

"That look in your eyes will be the death of me." I take one of her pouty lips between my teeth. "I've dreamt about this for months, wondering what it would be like to feel you wrapped around my cock. How wet you would be for me."

"Then let me show you," she whispers, and her lips attack mine. Roughly. Furiously.

I pull out her grip because I almost lose it right here. "Be patient. I have a surprise."

"I like surprises."

"I know." I kiss her forehead quickly, and I walk to the closet. Leaving her for even a second feels like a crime against humanity.

When I return, two of my silk neckties are wrapped in my palm. And my Trash Titans T-shirt lies abandoned at the foot of the bed, her black panties beside them.

Avery welcomes me with every flawless inch of her exposed skin on our sheets.

I'll have to ask her to keep that tee on in the future if she's willing to truly give us a chance. I want to see her riding me in that thing and play out a hidden fantasy.

The wickedness returns to her eyes when she spots the ties, challenging me.

A merciless taunt takes her voice. "Can you not fuck me without one of those ridiculous ties?"

"I can fuck you every way you like, Avery." I make my way over to the bed, towering over her as she lies before me, shamelessly naked and on display. "Besides, we both know this is much more than a *fuck*, Avery."

Her cheeks flush. I delight in the blush I bring to her skin.

"What if that's all I want?" she teases.

"Too bad." I smile, and she mirrors my playful grin.

I know this is another game of ours, and I'm happy to continue playing it. I just hope that when she's ready, Avery will admit there's more here than our battles.

I climb onto the bed and lean over her. My hands return to

the spots I know to make her squirm. Avery spreads her knees in anticipation, revealing the wetness already pooling there.

I suck on one of her tender breasts, and she moans.

"Now that I've tasted you, Avery, *eres mía.*"

I grasp her wrists and drag her up the bed, her body not resisting a single one of my touches.

"What are you going to do?" she protests unconvincingly.

"Remember trust?" I remind her. "You loved coming around my fingers yesterday, I promise you'll love this too."

Avery's stare meets mine, and she hesitates with her next words, probably realizing that her smart mouth can take away the pleasure still awaiting her. Her supple curves beneath me are testing me. I want to spread her legs right here and drive my bare cock into her swollen center. Instead, I breathe her in and let the wetness between her legs grind into my thigh.

I wrap one of the ties around her left wrist, then secure her to the headboard.

Her eyes bulge at the new restraint. "I've never done *this* before," she whispers.

"Me either." I've never wanted to ruin one of my *precious* ties, but I would burn my entire closet down for her. "Only with you. Do you trust me, Ave?"

Her free hand relaxes into mine. "I want this."

She nods to me, and I continue. I gently grab her other wrist, which I also tie to the wooden headboard.

"Do you know what you're doing?"

"I've practiced." I connect her mouth to mine like two points on a map and pull my body above hers.

My gorgeous woman is splayed out before me, needy and at my mercy.

"When did you practice this?"

I travel down the length of her body. "Every time you mentioned my tie, I thought about how beautiful you would look like this."

I cover her curves with kisses until I return to my favorite place. "Every jab." Another kiss. "Every bet."

I trace the fingers of my right hand down her slit in soft, taunting strokes.

"Luca." A warning from her. Avery's hips begin to rock against me.

I laugh at her pointed stare. "Relax, *cariño*."

My fingers return to the familiar rhythm she enjoys on her clit.

I reach up and trace the other hand between each of her breasts, the hardness of her nipples rough against my palm. My touch grows more deliberate, drawing out her building pleasure.

"You're too good at that," she exhales. "It's too much —please."

Those familiar loud gasps fill our bedroom, and it's fucking music to my ears.

I slip two of my fingers inside her before curling deep into her core, my thumb keeping pace on her clit.

"I want you to come, Avery," I tell her. "I want your pussy to drench my fingers before I fill every inch of you with my cock."

The words flare something wild within her. That lovely fucking determination returns to her eyes as my rhythm picks up. Avery's restrained arms drag across the pillows.

"Luca." She keeps fighting her release, but I'm determined to get her there. "I can't."

I climb up her body and lace the hand working her breasts into her hair, bringing her forehead to mine. "I bet you can."

The challenge is her undoing. A piercing cry fills the room as her orgasm unfolds. The pulsing of her tight cunt around my fingers is extraordinary.

A sheen of sweat coats her body, and seeing her undone like this, forces a primal possession into my veins. I want to mark her as my own and have her do the same to me.

I remove my fingers from her and stand at the edge of the

bed. Through her intoxicated haze, Avery watches my hands travel toward the place she's been so eager to acquaint herself with. She traces my chest with her eyes, her mouth parting as my hands pull down my sweatpants, stripping myself bare before her.

Those pouty lips drop open at the sight of my thick length throbbing between us. My cock is the most rigid it's ever been, the swollen tip is dripping, begging to fill every inch of her. I catch Avery's eyes broaden.

"*Wow.*"

I laugh at her awestruck expression. "What, Ave?"

"I know you'd be big, but that's…" She stares more intent-ly. The pitch-black of her irises swallowing the hazel of her eyes.

"That's?" I wait for her to finish my sentence.

"Bigger than I imagined."

I suck in a breath, trying not to focus on the aching in my dick. I don't want this to end too soon. "So, we've both been thinking about this for quite some time?"

"*Yes.*" Her cheeks turn a deeper shade of red.

"Are you ready for me, my girl?"

"Very." She nods, and I walk over to the nightstand, my fingers reaching for a foiled wrapper in the drawer. Avery watches me intently, her lower lip trapped between her teeth.

"I'm on the pill." The words slip from her like a loose arrow, causing my heart to race. "And I'm all clear after my physical a few weeks ago."

Is this really fucking happening right now, or am I in some kind of fever dream?

"What are you saying, Ave?"

"I want all of you, I mean, *obviously* only if you—" She tries to hide her embarrassment in the pillows.

This shy and bashful side I've never seen before makes my pulse vibrate. I return to the bed and abandon the wrapper on the floor.

"I got tested after we kissed on the boat, and there hasn't been anyone since then," I say.

"On the *boat*?"

"Frankly, there wasn't anyone before then either, but—"

"You talk way too much, Navarro." A blaze lights up her eyes, tempting me.

She's so alluring in her restraints. I don't fucking know how I'm going to last inside of her.

"And *you* seem to fucking love it." I smile.

I close the distance between us, pulling my body over hers, my fingers taking her jaw and holding her face still. My cock probes the wetness dripping messily between her thighs.

"I *do* love it," she says, and a guttural groan leaves my throat.

Love.

That precious word escaping from her is the final straw.

Chapter 30
Avery

LUCA BRINGS HIS FINGERS TO MY MOUTH, AND I HUNGRILY LICK each of them before he returns to a steady rhythm on my swollen clit. The restraints intensify the sensation of another climax building within me.

How can I hate something and love it so fucking much at the same time? Maybe these ties do have a purpose.

I want him.

I need him.

He works my body so well, not missing a beat, and I feel myself easily giving in to his touches.

Luca lowers his face to mine and tenderly kisses me before whispering, "Remember when I said you'd beg for me?"

A moan erupts from me. *Is he fucking kidding right now?*

"That's not happening." I glower.

Luca stills entirely, and my body betrays me. I let out another irate groan as my hips follow desperately after him. I'm almost embarrassed at how unhinged I am. Yet, every inch of my body is most definitely begging for more.

"Last night, you seemed to want it a lot." My cheeks heat at the reminder.

"So what?" I tease.

"If you want to be fucked, Ave…" My favorite boyish grin morphs into something dark and tempestuous. "You're going to have to ask nicely."

No part of me wants to make this a game. I need him.

A demanding cry breaks from me, and reluctantly I spill the desire from my lips. "Fuck. Me."

My wetness sticks to the flesh of my thighs as I twist and turn in the tempting distance of his body. Luca takes one of his large hands to my jaw and grips me tightly. I want to feel his fingers around my neck instead. I gently pull at the bonds cursing the fact I can't reach down and stroke him.

He's driving me fucking wild.

"Like you mean it."

"Luca." I bite in an exasperated tone. He continues to hover above me, his large hand still cupping my face, and a devious expression drips across his features.

"Yes, *Avery?*" he says plainly.

"Mr. Navarro," I bite. "Please fuck me, very fucking hard."

There is no use playing coy. I ache for him.

Luca takes that as his cue to drive one deep thrust into me. A pleasurable sting throbs through me. I don't think I've ever been this full before. My walls convulse around him as he continues to edge into me. *I will take all of him.*

"Fuck, you feel—" Luca whimpers and sucks in another gasp against me. "Is this okay?"

I nod.

"You're fucking perfect."

When he finally reaches my hilt, I struggle to comprehend where he ends and I begin. The room starts to spin around me. I'm drunk with need.

I instinctively reach one of my hands for him, but the ties only constrict tighter around my wrist. He watches my struggle with a half smirk. It turns me on more knowing that he can do whatever he wants with me. But I trust him.

My body trusts him.

Luca drags himself out of me in a frustratingly slow motion.

"Please, Luca." I yank at the restraints again, hoping they'll give way. But he sends another hard thrust into my sopping wetness, and I melt beneath him.

"You say *please* so well." He smiles.

The resistant fight in me returns, but I give in. The way he knows me so well is unlocking every stubborn latch inside me.

"*Luca*," I let out an exasperated moan.

"Be patient, Avery," he demands.

Fuck me. Now. I want to scream it in his gorgeous face. But I'm unable to form sentences. The tension in my jaw begins to loosen. As if Luca can read my desperation, he breaks from the slow, tortuous strokes with another slam of his cock. The collision of his hips becomes more aggressive.

I wrap around him as though he were made just for me.

He must be.

"You feel like heaven itself, Ave," he says against my damp flesh.

I relish in the sound of the name I didn't allow him to speak for months. I was so fucking wrong. He should've been saying it the entire time. Especially when it sounds this good.

"Don't stop."

Luca's warm palm returns to my cheek, and he swallows each of my haggard moans with his kisses. The brutal pounding of our flesh is the only music in the room. My eyes sting with tears; the pleasure coiling in my core is becoming unbearable. I ache for him to give me my release.

His glazed eyes return to mine. "Say my name, Ave. I love it when you say my name."

"Luca," I moan.

"Just like that." His voice rumbles through me.

The praise flames my determination to bring him over the edge with me. Luca's free hand works its way down my thigh and bends the length of my right leg to his side, my knee tucked under his chest. His hand returns above me, slamming into the support of the headboard. The new position pushes him deeper into my core, his rigid cock hitting my most sensitive spot.

"Harder." I wince as Luca fills the depth of me again and again.

"I should've known you'd be as demanding when I fucked you." Luca pinches my bottom lip with his teeth. "You were quite needy when you rode my face."

The words heat my cheeks. "And *I* should've known you wouldn't be able to shut up."

"You want it, *cariño*." He smiles. "I can see how fucking wild it makes you knowing I'm obsessed with your pussy."

I do want it.

Luca Navarro knows me like the back of his gorgeous hands. His sweat drips across my flesh, and his words flood my core even more.

Instead, I whisper into his lips, "Show me how obsessed you really are."

The wave of my climax is on the brink, my walls milking each thrust of his hardness inside of me. But Luca does not relent.

As I approach the edge of my orgasm, he breaks pace on my clit and uses his fingers to release the tie securing my right wrist to the headboard. I immediately reach for his hand and fold both of my legs over the back of his thighs, pressing him deeper into me. His cock fills me with deliberate thrusts, and Luca refuses to break the thrilling claps even for a moment.

"Do you want me to fill this tight, pretty cunt with my cum, sweet girl?"

Luca pulls his heavy hand out of my grasp and peels his upper half away from me, not separating our connection. I watch how he kneels before me, his eyes scanning from my gaze to where he and I meet. The act is like a shock to my system.

Me and him.

Together.

He lands a soft smack against my pulsating clit with his fingers in a split second before returning his hand to mine.

That was so fucking hot. My mouth dries entirely, and all I can do is nod furiously.

The successive motions play out in front of me as though I'm barely lucid in my own body. I pull Luca's warm palm up to my throat and wrap his fingers around my flushed skin.

A wave of fire rushes through my blood that I didn't know was there. The tension in me rages in every molecule of my being.

"More." Another begging rasps from me. "Please, I need…"

Turbulence unravels in my body as he gently squeezes my neck. This is definitely the good kind of choking. A darkened haze begins to invade the edges of my vision. My toes curl, my body becoming more rigid in anticipation of my fall.

"Good fucking girl, Ave." The grip of his fingers tighten. "Look at you, taking all of me like I was made for you."

You are.

My scream rips through me, and I crash. My body vibrates with him, and my walls convulse around his thick length. Every undiscovered edge of my being shatters as his orgasm joins mine. Hot, thick cum fills me to the brim, and I love feeling absolutely inundated with him.

I'm still convulsing around him when he finally withdraws from my swollen center. His cum spills out onto my thighs. He drops his head to mine and plants soft kisses all over my face. I smile into him.

We fall somewhere into our haze. I don't know how long he holds my limp body in his warm embrace, but I drift to the sounds of our breathing. Our heartbeats sync.

Luca unties the remaining knot binding me to the headboard and sends kisses up the strained muscles in my arm.

"Luca?" I manage to say, but my words disappear off my tongue when my eyes meet his tender stare.

"I know," he says.

"Hmm?"

"You and me, Ave, is so much better than you versus me."

Chapter 31
Luca

"Listen here, Mr. Navarro, I'm beginning to think you brought me here to drain my remaining sanity, *not* to feed me breakfast as promised."

Avery straddles me, her hands pinning my arms overhead like hers were only minutes before. I am so fucking content with her never-fading smile. I wrestle beneath her grip and sit up, hugging her close to me.

"What are we going to do, Ms. Soko?" I tease, and she wriggles in my arms. "If we have a whole day ahead of us and you're already drained."

"Refuel," she laughs and takes a big bite out of my shoulder.

The lustful sting of her teeth on my flesh makes me want to throw her over my knee and land a firm palm on her bare ass.

"Was that enough?" I ask as she pulls away.

"Never!" she yells back, covering my arms in more tender nips.

My fingers tickle up her sides. A cackle of laughter escapes her until she finally worms her way out of my grasp and runs toward the closet. I savor her naked body before it escapes from view.

I follow after her, and we take a quick shower before finding our clothes. I pull on a clean pair of boxers and sweatpants while Avery digs through her new pile of clothes in the drawers.

"If I have a whole closet here, I better get some pajamas soon," she says, one of my button-downs finding its way back onto her slender shoulders.

"Personally, you wearing this is so much better than any pajamas." I stand over her, and my fingers fasten the buttons of the two-thousand-dollar shirt I bought during my second year at Douglas & Draper.

"I'm glad you finally understand that I have exquisite taste." She laughs and pulls on a pair of her new cotton shorts.

"Your taste has always been exquisite."

"What do you think?" She smiles up at me.

"The only thing that could make this better is if you take it off."

Avery laughs. "We'll eat first and then you can taste *me* later."

"You're the boss." I kiss her forehead.

Being with Avery is so much *more* than the way we mesh, *more* than the silence of the world around us when she speaks. The glistening joy in her eyes is something I want to see every day. When I'm around her, I feel the most happiness. For the first time, in a long time, the fragments of my worth reflect themselves in her smile, not in my career success.

I brush a stray blonde wave out of her face and take her hand in mine, leading her out our bedroom door. We walk to the kitchen and are greeted at the stove by Nico standing in nothing but a pair of mismatched socks and running shorts.

My running shorts.

"Nico? Why are you here?" He's supposed to be on a once-in-a-lifetime hiking trip in the Poconos.

"Hello to you too, bro." He spoons surely cold eggs into his mouth directly from the frying pan. "You know, I'm glad there was an actual person with you in that room because I don't think I want my virtual reality headset back after what I heard."

Nico can't resist trying to embarrass me. I absolutely deserve payback considering how many of his morning-afters I've spoiled. I can't help but share stories of that ridiculous stuffed frog he kept glued to his side all through his preteen years.

"Don't worry, we thoroughly disinfected it." Avery's voice chimes in from behind me as she joins my side. My grin widens.

I love the way she's wrapped in something of mine. She stands next to me, not a trace of hesitation on her features.

"Avery, this is my very annoying little brother, Nico."

Nico abandons our breakfast and walks around to greet her. "It's nice to finally meet you, Avery. I know Luca has probably told you so much about me, so I won't go into details."

Avery's eyebrow quirks up to me, feigning confusion on her face. "You never told me you had any siblings."

Nico laughs at the tinge of sarcasm in her voice, and she joins him, brushing away his extended hand in favor of a hug.

"I'm going to like you," Nico says to her and gives me an approving nod.

I think so too, brother.

"Which one of you is responsible for the decorations?" she asks. "The art here is beautiful."

"That would be me," Nico replies.

Avery walks around the living room until her eyes land on something on one of the shelves. She picks up a small horse figurine that Nico placed there.

"Is this from Sweden?"

"Yeah, how'd you know?" Nico smiles. He loves to talk about his travels, and since Avery's been around the world, it makes sense that she would too.

"I visited Stockholm as a kid, and my dad let me pick one out just like this." She sighs and bites her lip slightly. When her eyes meet mine, the expression vanishes.

I t TURNS out the pair of them are quick to form a friendship. While I make us a feast consisting of lots of cheesy scrambled eggs, avocado toast, and extra-large mugs of coffee at Avery's request, they sit together, yelling at the television. A loud video game plays on the screen, and their hands work the controllers to a pulp.

They have been at it for almost an hour, pulling me into their conversations as they attack animated figures they claim are their cursed enemies. Avery's gales of laughter fill my apartment. Her charming smile refuses to leave her face even as she yips when she shoots down an enemy.

I get a taste of what life should have been like all along. The sun drenching my living room is suddenly brighter, the tension in my body gone after the release with Avery.

She turns to me, and her messy hair trails behind her as she sends me a wink, followed by one of those needy looks at the sight of my bare chest. It makes me want to pick my brother up by the nape of his neck and throw him out of this apartment.

However, I—unlike my storm of a woman—am a patient man. I remember when I stayed celibate for my entire senior year of college to win a bet. Yet no bet could keep me away from her.

As if Avery can read my thoughts, she places one of her fingers onto her lips, her tongue giving it a slow lick, and blood instantly rushes to my cock.

The corners of my mouth lift slightly, and I bring the spatula down on the counter in a smack. She accepts the challenge with the burning flame in her eyes.

My brother turns to both of us. "Can you please stop the telepathic fucking right now? We're losing!"

Without hesitation, Avery returns her eyes to the screen, giving Nico a nudge with her shoulder. I join them on the couch, placing the assortment of food on the coffee table.

"I don't understand how you became such fast friends with my brother. It took you months to stop sparring with me."

"I've stopped sparring with you?" Avery asks.

"He loves being given a hard time," Nico says.

"I absolutely do not."

Avery laughs. "I should really bring Lily around sometime. I think we'd all have a great time together."

"Who's Lily?"

My voice is heavy with warning. "No."

Avery ignores me. "She's my best friend and my roommate."

Nico looks at me with a smirk, and I glare at him. There's no fucking way my brother is getting anywhere close to Avery's best friend.

"You know, it *is* regrettable we didn't meet much sooner," Avery continues. "Nico could've given me ammunition."

"I would've given you a huge warning about him," my brother says.

"Nico," I scold. *What is with him today?*

"Relax." His gaze doesn't break from the screen. "No sane woman should be kept in the dark about your unconscionable tie collection."

"Okay, right?" she chimes in. "Who needs over a hundred ties?"

"You *both* love my ties." I come to my own defense. "Because neither of you can stop talking about them."

"I'm sure Avery would love to borrow one when you attend one of your stuffy events together."

"If he could part with it for that long."

They giggle like children.

"Avery's already familiar with the fit," I say.

She shoots me a playful scowl, and I know I'll make her beg me to use another one on her later.

THE REST of the weekend passes in a lustful blur. Nico leaves Avery and me to the privacy of our apartment. We stuff ourselves full of meals we cooked together after I worshipped her body in the bath, on the floor of the living room, in my office, once against the living room windows, and on the granite countertops of the kitchen.

Having Avery be the first woman to join me in my space finally makes it feel like a home, laced with her sultry smell and the syrupy sound of her voice.

When Sunday evening finally rolls around, we share dinner in the kitchen before I let her escape from my clutches.

"Not trying to spoil the mood, but I've been dying to ask. Has the money I brought in this past month been making an impact?"

The sobering reality of returning to work tomorrow hits me. Neither of us has mentioned work all weekend. I haven't seen my phone since we walked into my apartment.

"You could never spoil anything," I say, reassuringly. "You've managed to help keep ORO afloat for a few more months."

The amount of fundraising capital Avery brought in is giving ORO the runway we need to start seeing profits from Ocean Tidy. We might be okay after all.

"Of course, I did." She laughs.

"I don't know if I've said this already, but thank you for being here for me," I say. "I really don't know how I could've navigated this without you."

"ORO still means the world to me, even after what happened with Joanna," Avery says. "Being able to get back to doing what I love has made me feel like myself again."

"It makes me happy to know you're happy." I give her a quick kiss on the cheek before clearing away our dishes.

The way her face lights up makes me certain that my initial desire to hire her as a development analyst was a smart one. But now that we've worked together for over two months, I know her talents would've been wasted at such an entry-level position. Avery deserves to stand at my side, the way she has been these past few weeks, and shine.

"You know, this is one of the first weekends in years that I haven't checked my email," I say.

"Me too!"

"We should try it more often," I suggest.

The words give me an unusual thrill of excitement. Is this what normal feels like? Sharing a life on the weekends with the people who make you happy?

After another hour, Avery is finally ready to call it a night.

"I should get going. Lily's probably filed a missing person's report since I haven't checked in with her."

I pull her into my arms again and hold her close. We stand together for a few moments before she wriggles out of my grasp.

"If I haven't made my intentions clear. You're it, Ave."

She hesitates and looks up at me beneath her dark lashes. "I—"

"I know you need to take some time." I take her hands in mine.

"I do."

"I'll go at whatever pace you want," I assure her.

A smile returns to her beautiful face. "Then, I'll see you tomorrow morning for our run?"

"I can't wait." I gently squeeze her fingers.

I waited for her this long, and now that I've shown her what it's like when we're together, I won't let her slip away from me again.

I cup her cheeks, giving her one last deep kiss to savor her taste before she leaves me in the sudden cold of my apartment.

I tidy up the mess we've left behind, and her explosion of clothes in our closet, and decide to catch up on some rest while I prepare for tomorrow. My phone screen greets me with pitch darkness, refusing to turn on after I pull it from the depths of my work bag. I can't recall the last time my phone died on me because of my neglect. I set it on the charger and wait for it to power on.

My head meets the pillow that now smells like Avery. I want to bottle the smell and keep it by my nightstand.

A rapid attack of loud notifications soon fills the room. Tightness forms in my chest. I sit up again and crane my neck over the screen.

Missed call after missed call from ORO's board members. An ascension of indiscernible text messages bombards my screen. My email strains under the growing list of unopened communications.

Did the board finally discover Jo's mistakes before we fully repaired them?

I scan the messages for any clues that can help me get ahead of the new crisis on my hands.

A subject line finally catches my eye:

INVITATION TO JOANNA BENBART'S FUNERAL

Chapter 32

Avery

LILY IS SITTING IN THE SUN-DRENCHED CORNER OF THE CAFÉ Luca usually frequents. I scan my head hoping to see him here, but my luck falls short. Lily's dark hair knotted in a messy bun, her focus directed at her laptop. Her eyeliner is painted into a thick cat eye today, and she's stained freckles on her nose. She doesn't see me come in.

I join the line, anxious for the warmth of coffee to fill my belly.

We're in the final month of the Ocean Tidy project for the Ellington Grant, and I've been focusing on the presentation. It seems ORO's saltwater issue has finally been resolved, and we've overhauled our testing data results.

Nerves still linger in me over what will happen after Willa reviews our completed project. Our work could create an incredible impact, saving the oceans from six million square kilometers of floating debris. Plus, there are the profits from the recycled material and what that could mean for ORO's future.

But I brush all that away, my mind drifting back to Luca.

I spent Sunday night helping Lily finish an essay for her upcoming midterm exam over a very large glass of wine. We only broached the topic of my worries about turning the games Luca and I play into something more. I still juggle his intentions in my mind. *You're it, Ave.* But the fear of missing out on my career in favor of caring for someone else has been slowly sending me into a spiral. But Lily was adamant about making sure I follow my heart, not just the rules I've created to keep myself on track.

"Hey, Lil." I join her at the snug table facing the busy street.

"Have you heard anything?" she asks, taking the coffee I bought only moments ago and pressing it to her lips.

Always straight to the point.

"Still nothing," I admit.

After the brief text exchange from Luca the night I got home, I haven't seen or heard from him in over two days. I missed him on the run yesterday.

I check my phone again and anxiously open our text thread, but the same messages still sit there.

LUCA

Urgent work meeting outside the city. I'll call when I can.

AVERY

Hope everything's okay. Let me know if I can do anything.

LUCA

I will, cariño.

"Let's walk through the situation." Lily pulls out a pen and her notebook. "Shall we?"

"It's honestly no big deal, Lil." I shrug it off, but the nagging feeling in my gut persists.

"You know, the last time I dated my coworker—"

"That wasn't your coworker, that was a man who wore a Grinch T-shirt unironically and played guitar outside your bar."

"So what? He was hot!" She laughs. "Anyway, I enjoyed

every single minute of it. Maybe you should give your boss a chance."

"He's most definitely *not* my boss."

"But don't you wish he was?" Lily gives me one of her signature winks.

I remember the way Luca ordered me around in bed and the thrill of doing what he said. It sends a familiar heat down my back.

"No," I lie, but the grin on my face gives me away.

"I'm reconsidering my career options if a *sexathon* is involved in the kind of work-life balance you've been receiving." Lily snorts.

"Well, now that you mention it"—I take a sip of my coffee—"there was a lot of balancing required during the majority of the receiving."

We snicker loudly.

I fill her in on some more of the raunchy details from the weekend. The memories are a welcome distraction from the worry building in me. After I recap the various uses we found for Luca's ties, Lily gasps.

"Who knew my little Ave is so kinky?" Lily's palms slowly clap together, building into a round of applause. A few people at neighboring tables gawk at us, and Lily meets them with a glare.

I giggle at the scene.

"Alright." Her laptop is now closed, and her eyes return to mine. "So why haven't you called your sexy suit? He clearly wants to be with you!"

"I'm giving him space," I say. "If I had a work emergency, I wouldn't want to be disturbed."

The words do little to soothe the pang of concern in my chest. I know everything is probably fine, but with ORO's uncertain financial issues, I worry something serious happened. Either way, when Luca was ready to bring me in, I won't let him deal with it alone.

Luca Navarro.

I smile at his name.

"Ave, just take the risk and reach out," Lily says. "Not everyone is like you."

"Luca is."

Lily sighs. "Then you're lying to yourself if you think you'd want to be alone during an emergency."

The words hit me, and my muscles tighten at her words. "You don't need to be right all the time, you know?"

"I do." She smiles. "I know you're used to denying yourself some much-needed companionship. Other than me, of course. We both have worked our entire lives trying to fulfill these expectations of ourselves. But it's okay to bring someone along for the ride—that's how we found each other."

"Lil, you're gonna make me cry."

I'm so thankful for my friendship I have with Lily, who is like the sister I always wanted. If I managed to let Lily in and trust she wouldn't ever abandon me, maybe I could do the same for Luca.

Just *trust*.

"Maybe it's okay to admit you don't need to spend your days with only vibrator-induced orgasms."

"Lily!" I laugh, though my eyes now burn with tears.

The past few months have shown me I'm more than my career. The dream I shared with my dad, to become an activist like Joanna Benbart, hasn't changed. But I can have a life of my own too.

Since coming to terms with Joanna's rejection, I realized I only idolized her because it felt like keeping the memory of my dad alive. But everything he taught me, to care for the world and inspire others will never change. It'll be a part of me for the rest of my life, and I'll share it with others.

The friends I have found along the way—Matthew, Robert,

Ollie, Molly, even Hana and Jamie—have helped ground me to myself even while we've tried to change the world together.

And of course, there's Luca.

The person who challenges me and approaches me as his equal.

Luca, who could have been a prolonged adversary, became my partner.

My partner.

The words feel so safe inside my mind.

Why am I sitting here hesitating?

I spent months learning exactly how to make Luca Navarro answer me. And I'm not going to change now.

"I'm going to call him on my way back to the office!"

Lily is already on her feet. She busses our coffee cups to the counter. I pack up her things into her tote, putting her sticker-clad laptop between the stacks of Zoe Mona novellas she carries around.

I'm beginning to wonder if she just hands these out to people.

We barely make it out of the cafe when I get a call from Matthew.

"Hey, Matthew, I'm heading back now. Did Robert change his mind about the coffee?" I say as Lily and I walk down the sidewalk.

"Hey, Ave. Not sure if you checked your email, but you don't need to come back to the office for the rest of the day."

"What? Is Plastech okay? Is ORO okay?" Worry is thick in my voice.

Luca would've told me if ORO was shutting down, *wouldn't he?* I freeze, waiting for Matthew's response. Lily's worried expression mirrors mine.

"Yes, everything's fine. Umm. I mean…" He pauses. "Ave, I'm sorry to be the person to tell you this, but Joanna died this weekend."

My watch clasp snags my skin as I lower my phone from my

ear. My thoughts attempt to piece together the news while an abyss breaks into me, sinking into my bones.

Lily pulls the phone from my hand and takes over the call with Matthew. Loud ringing screeches in my ears.

"The funeral is Friday. They emailed the details to everyone," she says, hanging up the call and tucking my phone into my tote before pulling me into a hug.

The tears I expect don't come.

Joanna Benbart, CEO of the Oceanic Research Organization. Legendary environmental activist. My dad's idol. The person whose life's work shaped the path I am on today.

Gone.

Joanna's the second person I've lost. Yet, what I'm feeling right now doesn't even compare to how I felt when my dad died. Instead, it's a dull ache invading the gaping hole where the pain of his loss still lives within me.

I want to reach into the hollow sadness inside me. Grasp the girl trapped amid the wreckage and pull her into an endless embrace like Lily is doing to me right now.

Instead, I pull out of her warm grasp and stand in the middle of the striped crosswalk, a nagging itch at the top of my stomach.

Lily studies my face. I can feel her eyes trace every crease, anxiously trying to read my expression. A car honks at us, and she throws her middle finger at him before wrapping one of her arms around me and guiding me back to the curb. She's been here with me once before, the only witness to how I handle death.

When my dad died, I mended the pieces of him that clung to me, ensuring they would never rip away from me. I constructed the memories of him into the force that propelled me through life.

Right now, my thoughts are overwhelmed with muddled feelings about Joanna. Not only did she impact my life, but she influenced a generation of people who will continue to enact change on her behalf.

I wish the memory of her wasn't tainted by our few interactions. Especially now that I understand so much of her anger probably came from ORO's instability. If I'd been in her shoes on the day I walked into her office, I also would have indulged in my short fuse if the thing I loved were falling apart.

But Joanna inspired me, she made me want to become a better person, and that is how I hope to remember her. Her death is a dull sting in my chest, like salt on a wound that never healed. A wound I knew I could plan around, build around, and pull away from so it wouldn't break me.

"I'm so sorry, Ave." Lily pulls me into another hug.

"Do you think he knows?" I finally manage to say.

"Luca?"

I nod. Luca knows the impact Joanna created in my life.

If Jo passed over the weekend, was he aware this entire time? Did he not trust me enough to tell me? Why would he keep this from me?

"It wouldn't change anything," Lily pulls me from my thoughts. She knows I'm already searching for a way out of the commitment I want to make to him.

A large part of me wants to sink into my familiar and safe solitude.

But Luca has started to mean too much, too fast. Life can have a way of feeling like a bad dream. I just thought Luca would be here to help pull me from a nightmare.

Chapter 33
Luca

A BRISK WIND WHIPS AT MY FACE AS I AWAIT THE PROCESSION. The chairs lining the small green hill overlooking the Atlantic are crammed with activists, colleagues, business partners, and donors. Some guests wipe tears from their swollen eyes. Others flock around in their raven attire, silently squawking beneath the cloudy sky.

The high tide rocks against the cliffside, dulling out the rumor-filled whispers coursing through the crowd.

Who will take over for Joanna?

Will ORO dissolve?

What will happen to the contributions people already sent in this year?

Is the board already interviewing for the CEO?

Acid pricks my throat.

The Benbart Estate refused to greenlight the news of Joanna's cardiac arrest for days, giving me time to fix things.

I made the late-night drive to the edge of Long Island on Sunday night. The board immediately entered into back-to-back sessions to crisis manage the future of the Oceanic Research Organization. It didn't take them long to find the financial gaps

Joanna had been covering up, even with the money Avery and I brought in.

I used my growing influence at ORO and the fundraising work I've been doing with Avery to repair Joanna's financial mistakes. It took a while but I convinced the board not to dismantle the organization.

There was little argument from the members when they understood how much capital the new strategy we've developed could bring in.

I also pushed forward the approval of the merger between Plastech and ORO, under the stipulation that Willa awards us the five-million-dollar Ellington Grant. This way, all the profit the Ocean Tidy project could generate can be used to help ORO as well as sustain the expansion of Plastech's small-community projects.

Yet stomaching Joanna's funeral without Avery has been the worst part of the past few days. I need her at my side, standing tall with me as I face the interminable expanse ahead.

I stretch my neck, scanning the crowd for her familiar face, but I don't see her in the throng of people. Everyone at ORO was invited to the funeral, and I hope she'll meet me here today so I can apologize.

I should've called her the instant I found out the news and brought her with me on the trip here.

I didn't call her because I couldn't lie to her, even though I'm certain Avery would never betray my trust. I simply didn't have the heart to explain why I needed the space to process the emotional and operational nightmare the past few days have been.

Still, I should have found a moment between the back-to-back meetings to send her a message. Regret weighs down my exhausted mind.

In the distance, the procession finally rolls in, making the sluggish drive down the cliffside highway.

Molly joins the empty chair beside me, her eyes sullen from the draining day, and I pass her the handkerchief from the chest pocket of my suit.

Charles Benbart sits in a wheelchair near the stage with two nurses. A huge blanket is draped over him, protecting him from the crisp wind. His elderly body shivers. I hope his presence today means Joanna took the time to resolve their issues before she passed.

The sound of many bodies standing is quickly replaced with the voice of an elderly woman standing before the crowd.

"When I was seventeen years old, Joanna taught me an important lesson that I want to share with you today." The woman adjusts her eyeglasses before continuing to read from the note card. "In the thick of her youth, she told me the world we want to create requires an iron-clad exterior and an endless well of hope—because no one would care about our beautiful planet, our home, until it's too late."

Molly's body shudders with a sob, and I drape my arm over her, steadying my friend.

The woman's voice grows, waves of emotion bursting through every word. "Joanna, I promise all of us here will not forget to care. We'll not buck at the challenges ahead. We'll not soil the impact your determination made on the world that remains here, waiting for us to seize the reins of change."

Change.

In the end, Joanna's cynicism was her downfall, with her thinking ORO couldn't be saved. That we couldn't make an impact. The most important thing I've learned over the past two months is that she was wrong. Joanna inspired droves of people to believe in something bigger than themselves.

Her privilege distorted her understanding of the impact she created, refusing to acknowledge that ORO's sustainability didn't need to come from her own hands. Instead, ORO survived for countless years because others believed in Joanna's mission.

We've all come together to make a lasting impact, and each of us has contributed to the bigger picture.

I've never felt prouder to be part of a team. My law days were filled with isolation and silly hierarchy that deprived me of a community at work.

My old career stole weekends from me, like the one I had with Avery, and kept me at arm's length from the people I cared about. I've been able to put that behind me, embracing the drive for my new job.

Joanna lost sight of the impact her actions truly made, and I refuse to do the same. As I stand here witnessing person after person speak on the influence she had on their lives, I am reminded of why I joined ORO.

It's because of people like Molly, who never wavered through the worst of Joanna's hell, relentlessly believing in a woman who dedicated her life to saving the planet's oceans.

People like Matthew, who risked failure so they could leave behind something meaningful for future generations.

People like *my* Avery, who are driven by the pure will to continue to convince others to stand up for what is right in the world, even when most of us can barely look away from ourselves to care about anything else.

Joanna built a generation of those who will take over her fight.

And I'll stand beside them.

The memorialization comes to an end, and guests disperse to their vehicles or to pay their final respects.

I walk Molly to her car before heading back to the hotel, unable to stomach a three-hour drive to the city right now.

"You sure you don't want a ride back?" she asks.

"I could really use the walk."

"I know what I'm about to say will be hard for you to hear, but try to let yourself grieve, at least for a day." Molly opens her car door and gets in. "I'll field the calls and draft your CEO announcement—"

"Molly, thank you," I say before she sends herself down a spiral of tasks. "Get some rest, and we'll catch up in the morning."

I say my final goodbyes to a few people in the parking lot, beginning the long walk back to the hotel, when I see *her*.

Avery sits on the hood of a car, legs pressed to her chest, as she searches for something in the crowds of vehicles. She wears a thick knitted sweater and a dark pair of jeans. I instantly calm at the mere sight of her. Dread is replaced with a need to wrap her into my arms, melding us into one.

When her eyes finally land on me, an exhausted smile lights up her features. It's in this moment, with the salt air breezing through her hair and that committed gaze unwavering from me, that everything finally clicks into place.

You're it, Ave. My own words echo in my mind, and I've never been more certain of the truth.

I spent the better part of my adult life missing out on deeper connections. I chose my career over finding something with meaning. Surviving only on the love my family would share with me and the rush of my overworked lifestyle. But I never tried to find someone to share my life with.

I realize now that it's not because I had no time for love.

But simply that I never found a love that tastes like *her*.

A love that smells the way she does after a run. A love that curves its eyebrow when it's curious. A love whose temper builds like a storm. Love never held me at its mercy: willing, wanting, needing.

Until her.

She glides off the car's hood and sits in the driver's seat, leaning over to where I stand.

"Get in," she says.

Chapter 34
Avery

My fingers run through the gritty sand. Luca sits beside me near the coastline, the waves bringing thick, white foam to our feet with each wipe of the tide. He hasn't veered out of my line of sight since we exited the rental car I drove here to see him.

Three hours spent behind a wheel, trudging down a straight highway, gave me enough time to perfect the confession of my feelings for him, which I'd planned to give when I arrived. But now that we're together, I drift to the sound of the jagged waves, unable to piece together the words; they're misplaced inside me like scattered Scrabble tiles.

Luca's fingers find their way to mine, interlocking in an unbreakable grip. Magnificent bursts of reds and oranges are reflected in the depths of his eyes, which are wrinkled from exhaustion, as the sun mellows out the remainder of the day.

Luca breaks the silence between us.

"I need to tell you the full extent of my work on the oil case."

"You don't have to do that right now," I assure him but deep down, I'm curious.

"No," he explains, "I know we need to trust each other. I

need you to understand everything that happened and then decide if *us* is something you might want."

"I want to trust you. I really do."

He brings my hands to his lips. "A career in law can convince you that you're embarking on a just cause, defending what's right, being a good man. I won cases for my clients at the cost of friendships and spending time with my family." The words are unrehearsed, rushed like a weighted confession finally being set free. "And I told myself that it was worth it, that for all the draining years I put in, it was enough to fill the loneliness inside of me.

"Until the days I sacrificed felt meaningless when one of my senior partners assigned me to a case for Shift Industries. It was a simple acquisition deal. Shift wanted to acquire another company with ten thousand acres of land."

Luca cringes.

I nod, urging him to go on.

Luca tells me how a couple months after he successfully closed the case, Shift demolished all the solar panels on the land, instead choosing to drill for oil. A press release was put out about a discovery of a collection of oil deposits across the land, which happened to be near a small town on a marsh. The news spiraled into something more only a few weeks after the first announcement: a disastrous oil spill. The guilt still weighs heavy on his mind, crushing the caring man I've come to respect under his stone exterior.

But I refuse to let him take the blame for an unfortunate mistake. I feel like an old part of me would recoil at the confession, but I sit beside him, unmoving, our hands still locked together.

"You didn't do anything wrong, Luca."

"But I did," he says. "I played a role in a tragic outcome."

"*No*. You were doing your job, and it had nothing to do with the spill. You couldn't have predicted that Shift was going to drill on the land or mismanage their machinery. Luca, what happened is horrible, but there's a reason ORO exists, to help situations like this."

"When I took the job, I felt like an imposter," he says.

"That's the furthest thing from the truth. You're caring, hard-working, and generous. You've committed tirelessly to make sure no one at ORO had to lose their livelihood. And to think I considered you just a heartless suit," I try to joke.

"I was, Ave."

My fingers reach for the chiseled line of his jaw, stroking it gently.

"No, you weren't, Luca. I was wrong to judge you over something I didn't understand. And you're wrong to keep letting this weigh on your conscience. Forgive yourself and acknowl-edge how much *you've* done to make amends for something you didn't even cause."

Luca's gaze melts into mine. "Everything *we've* done, Ave. You and me, and our teams. I couldn't have done everything on my own."

I shatter at the intimate declaration, and Luca pulls me into his arms, settling my body in his lap. The knowledge renders me speechless, even more so than when we sat here in our own quiet. But something more important staggers me: my amplified admiration for the man beside me.

A man who let me make assumptions about him and proved me wrong.

These past few months, I have grappled with who I should have been and who I've slowly started to become. Little did I know Luca was walking the same ragged path, lost somewhere in the world, waiting for someone to stroll alongside him.

"Look, Avery, I'm so sorry. I should have called you when I found out about Joanna." His voice is raw and desperate.

I face him, wiping the stinging tears off my cheeks. Only inches separate us now.

"If this, *us*—" I hesitate. "I need you to promise me you won't drop off the face of the earth when life tangles together again. I can't be abandoned by someone that matters so much to me."

The disappointment from my mother's reclusion is too familiar, and I refuse to allow Luca, who has been pushing new breath into my lungs, to leave me in the suffocating bonds of dismay when I need him most.

"I'll stand at your side through it all, Ave," he says. "I promise."

I leap off the surface of my heart and free fall into believing him. I savor the reality of Luca Navarro drumming against my skin, and in my plummet into the deep end, I finally feel *safe*.

"I never told you why I wanted to work in conservation," I say. "Not just my respect for Joanna's work, but the *real* reason."

The reason I've just come to terms with recently.

Luca looks at me as though my words will be the most important ones he's ever heard. I collect the loose threads of memories inside me.

"I grew up by the forest, my small, beautiful existence filled with just my dad, my mom, and me." I inhale a calming breath, savoring the truth I haven't spoken in so long. "My dad was my best friend, one of the most incredible people to walk the earth.

"Once I was big enough to hold up my own protest sign, Dad took me to every environmental meet-up around the Northeast until I got the chance to witness his idol, Joanna Benbart, lead a crowd in New York City. She commanded everyone's attention, tearing into the lost and overwhelmed people standing in the group and pulling us into a united community for the betterment of the world.

"On the ride home, Dad's smile was the biggest I'd ever seen as he told me that I would be the voice of the next generation. His ambitious Ave would become an activist like Joanna." My tears dispel as the liberation of sharing this with Luca overtakes me. "And I committed every ounce of my being to that dream. Setting myself on track for a full ride at UNC in environmental studies, work at a conservation nonprofit, followed by my Ivy League master's program."

Luca nods, already knowing how successful I had been at school.

"But five years ago, I learned what people meant when they say life can flash before you in the blink of an eye.

"I sat alone in the Davis Library, the final term of my senior year, studying for a statistics final. I almost ignored the call when my mom's name flashed across my screen, antsy to cram for the exam. But I answered it anyway before listening to broken sobs on the line."

It was like a suffocating dream, but it was my harsh reality.

"My dad was scheduled to come home in two days from a *Global Planet Magazine* photography expedition in Greenland. The temperatures were too unpredictable, too volatile. His group of photographers stood with him on the edge of an ice cap when the base gave way underneath him. By the time his team was able to pull my dad out of the subzero waters, he was too cold and they were too far from camp."

I heave a sigh, and the rest of my truth scrapes against my chest, clamoring to get free. "After that call, my mom shut down, pulling away from me. I only got through those times by throwing myself at my commitment to him. Making a difference. I didn't take time off. I buried myself in work. It was easier to hold on to something practical like my new job rather than deal with the hollowness that still nags inside me."

The sun has nearly drowned in the horizon.

"Work can be an easy distraction when you feel disconnected from your life."

I nod before I continue.

"And then it all came crashing down again. The first time I

truly felt like I let down my dad was when you called me with the news that I didn't get to work with Joanna."

"Avery, I didn't—"

"I understand it wasn't up to you." I smile. "But I somehow managed to be at ORO, thinking this was my chance to try again. And when I finally got up the nerve to tell Joanna of her impact on my life, she ejected me from her office, barely remembering my name.

"I held on to Joanna's approval and acceptance as though it were my dad's. I wanted her to assure me that the work I've done since he died was enough. That I was living out our dream."

"Avery." He pulls my face to his and our foreheads touch. "Joanna spent the last years of her life thinking her efforts amounted to nothing. She neglected ORO for years when she lost sight of what was important. It's the reason the company's been struggling financially."

"That's so sad." My brows crinkle in disbelief, and I pull back and stare into my favorite deep autumn eyes. The soft pace of his heartbeat steadies me.

"Joanna buckled under the expansion, refusing to ask for help. She wanted to govern ORO alone even if it meant running it into the ground. When Joanna met you, I think she detested the hope within you, the way you refused to stop believing in the cause."

My chest constricts with understanding.

"But, unlike Joanna, we're not alone. We can and will do this together. I never want you to doubt yourself or feel like you've disappointed your father." Luca's lips press to my fingers. "You're an astonishing gift to this world. To have you at my side, leading the way, would be an honor."

"And I want to stand beside you, Luca," I admit and fall deeper into his arms. "I wish Plastech didn't have to move out after Ocean Tidy concludes. I'll miss torturing you around the office every day."

Luca smiles. "You don't have to move out of the ORO offices."

"What?"

"I trust you to keep this between us, but Matthew and I discussed merging a couple of weeks ago. It makes the most sense for day-to-day operations of Ocean Tidy," he explains. "Now that I'm going to be CEO, I got the plans approved—obviously, *if* Willa determines we're worthy of the grant."

Wow. "CEO?"

He nods in response.

"That's amazing, Luca," I say. "You're the best person for the job."

Thoughts of our future intertwine in my mind. What does this mean for my role on the Plastech team? Helping ORO get back on track has been such a rewarding part of the last month, my career feeling exactly how I wanted it to with Luca at my side.

He doesn't take his eyes off of me, and I break into a smile, a weight lifting within me. "What does all of this mean for us?"

"What do you want, Ave?"

"I want to stop pretending *us* is another game," I confess.

"Good," Luca says. "I don't want to miss a single moment together. Truthfully, Ave, I never thought I could love someone as much as I love you. *Te amo, cariño.*"

I love you. I love you.

Luca Navarro loves *me.*

The world finally settles on an even axis. My lips crash into his, mimicking the raging ocean beside us. Each touch reconstructs the pieces of me I have struggled to grasp and keep steady. But I no longer reach for them alone; instead, I have him.

"I love you, Avery." He repeats the words, and they are suddenly my favorite combination of the alphabet.

"I love you, Luca."

In that moment, I allow myself to cling to our potential. The battles between us conquered with the love in our hearts. I trace the lines of his palms like I'm studying a map and wrap his hand in my own, savoring the warmth I want to sink into forever.

Later, I pull my phone out of the glove compartment and text my mom to let her know I'll come see her in the next few weeks. Mom may be struggling to move past Dad's death, but I'm not going to put our relationship on hold because of my career.

I'm finally going to take my life back into my own hands.

Chapter 35
Luca

One month later

Horns and saxophones wreak pandemonium across the ORO offices at 8:00 a.m. sharp.

Willa let us know, last night, that we should expect her early this morning for her verdict on our testing and deployment strategy for Ocean Tidy. The team presented the results to Willa at our offices last week. Avery did an excellent job articulating the combined ideas and the way they would create the impact Willa wanted. I'm certain we're about to hear some good news.

We've been here for an hour, loading up on coffee and scones in anticipation of finding out Ocean Tidy's fate today.

"Gonna take a guess and assume Willa has arrived," Ollie yells over the squawking noise and the scraping of our chairs as we shuffle into the lobby. "Unless this is Luca's horrid attempt to encourage us to get here early."

"He would be a hypocrite if he tried to get us here before he strolls in himself at nine o'clock," says Molly.

Avery's lips crease into a smile at the truth of Molly's

comment; our lengthy mornings together are now a welcome disruption in my typically early schedule.

When your organization is stocked with as many intelligent people as ORO, you can sleep in sometimes. It also hasn't taken them long to pick up on the clues surrounding my new relationship status with Avery, but we haven't officially confirmed their suspicions yet.

In the middle of the reception area, Willa is flanked by an ensemble of musicians wearing navy-blue uniforms and bow ties that clash with the ivory jumpsuit and bright-orange hard hat on Willa's head. One of those comically oversized checks you see on game shows rests on the floor by her feet.

Relief washes over me with the understanding that everything will be okay.

Over the past month, Avery and I have worked tirelessly to secure more than enough funding to give ORO an operational buffer for the following year. However, deep down, I knew this grant would be the deciding factor in ORO's future. The expected revenue from the Ocean Tidy project being deployed is invaluable to all of us here.

The final weight in my chest unburdens itself at the sight of Willa's smiling face.

As the rest of our team makes it onto the floor, Willa raises her hand in the air and closes her fingers into a fist, silencing the band.

"Hello! Luca, dear. Come join me," Willa says.

I approach her and stand before her as the CEO of our organization. I look back at my team, their faces lit up with delighted anticipation.

Avery stands among them and lifts a small thumbs-up into the air, cheering me on.

"I had to deliver my congratulations in person." Willa's wrinkled hand squeezes my arm before her gaze quickly snags from me to Avery, and she gives us a barely discernible wink. "Stunning presentation, Avery. I knew you two would suit each other!"

Am I being paranoid, or does she know that Avery and I are together?

Willa continues, "As I said in the beginning, collaboration and teamwork is the most fruitful way to birth new ideas. I am happy to announce the Ellington Foundation will be breaking ground"—she taps her hard hat— "on the Ocean Tidy Project through its deployment and maintenance."

Willa makes a great strain to lift the check and throw it in my arms. The paper tickles the pads of my fingers.

My office erupts with applause, and the band plays a more peaceful tune.

"Thank you on behalf of the entire team at ORO and Plastech," I tell Willa. "We sincerely appreciate your confidence and support in our fight against ocean pollution."

"Yes! I'm glad you will be the faces of the future. Now, let's capture this wonderful memory before I forget it. Old age isn't a dear friend of mine, and I didn't wear this hard hat for nothing!" she squawks, ushering us around her.

We all squeeze in together. Avery slips in beside me, and I wrap my arm around her waist. Her radiant expression meets mine with a proud nod.

"Let's say 'Trash Titans' on three!" Avery jeers.

"We should say 'Sea Men' for the real winners, or did you forget that we beat you, sour lamb?" Ollie laughs back.

"It was Rameses," Avery says.

"Are these new projects I should hear about?" Willa stands in the center of our laughter.

"Ignore them," I say behind my own chuckle. "My team has too many inside jokes."

The photographer, who seems to appear out of nowhere, raises their camera, and on the count of three, each of us screams out our team names, and Willa screams her own name in the incoherent noise.

My first achievement as the CEO isn't commemorated like the framed artifacts at Douglas & Draper, with plaques devoid of faces watching your every move. Instead, a smile wraps my features, my proud grip surrounding Avery.

"Do they accept checks of this size at the bank? I'll have to give them a call." Molly tries to lift the cardboard monstrosity while already pulling out her phone.

"Oh, don't be silly, dear." Willa walks over to the check. "This check is made of biodegradable materials packed with individual grass seeds. Once it composts, it becomes a patch of grass. Isn't that neat?" The number of random projects Willa invests in will never not surprise me. "Obviously, the real money will be wired."

I hand the check to Matthew, who is the only one of us who owns a house with a backyard.

"Luca, be a dear and set me up with your counsel so we can wrap up these contracts." Willa turns to me, giddy, then begins walking toward my empty office.

WHEN WE FINALIZE the remainder of the contracts, I join my team in the conference room. Champagne fills an assortment of coffee cups. Molly and Ollie are heaving with laughter. Robert is playing some kind of game with Hana and Jamie. Matthew is on the phone, chattering to someone about the news.

I consider each person in this room a partner. We may disagree on some things, like appropriate work attire, but at the end of the day, I respect each member of my team, my new friends.

Amid the celebrations sits *my* Avery. She seems content, just like she has made me feel every day since we've been together.

Her blonde hair tickles her face; she's been letting her waves show more, and it is another one of my favorite looks on her.

Since our talk at the beach, Avery has spent most of her time outside of the office with me. A few times, I've dropped her off at her apartment to spend time with Lily and pick up more clothes. She still refuses to have me take her shopping or accept when I've put my card into her purse. But I'm hoping I can change her mind about that.

During those nights alone, I spent time with Nico. We've started to do a weekly yoga session followed by drinks and it's been great sharing more moments together. It's also a welcome distraction for the moments when I miss Avery occupying our bed.

Molly pulls away from her fit with Ollie and catches sight of me in the doorway, gesturing me to come in. She's been an irreplaceable right hand during my transition to CEO, and the bonus hitting her bank account tomorrow morning is worth every single penny.

"There's a policy about champagne in the office." I try to remain professional since I *am* still their boss. An eerie silence falls around the room, reminding me of my first month at ORO.

I shatter my stoic farce and say, "It's against policy to pop the champagne without me."

My team laughs, and I join them. The melody of our exuberance is music to my ears.

For the past few months, each of us has poured our all into this project, so if that means my stomach is going to be full of bubbly gold before 11:00 a.m., then so be it.

"Ey, there 'e is!" Ollie pulls an ORO-branded fleece vest off the table and brings an entire bottle of champagne toward me. "Don't worry, friend, I knew you'd come around."

He drapes the vest over my Italian silk blazer and thrusts the bottle into my hand.

"Isn't this entirely too much champagne?" I set it down and

shrug off the horrid vest onto a nearby chair. I may have a newfound care for my colleagues, but that wretched thing will not be anywhere near me.

"Speak for yourself." He chortles and returns to the celebration.

"Here, you can share with me," Avery says, passing me the Trash Titans mug filled with champagne and settling herself at my side, the familiar sweet-ocean scent of her luring me close. A beautiful grin has been stuck on her face since the announcement.

We rest our hands on the credenza behind us, our fingers looped together out of sight from our team.

"Good work, Mr. CEO," Avery says.

"I couldn't have done it without you," I reply.

"True." She tilts her head onto my shoulder for a fleeting moment before pulling away.

And I am really regretting the *no public displays of affection at work unless it's in the privacy of my office with the blinds closed* rule we created for ourselves.

I have simply fallen off the deep end with my love for her, and having her near me at every possible opportunity is becoming a necessity.

My brilliant and exquisite Avery.

"Are you going to give a speech?" she teases, but little does she know that I am.

I nod to Matthew, who is watching Avery and me with a smile. He nods back at my unspoken intentions.

I clear my throat, calling everyone's attention. "I wanted to say thank you for all the work you have contributed to the Ocean Tidy project. The Ellington Grant would not have been secured without every single one of you," I say and tip my mug to Matthew.

"There's another cause for celebration. We've been eager to announce this for some time but had to wait until the final board approval." I pause and turn to Avery. "Plastech is now officially a part of ORO."

Avery smiles, tipping her glass slightly in the air.

"What? This is so exciting." Molly looks toward Matthew.

It seems Ave and I weren't the only ones who gained more in this project than the grant.

"That means we don't have to leave all the snacks and that fancy-dandy coffee machine now!" Ollie says brightly.

"So everyone is happy with this?" Matthew turns toward his team.

"It makes the most logistical sense." Robert takes a sip of his champagne, nodding silently.

"Of course." Avery smiles.

"Aye! It's for the best—now I won't have to steal all these chairs!" Ollie slides into one of the seats and spins himself across the office, making the entire team laugh.

"Steal the chairs?" I try to clarify.

"Oh, ignore him." She looks at me.

Matthew and the rest of the ORO team burst into celebratory applause before returning to their conversations. I walk back to where Avery is perched on the edge of the credenza.

"Ave, can I speak with you in private?" I say in a hushed tone.

"We said not at work." She gives me a coy smile.

"That's for later. This is something else."

"Ooh, a surprise? Okay, let's go." She follows me into the hallway, her fingertips inconspicuously brushing my hand as we walk toward my office. Once inside, I lead her to stand beside my desk.

"I was waiting to surprise you with this at our celebratory dinner this evening, but—" I collect the employment contract next to my computer and hand it to her.

"Since Plastech is going to be so focused on Ocean Tidy, I

wanted to offer you the position as head of development for the Oceanic Research Organization."

"Seriously?" Her face lights up, and she takes the papers from my hands.

"I need you," I admit. "You're so remarkably talented, Avery. The connections you've fostered. The fundraising you've done. There aren't enough *thank-yous* I could shower you in to make you understand how much you've impacted my life. Not only do you inspire me every day, but you inspire everyone around you. You truly remind people of a greater purpose. I've always wanted you on my team, Ave."

She continues to scan the contract, her eyes not widening at the salary offer in front of her—a number equivalent to my own. There was no way in hell I would allow her to work here without being my equal in every sense.

I grow antsy in the silence, hoping she will accept.

"What do you say?"

Chapter 36
Avery

My chest rises and falls in an arrangement of calming breaths.

I deserve this.

Each of my inhales morphs into a thick wave of warmth filling my lungs. I take in the sight of Luca's slightly unkempt hair and the hint of scruff on his jaw. He's been worrying less about looking neat, which somehow makes him look more handsome. My adoration for him makes my lips curve at the edges.

When I scan everything outlined in my contract, the possibility of all the projects I could help bring to life, and the connections I could continue to cultivate launch an exciting crackle through me. This role is crafted perfectly for me. It would allow me to make the impact I've always wanted to make and build a lasting ecosystem of change with the man I love.

I try to keep my demeanor calm at seeing my new salary. That's a whole lot of zeros.

"What do you say?" Luca looks at me with anticipation.

"I want to make one thing clear," I demand in my most neutral tone. "I will *not* be taking orders from you."

"No orders…in what context are you referring to?" He gives me a naughty smirk, and his fingers run through his hair.

My arrogant, handsome *prick.*

"I'm not calling you my boss," I declare.

"Trust me, Avery, I know who, out of both of us, will be calling the shots." He pulls my body close to his in a heated embrace and whispers, "Unless, obviously, you find yourself between our sheets."

"If you keep it up, I may take over that privilege too." I pull away slightly to face him, and he yanks me closer.

My weight shifts in my stance, and confidence roots me into the ground. I rest my hand on my hip. I know Luca—he would bend the world at my whim instead of giving me a no.

"Not your boss, your partner," he assures me.

I summon every ounce of willpower to keep my eyes off his lips.

I will not kiss him right now.

Focus, Avery.

Focus.

His hand rises to caress my face, and my head instinctively nudges toward his touch.

My voice is finally steady. "And I want an endless supply of toffee syrup."

"Already done. I wasn't kidding when I said I need you," he says, full of conviction.

He chuckles, now pulling both of my hands into his and holding them as though he would never let them go. "Does this mean you're ready to say yes?"

A very different man stands before me than the one who interviewed me all those months ago.

"Yes. This is what I want." I nod, pride snaking its way through my body.

Luca covers me in kisses that make my knees weak, and one of his hands interlaces with mine.

I can't imagine ever getting tired of this.

"Good, because I have another surprise for you!" He lights up.

"Luca, if you purchase one more item of clothing that I've been window-shopping for online, our closet will implode."

"How quick you are to implode is one of the reasons I love you. But it's something better than the clothes I *know* you like."

My heart rate quickens in anticipation. I rack my mind, trying to decipher what possible surprise he could have conjured up this time.

His fingers unlace from mine, and a familiar posture snaps into his body as he walks over to the top drawer of his desk. A deep burgundy tie slowly unravels in his hand, the deep browns of his eyes now locked on me in my favorite challenging gaze. My blood thrums with adrenaline as every molecule within me lights up like a swarm of fireflies.

"Seriously, Navarro?" I bite. "It's not even noon! And we're at the office!" My head swivels toward the door, trying to see if anyone can notice us.

"Glad my ties evoke such a passionate reaction from you." He smiles. "Sadly, *cariño*, this one will only be used to cover your beautiful eyes briefly."

"Can't you just tell me what it is?" I sigh, my arms dropping at my sides in exasperation.

Luca walks over to me. "Be patient, it'll be worth it."

"Fine." I don't hesitate to turn around, trusting him completely. "But you better not mess up the new head of development's hair!"

Luca stands behind me, his breath heating my skin and causing the hairs on the back of my nape to perk up. He gently brings the tie to my eyes, blocking the room from view. He kisses my neck tenderly, and I naturally crane into him, a quiet moan escapes me. I can feel him stiffen against my body, his earthy smell suddenly occupying my mind entirely. My hips press firmly against the bulge in his pants.

For the past month, I haven't been able to help myself around him.

"You're distracting me from *your* surprise, Ave."

He pulls away from me and replaces the length of him with a steadying palm on my lower back, guiding me forward. I hear him open the door and begin walking me down the hall.

"Are we going toward the conference room?"

"Do you really think I'd crack that easily?" He brings me to a halt then twirls me around in countless circles like I'm a child gearing up to play hide-and-go-seek.

"What *are* you doing?" I say, suddenly dizzy. I reach for the blindfold.

"No more guessing." He plants a small smack onto my ass before his hand returns to my back.

"Hey!" I yelp, laughter escaping me from the excitement.

He walks me through an indiscernible maze, and I keep the remainder of my guesses to myself, trying to map my way through the office. In a succession of three more turns, one of which I could have sworn was the kitchen, we reach our destination.

Luca's fingers undo the blindfold to reveal Joanna's old office. Except the space has been completely remodeled.

The shades are rolled open to reveal the expansive skyline overlooking Central Park. Each piece of Joanna's furniture has been replaced with modern fixtures. New oak-colored cabinets line one of the walls, nestled with plants and small picture frames. A cozy, plush white chair is positioned behind the sleekly crafted desk.

"Did you blindfold me just to show me your new office?" I spin around.

"I redesigned this space last week." He places a key card into my hand. "This office is yours."

I stagger back at his words. *This* office is *mine*? "But how'd you know I was going to say yes?"

"Because I know *you*, Avery Soko," he says.

I walk through the office, glancing at the framed photographs, and my hands clasp at my chest.

Three pictures sit on the shelf.

The first is the one Willa's photographer took only hours before.

The team. *Our* team.

"What? This was just taken—"

"Nothing our new printers couldn't take care of in a few minutes. I wanted you to have a picture of our team."

Happiness seeps through our captured image, and I know my decision to become the head of development is the right one.

The next photograph I haven't seen before. I pull it close, and I recognize my dad and myself in the shades of black and white. My hair is tied up in a ponytail, and we're wearing matching tees that I cannot recall.

Me and dad.

My heart hammers against my ribcage.

"Where's this one from?" I hold it up to him.

"Turns out Burlington has an avid environmental activist community. It took a researcher only a few hours to find a photo of you together from a local newspaper."

"You hired someone?" My voice cracks.

"Don't make me remind you of the countless things I would do for you, my love, or I'll have to use this tie in other ways." He smirks, lifting the fabric still in his hand.

The tears return, and I laugh them off. Luca brushes the salty droplets off my cheeks and nudges his head toward the final photograph.

The third picture is just of Luca and me. My legs are draped over his body, a game controller in one of my hands as I yell out at the television. Luca's gaze is locked on me with a wide smile painting his features.

Our first picture as a couple.

My heart feels like it might actually tear to shreds from the overwhelming amount of love coursing through me.

"Nico took that one," Luca says, and my attention returns to him.

"I love it." I laugh through another fit of tears.

He smiles. "Turn the frame over."

I do as he instructs, and on the back is the scribble of his handwriting.

Our Apartment

"Luca—"

"There's one final surprise for you over there." He gestures at my desk.

Anticipation bubbles through me. I walk over, running my fingers across the polished grain of oak wood. I pick up the neatly folded paper sitting on top of a black velvet rectangular box. My heart races as I shake the envelope slightly, unable to figure out what's inside.

"The box first," he instructs.

I open the black box to reveal an emerald tennis bracelet. My eyes shoot open at the intricate design. The gems shimmer dazzlingly under the afternoon sun, sending a rainbow of greens onto my skin.

"Luca!" I gasp.

He walks over and secures the clasp onto the wrist that doesn't wear a watch, his lips pressing firmly to each of my fingers.

"Consider it a temporary placeholder."

My blood thrums against my skin. His gaze falls to the envelope in my hand, and he tips his head to the side, indicating that I'm ready for my next surprise.

I peel open the edges.

"A key?" I pull out the jagged metal and hold it up in front of us.

Luca takes my hand in his and leans in close. "Avery, if you're ready, I want to make a home with you."

"But my lease—"

"It's already taken care of," he says. I melt into his arms as he pulls me toward him. "I asked for Lily's blessing and paid the entirety of your rent through the next six months. I don't want to spend another night without you, Ave."

My mind feels as if I'm in the driver's seat of a race car going a hundred miles an hour.

I'm ready to commit my all to him like I've done with everything I've loved my entire life. I know I am. I don't hesitate for a single moment.

"Yes."

I smile as Luca Navarro kisses me softly.

His forehead meets mine, and he whispers, "You and me."

"You and me."

The end.

Epilogue
Avery

Some time later.

MUSIC PLAYS SOFTLY THROUGH THE CAR SPEAKERS AS OUR summer beach house comes into view. I'm sure most people, including myself, would call this charming home an actual mansion—especially since it can probably fit four of our apartments inside. I found the place in Montauk by accident. It was way out of our price range, but Luca insisted that we rent it for the season. Refusing him was not an option. Secretly, or not so *secretly*, I'm glad for it.

I love this place.

The white planks of wood wrap around the stunning deck that leads to the front door, exposing itself to a small garden patch of flowers.

The memory of the first weekend we stayed here plays in my mind every time we pull into the driveway. We gardened for most of the afternoon, each of us stripping off a layer of clothing as the day wore on. Thankfully, our abode has a ton of privacy because our garden became privy to some very, very inappropriate behavior.

Now excess bundles of rosemary and thyme line the stony path leading to the front door. Where the path begins, there is a small wooden gate that separates us from the golden, sandy beaches. It always brings a smile to my face.

A bittersweet feeling settles into my stomach that this is our last weekend here. We're going to say goodbye to the slice of heaven we found together.

There's nothing I can do except soak in every minute with Luca, watching the tide slowly leave the shore and the gorgeous sunsets that consume the never-ending skyline.

"Do we have to return the keys on Sunday? I'm going to miss this place so much." I turn my head away from the scenery and look over at Luca in the driver's seat. He parks our car in front of the house and gravel crunches loudly under the tires.

"Sorry. Me too."

"I wish it wasn't for sale. I wonder if the new owners will rent it next year?"

"I'm sure we could convince them." He smiles at me.

I squeal a bit at the thought of us coming back here every summer. It could be another one of our new traditions together.

Luca pulls the keys out of the ignition and reaches one of his warm palms over to my bare knee, giving it a gentle squeeze. The entire summer I wore dresses and skirts, aching for these exact moments when he'd tease the hem of my skirt and rub his fingers on my skin, making my entire body come alive.

We climb out of the car, and the smell of the sea cleanses the stress from the week.

We only come out here on the weekends, opting to join the rest of the team in working a summer schedule. Since the Ocean Tidy deployment is doing so well, we sometimes even take a full Friday off. We've brought in more than enough revenue to keep ORO afloat and fund a dozen new projects.

I throw my legs out of the passenger door and hesitate in my seat, watching Luca pull our suitcases from the trunk before turning to the house. I could make this place a forever home. Especially when Lily and Nico make the trip with us. The few dinners the four of us have shared have been some of my favorite recent memories.

"Ave, go unlock the house. I'll grab the bags." My attention snaps back to him and he tosses me the keys.

His hair is slightly disheveled due to the brisk wind. I have not yet figured out the secret to his soft yet rugged handsomeness. Maybe I never will.

The material of his pressed blue shirt stretches against his lean muscles. He's wearing jeans today after losing a bet we made last week, and the denim material sits tautly on his muscular legs. But it's not quite *him*. The suits are much better.

"Mr. Navarro, *te ves bien. Te ves muy bien.*"

The weekly Spanish classes I'm taking online have somewhat paid off. I struggle a lot with tenses, but Luca has been a patient teacher. Even when we ignore most of my study sessions in favor of our favorite distraction.

"*Tú también, cariño.*" He winks at me.

A grin spreads on my face. I turn to make my way up the cobbled pathway. A giant vine creeps up the side of the white house, wrapping itself around the metal gutters. Seagulls sing above while the waves crash softly on the beach.

I unlock the door and am instantly flooded with orange and pink light shimmering throughout the living room. The floor-to-ceiling glass sliding doors facing the beach capture the sunset in a mesmerizing way against all the light wood fixtures, the tall, curved ceilings, the stone fireplace we haven't even lit once, and the rows and rows of books that line the ledges by the windows.

This place exudes beauty and serenity and I try to take it all in. To memorize every nook and cranny of this house. To remember each spot we shared a kiss or more.

A smell I can't place draws me to the expansive chef's kitchen. A charcuterie board with a variety of cheeses, fruits, and chocolates sits on the oak breakfast table with a bottle of champagne chilling in the middle.

Did he do this or maybe the owners left it?

Luca wouldn't have had time to do this if he had been with me all day.

I rush back into the living room where Luca's setting our bags down.

"For someone who complains about how much space my suits take up, you're the one who needs to bring two full suitcases—"

I cut him off. "Luca, there are snacks in the kitchen."

"There are usually snacks in the kitchen."

"*No.* This time there are fancy snacks in the kitchen. Did you plan this or is there a ghost in here that loves brie as much as I do?"

"Are you thinking of a good excuse to use when all the brie and honey mysteriously disappear?"

I laugh. "Hey, it's your mom's fault for getting me obsessed at Christmas."

"She's buying an entire wheel just for you next year."

Luca finally manages to strip all of the bags off his body. He walks over to me and taps one of his large fingers on my nose before kissing me.

"Perfect, that means I won't have to share." My lips curve against his lips.

"Have all the snacks your tender heart desires, we're celebrating our last weekend renting the house."

I try not to think about Monday. Instead, I inch closer to his chest and the sound of his heart thrumming beneath his clothes.

"Wait, why did you say *renting* weird?" I push away from him, and my thighs hit the back of the couch.

He peers down at me with my favorite boyish grin.

Think, Avery. Think.

All week he was impassive when I asked him about being

upset over our last weekend here. Come to think of it, he has been leaving some stuff here every weekend.

Wait.

I hesitate. "Luca…"

"Yes?"

My mind is running at lightning speed. "You didn't!"

"What?" He smiles at me, trying to play coy. If only those gorgeous eyes of his didn't reveal every single thing he's thinking.

"I'm going to take a wild guess right now."

He nods for me to continue.

"Smiling man. Elevated heart rate. Not nearly as sad as I am."

"Hey!" He laughs.

"Did you buy this house?"

He takes my hands in his. "You know, it's more fun when you don't guess your surprises."

I squeal at the top of my lungs and collide my mouth with his. After our kiss breaks, I shoot one of my fists into his strong arms. "You let me spend the entirety of last week rambling on about how much I was going to miss this place?"

"I love your rambling."

"But this house is huge! How long have you known? What are we going to do with all of this space? How much did this cost? It has six bedrooms, six! You have to let me—"

"I'm sure we can think of all the different ways to fill the bedrooms, Ave." He kisses me on the forehead before all the questions can tumble out of me. My entire body relaxes, and we melt into each other's embrace.

My happiness isn't for the house or the full kitchen. The only thing I can focus on is the absolute thrill of anticipating the memories we will create here, *together*.

I can already hear the sounds of laughter filling the walls. Our friends and family joining on the weekends. Maybe, sometime in the future, Little Lucas running around on the hardwood floors.

Do they make suits for toddlers?

I'm going to have to get multiple if they do.

Is our daughter going to love swimming as much as I do?

Will we get to float together in the salt water under the stars?

I sure hope none of them have my temper.

My thoughts spiral with what life will look like for us. A future where I can pass on all the things my dad taught me down to the next generation.

But for now, I savor the moment of our life being just us. Because, at the end of the day, that is the true gift.

I pull out of Luca's hug. "What about our apartment in the city? I can't imagine living hours away from Lily. She doesn't come out here enough, and I would miss the team too much to work remotely."

"We're not selling the apartment. We'll keep doing what we've been doing. Driving out here whenever we want to."

My lips meet Luca's again. Our tongues intertwine in their favorite dance while we inhale each other's air. I don't know why I ever thought our kisses would calm after we spent more time together; our wildness always leaves me wanting more.

Luca pulls away just as my breathing becomes more ragged. "As much as I'd love to throw you onto this floor and christen this house as the official owners. We shouldn't miss the sunset."

He interlocks his fingers with mine, and I try to calm the current firing through me. He guides me to the sliding living room doors and glides them open for us to enter the porch facing the beach. Instantly, the smell of fire intertwines with the sea. I scan the beach to find a bonfire blazing close to us.

I point to the abandoned pit. "I thought this was a private beach?"

There aren't any neighbors for at least a mile.

"It is," he says.

I turn to face him, but his expression reveals nothing.

"Is this another surprise? Because it's going to be hard to top buying me a house."

I hope it is another surprise because they always end in my favor.

"Let's go check it out." He leads the way.

We approach the raging bonfire. "Are you going to sacrifice me? Is that what this is?"

"If I told you that, then it wouldn't make for a good surprise now. Would it?"

He tries to pick me up, but I duck under his arms. Our laughter gets lost in the wind and waves. I run toward the dancing fire like a bird taking flight. The crackling flames become louder with each step.

I stop running when the heat radiating from the bonfire reaches my body, evaporating the last remnant of chill in my bones. My fingers trace the embers that float into the sky, which is now a vibrant cotton candy pink.

The weight of his arms drapes around me from behind. My favorite smell, that woodsy tinge on Luca's skin, intertwines with the briny sea and ash. We stand together. His large hands rub over my pebbled skin, each caress pulling me closer to his chest. The sand beneath my feet begins to give way as I lean further into him, each tiny grain tickling my legs. There's nowhere I would rather be than with him right now.

"You're stunning tonight," he whispers in my ear. His breath ignites every nerve in my body. I need him.

"Not every night?" I gently nudge him with my elbow.

"Every night." He kisses me on my cheek and then drops his arms. And suddenly his presence is gone.

"Hey, where did you g—"

But my words are lost at the sight of Luca down on one knee, the velvet box in his hands housing a ring on a dark fabric cush-

358 Kels & Denise Stone

ion. Small, jagged stones decorate one side of the large single stone resting on a gold band. If a ring could reflect the inside of a person, this one matches everything about me. Simple, magnificent, a little imperfect.

My brain starts to piece together each minute clue. No wonder he was being so weird yesterday about his bag.

"Ave." He beams up at me.

"I knew it."

"You haven't even let me finish." Luca smiles his heart-melting smile.

I'm cemented into the sand as I watch this enchanting man on his knees before me. The glint of the fire reflects in his deep-brown eyes. His shaggy hair moves with the gentle breeze of the evening.

Luca takes one of my cold, shaking hands into his warm fingers. The pulse in my veins grows.

Am I breathing? I honestly can't tell.

"I won't tell you what you already know." He looks up at me with delight written all over his handsome features. "That you're the sun that I welcome each of my mornings with, that you're the other half of me, that I would spend an eternity making you smile."

A giggle fights itself out of me. One filled with only pure joy at his truth. I'm stuck somewhere between the burning tears pouring from my eyes and the swelling happiness bursting out of my chest.

I manage to give him some kind of response instead of standing here succumbing to my emotions. "I love you, Luca."

"I love *you*, Avery."

He brings my hand to his lips and kisses each one of my fingers gently. I give his hand a tight, unbreakable squeeze. I know right now, like I think I've always known, that I will never let go of him.

Luca's eyes trail back to me, soaking me in before he says

the most captivating words I've ever heard. "Avery Soko, will you marry me?"

"Yes." I nod. "Yes. Yes. Yes."

I don't know how many times I say it, but handsome lines crease his face.

I try to pull him up toward me, my fit of laughter and tears refusing to let up. "You're getting your new jeans dirty!"

Instead, he gently yanks me into the sand beside him, and I collapse in front of him.

He chuckles. "It doesn't matter."

Luca places the elegant ring on my left hand, and the delicate gems gleam from the bonfire flames. We kneel in front of each other, our smiles bright enough that they could be seen from outer space.

I try to joke because my brain and heart are refusing to express themselves accurately. "You suddenly don't care about your clothes?"

"Oh, Ave, do you always have something to say?"

"Yes. Are you ready to deal with it for the rest of your life?"

Luca breaks into my favorite smile. "You bet."

Spanish Glossary

We worked closely with people of Mexican heritage to reflect the Spanish dialect commonly used in Mexico and the U.S. However, some of the translations are intentionally not literal as it is mostly informal and, in some cases, slang. The dialogue, food, and familial interactions are depicted from lived experiences. The glossary below includes the Spanish and English text to help map the interactions across the book.

Hope you enjoy it!

<u>Appears in multiple places in the text</u>
Cariño
Darling or sweetheart

<u>Chapter 5 - Luca:</u>
Todavía no. ¿Por qué?
Not yet. Why?
Arriba, abajo, al centro, y adentro
Up, down, to the center, and inside

<u>Chapter 10 - Luca:</u>

¡No haces nada!

You don't do anything!

No mames.

Stop fucking around.

Chapter 21 - Luca:

No fue tu culpa.

It wasn't your fault.

Mijo,

Shorthand for **son.**

¿Y tú?

And you?

Y por eso no estás casado

And that's why you are not married.

Tal vez si tuviera algunos nietos.

Maybe if I had some grandchildren.

Chapter 25 - Luca:

Aye, Miguel. ¿Cómo estás?

Hey, Miguel. How are you?

Ooooh, Luca. ¿Quién es la señorita?

Ooooh. Who is the lady, Luca?

Es mi futura novia.

She is my future girlfriend.

¿Y ella lo sabe?

Does she know that?

Pendejo.

Dumbass.

"No te creas. ¿Qué les puedo dar?"

Just kidding. What can I get for you both?

Dame cuatro tacos de nopales, una torta de pollo asado, y dos mulitas de rajas. Ah, y una horchata, por favor.

Give me four nopales tacos, one grilled chicken torta, and two vegetarian mulitas. Ah, and one horchata, please.

¿Si, y para la señorita? Tal vez una cerveza, para que te pueda soportar.

Yes, and for the lady? Maybe a beer, so that she can put up with you?

No, gracias. Un agua, por favor.

No, thanks. One water, please.

Agua and *una cerveza*

Water and one beer.

Chapter 29 - Luca:

eres mía

You are mine.

Chapter 34 - Avery:

Te amo.

I love you.

Epilogue - Avery:

te ves bien. Te ves muy bien

You look good. You look very good.

Tú también.

You as well.

Acknowledgments

An immense thank you to our team of editors, Manu Shadow Velasco at Tessera Editorial and Caroline Acebo. They held our hands as we navigated the world of becoming authors for the first time. Thank you for making Luca and Avery the best characters they could be while they fell in love. We promise that our next first draft will be exemplary (and, for the most part, in the correct tense). Thank you to our cover artists and designers who put up with our countless revisions as we tried to create the best book possible. Your endless patience and skills are some things we never took for granted.

Thank you to our beta reader, Luzangel Valles, and our sensitivity reader, Nataly Solis, for the incredibly helpful feedback and for being the first readers to fall in love with Luca.

Thank you to the organizations who are working to protect the world's oceans like Ocean Conservancy, Oceana, Environmental Defense Fund, Coral Reef Alliance, Project AWARE, and many more.

Thank you to our partners, who we severely neglected these past few months. We yelled at you, and you still made sure we were fed and watered every single day, even when we refused to spend time with you in favor of *Luvery*. Thank you for inspiring us, in more ways than one. Ahem…

(And if that's not the most book boyfriend behavior, we don't know what is.)

Thank you, most importantly, to the incredible readers on BookTok, Bookstagram, BookTube, Book Twitter, book blogs, book podcasts, and book clubs. If it weren't for all of you, our love for books and dreams of writing would have remained hidden away. Thank you to the friends we made along the way who encouraged us to follow our passions. Thank you to the wonderfully supportive community that has been here since the very beginning. Thank you to the good girls who join the Between The Sheets podcast. Thank you to the friends on @authorkelsdenisestone. None of this would have been possible without you.

Lastly, thank *you*, the reader, for giving our debut novel a chance. We hope you loved meeting Avery and Luca as much as we loved writing them. We appreciate the opportunity to share their love story with you and are tremendously excited for you to join our romance journey.

D: Wow, Kels, we actually did it! Thank you for not abandoning me through hours of crying and panic as we navigated this process together. I couldn't have done it without you. You're the Lily to my Avery, and I'm so glad we met.

K: I knew we could! *insert feelings*

Playlist

"Good Days" by SZA
"Small Talk" by Majid Jordan
"So Good" by Omar Apollo
"Latch" by Disclosure, Sam Smith
"3:15 (Breathe)" by Russ
"Beige" by Yoke Lore
"Cariño" by The Marías
"I Dare You" by The xx
"La Curiosidad" by Jay Wheeler, DJ Nelson, Myke Towers
"I Fall Apart" by FLETCHER
"Rather Be" by H.E.R.
"Ella Quiere Beber (Remix)" by Anuel AA, Romeo Santos
"Está Dañada" by Ivan Cornejo
"Falling in Love at a Coffee Shop" by Landon Pigg
"Morning Sex" by Ralph Castelli
"Honesty" by Pink Sweat$
"Kiss U Right Now" by Duckwrth
"La Noche de Anoche" by Bad Bunny, ROSALÍA
"Water Under the Bridge" by Adele
"Help Me Lose My Mind" by Disclosure, London Grammar
"Gonna Love Me" by Teyana Taylor
"Beauty & Essex" by Free Nationals, Daniel Caesar, Unknown Mortal Orchestra
"Never Tear Us Apart" by Bishop Briggs
"I Wanna Be Yours" by Arctic Monkeys
"By The Sea" by Anna Phoebe
"Through The Echoes" by Paolo Nutini
"Home" by Matthew Hall

About The Authors

Kels & Denise are authors, best friends, and the definition of the found family trope. The pair bonded over their love for romance and turned all their late-night chats into writing together. Their love for storytelling morphed into writing strong heroines and rugged, swoon-worthy love interests with lots of dirty talk. While Kels travels the world with her high-school-sweetheart husband, Denise is making her way through every restaurant with her boyfriend.

Stay in touch!
@authorkelsdenisestone
kelsdenisestone.com

Join our newsletter *The Sticky Note*
kelsdenisestone.com/the-sticky-note
Join our Patreon for exclusive content

Also by Kels & Denise Stone

Perks & Benefits Series:

Water Under the Bridge

Workplace Romance, Avery and Luca's Story

Our Scorching Summer

Friends to Lovers Romance, Lily and Nico's Story

On Cloud Nine

Fake Dating Romance, Molly and Matthew's Story

Falling for Meadow

Small Town Romance, Ollie & Meadow's Story

The Hastings Series:

Close Knit

Sports Romance

Printed in Great Britain
by Amazon

59199765R00219